KEEPER OF SECRETS

3/24/12
TO ROBERT
ON YOUR VISIT TO
THE 390TH
ENJOY +
SHARÉ

Jerry Dow (signature)

KEEPER OF SECRETS

GERALD "JERRY" DOW

TATE PUBLISHING & Enterprises

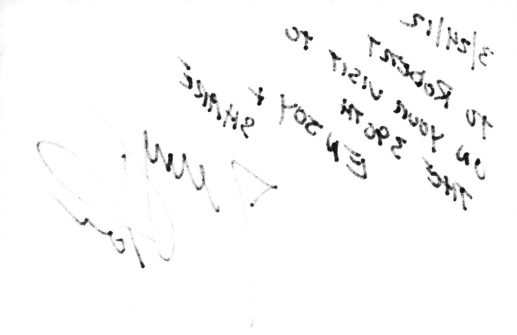

Published by Tate Publishing & Enterprises, LLC
127 E. Trade Center Terrace | Mustang, Oklahoma 73064 USA
1.888.361.9473 | www.tatepublishing.com

Tate Publishing is committed to excellence in the publishing industry. The company reflects the philosophy established by the founders, based on Psalm 68:11,
"The Lord gave the word and great was the company of those who published it."

Book design copyright © 2009 by Tate Publishing, LLC. All rights reserved.
Cover design by Tyler Evans
Interior design by Blake Brasor

Published in the United States of America

ISBN: 978-1-60799-936-2
1. Fiction, Action & Adventure
2. Fiction, Men's Adventure
10.04.13

DEDICATION

This story is dedicated to 390th Bombardment Group (H) and all who have served and are now serving in the military of the United States of America.

ACKNOWLEDGMENT

This story could not be told without the encouragement of many family members, especially my brother, Richard, true friends who have stood by me, such as Jane and Dave Brown, and those who have come alongside to lend a hand, like Desmond Hollopeter, my fellow teacher.

Thank you.

PREFACE

I watched, like so many others, the jets fly into the World Trade Center; I felt this was our Pearl Harbor, our wake-up call.

Those who responded to Pearl Harbor (Tom Brokaw rightfully called them the Greatest Generation) are fading, and a couple of generations have passed. For the most part, only their lessons remain, for those who are willing to learn. Then I wondered, *What would this generation be called? Were we going to pull another Vietnam or fight, both military and civilian, united in a common cause?* As I thought of the situation, this story evolved: the comparison of two generations, our current youth and those who went off to World War II.

Many think our strength is in wealth and technology, but I think it's our character, our will, and what we look to for our strength that are important. This story, among other things, deals with the main character, Jason Riley, and his relationship with God.

The reader is reminded that this is a work of fiction and I, like any human, should not and do not assume how the Almighty would or would not act, except via his Word. So the reader is left, so to speak, to read between the lines of what is truth and what is fiction. There is much of both to challenge the reader.

For God and country, both that I love, enjoy the read.

—*Gerald "Jerry" Dow*

War is an ugly thing, but not the ugliest of things: the decayed and degraded state of moral and patriotic feelings which thinks nothing worth a war, is worse ... A man who has nothing which he is willing to fight for, nothing which he cares more about than he does about his personal safety, is a miserable creature who has no chance of being free, unless made and kept so by the exertions of better men than himself.

—John Stuart Mill
"The Contest in America" April 1862
Harper's New Monthly Magazine,
Volume 24 issue 143, page 683, Harper & Bros., New York

INTRODUCTION

May 25, 1945

Silver shimmered from the midday sun against the bomber, catching Major Ramsey's eye before its familiar scream rumbled in his chest. His steps shifted weight from hip to hip and paced in aimless patterns until the control tower finished with landing instructions. He picked up the mic from the jeep seat and brushed its ribbed surface against his dry lips. "*Golden Eagle* Two, welcome to France."

"Roger that. We will follow your lead. Out."

With the screech of wheels, debris swirled and scattered in a whirlwind that followed the four massive engines. Off the starboard wing of the plane, a jeep raced alongside. At the end of the runway, Major Ramsey led the B-17 away from the construction that crowded the base. When the scream of the engine had silenced, the belly hatch swung open, and Colonel John Riley dropped to the hardstand, followed by three of his crewmembers.

Major Ramsey saluted and then extended his hand. "Good to see you, old friend. Everything is set."

Colonel Riley returned the salute and the two men embraced. "Good to see you, Joe. I never thought we would make it through this war alive."

"We almost didn't, John, but you and the Eighth Air Force still have Japan to deal with."

"There will be no Japan or Japanese invasion."

"You seem sure, John, just like Jason was about Normandy."

Upon hearing the name, the colonel paused for a few shallow breaths, saying, "I suggest that name be left unmentioned."

Major Ramsey took the overnight bag from the Colonel and wrapped his arm around Riley as they walked toward the jeep. "You're right. Jason is the last person we need to bring up. It's good to see you."

"You too, Joe. You too."

When they reached the jeep, the Colonel took the overnight bag. "Joe, let me introduce my crew. This is Lieutenant Bob Carmichael, my navigator, and Captain Jim Frank, second seat. Crew Chief Eugene Johnston. Gentlemen, this is Major Joe Ramsey. Joe and I were in the old 572nd."

As they shook hands, Lieutenant Carmichael said, "We heard rumors about the last 572nd mission. What about it, Major?"

The Colonel shot the Major a wicked stare before changing the subject. "What's all the activity about, Joe?"

"Getting ready to turn the base over to the French. We figure we'll have our POWs for a couple more weeks before the poor devils head home, with the war over and all."

"Poor devils?"

"Not much left of Germany. That's what I've been doing for the brass, evaluation reports on our effectiveness. In all, we did a good job."

"Yeah, a good job."

The jeep rolled toward the hangar that served as the terminal. Trivial conversations murmured below the hum of the jeep, but the Colonel remained lost in the silence of other thoughts. When they arrived, the Major handed the Colonel two maps; one was a road map, and the other was hand drawn.

"That's where you can find the crew."

The Colonel, looking down at the sketched map of the cemetery, turned away, embarrassed by his tears. He moved over to the driver's seat. "As always, Joe, you have gone the extra mile."

"Pay my respects to the crew. I'll keep these three in tow while you're gone."

\- \- \- \- \- \- \- \- \- \- \- \- \- \-

The visit to the crew at Normandy was a quick one, but the dead never complained, nor would they ever reveal the true purpose of the Colonel's trip. A few miles away, the Colonel glanced around his circumference before lowering the binoculars in satisfaction. With a tug of the wrist, the jagged rock that hid a package eased out of the field wall. Unwrapping the torn section of the rubber poncho, he found the 45 cal automatic and the cigar box, both in good condition. He automatically glanced at his hands to see if they were covered with blood, but the blood was now dry, while the memories of that night, nearly a year ago, were still fresh.

Fifteen minutes later, he pulled off the road and opened the road map, spreading it over the steering wheel and checking as if he were searching for directions in case anyone was looking. Reaching into the bag on the passenger seat, he removed the cigar box and the electrical tape. After reading the note inside for the last time, the Colonel sealed the box with trembling hands. A vow overcame the fright in his heart. Only the owner would open its sealed secret.

\- \- \- \- \- \- \- \- \- \- \- \- \- \-

Colonel Riley lifted his overnight bag out of the back of the jeep as he gave the thumbs-up to Captain Frank. He turned to Major Ramsey. "Thanks, Joe, for everything, and pass that on to the General. I would like to stay and visit, but I was hard-pressed even to get these few hours with the group packing up to ship Stateside."

"Hope it went well, John," Joe replied.

As the engine fought to come to life, Riley yelled, "I did get lost," nodding in assurance to himself more than Joe, effectively covering the bases if the jeep was spotted where it should not have been.

As the engine screamed to life, Joe shouted, "Well, you never did get lost when it counted!"

"Again, thanks, Joe!" Riley shouted back.

"Glad I could help! Strange, I miss flying that bucket of bolts!"

"What?" Riley turned.

"Have a good flight!" Ramsey said, waving Riley away.

"Roger that, Joe!" He gave a casual salute.

Major Ramsey watched the bomber lift off the runway and bank with a gentle tilt west toward the Channel, back to England.

JULY 4, 1999

Judge John Riley's wrinkled face told two stories. To most, it looked like a weathered old man's but pulsed with courage underneath its dry fissures. The bright, unmoving gaze had been shaped by B-17 bombings during World War II, impassioned arguments as mob prosecutor, and expeditious decisions as a federal judge. All had earned him a reputation of being incapable of fear. That was, until he met his nineteen-year-old grandson, Jason Riley, face-to-face. The paramedic's report of that first meeting was confused as to the cause of the Judge's medical emergency.

━ ━ ━ ━ ━ ━ ━ ━ ━ ━ ━ ━ ━ ━

Through the doctors' induced haze, Judge Riley heard the physician tell Emily, his wife of over fifty years, that the tests so far had ruled out the possibility of a stroke. Further tests would be needed to find the cause of his collapse. Drifting in and out of consciousness for the last twenty hours, he not only possessed that answer but, in part, what had happened to him and his crew on their last mission flying over Nazi-occupied France. The larger question that ate away at his mind was how it could have happened. He knew, more than ever, with Jason's arrival that he had to keep secret the cigar box and the truth, or many of those around him would die.

As Emily clasped his hand, Judge Riley drifted back into sleep and dreamed again of looking into the eager eyes of his teenage son, David, Jason's future father. What had moved him to tell David about the *Golden Eagle* when so many times before he had refused? Yes, it was the cigar box. He had grown callous over the years waiting for its owner. A safety deposit box would be its future home, but the task before him now was to get it from David.

"David, hand me the box," he demanded, reaching toward what the handsome youth held.

Pulling back, David protested, saying, "No, Dad. I'll open it if you don't tell me what's in it. I have a right to know." For the first time in his life, David openly defied his father.

The Judge raised his voice to hide his fear. "A right? This is no time for games, David."

David stepped back. "You've promised for years to tell me about your plane, the war, and now I'm going off to West Point," he pleaded while stepping back.

The Judge moved closer centering in on the pale blue eyes. "I never should have promised. It was an error."

"A promise is a promise."

As his hand crawled closer to the box, the Judge whispered, "I know, I know," stalling for time. "I guess there's no harm after all these years. First, have you opened the box, David?"

Below blond bangs, a slight smile moved across the young face as he sensed victory. "No, Dad," he replied in the cocky manner of youth, holding the box out in surrender. "Look for yourself."

Reaching for the second time, Judge Riley was aware of his pounding heart. He had to be careful not to show fear. David was no fool and possessed a natural ability to read people. "Did you tell anyone about the cigar box?"

"This is family business, Dad. Do you think that I have no loyalty?" with an indignant tone

"I was not questioning your loyalty, David, just checking your judgment." Moving closer, his whisper pierced the silence. "I take it by your answer that you've told no one. Correct?"

"Yes, sir, that is correct," David confirmed as the box slipped from his hand.

Riley glanced down to make sure the box was still sealed. "Fair enough. I'll tell you of the last mission of the *Golden Eagle*."

With wide eyes, David was transfixed by the emotional tale of death and terror on the *Golden Eagle* spun by his dad. The judge struggled, wiping away tears and stopping more than once to regain his composure. After ten minutes, the eyes of courage narrowed in pain, and David could take no more. He reached over and grabbed his dad's hand and rose slowly to his feet. "Dad, I'm sorry. You don't have to continue."

The Judge pointed to the chair. "You wanted to press the promise. So be it. Sit down."

At the end, a type of truce was made by promises to each other. The Judge vowed to somehow show David the contents of the cigar box. David promised to name his first son Jason Shawn, after his father's co-pilot who had saved his life.

— — — — — — — — — — — — — —

"Grandpa." As the Judge opened his eyes, he looked up. David's fulfilled promise stood before him, while his promise had died in the sands of Iraq.

"Jason, be careful." He grabbed Jason's hand.

"I'm always careful." But Jason's words were ignored as the old man drifted back asleep.

Emily, coming up behind Jason, wrapped her arms around him. "Why don't you go home, sweetheart, and unpack."

"Are you sure, Grandma? I can stay," Jason said without turning.

With a gentle grip she turned the young man around to face her. "Jason, how much sleep did you get last night?"

"About four hours."

She looked into his deep blue eyes. "Not much after two long days of driving. Like your grandfather said, be careful; don't get into an accident."

"If you need anything or if something happens, give me a call."

Emily stood on her tiptoes and kissed him on the forehead. "It's going to be good having you with us, Jason."

"I feel the same, Grandma."

- - - - - - - - - - - - - - - - -

As Jason walked out of the hospital's side door, a young nurse on a smoke break stopped him and asked, "So how's your grandfather doing?"

Jason's long hair tossed with a quick turn. "He seems okay, but they still don't know what happened."

"He has a lot of people praying for him. I'm not into that. To each his own." With that Nancy Baxter flipped the still-lit cigarette behind the bush.

"You're not the only one. I don't hold much stock in it."

"Word is that you just moved here. I can tell you, the judge is well respected in Waterbury. You should be proud."

"Thank you. I am." Jason glanced down and away.

As she watched Jason cross the parking lot, she laughed at sexual thoughts that came unbidden. Under her breath, she sighed, "Women of Waterbury beware." She watched as Jason unlocked his pickup and started to turn away when the first bullet ripped into Jason's shoulder.

Jason bolted straight up and spun just as the second bullet slammed into his right arm. It threw him back with such force that his head cracked the driver's window. As he started to fall forward, the third bullet entered his left thigh. He straightened up again and then fell backward against the pickup. His mind told him to hit the ground, but he remained stuck to his pickup as if it were flypaper, suspended in time, unable to move or fall until finally the law of gravity took over and he slid down the side of his pickup in a smear of blood.

Nurse Baxter watched in horror at the spatter of blood. Jason jerked around like a puppet. Pools of blood formed around Jason's limp body and forced a scream from Nancy, who remained upright on the steps. "I'll get help! I'll-I'll get help!"

As hard as Jason tried, he could not lift his hand to reach out to her, nor could he make a sound. His surroundings swirled then slipped into cold blackness.

— — — — — — — — — — — — — —

Jason felt a jolt of pain as he tried to sit up and fell back to the mattress. He opened his eyes and saw his grandmother gazing down at him. "Hi, Grandma. What happened?"

"You gave everyone a scare, Jason. Now try not to move, sweetheart." Emily gently placed her hand on his chest.

Shaking his head, he asked again, "What happened?"

"You've been shot. Someone tried to kill you."

Closing his eyes against the pain, a mumble rose from his throat.

Emily pulled the sheet up to Jason's neck. "The doctor says you'll be fine. I tried to call your mother, but all I got was the answering machine. I didn't want to leave a message, so I'll try to call her again now."

Jason tried to sit up again, but this time his grandmother gently pushed him back down. "Grandma, please don't call her. She didn't like the idea of me moving here, and this will just set her off."

"The hospital needs information." She leaned closer to him, lowering her voice, as money was always a secretive subject to the Depression Generation.

Jason opened his eyes in less pain. "You mean they want to be paid. In my wallet is an insurance card. Give it to them and remind them that I'm a legal adult, not some kid."

She stood straight, as if rebuked. "You're right, Jason. You're not that little boy we last saw. I guess I'll have to get used to having another man around the house. A Detective Tucker is outside, waiting to talk to you."

"Sure, why not, but I don't have much to say."

She bent over and, for the second time that morning, kissed him on the forehead. "I'll go now and look in on your grandfather. I'll send in the detective."

A few seconds after she left, Detective Tucker, a slight man, thin and wiry, bespectacled with thin silver frames perched on a pointy nose, extended his hand to Jason.

Jason looked up and thought, *Great, I need a manly detective and I get a nerd.* After guessing no harm lay beneath the gesture, Jason made a fast and weak shake.

Tucker noted the slight tense of the shake, fighting to cling to his hand. "Jason, is that what you want me to call you?"

"That what all my teachers call me."

"Did you ever have a teacher called Sergeant David Tucker?"

"Can't say I have."

"Well, you have now, and the first thing you're going to learn, Jason, is it is like school. I ask the questions, and you give me the answers." Tucker removed a small notepad and pen from his inside pocket. "Okay, Jason. Tell me what you know. I'll interrupt to ask questionsand, when you're finished, I'll tell you what I've found out"

"Maybe I don't want to play school."

"It's up to you. I'm not the one someone is trying to kill."

"You do have a point."

"It's up to you, Jason."

"Well, I just got here from Seattle yesterday afternoon."

Tucker, writing down Seattle, prompted, "When and to do what?"

Jason found it hard to think as another surge of pain battered him. "I guess about two in the afternoon, yesterday. I am going to live with my grandparents, my father's parents, and go to Waterbury

Community College. When I got to their house, my grandfather had some type of attack and was rushed here."

"Your grandfather being Judge John Riley. Your father's dad?"

Jason winced in pain. "Yes. I stayed here till late last night and then went back to my grandparents' house to unpack. I still had my surfboards on the surf racks; I'm lucky they didn't get ripped off. I didn't see or talk with anyone. I came back here this morning. I was here maybe three or four hours. When I went out the side door, a nurse stopped me to ask about my grandfather."

Tucker flipped back a few pages in his notes. "That is Nancy Baxter from Emergency?"

Jason waited for the pain to go down then continued. "I don't know her name, but she's the one that came to help me. I was unlocking my pickup when what felt like a fist hit me in the back, right over my right shoulder. I spun around to see who hit me, and then my right arm flew back. I think I hit my head against the pickup."

"Maybe I should come back tomorrow. You seem to be having a rough time."

Jason held up his hand and said, "No, let's get this over with."

A brave or stubborn kid, Tucker thought. "Okay with me, Jason. You're correct about hitting your head; you have a smashed driver's side window to prove it."

"I remember trying to hit the ground, but I couldn't move. I finally ended up on the ground, looking up at the nurse. She was wigging out. Then I'm here."

Tucker walked over to the window and watched as Jason's pickup was loaded onto the flatbed tow truck. "Did you see anyone or hear any noise, Jason?"

With a little more energy in his voice, Jason replied, "That's what was weird. Not a sound, no one, nothing, not a thing, other than the nurse."

Tucker continued to stare down, absentmindedly clicking his ballpoint pen till Jason's repeating his name brought him back. "As I promised, you were shot three times by what appears to be a large-caliber gun. You were hit once from the back in your right shoulder, then again from the front through your right arm, and lastly through your left thigh."

Jason pushed himself up on his left elbow. "You said 'what appears to be.' You have the bullets out of me. You should know, right?"

Tucker turned back to the window and, more to himself than to Jason, murmured, "There were no bullets, Jason."

"They're still in me?"

"I can assure you, with all the x-rays and the doctors' probing, there were no bullets." Tucker walked slowly over to Jason and peered into his bewildered eyes.

"I don't understand."

"There are *no* bullets, Jason, in you," Tucker whispered. "None hit your pickup or any other place. The only physical evidence is the cracked window from your head and your injuries."

Jason was mystified. "Was there blood?"

"Yeah, a lot, and in the right places and patterns to match all three of your wounds and what Nurse Baxter witnessed. Who would want to kill you?"

Jason was irritated. "No one. I just got here. Back home I have no enemies except maybe a few old girlfriends and some of their jealous boyfriends."

"That bullet scar says different. Doctors say it's less than a year old," Tucker said, pointing at his neck.

"Shows how much the doctors know; they can't tell the difference between a cut from a surfboard fin and a bullet." Jason was not about to tell him about Indonesia.

"Really, Jason? Should we warn the female population of Waterbury about you?"

Jason laughed. "Please, no warning."

The detective chuckled. "I may be duty bound to do so if the nursing staff here is any indication." Now smiling down at Jason, he continued, "Maybe it's only fair to sound the alarm."

Jason smiled to himself. *Two can play this game.* "I don't think that's necessary. Can you guarantee I won't be a target again?"

Tucker hesitated. "No, I can't. I think at this point it was probably a random shooting. You just happened to be in the wrong place at the wrong time. To be honest, Jason, I have no theories. I've never seen anything like this. I talked to your grandmother, and she was no help. With the condition your grandfather is in, I don't think I'll bother him."

"I guess I should thank you, for being honest if nothing else."

"Sorry, Jason, I know that doesn't mean much. My business card is on the night stand if you think of anything."

Tucker started to open the door.

"The last and only words my grandpa said to me, 'Jason, be careful.' And look at me." His hand trembled, and veins were visible between knotted tendons.

"What did he say, Jason?" Tucker asked as he walked around the side of the bed.

"He grabbed my hand just before I left his room and said, 'Jason, be careful.'"

"And what did you say?"

"Nothing really. He went right back to sleep."

"Don't you think that's odd? He tells you to be careful and then you get shot?"

Jason started to speak, then hesitated. In deep thought, he answered, "No, my grandmother had just said the same thing about my driving, so I figured he'd heard her."

"You're probably right, Jason. Maybe it means nothing." Tucker saw the flick of the lie in Jason's eyes, and his plans took an alternate course.

- - - - - - - - - - - - -

As Tucker entered the judge's hospital room, Emily excused herself. To Tucker's surprise, the Judge was sitting up and alert. "I have been expecting you, Detective. I heard about my grandson."

"Judge Riley, I'm Detective Sergeant Dave Tucker. I have been assigned to find out what happened to your grandson. Judge, from what I know about you, you could be running this investigation, so I'll skip the fifty questions. What do you know?"

The Judge gave Tucker a cold stare, making sure he knew who was going to set the ground rules. "All I know is, if I was shot three times, they would be burying me. Jason will be as good as new in a month. From what little we hear from his mother, losing surfing time will be his biggest pain."

"Sounds like you and his mother don't get along?"

"It is a family matter," the Judge said gruffly. "It has to do with Jason's father—my son, David—getting killed in the Gulf War. It has nothing to do with this." The Judge cut off eye contact, "Frankly, Tucker, I can't think of a thing that can help you."

"There was one thing, Judge," Tucker said, pulling out his notebook. "Why did you tell Jason to be careful?"

"It's always what the older generation tells the younger, but they don't seem to pay much attention." The Judge emitted a quiet, nervous laugh. "You have a good afternoon, Detective. Give my best to Chief Rogers."

Tucker replaced his pad and pen, knowing when he was being stonewalled. "Thank you, Judge. It was an honor to meet you, and I'll pass on your greeting to the chief."

As Tucker walked out, Emily started in. His gentle touch on her arm stopped her. "Mrs. Riley, may I have one more word with you?"

Emily paused, then returned to the corridor. "Why, of course, Sergeant Tucker."

"The chief and the Judge are old friends, so he'll want to know how the Judge reacted to the news of Jason being shot."

Emily unzipped her handbag and pulled out a handkerchief. "It was strange, like he already knew. When I told him Jason was shot in the parking lot, he didn't ask for any details except to ask how Jason was doing."

Tucker pulled out a pad and pen again. "Maybe someone had already told him."

Emily removed her glasses, wiping them absentmindedly. "No, I asked the hospital staff, and they said nothing was mentioned. They wanted to wait and see how Jason was doing first. They wanted me to tell John."

"It is strange that he didn't ask for details. It goes against his reputation."

Emily nodded.

"One more thing, Mrs. Riley. Jason said that your husband told him to be careful."

Emily replaced the glasses. "Yes, I told Jason the same thing right after my husband did. Jason hadn't gotten much sleep, and I didn't want him getting in an accident."

Tucker stopped writing in midsentence. "You said right *after*?"

Emily stuffed the handkerchief back in her handbag and zipped it closed. "Yes, just after my husband had told him the same thing."

Tucker continued to write for the next minute, then remembered Emily waiting in front of him and said, "Sorry, Mrs. Riley. Thank you for your time. I hope the Judge will be well soon."

As Tucker left the hospital, there were a few things he knew: Jason lied about the bullet scar and what his grandfather said. Judge Riley knew beforehand about Jason being shot. And in unknown exchanges of files, glances, and handshakes, the case would be transferred from him and closed. The latter happened three weeks later. The case was never to see the light of day.

Meanwhile, the cigar box and its secret remained secure in the bank vault.

THE PROFESSOR

Waterbury Community College claimed to be a two-year public college but was more like a glorified high school. The student body was made up mostly of those who elected to be underachievers, signing up and dropping classes as needed to satisfy overindulgent parents' minimum standards to live at home for free.

Professor Richard Richford's demand for excellence, along with his formal British accent and attire, was in sharp contrast with the rest of the staff. Students found him fair, sensitive, at times humorous, and even accepted a poor grade from him in good spirits. Parents and most of the staff held him in contempt for not embracing the popular self-esteem movement. In maintaining their chief accomplishment of pacification, the administration worried that his authoritative method would discourage student attendance, the sole criteria that gave them access to the taxpayers' wallets.

Glancing down from his campus office, Professor Richford laughed at the short-term delight the staff and administration were going to have from his disappearance. However, if they knew about what was about to happen to their most popular student, Jason Riley, their pleasure would be short-lived.

His thoughts drifted as he heard the slow, steady flap of sandals coming up the stairs. There wasn't the spring that twenty-year-old should have. It pained him as he reviewed in his mind all the old-young faces of flaming potential he looked at each day, washed away in waves of alcohol and drugs that left their drive, purpose, and zest for life in smoke. That would soon change for Jason Riley, but free will could change even these changes. He would have to be careful.

-- -- -- -- -- -- -- -- -- -- -- --

Jason stood outside the open door, flipping one hand through his long hair and biting the tip of a nail of the other. No one he knew had ever had been called by Professor Richford to his office. Foolishness overcame anxiety, and Jason's knock was met firmly. "Enter, young man."

The Professor turned, taking final stock of the adult boy who soon would become a man. Jason's shaggy natural blond hair was almost white due to extensive time in the ocean and sun. His blue eyes and white teeth glistened against the dark tan that ended where the wetsuit normally started. His t-shirt stretched tight across his chest and hung loose, clearing by inches the chiseled abdomen below, and his baggy surf trunks failed to hide the powerful thigh muscles bulging below them. Richford heard that surfing was one of the best sports for all-around fitness, and Jason had the grades and attendance to prove his devotion to the sport, as did Jason's friend Alex. It seemed, despite a history of alcohol and marijuana use since sixteen, Jason was a fine specimen of a young man. The Professor wondered how much, like the bullet scars, this had to do with Lieutenant Jason Riley rather than Jason Riley.

As the Professor sat down, he noticed the trademark of the surfer, the tan hands hanging from white arms. *Now*, he thought with a degree of sadness, *the process starts*. He knew the young man who stood before him at the moment would be no more.

"Please, sit down. Mr. Riley, you don't mind if I smoke, do you?"

"Only if it was some bud, and you didn't share, that would bother me a bit." Jason broke into a big smile.

Looking over his glasses, Richford said sternly, "Mr. Riley, I don't think your marijuana intake enhances your life or, for that matter, that group of misfits you elect to hang around with."

Jason put on a fake hurt expression. "Professor, how can you say my friends are misfits when most have had the opportunity to learn the history of this fine nation under your able instruction?"

"While I always enjoy our adolescent conversations, time is short, and we must get down to business." Pulling out his pipe, Richford smiled.

"I guess this is about my finals. I want you to know that I really did study. I know my grades don't always show that, but I did study for you."

"You studied for me?" Richford raised an eyebrow. "Why would you study for me, Mr. Riley?"

Jason felt his stomach clench with the question. "Maybe you remind me of my grandfather."

"Really. Should I take that as a compliment?" Richford opened the thin folder on the desk.

"Yes, he's one of hell of a person, a little bit of a Bible-thumper."

"I take it, Mr. Riley, that you're not a Bible-thumper."

Jason felt like he was in quicksand. "No way. I think all religions are the same: if you live a good life, you get to wherever. In fact, religion with its right and wrong is dangerous. We have to be open-minded. Just look how many religious wars there have been. I guess my opinion wouldn't make me one of the founding fathers of this nation, but then, we are far away from those times."

Richford pulled out his black leather tobacco pouch. "Well, Mr. Riley, as always, you seem to be the poster child by looks and mind-set of these times." Pinching the tobacco, he loaded his pipe and slid Jason's final across the desk. "You had the highest class score, and I'm forced to admit that you earned an A. I know that will ruin your 2.0 GPA, but all good things must come to an end."

Jason looked down, searching for words. "I thought you called me here to tell me the opposite. I mean, you don't invite students for praise. I mean, you don't ask students here, so I figured the worst."

Richford chuckled. "Actually, I didn't call you here to discuss your final but to give you a chance to learn history firsthand. Are you interested, Mr. Riley?"

A deep frown, like an ugly scar, creased Jason's forehead. "Maybe. I consider myself a go-for-it type of person."

As Richford stood, he picked up the folder and looked down at Jason. "Well, it's good to know that you are a 'go-for-it type of person,' Mr. Riley. What do you know about World War II?"

Jason cleared his throat. "That the Japanese attacked us at Pearl Harbor. I'm going to see *Pearl Harbor*, it comes out Memorial Day weekend. Anyways, we dropped a couple of atomic bombs on them, ending the war."

As the Professor walked around his desk, he kept eye contact with Jason and sat opposite him. "Let me be more exact, Mr. Riley. Tell me about Europe and Hitler," he said, handing Jason his final.

"Mostly from movies." Jason folded his final into quarters.

"Nothing from my class?"

"Sorry, Professor. Sure, a lot. We were fighting Adolph Hitler's Nazi Germany. The turning point was the invasion of France at Normandy, D-Day, and the Russians ended it in Berlin."

"I would not count on movies being very accurate about history, but I guess something is better than nothing." He tapped Jason gently on the knee.

Jason began digging out of his hole. "I'm sure most of what I know is from you. We all learned a lot."

Fishing around in his vest pocket, the Professor produced a small box of matches. "With the mind-set and the way your peers come dragging into class, I have my doubts, and their finals show it."

"We are not bad, Professor, just young."

"Really? What is your standard for good and bad, Mr. Riley?"

"I don't know. I guess what we all agree to at the time." Jason felt the warmth rise in his cheeks

"So I guess we can add situational ethics, along with open-mindedness, and the pursuit of pleasure to get close to modern America, or should I say progressive America?" Richford withdrew a single wooden match.

"You make it sound so bad, evil."

Richford held the match in front of Jason's face. "Far different from what this country was founded on, but let's get back to the subject at hand." Leaning forward with a gentle hand resting on Jason's knee, Richford looked deep through his eyes, into his heart. "What has your grandfather told you about the war and the *Golden Eagle*?"

Jason's spine tensed as he struggled for words. "He told me… nothing about it. I mean the war. Uh…you mean the bird, the golden eagle?"

Placing the pipe in his mouth, Richford snapped. "Come, Mr. Riley, you're telling me you didn't know that was the name of your grandfather's bomber?"

Jason's hand trembled; something was very wrong. "I'm sorry. I forgot its name. What little I know is from my dad. I was really young. He only told me about its last flight, but my mother got so mad at him, he never said another word about it."

"Why was that?"

"She was very much a peace-and-love type of person." His head dropped. "It didn't matter. My dad was killed in the Gulf War a short time later. Anyways, I was named after my grandfather's co-pilot who was killed saving my grandfather. There was something about a mysterious cigar box… I forgot most of it, but I did get this."

Rolling up his left t-shirt sleeve, Jason turned his arm in full view of the professor—a tattoo of the insignia of the 572nd Bomber Squadron. "It's from a leather coat patch my grandfather gave my dad. My mother flipped when she saw it, being so anti-military. She almost sent me here to finish my last two years of high school."

Adjusting his glasses, the Professor leaned forward for a closer examination of the colorful design. "So…you were what, sixteen when you got this tattoo?"

Jason rolled down his sleeve. "Yes, sir."

"And your grandfather's reaction to this tribute to his old outfit?

"Strange."

"How so, Mr. Riley?" The Professor replaced the matches back in his vest pocket. "Well, I arrived at my grandparents' house almost two years ago; in fact, it was 4th of July. The last time I'd seen my grandparents was when they buried my dad. There was a lot of tension; my mother blamed them for Dad getting killed, being in the Army, going to West Point and all. I remember it like yesterday, as I walked up the front-porch stairs, my grandmother came rushing out, gave me a bear hug, and over her shoulder I saw my grandfather staring at me, not saying a word. I don't know how he knew, but he grabbed my arm and pulled up my sleeve. When he saw the tattoo, he passed out. We never found out what happened to him, and he never said another thing about the tattoo."

Professor Richford snapped the match head with his fingernail, and it flared to life. "I guess your grandfather was nervous about seeing you."

"Are you kidding? My grandfather has nerves of steel…It was something bigger than fear."

The Professor moved the match over the bowl of the pipe and took a few quick puffs, drawing the flame to the tobacco. "That was some welcome to Waterbury."

"That was nothing compared to the next day, when someone tried to kill me. I got shot three times."

Shaking the match to kill the flame, Richford prompted, "Really, Mr. Riley, such a story."

Jason stood up and took his t-shirt off. "Look, see the two scars?"

"Put on your shirt and sit down, Mr. Riley. I believe you." Richford placed the dead match on the corner of the desk.

"You want to see the other scar?"

The Professor continued to look at the dead match, peering through its smoke, the room, and campus. "Warm and light, now dark and cold. Like us, Mr. Riley, like us."

Jason looked down at the dead match for the lesson, the message, but he couldn't see it, only the dead match. He repeated, "You want to see the other scar?"

The Professor looked up at Jason. "Your left thigh—no."

"Hey, what th—I didn't tell you that!"

"Lucky guesses maybe." *That was close. I better be careful* he thought. With controlled, relaxed puffs, Richford regained inner control. "Well, Jason, I'll take your word for it. I hope the smoke doesn't bother you."

"No, Professor, it smells kind of good."

Reaching, Richford pulled the folder toward himself. "I have a little surprise for you, Jason."

So now I'm Jason, not Mr. Riley. "I like surprises."

"That's good to hear, Jason." From the folder, Richford pulled out an airline ticket packet and handed it to Jason. "Inside are round-trip tickets for England and France." He pulled out a check and held it up in front Jason. "As you can see, this check is made out to you for five thousand dollars. It should cover all your expenses and some spending money."

"I don't get it. What for?" Jason said, bewildered.

"There is, shall we say, a foundation very keen on developing Godly character. It is in short supply, especially with public education being what it is. You, Jason, have been predestined, or selected, if you like, to learn from life experience such lessons." The Professor slid a single sheet of paper across the desk to Jason.

"This is very generous, Professor."

"I would like to take credit, Jason, but I'm only an ambassador." Richford looked at the single sheet with Jason. "It's very simple, Jason, and straightforward. You agree, for the Foundation of Time, to travel to England June third and then on the fifth to travel on to France, where you will remain until the twelfth. Or, if you choose, you can remain longer in Europe. You will focus on and participate in the events leading to and in the actual invasion of Normandy, France." The Professor removed his glasses and stared Jason in the eyes. "This is no surf trip but an experience in history."

Jason eyed the contract in suspicion. "I know there's a catch. What do I have to do, sign my life away?"

The Professor laughed. "Jason, that's what I like about you. You have a way of hitting the nail on the head."

Jason started to laugh, not because he found the situation funny, but out of embarrassment at the professor's reaction. "Sometimes you're very confusing, Professor."

Richford withdrew a fountain pen from an inside pocket and handed it to Jason. "I'm just a simple agent. I must ask you to sign this agreement for me; it simply says what I said. There is one little item, since you will be attending the D-Day anniversary ceremony on June sixth. You must be in suit and tie and have a short haircut, as you will be representing the Foundation. Any questions?"

Jason put the ticket and check back down on the desk, signed the document, and handed the pen back. "How did you know about my grandfather's bomber?"

"I have known your grandfather for years. When you get to England, I will meet you and explain what you will be doing and where you are staying."

Jason backed away. "Again, thank you, Professor"

"Jason, what will you be doing next year?"

"I don't know yet, maybe surfing around the world for a year or so, make it a tradition. I did that when I graduated from high school, so whatever comes easy."

The Professor dropped the single sheet of paper into the folder. "No use rushing important matters; the summer can be a lifetime."

Jason, still confused, stuck out his hand. "I guess I'll see you on your home turf, Professor."

"Well, very good then, Jason. Don't forget, a decent military-type haircut."

"You can count on me."

Richford moved his hand to Jason's shoulder. "We are, Jason, we are."

THE LIE

Alexander Morgan Benson Montgomery was never one to display the cultural refinement of his prestigious family. He flopped his thin frame onto the couch as if he were a scarecrow cut down from a post. What he lacked in physical comparison to Jason, he made up both in intelligence and his serious manner. Emily viewed him as an anchor in stabilizing Jason's adventurous nature. She guessed John must have also, because he treated Alex like a member of the family.

As Emily was taking the cookies from the oven, she continued to marvel at how John went out of his way for all of Jason's friends. It was not that John was unfriendly, but ever since Jason had come to live with them, he was more involved with Jason and his friends than she could ever remember him being with David.

As the smell of the cookies grew stronger, Alex sat up, for next to surfing and collecting baseball cards, eating was his favorite pleasure in life. Moving items aside on the coffee table to make room, he heard Grandma Emily, as he called her, wonder aloud what was keeping Jason.

As Alex stuffed the first cookie in his mouth, the front door burst open, and an excited Jason made his entrance. Jumping over the back of the couch, Jason landed next to Alex, giving him a high five. "Dude, I'm going to Europe!"

Alex asked with a laugh, "How is a poor surfer boy like you going to Europe? You're as poor as a church mouse."

Scooping up a couple of cookies, Jason answered, "Because Professor Richford knows a genius when he sees one." Holding up the plane tickets, Jason put the five thousand-dollar check in front of Alex's nose.

Alex snatched the check from Jason. "Look here, young one; this check should have my name on it, if being a genius is what is needed. So don't lie to your elder. What gives?"

Jason, catching the broken cookie in midair, said, "Alex, bro, don't give me that elder crap. Two months doesn't give you any juice with this stud, but I do need your computer talents."

His tightened cheeks relaxed, the smile that spread across his face vanished, and Alex gazed through the wall. "My talent is yours. Spew on."

Jason dropped back on the couch and stared up at the ceiling, talking more to himself than Alex. "There's more to this than the Professor is letting on, and somehow my grandfather is involved."

For the next twenty minutes, Jason told Alex about his meeting with Professor Richford, the little he knew about *Golden Eagle*, and, as happens between best friends, his deep feelings and fears. Alex was careful only to interrupt to ask a few needed questions in order not to break the spell of the rare time when Jason let out his true feelings.

"So, Alex, I guess it's time to talk with my grandfather. What do you think?"

Alex took his saliva-covered finger out of his mouth and sponged up cookie crumbs from the plate. For a few seconds, he studied his finger as if a lab specimen and then sucked it clean. "We can ask him, but don't hold your breath. The best we can hope for is that I get some hits on this Foundation of Time or the 572nd Bomb Squadron."

Jason jumped up. "Well, bro, let's get a few waves, then when we get back, we'll talk to my grandfather."

Alex pulled up his six-four frame. "Bad news, the waves are small, but at least we'll get wet."

As Jason reached to open the front door, it opened, and there stood his grandfather.

"Well, there must have been an earthquake if you two aren't surfing yet." His voice was heavy and raspy.

"We would," Alex said, "but Jason had to meet Professor Richford. He gave him a trip to Europe."

All color drained from the old man's face, and he began to tremble. Jason and Alex grabbed him, fearing the Judge would drop before them. Emily, hearing the commotion of the boys, came running in from the kitchen just as Jason and Alex lowered the Judge to the couch.

"John, what is the matter?"

The Judge regained composure. "Nothing, dear, just a little faint for a second. It must be old age." With a little effort, he stood up.

"Don't get up," Jason said. "It's better if you rest for a few minutes, Grandpa."

"Death will soon give us all the rest we need. Right now, I need to hear about this Professor Richford deal."

"Grandpa, maybe after we go surfing."

"No, now, Jason. Stay right here." The Judge pushed himself up while yelling for Emily. He led her by the arm onto the front porch. While Jason and Alex couldn't hear what was said, they saw serious animation through the white-lace curtains. Then the Judge came back in the house smiling. Jason gave Alex a quick glance as his stomach knotted for the second time that day.

As the Judge sat down across from the boys, his body relaxed.

"Now, what were we talking about? Oh yes, it was about this trip of Professor Richford's."

Alex, sensing danger, started to stand, but the firm old hand on his shoulder drove him back down. "Now, Alex, you don't have to go. There are no secrets between friends. Right, Jason?"

Jason looked at his grandfather in shock; before him was a person he had never known. "Yeah, right, Grandpa, no secrets between us. As I said, we were just on our way surfing, maybe later."

They all stood at once, two to escape and one to capture.

"Jason, there is no later; there is only now."

As Jason turned to walk away, he was hit with the words.

"You want to hear about the *Golden Eagle*, don't you?"

Jason and Alex sank slowly down. "So here's the deal, Jason." A slight smile crossed the Judge's face. "You tell me every detail of your meeting with Professor Richford—I mean every word—and I will tell you about the last flight of the *Golden Eagle*. Do we have a deal?"

"Sure, Grandpa, sure."

For the second time, Alex started to stand and was met with the firm hand. "Alex, my boy, you seem to be making a habit of standing to leave when you're my guest. Anything wrong, son?"

Yeah, he thought, *there is a lot wrong, but what it is I don't know.* With a dry mouth, he said, "No, nothing, Judge. I've already heard the story, so—"

"So you'll be able to make sure Jason doesn't forget anything. I'm sure you want to hear about the *Golden Eagle* too, right?"

"Sure," Alex whispered.

Alex watched, tortured with waves of pain that followed each question tossed at Jason, but that pain seared every nerve as the Judge's attention turned to him. They both confessed later that if Jason's grandmother had not returned, the Judge might have worked them over for hours.

The Judge excused himself and left the room. Alex leaned over to Jason. "What is going on?"

Jason shook his head. "I don't know, Alex, but it's our turn next. Be alert."

When the Judge returned, he placed a beat-up cigar box on the coffee table gingerly, as if it were a deadly bomb. For a full minute, not a word was said. The three of them stared at the box. It was old, battered, and obviously a lot of effort had been used to seal it closed by the thick wrapping with black electrical tape.

"Well, boys, I guess it's my turn. First, let's clear the air about the person you call Professor Richard Richford. He is really Colonel Richard Steel of G2, or military intelligence to you."

Alex's eyes moved from the box to the Judge. "You're not telling us you know him from World War II?"

"That's correct, Alex. I know, he seems to have a way of keeping age at bay."

"Grandpa, no disrespect, but I find this hard to believe. He looks forty at most. I really don't think Professor Richford can be the same person you knew in WWII. Grandpa, you're talking, what, sixty years ago?"

Judge Riley held up his palm in a placating manner. "Back up, Jason. Your Professor Richford even told you he knew me. What he failed to tell you is how and under what name, but fair enough. Remember when you came to live here?"

"How could I forget!"

"You were not my only visitor at the hospital that day. Your Professor Richford came by to pay his respects. Colonel Richard Steel and Professor Richard Richford are the same person. I state that unequivocally."

"What you're saying is very disturbing. You're making him sound evil."

"Evil, that is to be seen, but what I do know, Jason, is I love you, as much as I loved your dad. I just want to protect you; there are issues between the Colonel and me that go back to 1944 and are still of the highest national security."

Now Alex leaned forward. "Maybe we can talk with Professor Richford."

"Alex, Jason, your professor is long gone and, knowing him, without a trace. So you are stuck with my word on the matter, but let's move on to the *Golden Eagle.*"

Reaching over, the judge picked up the box and held it at eye level, first in front of Jason and then in front of Alex. "I want you both to think really hard. Have you ever seen this box before?"

As the Judge lowered the cigar box back to the table, Alex spoke up, shaking his head. "Looks a little beat up to me, but I've never seen it before."

Jason stared down at the box. "Neither have I. What is it?"

Judge Riley pointed to the cigar box. "That, young men, is all that remains of the *Golden Eagle.* Except for us who flew her, it has not been opened since I sealed it."

Jason felt the soft edges of the faded box as he held it up to the light. "What's in it?

"Well, I think, Jason, you know more about that than I do."

"Whatever."

"Well, boys, there are few odds and ends I grabbed before the *Golden Eagle* went up in flames: a note, a picture of the crew, a photo of your grandmother, and maybe a few small items I've forgotten. The main item was already wrapped watertight and placed in the box by Lieutenant Jason Riley to keep it safe for him."

"Wow, this is like a time capsule!" exclaimed Alex. "Let's open it up."

Jason looked over the box with pierced eyes and a heavy breath. "Why hasn't he contacted you, Grandpa, to get it back? He died, right?"

"Once I thought he was dead, but now I know he will come, Jason. Soon." The Judge picked it up and balanced it on his fingertips, looking over it into Jason's eye for a clue that he recognized the box but found none, remembering the plea made to him to lie to Jason about the last mission. The Judge gently put the box beside him. "I'll tell you what, when you come back Jason from your trip, we will open it up."

"The story, Grandpa, the story"

The Judge's jaw sagged, and he leaned back in his chair while the anger burned inside against the Colonel. "Well, I guess it's time for the story to begin. A little background first, I'll try not to bore you. I was a B-17 bomber pilot, with the Eighth Army Air Force, sometimes called the Mighty Eighth. I was assigned to the 390th Bomber Group at Parham Airfield near Framlingham, England. One of the five bomb squadrons of the 390th was the 572nd, as your colorful tattoo testifies to, Jason. I never told you, but that is one fine tattoo."

Jason felt his eyes stretch as they darted toward Alex.

"The *Golden Eagle* was a B-17F, a four-engine monster that could take a beating. It took a crew of ten to fly and deliver a load of bombs to its targets, protected with twelve Browning fifty-caliber machine guns. I was the old man of the crew at twenty-three; the First Lieutenant co-pilot and the Second Lieutenant bombardier were your age. The other officer was our navigator, also a Second Lieutenant, a twenty-one-year-old. The six enlisted crew ranged in age from nineteen to twenty-one. There was the tail gunner, the two-side gunners called waist gunners, the ball turret gunner and the radio operator who also operated single fifty-calibers, and the flight engineer who manned the top gun turret.

"For nearly half a year, we flew over twenty-seven missions. At first, crews would rotate back Stateside after twenty-five missions, but with a casualty rate of over sixty percent, command kept extending the number of missions up to thirty, and on the day before our last mission, it was extended again to thirty-five. During that period, I made two emergency landings but never lost any crewmember. The only loss to the crew was after our second mission. My co-pilot was killed in an auto accident, of all the dumb luck, but that is how your namesake became my co-pilot. We were feeling pretty lucky until Monday, June fifth rolled around."

"So Lieutenant Riley was a replacement?" Jason asked.

"That's right, Jason, but don't think less of him. He was one of the best pilots around. Anyway, as the invasion of Normandy, codenamed Overlord, or D-Day to you, drew near, the preparation missions were relentless. The group mission, on the day before D-Day, was the Luftwaffe airbase at Abbeville, France. Except for the 572nd, we had a special mission. We were to break off and attack Field Marshal Rommel's B Army Headquarters, a hundred miles south. It was later determined that our successful bombing eliminated his intelligence staff, which had just pieced together the invasion plans."

"Wow, so you saved the invasion," Alex exclaimed.

"On our approach, all hell broke loose. Flak took out a third of the squadron; as we made our turn after the bomb run, a dozen fighters jumped us. We got shot up so bad that we couldn't make it back over the Channel. Somehow, Lieutenant Riley knew about the invasion location and time, so we headed to a small town in the Normandy area where I was able to land in a field. We hooked up with the French Resistance, and they split us up and hid us until our troops landed. As for the *Golden Eagle*, she was smashed up pretty bad, so, to prevent her and any part of the Norden bombsight and gyro from falling into the enemy hands, we set her on fire. End of story."

"Gee, Judge, that was exciting," Alex said.

"This doesn't make any sense," Jason said in disbelief. "Grandpa, my dad told me that I was named after your co-pilot because he died saving your life."

The Judge sensed he was at a critical juncture in his lie. "Well, he did, Jason. The fact is that he saved all our lives by directing us toward Normandy."

Jason frowned. "I thought it was more dramatic than that. If you thought Lieutenant Riley died, why would you protect or even keep the cigar box for him?"

The Judge glanced at the cigar box and then Jason. "Well, some of us made it back right away; for others, it took months. Some were captured and became POWs, like Lieutenant Riley was, and were released at the end of the war. With us scattered to the four winds and the war over, we just drifted apart."

Jason moved closer to his grandfather. "This sounds different than what my father told me."

Alex joined in. "The invasion was one of the biggest secrets of the war; how could Lieutenant Riley know?"

The judge pulled the box closer. "You were a young boy, Jason, and stories normally sound bigger than they really are. Alex, I really don't know the answer to your question."

"I guess," Jason said bitterly.

As the Judge stood up, he held the box tightly. "Jason, how were your other grades this semester?"

As Jason was about to reply, Alex looked down. His grades, or lack of, always brought on a war at his house.

"Besides history, a couple of C's and one other A."

The Judge looked down. "I hope French was the A."

Jason was happy to reply that it was, because, for some reason, it was the only subject his grandfather pressured him to take.

"Jason, you still have your passport?" The judge said as if an afterthought.

"I lost it."

"Could you leave your tickets here, please? I need to look at the dates and see about getting you a replacement, I don't think we—*you* have much time." The Judge pointed to the coffee table.

"Well, the waves are calling, Alex." Jason dropped the tickets on the table, and Alex and Jason rushed from the house.

As the front door slammed behind the boys, Emily came in from the kitchen. "I take it you've cleared everything?"

"It's clear to me now." The Judge walked over to her and wrapped his arms around her. He rested his head on her shoulder and started to cry.

"John, we have to talk."

"Emily, I wish I could, but I can't. I just need you to love and trust me and hold me tight right now." His hands clasped her tighter.

"After near sixty years, John, should I now change?" Emily knew that at times a mother's love was needed for a husband too.

THE CREW

Hunger drove Jason out of the water, but with Alex, hunger was a constant companion he had made peace with. They talked of great surf sessions and looked forward to a summer of no wetsuits and trunking it.

Alex shook his head like a wet dog. "How long you going to be gone, Jason?"

Jason came up behind Alex and unzipped his friend's wetsuit. "At least a week, maybe longer. I'll give you a call."

"You gonna bring a board?" Alex said, unzipping Jason's wetsuit.

"No, I don't know what the professor has planned. I'll rent one if I have time," he said, placing his board on the surf racks.

"Nothing like your own stick though."

Jason pulled on the rubber strap and slipped the hook into the hole in the rack to hold his board in place. "You're right, Alex, but I don't know the plan."

Alex stepped on his wetsuit to pull his leg free. "Did you hear the Rodent knocked up his girlfriend?"

Jason threw his wetsuit in the pickup bed and ducked as Alex's suit flew past his head. "Betty?"

"Yeah, he's bummed."

"I think he's working right now. Do you have any money?" He picked up Alex's wetsuit and put it in the pickup bed.

Alex reached into his pocket, pulling out a crumpled bill and some loose change. "Maybe a dollar or two."

"Alex, you're from one of the richest families around, and you live like a bum."

Alex threw himself into the passenger seat. "You said 'family,' not me. My dad has this thing about not spoiling me. If I had big bucks, do you think I'd be working down at Ace Hardware?"

- - - - - - - - - - - - - - - -

By the time they got to McDonald's, they'd combined their money for a total of $4.27, which included the 76 cents found after pulling Jason's pickup apart.

"Well, Jason, let's hope the Midget is on duty."

Alex positioned his hands to his eyes as if looking through binoculars. "I don't see him; maybe he's standing behind the counter."

"Everyone's a midget next to you, and keep your mouth shut or we won't be eating." Jason punched his friend's arm.

Steven "Rodent" McBeth was known for both his flaming red hair and a fiery temper to match. Anyone with any good sense, friend or foe, never, ever called him Midget to his face, and only those he called friend used Rodent, his nickname. Alex and Rodent shared the distinction of having the two largest and oldest family plots in Waterbury Cemetery and of being the only two of the crew from Waterbury, or from California, for that matter.

Rodent turned around just as Jason and Alex walked up to the counter. "Don't come any closer, Alex. You know I hate standing close to you. It hurts my neck looking up at your ugly face."

"What are you up to, four feet now?" Alex said as he placed his hand on Rodent's head.

"You're thinking about someone else. I'm five foot seven, and I still have a growth spurt coming up. I'm a late bloomer." Rodent slapped Alex's hand away.

Jason rubbed his stomach. "If we didn't need to feed these two handsome bodies, I would tell you that at nineteen, almost twenty, your blooming days are over."

Rodent's eyes darted around for the manager, then back to Jason. "Well, you better make it fast. You're in luck; the coast is clear."

"Fast is our middle name, especially as hungry as we are." Alex plopped down the $4.27.

Rodent pulled the mic to his mouth. "Tom, I need two specials."

Alex saw Thomas "Tom" Walker come from the back and glared up at the menu.

"What is *he* doing here?" Alex pointed at Tom.

"Alex, this is our newest team member."

"You have to be kidding, and Mr. W. must be losing his mind to hire him. He eats more than me; this place can't afford him!"

A middle finger flipped up in Alex's face. "I use the food to move these swift feet, not to grow uglier like you."

Alex swiped a hand over the counter at Tom. "You keep that up, and Waterbury will be looking for a new quarterback," he growled.

Tom looked down at the Rodent. "What's a special?"

"That is when our friends, you know, like Alex and Jason come in; it's three hamburgers, a large fry, and drink, times two."

"There is *nothing* like that on the menu," Tom said, pointing at the menu.

Rodent huffed a sigh and shook his head. "Figure it out, Tom. It's a favor to our *special* friends; get it?"

Tom's voice rose as his head and hand bobbed in unison, "I got it, but it sounds like stealing to me."

"Would you believe we have another preacher among us?" Rodent slapped his forehead.

"What's the matter with the Preacher? You guys are just jealous because he has faith and all you guys have are dumb ideas!" Tom yelled, throwing his hat on the counter.

"Well, speaking of his holiness." Rodent bowed down.

In came the Ox, Reb, and, with a big smile spread across his face, the Preacher. "My loyal subjects, your respect warms this humble heart." Preacher waved his hand at his four friends to stand who also had mockingly bowed down.

"Your loyal subjects are a bunch of crooks, and you should see them trying to steal food," Tom chimed in.

That was the final straw for the Rodent. He held out his hand. "You can kiss his ring," he said before turning, "and then you can kiss *this*." Rodent's protruding bulge began backing into Tom until he found Alex's arms wrapped around his chest, pinning his arms. "Leave me alone, or you'll be eating crab, Alex."

Walking around the counter, the Preacher faced Rodent. "We've talked about your temper thing, right?" He turned to Alex. "Let him go, Alex." He turned back to Rodent. "What do you want to do? If you want a piece of Tom, then you start with me. Rodent."

There was silence as Alex released his grip and Rodent stood there, flush with veins pulsing from his neck. To the curious bystander, Nathan "Preacher" Campbell and Rodent would seem an even match: they were the same age, but Preacher, while having a four-inch advantage, lacked the ten pounds of additional muscle stretching up Rodent's chest and out his arms. Those that looked on knew different by experience and sighed at the distance now between them.

It had happened last October, after the big cross-county rival football game. A small "after the game" party had swelled to hundreds. Eventually, the neighbors called the police, as the noise grew and the beer bottles started breaking. As the crew was leaving, a few drunken words were exchanged, many thought started by Rodent, when a half dozen of the rival defensive line blocked their path. What exactly happened next never could be agreed upon, since none of the crew was sober except Preacher. There was general agreement that Preacher pleaded, almost begged on behalf of his friends, and that within ten seconds of the opposing team rejecting his offer and promises to beat the crew to a pulp, three of the defensive line lay on the ground in great pain and three others were running away.

Rodent struck out his hand. "Sorry, Tom, this temper thing. Let's shake, friend."

There was a collective sigh of relief as Preacher embraced Rodent. The love fest came to a halt with the earth-shattering yell of Reb. The yell brought Mr. Winfield, the owner/manager, out from the back, where he had slipped in. "If you ever do that rebel yell again, Jackson, when there are customers here, I'll sit on you and crush you like a rodent. No offense, Steven."

It was a threat to be taken seriously, since Winfield weighed way over three hundred pounds. Every tie he wore struggled to make it halfway down to his belt. Winfield pointed at Preacher. "Well, Mr. Nathan Campbell, or, as the group of misfits like to you call you, Preacher, I take it, since you are on my side of the counter, have you decided to improve my sorry staff?"

"Mr. Winfield, this is remarkable, and twice in one day we're called misfits."

"Jason, who would the other intelligent person be that has correctly identified the pride of Waterbury Community College?" Winfield said.

"None other than the honorable Professor Richard Richford of that fine institute. While he, like you, has misidentified this fine group of American youth, he did recognize *my* genius."

Jason pulled out his wallet and unfolded the check, holding it up for all to see. "Please note the amount of five thousand dollars, and along with this came a round-trip ticket to Europe." Jason spent the next few minutes briefly recounting his meeting with Professor Richford.

Paul "Ox" Sorenson pulled out a cigar and held its tip to the ceiling. "This is surely an event worthy of lighting up a fine cigar, and, Reb, I think a good yell is in order."

Billy Ray "Reb" Jackson let out a yell that made most cover their ears and sent out a series of cheers and shouts.

Winfield waved his hands in the air to quiet everyone down. "I must be the only McDonald's in the nation that can go without customers for fifteen minutes. Steven and Tom get back in the kitchen, and I'll take the orders. This treat is on me in celebration of Jason's ability to fool the good professor. There's only one condition. Ox, you *cannot* smoke that cigar in here."

Ox dropped his hand and placed the cigar back in his shirt pocket. "You got it, Mr. W"

As he started to take orders, Winfield looked up at the door. "You mention free food and it figures the rest would show up. You guys remind me of seagulls."

Into the confusion and pushing in line came Gerald "Jerry" Zandi and Ray Stone. Tom and Ox nodded at their fellow warriors from the football field. Tom and Ox hailed from Indiana, Jerry from Maine, and Ray from New York. All had once been themselves lost in the halls of school but found comfort digging their fingers and feet into the football field, where they all learned to swagger and hoot in unison.

Jerry pushed ahead of Preacher. "Have you heard about Steve and Betty, Mr. W?"

"No. What about them?"

Preacher gave Jerry a kick to his ankle. "Oh, they've been going out for the last six months. Did I hear something about Jason going to Europe?"

"Nope, I didn't know that, and as for Jason going to Europe, ask him."

As Rodent and Tom finished the orders, the night crew came on duty. Winfield was in good humor and released the two. "Well, join your friends. That way I can poison the whole lot of you and improve Waterbury."

Winfield watched the exchange of elbows and sardonic glances as well as the easy laughter that followed. The absence of tension and precaution of the conglomeration brought a smile to his silent chuckle. *How wise of Professor Richford to acknowledge Jason with this opportunity. He is a natural leader.* In another time, they would rise to greatness. Now the permissive and indulgent parents—with too little faith and too much materialism, mediocrity, drugs, and sexual diseases—would doom their dreams. A cold chill gushed through his veins and soured the dream. He knew—he sensed, without knowing, that something or someone would change, and nothing could stop it. He glanced at his watch and flipped its band around as its plastic top slid against the matted hair of his arm.

Five days later, at CIA headquarters in Langley, Virginia, the deputy director of special operations re-read the e-mail. "Be advised, that on this date, retired Federal Judge John Riley picked up two expedited passports, one for himself and for a Jason Riley. Scan copies of the applications are attached, along with confirmed airline reservations."

Aaron Odin leaned back, folded his hands against his mouth, and exhaled. *Well, after so many years, is the old fox making his move? If so, where's he going?* He picked up the phone. "Director. Aaron here. We have activity on *Golden Eagle*. I need a surveillance team on Judge Riley and some computer time...No. Nothing for sure. He applied for a passport for himself, and I would guess by last name and age, for his grandson too...That's right. Used his address for the boy also, so he must be living with Riley." He paused again, sucking his lower lip in his mouth. "You're right. He's not a boy; he is almost twenty-one...I agree; I don't think it's anything, just a vacation or some type of trip with his grandson, but we can't take a chance. We have no choice really...I understand. You will know everything as soon as I know...That's right. I'll call you when I find out more, and thank you, sir."

Aaron put the phone down and turned his chair. He took the color photo off his credenza. He smiled at his smile in the photo, at fourteen with four trout, alongside of a prouder father. "That was a great trip, Dad." He put the photo back down and walked over to the wall safe and pulled out the summary report of the *Golden Eagle*.

He started to read the summary for the fifth time that hour but stood and paced before he could finish. As he reviewed his notes, he bit into his knuckle and then threw the pad across the office in fury.

"Jason Riley, you're as good as dead! You won't ruin my career like you did Dad's."

THE LAST NIGHT

The last two weeks had flown by since his visit with the professor—a shopping spree, a few parties in his honor, and a visit with his mother and his younger brother, Troy. It had not taken ten minutes for his mother to narrow her eyes and tighten her lips at his new haircut. He explained to her that it was part of the agreement for the trip, but her hands flew up as her steps shuffled from couch to chair, shifting a leg an inch here, fluffing a pillow another inch there.

"Who gave you this trip, some Nazi war vets? Why can't you look more like Troy?"

She pushed all of Jason's buttons. "Maybe because I don't want to look like some drugged-out hippie left over from Woodstock." He snarled.

She turned to the final chair. "What's wrong with Woodstock? It happens to be one of the cultural milestones of this country. I guess your grandfather would have you repeal the free-speech movement, women's rights, and abortion. I knew it was a mistake to let you live with them."

Jason felt his nerves sear. Words began forming under his tongue he could not bite, so he rushed out of the house, slamming the door in his wake. He walked around the block to cool down. The community looked different. The gap between the sidewalks seemed vast and empty, and a cold breeze chilled the air. He had grown up knowing what to say, when and how, now that comfort had cracked, leaving him with booming arguments and desolate silence of the street. Gazing down the block was like gazing through a room of mirrors, and vertigo forced him to sit. *Maybe Mom is right; living with my grandparents has unsettled this balance.*

While any potential arguments remained smoldering, the rest of that first day could not prevent his mother's and brother's comments, beliefs, and idiosyncrasies slipping under his skin to the bone. The next day, Jason called the airlines and was more than willing to pay the extra fee to change his ticket. He could handle them four days, but a week would boil his blood.

--- --- --- --- --- --- --- --- ---

As Jason finished packing, he heard his grandfather's steps against the stairs. A soft rap on the door followed. "Come in, Grandpa." Jason closed the two suitcases. "All packed; I could have done this later."

The Judge bent down and tugged on the suitcase handle, but it remained grounded. "What did you pack, bricks? I figured with your friends all coming over, and knowing them, they will want to, shall we say, have a few adult beverages with you after the movie. It's better to be ready now than rushing around in the middle of the night. What movie are you going to see?"

"*Pearl Harbor.* It just came out." Jason lifted the suitcases off his bed. "That should do it. I hope you got my passport?"

"It was a rush, but I got it. I left it out in the glove box; it should be safe. I take it that I'm still giving you a ride to the airport?" The Judge dropped a hand in his pocket and felt the two passports.

"I wouldn't want anyone but you to drive me." Jason gave his grandfather a hug and felt the old man tremble. Jason felt the warmth rise in his face and wanted to hide. There was a sense of shame, but why? *What happened to Grandpa?* His entire behavior since the meeting with the professor had been beyond strange, as Jason once knew it. At Emily's call, both men's heads lifted before their arms dropped to their sides.

The Judge wiped away a tear, its warmth smearing the back of his hand. "Jason, I guess we better go down and help your grandmother, but before we do, this may be our last chance alone, and I wanted to tell you, I love you like your father. The last thing I would ever want is for anything to happen to you or your friends. Now, what did I say?"

Jason felt the room shrink as he gazed into the Judge's face. His thoughts refocused, but the gaze of the Judge swallowed his vision. He cleared his throat. "That you love me as much as my dad, that you don't want anything bad to happen to me or my friends."

The old man pulled Jason forward in another hug and whispered in his ear. "Remember—whatever happens, we love and trust it to be true."

"I know, Grandpa, I know."

"Well, we better get going before your grandmother starts yelling." He pushed Jason away gently.

The open house for all his friends was the usual overkill by his grandmother. He marveled how, at her age, she could pull it off when women half her age would struggle.

"Thank goodness for paper plates," Emily exclaimed, pushing down the empty plates in the trash bag. "I have never, John, seen such eating in all my life. Even the girls eat like men!"

"I think they just ate us out of house and home." The Judge jokingly turned his empty pockets inside out.

"What was the final count, John?

The Judge continued tying up the bags. "I think about twelve thousand . . . half of Waterbury."

Emily wiped down the counter. "It seems like it."

Suddenly the kitchen was full as the crew barged in.

"That was great. Can we help you clean up, Grandma Emily?"

"Thank you, Alex, but somehow I think having you boys helping would be more like having a bull in a china shop. What I would like, Jason, is a picture of you boys."

"Okay, Grandma, but first let me get everyone else going, then we'll take a group picture of the crew, then we're going to the movie and, you know, for a final private goodbye." Jason bent down and kissed his grandmother on the forehead and waved Alex over. "Alex, come on and give me a hand."

- - - - - - - - - - - - - -

After ten minutes of ushering everyone out but the crew, Jason pulled Alex into his grandfather's study. "What is the latest you found out?"

Alex pulled out a piece of paper and reported, "There is nothing about the Foundation, but, like I said before, there is a ton on the 390th Bomber Group. They have their own Web site and a museum in Tucson, but there is no mention of the 572nd as part of that group. I even tried the Air Force Historical Research Agency at Maxwell AFB but hit a brick wall. No *Golden Eagle*, no John Riley, Jason Riley, no 572nd. I guess we didn't listen too well."

"Yeah, Alex, we got my grandfather's name wrong and my tattoo isn't real . . . give me a break. Next there will be no Field Marshall Rommel." A sneer curled Jason's mouth.

"What was your grandmother able to tell you?"

"What she was able or would; there is a difference, you know. When I asked her if Grandpa went to any reunions to see any of his old crew, she said, 'What crew?' When I said from the *Golden Eagle*, she said that I would have to talk with my grandfather about it."

"Maybe you shouldn't go, Jason." He placed his hand on Jason's shoulder.

"Can't. I've already spent over a thousand dollars of the five. If I don't go, I'll have to pay it back." Irritated, Jason pushed Alex's hand away. "Besides, I want to get to the bottom of this. I guess when I'm in England, I'll have to do some of my own research not on the Professor's agenda."

- - - - - - - - - - - - - - -

Emily aimed the Polaroid and fired away. "John, get back there. I want to take another shot. I'll give you one if you behave." Emily looked down at the developed photos. "I have never seen a finer-looking group of young men."

The crew pushed and shoved to look at the photo. Jerry finally held the photo up so they could all see and said, "Alex, did anyone ever tell you fluorescent clothing is out? That is one ugly green t-shirt."

Emily took the photo back and wrote "eleven copies" in the margin. "I'll take it in tomorrow and have a copy made for each of you. Don't forget to drop by to get them, even if Jason's not here." She picked up the other photo. "John, as promised, this one is yours."

Jason whistled. "Well, it's getting late. We'll miss the movie. Duty calls; everyone to your vehicles and mount up." With that, the crew bade goodbye with hugs, kisses, and handshakes, thanking the Judge and Emily.

Just as Jason headed out the door, his grandmother yelled, "Jason, don't you dare leave yet." She walked over and grabbed him by the ear. "You come in here now."

"You're making me look bad in front of the guys, Grandma. They're watching!" Jason protested.

"Be quiet," she snapped, followed by a snicker, "or they'll have a lot more to talk about." She clasped Jason in a tight hug. "Seriously, Jason, I'm not going to get up tomorrow morning. It is too early, so I'll say goodbye to you now. I want to ask you to talk with your grandfather on the way to the airport; he is really worried about this trip. I've never seen him so upset."

Jason patted her shoulder. "I know. I even asked him if I should go, and he said I had no choice. I'm worried, not only about Grandpa, but about my friends. I just have this feeling, and I can't put my finger on it."

She looked into his deep blue eyes. "Jason, dear, love conquers fear. If you could transfer my love for you, there would be victories in every area of your life. Remember, you're loved, and this will always be your home." Jason kissed his grandmother on the cheek as the car horns started honking.

"Good Lord, get out there, Jason, before they have the neighborhood up in arms. Oh, and take that skateboard on the couch. I think it belongs to Preacher." Heading out the door, Jason gave thumbs-up to his grandmother.

As the door slammed, Emily walked over and sat down next to the Judge. "John, do you want to talk?"

Standing up, he replied, "Emily, it's not that I don't want to talk, it's…I can't. Maybe when Jason comes back we can all sit down and talk it over. I told Jason and Alex I'll show then what is in the cigar box."

"I wouldn't mind seeing what is in it, and I'm relieved to hear you think he *is* coming back. The way you have been acting recently, it was like you thought he wasn't."

He'll be back, or we wouldn't be here he thought. "I'm tired, and I have to get up early." Bending down before she could ask another question, he kissed her and said goodnight, leaving her to her thoughts.

After a major stop for a couple of twelve packs, a bottle of Wild Turkey, and Jim Beam, the crew went up the hill to their favorite drinking spot, Waterbury Cemetery. The hilltop World War II memorial provided not only a breathtaking view overlooking the town and ocean, but of both the paved and the dirt road, which, from opposite directions, went up the cemetery hill. The few times police came to check out reports of lights or noise or, as the crew called it, being harassed, they found only the telltale sign of bottles and beer cans.

"Reb, you're lookout, and make sure you give us plenty of warning," Jason said.

"You have to be kidding, Jason. Preacher is here; he is always the lookout."

"Not this time, so stay alert. Last thing I need tonight is to be caught by the pigs; worst yet is us running head-on into them with our lights off, so make sure you call out the right road."

As a joint was passed around, Tom waved it on without taking a hit. While that was normal for Preacher, who rarely came with the crew on what they called "missions," it was quickly noted by Reb. "What's going on, Tom? You had one beer. What, are you getting religion?"

Tom threw his empty can in the bag. "You know, the Preacher makes sense; what the hell are we here for? Just to get drunk, stoned, and act like oversexed dogs? What a great purpose."

From the ground, Rodent added, "Well, I wish it was just getting drunk and stoned. That oversexed dog part I could leave out, Betty being pregnant. So here I'm working at McDonald's at minimum wage."

Ox placed his hand on Rodent's shoulder, blowing cigar smoke like a dragon, and almost vomited as he talked. "What happened? Did you flunk the safe sex-class or miss the 'condom on the banana' lesson?"

"There's always Planned Parenthood, your local birth-control center," Ray piped up.

"I don't want to hear that murdering talk!" Preacher, red faced, jumped up.

Normally, Jason would have been wiped out at that point but felt the beer agitating his head. "Sorry to hear about that, Rodent, but let's not get into the abortion debate when we've all been drinking. The last thing I want to do tonight is break up a fight."

Alex staggered and slurred. "Jason's right, yeah, right, not a time for us to … to fight about, over our sorry, wasted lives." He kicked Jerry and said, "Get up, you slob."

Jerry shook his head groggily. "What's going on?"

"What's going on? I'll tell you what's going on. Look around, what do you see? The graves of those like us, teenagers, young adults, yet they had the courage to do what was right. We don't even know what's right. We are so … we are … are so open-minded, our brains have fell, I mean, fallen out. No right or wrong with us, no good or evil. Tom is right; the only one among us who has a clue is the Preacher, and we mock him."

Ray laughed and cheered Alex. "Preach it, Alex, you drunk!"

Jason yelled, "This is getting a little too serious and the fog is rolling in, so it's time for my famous magic act. Shut up, Alex; I need your help."

- - - - - - - - - - - - - - - -

The Judge lay silent in bed and listened to Emily's light snoring, wishing for sleep. On the first ring, the Judge answered and heard a familiar voice say, "Judge Riley?"

His throat tensed. "Yes."

"It is time. I'll meet you at the bottom of the cemetery hill on the paved road in a half hour."

Hearing Emily move, Judge Riley whispered, "Yes, I understand, but you have the wrong number," and with a trembling hand he replaced the receiver.

Emily turned over and mumbled, "Who was that, John?"

The Judge stood. "Wrong number, Emily. I'm not feeling well. I'll take the alarm clock and my clothes downstairs to sleep. I don't want to bother you in the morning."

Emily reached out. "You don't have to leave."

He patted her hand. "I think it best I go downstairs."

- - - - - - - - - - - - - - - -

Three times a day, the surveillance vehicle was changed; tonight it was a dark blue van. The team had already used dozens of rolls of film on Jason and his friends. They were just settling in for another long, boring night when the Judge's short phone conversation transferred into their ear sets. After a short discussion via secured satellite, the decision was made to set up along the main cemetery road to intercept the Judge rather than risk following him.

END OF THE PARTY

The Judge went into his study and pulled out the guest bed, fluffing the pillows and pulling the sheets aside. Once done, he got dressed and snuck up to Jason's room. The suitcases lay at the base of his bed. Pain shot through his arms as he tugged on both handles, so after lugging one down the stairs in thuds, he heaved it in the car trunk and returned for the other. Down in the basement, he went directly behind the furnace, where he removed a loose stone from the wall and took the cigar box and a heavy wrapped bundle. Placing both on the workbench, he opened a penknife and cut the tape that sealed the cigar box with a delicate slice.

Lifting the lid, he first took out two photos. A yellow tint clouded the faces and background, but the photos themselves remained unbent and shiny. He smiled down at the smiling face of a young woman, then placed the other photo next to the Polaroid taken earlier that evening. With careful dexterity, he taped the brittle note onto a piece of cardboard. He didn't have to read it; he knew the blocked printed list by heart: *D-Day tomorrow, Pres. Roosevelt dies April '45, two atomic bombs on Japan ends war with no invasion, Pres.*

John Kennedy, Pres. Jimmy Carter, Pres. Ronald Reagan, Pres. George Bush, Pres. James Strong.

He tried to lift out the well-sealed package, but it was jammed against all sides. Turning the box upside down, he hit the bottom until it dumped on the bench. A quarter pinged against the bench top and rolled toward him. He picked up the New York State quarter with the current year 2001 imprint on it, fifty years old and discolored, yet just issued. His head shook. "How could I forget about it? I should have known it was now."

Once satisfied that nothing had penetrated the protective packaging, he set it aside and picked up the black-and-white photo of the crew of the *Golden Eagle*. As he stared at the faces of the smiling crew, he picked up the color Polaroid and compared them while bitter tears rolled down his cheeks.

His eyes narrowed as the blood rushed to his fingers. He unwrapped the 45 cal automatic, slammed home a full clip, pulled back on the slide, and chambered a round. Standing, he placed an extra clip in his jacket pocket and jammed the forty-five into his waistband. He would finally deal with Colonel Steel, once and for all.

Placing the contents back in the box, the Judge placed it back in the hole and replaced the loose stone so it would not give away the hiding place. The last thing he needed was to get Emily involved in the deadly business.

The Judge used a penlight to check his watch, twenty minutes before midnight; he was running a few minutes late. A word of praise passed the Judge's lip when the car started on the first turn of the key. Using only the moonlight to guide him, the Judge backed out of the long driveway. Halfway down the block the two eyes of the car flooded the road as he flipped a switch.

Lieutenant Jason Riley staggered up the dark, moonlit dirt road toward the barracks, falling farther behind Alex and Jerry by the minute. "You guys, wait up. I need to take a piss." Seeing them continue forward as if not hearing, he mumbled to himself as he entered the woods, "You call yourselves friends."

As he unbuttoned his fly, the full effect of a heavy night of drinking hit him. He passed out, falling into the tall, soft grass.

The Judge saw the quick flash of the penlight and pulled up behind the dark sedan with the professor standing next to it. Judge Riley, with one hand, pushed closed the door and with the other shot down toward his waistband to grasp the perforated handle of the 45 cal automatic. He would not back down. He would kill Colonel Steel and maybe save the crew, the *Golden Eagle*, and Jason.

The Colonel extended his hand toward the Judge. "I know this is difficult." As the judge made the mistake and extended his hand, the Colonel clasped it, spun around, and, in one fluid motion removed the 45 cal automatic out of the Judge's waistband. "I'm disappointed, but you are not the first."

The Judge's body remained locked, and his mouth gaped. "I can't let you kill them again."

"I need the extra clip and Jason's passport." Steel held out his hand.

"Is there any other way?" Defeated, the Judge reached into his jacket pocket and handed him the clip. The Colonel removed the clip from the 45 cal automatic, removed the bullets from the clip, then the same with the spare clip. With flare he pulled the automatic's slide back, catching the ejected bullet in midair. "Not bad for an eight hundred-year-old," he said. Opening the back door of the judge's car, Steel continued. "I wouldn't try taking this to London. The airlines get very sensitive about such things." He threw the gun, bullets, and a large envelope on the backseat.

"You didn't answer my question." The Judge leaned against his car for support.

"Is there any other way, you ask? I have no idea; all I know is that this is the way it is going to be."

"You seem to forget, I was there, and I know you shot Jason at the hospital."

"You're wrong; you were there part of the time. I have always been there. Again, I need Jason's passport."

The passport appeared under the Colonel's nose. "I guess he will need this."

"You'll get it back with all the proper dates and stamps. As far as me shooting Jason in Waterbury, the Germans shot him. If I had not been there, he would have died."

"Germans tried to kill him in Waterbury?"

"No, in France during the war." The Judge opened his mouth. The expatriated Colonel continued. "Look, in a few days, you will have answers. Until then, continue to have faith in God … One more thing: I never killed the crew, nor would I have ever been instructed to do so." The Colonel looked up the hill that was bathed in full moonlight. "The fog will be rolling in; it is that time. Stay here and go up when you see me drive down. On the backseat is an envelope with instructions, money." Reaching into his pocket, the Colonel pulled out a couple of plastic bags. "You'll need them on the hill."

As the Colonel turned to walk away, he paused. "Watch out for yourself. You seem to have picked up a blue van as an escort." The Judge continued to lean against his car for fear he would faint. He watched the Colonel drive away with his lights off.

– – – – – – – – – – – – –

The driver in the blue van tapped the plug into his ear. "All I'm getting is static."

In the rear of the van, the operator hit the sophisticated equipment. "Yeah, the best equipment in the world, my foot. What do you want me to do?"

The agent with the large telephoto lens said, "Not to knock over the camera for a start. Did you see that guy take the weapon from the Judge? A real pro."

The agent in the passenger seat yelled, "We've been ordered to stay on the Judge. Let's hope the photos identify our mystery guest."

"I need a quarter for Jason," Alex said, slurring.

Jason pulled the bottle of Wild Turkey from Alex's hand and took a couple of quick slugs. "As I said, this is getting a little serious." Pushing the light button on his watch, he peered at the face blearily. "It's almost midnight, so it's time for my famous magic act before we lose the moonlight and the fog rolls in."

Preacher flipped a quarter to Jason. "Here is a new one, just issued for the cause."

Jason placed the New York quarter in his right palm and held it up for the crew to see. As he passed his hand across his face, he snapped the quarter in his mouth, pushing it over with his tongue between his gum and cheek. "Now you see it, now you don't." He held up his hands to show the quarter was gone.

Alex became pale with sweat. He managed to mumble, "Professor." Jason turned around as the Professor walked out of the fog.

As the Colonel drove by, he flashed his high beams. A few minutes later, the Judge pulled into the cemetery parking lot. *Strange, only Jason's pickup is here.* Reaching over, he grabbed the plastic trash bags while reaching into his pocket for the penlight. As he walked up to the war memorial, the fog was so heavy there was hardly any visibility.

Turning on the penlight, the Judge picked up the pile of Jason's clothing, making a mental inventory as he placed them in one of the plastic bags. After a minute, he located Jason's watch and three rings. As he walked around the area, he picked up a couple of beer cans, a lot less than expected. The Judge was about to leave when his light reflected off the Wild Turkey bottle. As the judge bent down to pick it up, he noticed the brown liquor had poured out and filled the familiar name engraved in the flat granite gravestone. The old man fell to the ground where he remained emotionally spent until the fog lifted and the full moon again bathed the grave in soft light.

As the Judge drank his second cup of coffee in the 7–11 parking lot, he reread the instructions the Colonel had left and then headed for the airport. In the underground lot, Judge Riley backed into the space, almost hitting the concrete wall. Unlocking the trunk, he removed Jason's clothing and personal effects from the plastic bag and repacked them in one of the suitcases, along with consolidating needed clothes into one suitcase. He got back in the car and drove up to the departure level and summoned a skycap, handing him his tickets.

At the ticket counter, the skycap lifted the suitcases off the cart and placed them on the scale, then departed, happy with the generous tip. Midway through the check-in process, the ticket agent rechecked the computer screen. "There must be an error. Sir, I don't show you on this flight; I have a Jason Riley."

"There must be a name error, and I am John Riley," he said in his most sincere voice.

The agent continued punching the keyboard. "Mr. Riley, I have you for tomorrow, the fourth, not today."

Taking the tickets back, the Judge smiled. "I guess it is old age. Those suitcases nearly killed me; can I leave them here?"

The agent was about to say no and then changed her mind. "Let me check."

A few minutes later she came back. "If it's all right with you, we can forward your suitcases all the way to London. Tomorrow your flights look like they'll be full. If you'll please give me your tickets, I'll process you now for tomorrow."

Judge Riley was about to say no when his eye caught a reflection off the plastic sign. *The Colonel was right. The hunt is on again.* "Thank you very much; that would be very kind of you."

A few minutes later, he headed to the boarding gate with his boarding pass visibly in hand. He hid behind the first pillar and watched his tail push his way to the front of the counter in a panic.

Reaching the counter, the CIA agent displayed his fake FBI identification and, in a rude manner, demanded to know where the old man was going.

The ticket agent was impressed with his credentials but not with his manner. "Whom are you talking about?"

"Mr. Riley."

The ticket agent continued to smile, but inside she felt the opposite "A Mr. Riley is scheduled for a connecting flight to London."

"I need to get on that flight now! Do you understand?"

In a calm voice, the ticketing agent replied, "Yes, sir. There is time." She pointed over his shoulder. "If you will get in line, there are only few people waiting. Another agent or I will take care of you when it is your turn."

"You don't understand. I need to get on it *now*." He pounded the counter.

With narrowed eyebrows, the ticket agent flattened her tone. "There's a lot of room, sir, and I have other passengers who are waiting."

The imposter glanced over his shoulder at the line of glaring faces behind him. Returning a cold stare, he stomped back to the end of the line. Pulling out his cell phone, he reported his assumption that the Judge had used Jason Riley's reservation to change his travel to today. Twenty minutes later, the same ticket agent stared across from him. "I want on the same flight as Jason Riley."

"Let me get this right. You want to be ticketed the same as Mr. Jason Riley, is that correct, sir?"

"You have trouble hearing?"

"Not at all, sir. I'm just making sure you get what you deserve."

A few minutes later, the imposter arrived at the gate that was already boarding. The Judge was about to hand over his boarding pass when he faked having forgotten something. Heads turned with the strange voice. "I forgot my newspaper; I'll be right back."

The CIA agent, deciding he had already drawn enough attention, continued in line and boarded the plane.

As the Judge walked past the ticket counter, he went over and thanked the helpful ticket agent. With a deadpan expression and automated voice, she replied. "Mr. Riley, I don't know why you are thanking me; I simply gave the FBI agent what he wanted."

- - - - - - - - - - - - - - - -

Emily picked up the Polaroid photo of Jason and John from the coffee table, wondering why she had written in the margin to have eleven copies made. Emily shrugged her shoulders. "Must be a senior moment," she said quietly. She was starting to worry about John when she heard the car pull into the barn that served as the garage. From the front porch, she waited. After five minutes, she wondered what was keeping him; she did not know that the Judge was hiding one of Jason's suitcases. Finally, as he appeared, she glanced at the man she loved so deeply and thought he had aged ten years in the last two weeks. As he took the first step, she said, "John, you look awful."

Out of breath, Judge Riley bent down and kissed Emily. "I feel like it; I had a rough night."

Holding open the door, Emily glanced around. "Where is Jason's truck?"

The Judge patted Emily's backside softly. "Up at the cemetery lot; it broke down. I'll go up later with Carl and see if I can get it started."

Emily jokingly slapped the Judge's hand away. "John, you must be careful; you are not a young chicken anymore. I take it that Jason got off okay?"

The Judge lifted his head and smiled. "Yes, he's on his way." Then his gaze dropped. "I love the smell of coffee. Even better, I love a good cup."

"One cup of coffee coming up." She gave him a quick peck on his cheek.

━ ━ ━ ━ ━ ━ ━ ━ ━ ━ ━ ━ ━ ━

"Have him continue on to London." Deputy Director Odin said, ending the conversation and slamming the phone down in the surveillance chief's ear. He began dialing and muttering. "Screw up a simple job of watching an old man."

"Hello, Director, Aaron here. I need about a half hour of your time. We have a lot of activity on *Golden Eagle*. I think we'll have to bring the President in on this."

The Deputy looked at his watch while waiting. "An hour and half will be fine. I'll let Sally know where we will be meeting. I'm having everything moved from storage. I'll see you then."

Aaron walked out to his secretary. "Mary, I need Robert Higgins up here now. Tell him to cancel all his plans for the weekend—no, make that for the next two weeks."

A WAKE-UP CALL

May 1942, landowner Percy Kindred, along with his brother, Herman, received the requisitions from the Air Ministry that would transform Crabbs and Park Farms to Parham Airfield. Eight miles of hedgerows were ripped out, along with fifteen hundred trees, replace with four and a half million bricks and a half million tons of concrete to help create what was officially called Farmlingham Station 153, home of the USAAF 390th Bombardment Group (Heavy). Parham, as the locals called it, was not unique among the forty bomber bases of the Eighth Army Air Force. Nearly all were built in the middle of farmland scattered over the northeastern part of England. Parham's uniqueness lay in its proximity to the North Sea and Germany, the closest bomber base to both boundaries.

The base itself spread over a thousand acres; this was to prevent German air attacks from knocking it totally out. Circling the three runways were the taxi runways with offshoots of large concrete circles called hardstands that held the B-17 bombers. Living quarters of squadrons and support units of over three thousand personnel, along with work areas, were also spread far apart to make the base a difficult target.

Up the road from Site 5, home of the 458th Sub-Depot, was Site 8. Thirty-four Nissen huts dotted the site of the 572nd Bombardment Squadron (H) and bunked the crew of the *Golden Eagle*. The enlisted huts each held two crews of six men while the officers' huts held three crews of four, making an even dozen to crowd under the roves of sheet metal. You could fry an egg on its surface in the summer, but knives of icicles hung from its corners in the winter. The thin layer of insulation forced the soldiers to sleep with long underwear under coats and blankets. The one small wood stove often went out within a few hours, as the men slipped their heads under the blankets, and the waiting began for the man who would rekindle the fire, just to sleep the last hours of the early morning.

When no one responded to his pounding on the back door, the Corporal went in yelling, "Lieutenant Riley! Lieutenant Riley!"

Alex pulled the pillow over his head, moaning. "Please, Jason, answer him. Make him go away before he splits my head open."

Jason forced his head to lift a few inches off the pillow. "What is it?"

The Corporal stood at the foot of his bed. "Sir, you need to report to group commander's office at 0700 hours."

Jason let his head fall back on the pillow. "Okay, okay, just go away." Dismissed, the corporal made a beeline for the front door.

Jason lay there, half in, half out of sleep when suddenly he jumped up, holding his head at the same time, and almost stepping in the pool of vomit on the floor. Looking down, he almost threw up again, and then he spotted the new quarter that the Preacher had given him. Picking it out, he wiped it clean with the blanket. Suddenly he dropped the quarter on the bed and, as he realized he was in a Quonset hut, yelled out, "Where am I?"

Alex pulled the pillow off his head and growled, "Jason, give me a break. Go bother Jerry."

Jason looked around, spotting Jerry staring up at the ceiling. "Jerry, Jerry, get up."

"Yeah, Jason. What are you, nature boy?"

Jason sat on the bed next to Jerry. "Something is wrong."

"I'll tell you what's wrong, Jason, you're naked." He threw the blankets aside and jumped up, asking, "What happened to you?"

"You tell me!" Jason shouted.

Jerry stood looking down at Jason. "Shut up, Jason, you'll wake the other crews. Your feet, hands, and face are all brown."

"What are you talking about?" Jason shook his head. "Wow, that Wild Turkey is murder."

"You're telling me that eating turkey made you look like that?"

"Are you crazy, Jerry? How'd we get here?" Jason jumped up and cried.

Jerry backed across the aisle closer to Alex's bunk. "I'm not crazy; you're the one standing naked, looking like a freak. To answer your question, we walked here; you were too drunk. Your bike is still at the club."

"This is a joke, right Jerry?"

Jerry looked down at Alex while trying to keep an eye on Jason. "What did you use, Jason, leather stain?"

"What are you talking about?" Jason felt sick and sat back down on his bed.

"Your hands and feet, your face."

"No, you idiot, not my tan, this place," Jason pleaded, almost crying.

Jerry decided not to wake Alex and instead walked over to Jason. "You better stop acting crazy; you got about fifty minutes to report or the old man will chew your backside off if you're late"

Jason's eyes fell to his wrist. "Where's my watch?"

"Right where you always leave it." Jerry lifted the lid of Jason's footlocker. "It's not here, and your wallet is missing too."

"Look, dude, you better give me my watch and wallet." Then he noticed his bare fingers. "Where are my rings?"

Jerry closed the lid and put up his palms facing Jason and slowly backed over to Alex's bed. He shook Alex. "Alex, get up, get up. We have problems."

"Give me a break, Jerry." Alex struggled out of bed and grabbed his head. "Jason, what's the problem?"

"What's the problem? My watch is missing; my wallet and rings too. I'm standing here naked, and I don't know where the hell I am!" He slowly stood and walked toward Alex.

Alex pushed Jason aside and reached down into Jason's footlocker, got a pair of boxers out, and threw them at him. "Have mercy; let's not shout. And put those on."

"Whose are these?" Jason held up the brown boxers.

"They came out of your locker; figure it out."

"I don't have any locker, but I'll put them on rather than stand here naked. This is the worst hangover, ever."

Putting on the boxers, he sat back down on his bed with Jerry and Alex sitting across from him.

"Alex, Jason needs to see the old man at 0700, and look at him."

"Wow, Jason, what did you do to yourself, use stain?"

"What you two did, not me."

"We're not going to get anyplace, Alex. Jason is still drunk, not making any sense."

"Listen, Jason," Alex said, "as your friend, the Lord knows I have tried to keep you out of trouble. Hate to lose one of, if not the best pilot in this group, so don't be a royal pain. Let's get ready."

"This is a joke, right?" Jason attempted his best smile.

Their attention turned to the knock on door.

"Who dares knock at our door!" Jerry yelled.

"Sorenson, sir," A deep military voice responded.

Alex glanced at Jerry, who winked and nodded toward Jason. "Sergeant, please come in; we may need your assistance."

"Look at you, Ox, uniform and all. You're in on this too?"

"Is this your attempt to get grounded, Lieutenant Riley?" Ox said.

Alex stood and waved Ox closer. "Sergeant Sorenson, Ox. First, don't even ask about the tan, we don't know. What we do know is our most esteemed co-pilot, has a major hangover, if not still drunk. This would not be a big deal with us being on down status, except your fearless leader has less than fifty minutes to report to the group commander."

Jerry walked over to his area and pulled on his trousers. "What brings you here, Sorenson?"

The Sergeant stood at semi-attention. "Walker wanted Lieutenant Montgomery to check out the bombsight for sign off."

Alex, now putting on his trousers, winked at Ox. "I take it can wait and you don't mind getting a little wet."

Ox gave a big smile. "It would be a pleasure to assist you, sir."

The three jumped Jason, carrying him screaming out of the rear of the hut. Fifteen minutes later, the four looked like drowned rats, except that Jason had a few razor nicks. His friends pushed Jason back into the hut.

"You do know how to dry off? Ox, keep an eye on him while we get dressed." Alex threw a towel at Jason.

"Come on, Jason, get it in gear; you have a half hour until 0700 hours." Jerry strapped on his watch.

"Okay, I'll go along with this joke. I don't know how you guys pulled this off, but this is great."

Jerry walked over to Jason's pole rack. "Sergeant, thank you for your help. If you will stand by outside, I think we can handle it from here."

Alex lifted the footlocker lid. "Jason, we will do this by the numbers: dry shorts, socks, belt, hat, t-shirt, watch, wallet, comb, pen, handkerchief, and bars."

"I like the bar part," Jason quipped.

Alex threw Jason's bars to Jerry. "Put those on him. Jason, where's your wallet and watch?"

"Where you guys hid them."

Jerry pulled Jason's trousers, shirt, and tie off the rack. "Alex, his shoes are under the bunk."

Alex went over to the side of the bed and almost vomited. "Jerry, he puked on the floor."

"Sergeant Sorenson, I need your help!" Jerry yelled.

Ox rushed back in. "Yes, sir!"

"It seems Jason could not keep his booze down. Could you clean it up?" Jerry pointed to the pool of vomit.

"Is that an order?" Ox pinched his nose.

"Does it have to be?"

"No, I'm just kidding around; we are all in this together, from bullets to vomit."

Alex picked up Jason's shoes. "Look, Jason, you get dressed. I'll give your shoes a quick going over. Jerry will put on your bars, deal?"

"I'll play along with this, but I warn you not to mess up my trip."

– – – – – – – – – – – – – – –

Ox walked behind Jason as Jerry and Alex kept Jason between them. "Look, guys, this joke has gone too far. I need to get to London, or I'll be in trouble."

Alex glanced over to Jason. "Look, Jason, maybe in a couple of weeks the whole crew can get a three-day pass and take the train, then we'll all go to London, so just hold it down."

Jason stopped midstride, causing Ox to walk into him. "Alex, I need to go now; you guys have already made me late for my flight."

Ox grabbed Jason from between Alex and Jerry and spun him around to face him. "You may be an officer, but you're crew. And in about one second, I'm going to pound you into the ground if you don't stop giving us a hard time. So shut up and get moving." He pushed Jason back.

Any thought they had of Jason causing any more trouble was lost at the crossroad as he saw the bombers. Several times Jason walked into them as he kept looking around, lost in the reality that it was no joke. Half a mile later, as they neared the administration building, bewilderment mixed with fear.

Just before entering the group headquarters, Alex and Jerry steadied Jason. Jerry tucked Jason's tie in as Alex wiped off his silver collar bar with his handkerchief.

Alex stepped back, examining Jason. "Jason, now don't go shooting off your mouth. You look terrible and you're already ten minutes late, so the old man is not going to be in a good mood as it is."

Jason, for the first time, noticed the gold bar on Alex's collar. "I outrank you."

Alex put both hands up to his face. "I don't believe this; we *are* in trouble." He turned to Sorenson. "Thanks for the help. Don't say a thing to the Captain; I'll talk with him and tell Walker I'll be over as soon as I can."

"You're the tannest pilot in England. Wait till the rest of the crew sees you." Ox said

"What about Alex? He surfs too." For the first time Jason really looked at Alex. "What happened to your tan, bro?"

"I must have lost it, like you lost your brains." Alex hissed as he pushed Jason through the door.

The Sergeant behind the desk looked up as Alex addressed him. "Lieutenant Jason Riley for Colonel Schilling."

The Sergeant waved for them to sit down. "Please have a seat. I'll tell the Colonel that the Lieutenant is here."

- - - - - - - - - - - - - - - -

Alex and Jerry jumped to attention. Jason looked up slowly at the towering figure, trying to remember what the gold leaf meant. He had seen it in a photo of his father. Just as the voice boomed, Jason remembered it was the rank of a major. He looked across at his friends' bodies and tightened his spine up to his tucked chin.

Major Odin gave Jason a cold stare. "Well, Lieutenant Riley, it's good to see you can finally get to your feet. How is that colorful tattoo doing? Is it sore?"

"Sir, it's been nearly five years since I got it," Jason said with a look of surprise.

"That's right, your medical record said you had it when you enlisted." He put his fingertip to his lips.

"What records?"

"What is with the tan; where have you been?"

"California," which caused Jerry to kick Jason's ankle with the side of his shoe.

"Lieutenant Zandi?" Major Odin gave Jerry a dirty look.

"Yes, sir, Lieutenant Zandi, sir."

"Lieutenant Zandi, I suggest you let Lieutenant Riley dig his own hole." He turned his attention back to Jason. "After the Colonel is done with you, Lieutenant, I want you to drop by my section. We need to talk a little about how the war is going."

"But Major, I don't know anything about this war except from movies. If I hadn't seen *Pearl Harbor* or *Saving Private Ryan*, a few History Channel shows, I'd know zip. I was just starting to study it in college. I mean, I'm not completely dumb; I know a little about the Manhattan Project and Ultra, D-Day at Normandy, or Overlord."

Having taken out a small notepad, Odin wrote, "Manhattan Project, Ultra, Normandy. What is Normandy, for example?"

Jason found his question both strange and exciting as he watched the Major take notes. "Overlord, D-Day, you know, the invasion at Normandy, you know June 6."

Finishing a few more notes, Odin said, "Why of course, how could I forget?"

"Glad I could help, Major … is that right?"

Smiling, Major Odin tucked the pad and pencil back in his shirt pocket, trying to hide his pleasure that soon he would have enough to rid the 390th of this hotshot pilot. Calmly he patted Jason's shoulder. "That's all right; please don't forget to drop in for a chat." He did an about-face and walked away.

Alex flew into rage. "Are you crazy? Screwing around with Major Odin. He'll nail you as being unfit for flight duty with foolish talk about California and New York."

"What's the big deal?"

Jerry spun him around. "Major Odin, he's not just any Major. He's a Group G2 officer; he can make big trouble for you and for us. Are you out of your mind?"

"Maybe, just maybe." Jason sank back down.

- - - - - - - - - - - - - - -

The Sergeant, now accompanied by two military police, stood before Jason. "Sir, the Colonel is ready for you."

As Jason stood up, the MPs took up positions on each side of him, with the Sergeant leading the way, the procession looked like a prisoner being led to the gallows. Coming to a door, the Sergeant knocked, and opened it at the same time. As Jason stepped into the office, the MPs closed the door, and he heard it lock behind him.

"Jerry, did you see them lock the door?" Alex whispered.

"It looks like they are going to arrest him, Alex."

"I don't remember us doing anything last night, do you?"

"No, we didn't do a thing. Jason didn't either. At least I don't think so." Jerry wiped his palms on his trousers.

"Last I saw Jason, he was yelling and wandered into the woods. He was too drunk to go anyplace. If we did anything at the club, they would be calling us all in."

As they settled in for the wait, the Sergeant walked over. "Sirs, the Colonel asked me to convey to you that you are to return to your barracks or duties. Your waiting is not needed."

THE PURSUERS

The CIA Director walked through the underground warehouse, stopping at the double doors to the conference room where the guards checked his identification. As he entered, everyone stood up. Deputy Director Odin introduced Higgins, "I don't know if you have met Robert Higgins."

"No, only by reputation. Glad to meet you." They shook hands then settled down among the mound of file folders stacked on the conference table.

"I take it, Mr. Higgins, that you are now familiar with all of these," the Director said, waving his hands toward the stack of files.

Higgins pushed his reading glasses back up the bridge of his nose. "I'm afraid not. The deputy spent the last fifteen minutes giving me an overview and the theory. I find this impossible to believe. Shouldn't this be an Army or Air Force case anyways?"

The Director whistled as he looked at the color sketch and photo that had just come in. "Go on ahead, Aaron. Tell him how it landed in your lap."

Aaron drummed the yellow pad in front of him with his pen.

"Where to start? My father was the intelligence officer for the 390th Bomber Group. He started the investigation into the *Golden Eagle* and the disappearance of Lieutenant Jason Riley. The army wanted to get rid of the security embarrassment, so they came up with the solution. They shipped both my father and the case to the OSS, our predecessor, ending his military career; it was a case of strangling the messenger. Little was done with the case; my father kept track of the Judge and updated information as needed. The agency couldn't care less; the case was always treated as inactive. When my father retired in 88, I had been with the agency for a dozen years, and so I was assigned the case to do with as I liked, a military case no one wanted."

"So you came up with this theory." Higgins slid a folder across to himself.

"No, after his retirement, my father spent the last three years of his life coming here, going over these files, and came up with this theory of what happened. I made him promise not to tell anyone. I had a career, so we exchanged promises: he wouldn't tell anyone his theory, and I would keep track of Judge Riley until he died."

"This theory is pretty wild, so who would blame you. I take it that brings us here now." Higgins pulled out a cigarette.

The Director held up the enlarged passport photo of Jason and slid it across to Higgins. "When I came on, I reviewed all the cases, both active and inactive. I forced the theory out of Aaron. I found it had some merit, so I was willing to commit resources if Aaron ever requested them."

Higgins' cigarette shook in his hand as he looked at the photo. How could this be the same stupid kid from close to three years ago that he saved in Indonesia, or did the kid save him? He never put Jason's name or the "event" in any report that could get him in big trouble. He had to remain calm. "Not much cost, and it's easy to keep track of a federal judge. Then when he retired, he lived a quiet life, which until—"

"Until two weeks ago." Aaron took over from the Director. He slid over the two passport applications. "The Judge applied for two passports, renewal for himself and a replacement for his grandson, who lives with him and his wife and goes to the community college. At first, I was thinking, no big deal, he's going on a trip and taking his grandson along. Then I noticed they were traveling one day apart, not a normal vacation together. The Director authorized a surveillance team for a week and for our computer system to pull up everything, not only travel plans, but credit cards, reservations; I mean *everything*."

The director pulled over another photo. "As I said, Mr. Higgins, I found the theory sound but unbelievable at the same time. Aaron, tell Mr. Higgins about the Judge's abilities."

"I found out that the Judge won $460,540 in November of 1988 and $200,845 in November 2000. Most people wouldn't even report it, since the winnings were offshore, but if one thing is true about Judge Riley, it is that he's a pillar of integrity." He pushed a thick file marked "John Riley tax returns" before Higgins. "Those were not the first, Robert. Our Judge is not a gambler, per his periodic FBI investigations, yet in November 1960 he won $412,400, November 1976 he won $325,540 and November 1988 the big one, $650,000. Any guesses why November?"

"Needs money for Christmas shopping?" Higgins shrugged.

"Our friends on the other side of the law hit pay dirt. They tracked down a number of casinos offshore, and we lucked out; many still had records of our non-gambling Judge. It seems Judge Riley has the great ability, against great odds, to predict presidential elections way before the early primaries. So much for theory."

"Well, it is an impressive theory but not proof."

"Not hard, Mr. Higgins, if someone from the future can tell you who is going to be President." The Director reached toward Aaron. "Your father's notes from June 3, 1944, I want to reference a little from them."

Aaron withdrew the protective cover sheet out of the folder that held the small notepad page from so many years before. Wiping an unwanted tear away, he said, "Sorry, sir," and handed the note to the Director.

The Director glanced at the note and was impressed again with what it said. "Mr. Higgins, have you seen *Saving Private Ryan* or *Pearl Harbor?*"

"*Private Ryan*, yes, but *Pearl Harbor* just came out, so not yet."

The Deputy started to speak, but the Director smiled and held up his hand. "Please, let me have the honor, Aaron. Mr. Higgins, it seems our boy Jason did—in fact, last night. Let me read a note that Aaron's father wrote on June 3, 1944. I quote: 'This morning I came upon Lieutenant Jason Riley waiting outside the CO's office to meet with a Colonel Richard Steel from Eighth staff. He was strange in both appearance and manner. He was very hung over, if not drunk, and while there wasn't any smell of alcohol, his eyes were red. And even more strange, he had a deep tan, which he claimed he got in California. When I asked him how the war was going, he claimed to know nothing except from a couple of movies, *Pearl Harbor* and *Saving Private Ryan*, neither of which I nor anyone in my section have ever heard of, and Lieutenant Riley continued to mumble on about a Manhattan Project, Ultra, and that the invasion would be at Normandy and code-named Overlord. I plan on taking Lieutenant Riley to see the operations CO for an interview. I feel he should be grounded and reassigned.' End of quote." With that, the director slid the note across to Higgins.

Higgins picked it up and, within a few seconds, let it drop back on the table. "This is impossible."

"Mr. Higgins, as I said earlier, when I came on board this year, I reviewed the case, and it was *Saving Private Ryan* that convinced me that this had merit. How about this?" He slid over a color sketch and photo. "The sketch is the emblem of the 572nd Bomb Squadron that was designed in late 1942; the crew of the *Golden Eagle* was assigned to that outfit in January of 1944. Lieutenant Riley was assigned a short time later as a replacement. The color photo was taken last night and just came in this morning. The young man in the photo is Jason Riley, the Judge's grandson. Who the blurred young lady is holding up his sleeve, we have no idea, but that is not important; his tattoo is. It is the same as the sketch, and as to location and size, it matches Aaron's father's description of the tattoo on Lieutenant Jason Riley."

The Deputy continued. "It should be noted that the tattoo you're looking at, especially the color, was not available in the forties. That's what caused my father to take notice of Lieutenant Riley. He went so far as to check his medical enlistment records. They made reference to the tattoo in December of 1941, when Lieutenant Riley enlisted at eighteen. Needless to say, he was not even a pilot, and it was over a year before the 572nd was even formed, and those records disappeared along with everything else connected to Lieutenant Riley."

Higgins took off his glasses. "Because this grandson has the same tattoo still does not prove that he is Lieutenant Riley—"

"Well, Robert," the Deputy said, "*you* explain how a lowly pilot, one of two hundred thousand pilots, knew the highest military secrets of the time. My father said, as you can imagine, that the high command went through the roof. They went crazy looking for the young Lieutenant."

"No one leaves without a trace." Higgins shook out another cigarette then realized the first still lay on the table.

"Robert, you're in denial. As for Lieutenant Riley, one day he's here, and the next he's gone without a trace. Everyone, I mean *everyone* was looking, including the French Resistance. The big fear was that the Germans would get him."

Higgins placed the photo of Jason back down, lit up, and, leaning back, thought to himself, *If they only knew that I know this stupid surfer and have seen his colorful tattoo,* as he watched the first smoke ring head up toward the ceiling air vents. "Tan hands on white arms.

So our boy Lieutenant Riley was a surfer; I guess he must have been the most tanned person in England. "

The Director stood and commented, "But here he is, or was, among us; it has to be him. I guess it's time to talk with the Judge and when and if we can, young Jason Riley."

"Jason seems to have disappeared again. The Judge we can grab." The Deputy waved away Higgins' smoke. "Under a lot more pressure in 1944 than we can apply today, he said nothing and is now too old to risk the use of any chemical treatment. Our best hope is that the Judge will lead us to him, but we spooked him."

The Director placed both hands on the conference table, leaned forward, and stared into Higgins' eyes. "The surveillance team has been a dismal failure; that's why, Mr. Higgins, you are here. You are going to take over field operations. Deputy Odin will continue to be the overall director. If this turns out to be what it appears, then we have someone who can control time; that means history and, possibly, the world, and we have no idea who or how, but we had better find out fast."

The Deputy hit the stack of reports. "These are the individual reports of each member of the surveillance team. I have read them a half dozen times. They are all screwed up, because while the Judge has been the target, they made reference for the last week of Jason Riley's large core group of friends. Yet in every photo, including those from last night, there are no friends. They show no one or weird photos or blurred faces."

"What is weird?" Higgins' cigarette stopped halfway to his lips. Odin picked up a couple photos off the table, and he threw them at Higgins. "Here is a girl with her arm around thin air and a guy who looks like he is talking to a ghost. When I called the team this morning, they couldn't remember writing their reports and all claim that Jason was a loner."

"I know a couple of those on the surveillance team. They are not screw-ups; far from it."

"Try this, Robert, the team leaders' report from last night. The Judge gets this strange call and sets up a meeting on the road to the local cemetery. So the team sets up on the road. They don't get one digital image or a sound. The best equipment in the world and all I end up with is a vague visual report of a mystery meeting. Then, due to heavy fog, all I get is one photo of the Judge pouring out his soul over a grave."

"Sounds like more than technical problems."

"An hour ago, I get this on whose grave it was." Odin handed Higgins a fax.

"No wonder the Judge was torn up. I thought bodies weren't shipped back during the war."

The Director walked to the door and turned. "Mr. Higgins, only three of us know about this, soon the president will make four. Trust no one, not even those on your team. Needless to say, there is no limit on personnel or funding that you need. Aaron, I'll give you a call when I set up our appointment with the President."

As the door closed, Odin walked to the far end of the conference room and picked up a hammer, crowbar, and bolt cutter off the top of a large crate. "About the body, you're wrong; they shipped them upon request, and his escort was none other than Judge Riley, or Major Riley. Robert, nothing is normal with this whole case. The Judge goes to the airport to check in to fly to London, even gets a boarding pass, and at the gate finds out he's booked for tomorrow and leaves. The only one who flew today was a surveillance team member; Jason, who was to fly out today, was a no-show."

Higgins looked at the photo of the Judge at the grave. "What's in the plastic bags next to him?"

"I have no idea. As I said, this has been all screwed up, that's why you're here." Odin cut the first metal band off the crate.

"Maybe Jason doesn't need a plane; the airlines are lousy for arriving on time. He'd be late for the war."

The four metal bands around the crate snapped off easily. As if to make up for that, the wooden crate lid was a bear to pry apart. Odin smashed his finger and stood looking at it as it bled. "I hope there's a thousandth of that much blood in here."

Once the sides had been pried away, a large olive green, metal case with a yellow warning notice stenciled on its side was revealed. Reading the security document first, Odin looked at a green gauge and hit a release valve, which caused a hissing sound. Higgins stepped back quickly.

"Don't worry, Robert," Odin said. "It's not a bomb. It's vacuum packed, like a coffee can. If that gauge had been red, it would mean that someone had previously opened it." As the Deputy flipped the last of the eight latches, the lid broke away from the rubber casket. Odin flipped up the cover and, as Higgins gasped, said, "Welcome to World War II, Higgins."

WELCOME BACK

Jason, who still had the presence of mind to read the sign on the door, now stood at attention, saluted, and announced, "Colonel Schilling, Lieutenant Riley reporting as ordered."

After ten seconds of staring at the back of the Colonel's head, Jason wondered if the movies had it wrong. *What the heck*, he thought. *I'll give it another try*. "Colonel Schilling, Lieutenant Riley reporting as ordered."

As the Colonel turned around, Jason's hand dropped, and his face paled. "Professor," he whispered and, regaining some composure, asked, "You're Colonel Fredrick Schilling?"

"Please, sit down, Lieutenant."

"It's Jason, sir." Jason collapsed into the chair.

"Well, that wasn't bad for a surfer. Where did you learn that?" Colonel Steel leaned over the desk.

Jason stuttered. "M-m-movies, and maybe seeing my father."

"You aren't Jason anymore; you are Lieutenant Jason Riley. This is both proper and best for you."

"How should I address you? Professor Richford or Colonel Schilling?"

Pulling out his pipe, "Neither, Lieutenant. Professor Richford does not exist, and while Colonel Schilling is the very real commanding officer of the 390th Bomb Group, I'm not him. Let me formally introduce myself. I am Colonel Richard Steel at this point in time, temporally assigned to the staff of General Jimmy Doolittle, Commander, Eighth Army Air Force, in G2 to be exact; that is military intelligence to you."

"My grandfather mentioned your name; you seem to like the name Richard." Jason tried to put on a brave smile but failed.

"I have my reasons, Lieutenant. Now I need to know everything you have seen, heard, and whom you have had contacted since midnight."

Jason looked down at the strange watch Alex had loaned him. "I can't even figure out this time thing. I think I got it down with this watch, but I see signs like 1300, 1700 hours."

"No problem; that is just an education issue. Continue on." Colonel Steel tapped tobacco into his pipe.

"When I woke up, someone was yelling that I had to be here, but I never saw him. Then I made a scene with Alex, Jerry, and Ox, you know from your classes, about being here."

"What was their reaction?"

Jason leaned back, a little more relaxed. "The same thing I was thinking, that they were either crazy or pulling a joke. They took me out of the hut, used a barrel of water on me, I guess it was their version of a cold shower and a rough shave. They made a big deal about my tan. Jerry said I looked like a freak. I got into it, told them it was from surfing, and I asked Alex where his tan went."

"What did Lieutenant Montgomery say?"

"Lieutenant Montgomery? He looked like I had lost my mind."

Pulling out a match, Colonel Steel struck the head with his fingernail. "See, some things never change. Continue, Lieutenant."

Jason took in the familiar smell. "They got me dressed in this uniform. As we walked, I told them I had to catch a flight to London and that they were going to get me in trouble. Ox got really mad. I thought he was going to deck me. So I shut up, then I realized this was no joke with the dozens of old planes, bombers, everyone in different types of uniform, on bikes, a lot of activity."

"What do you think now, Lieutenant?"

"As I said, I thought this was a joke, but this is way too elaborate. The crew couldn't pull it off. Then there's the ageless you, who seems to be pulling the strings."

"You give me more credit than I deserve, Lieutenant."

"Can we make it Jason? This is no joke—it feels more like a nightmare—and I hate the military. Alex said I'm First Lieutenant Jason Riley, his most esteemed co-pilot. I would guess he was influenced by our conversation with my grandfather about the *Golden Eagle*."

"Lieutenant, you were saying that you were on your way here…"

"When we got here, Alex told the Sergeant I was here. As we sat waiting, a Major, Jerry said he was Major Odin, group intelligence officer, asked me about my tattoo, and I made a few brief comments. I got the feeling he doesn't like me."

The Colonel walked around the desk, pulled up a chair inches from Jason, and said, "Lieutenant, you need to repeat every word you said to the Major," while tapping him gently on the knee.

"First, I was a little slow to stand at attention, and he said something about my backside. Then he asked if my colorful tattoo was sore. I told him no because I got it when I was sixteen. He said that that information was in my medical record. He then asked if I got my tan at Pearl Harbor. I told him California, and that is when Jerry kicked me in the ankle, to shut up. The Major told me to come to his office after this meeting, because he wants to talk about the war. I then said…"

The Colonel, seeing his panicked look, pulled out his pipe quickly. "What is it, Jason? I mean, Lieutenant."

"I told him I didn't know much about war except from movies, like

Pearl Harbor and *Saving Private Ryan*, and that I didn't study much in school about it. I also said I knew a little about the Ultra coding machine, the Manhattan Project, and that D-Day was at Normandy. He wrote down what I said and then acted strange. He patted me on the shoulder and told me not to forget to come see him."

"What did Lieutenant Montgomery and Zandi say or do?"

"Lieutenant Zandi, Jerry, as I said, kicked me, and when the major left, Alex was raging. He said the Major could have me taken off flight duty with crazy talk about California and New York. I hope they all thought I was babbling." Jason jumped up and screamed, "Wait a minute, why should I care?"

"Sit down, Lieutenant. I think you've gotten yourself in big trouble, or I should say, *we* are in trouble."

"Don't blame me!" Jason yelled angrily "You transported or beamed me here or whatever you call it—I don't know—some, sixty, seventy years, without asking me, ruining my life. I'm screwed. Why should I care about whatever you're up to?"

Colonel Steel stood with slow and deliberate purpose, pointing the stem of his pipe within inches in Jason's face. "Ruining your life, what a joke. You were well on your way doing that with your drugs, sex, and alcohol. I guess next you'll tell me I got you drunk at sixteen and made you get a tattoo; that is what started this with Major Odin."

"I'm out of here." Jason rushed for the door.

"Stop, Lieutenant! That door is locked, and I can assure you that either one or both of those MPs stationed on the other side will be duty bound to use whatever force is needed to restrain you and assist you in showing proper military respect to a superior officer. So sit down and shut up."

Jason stopped, realizing the truth of the statement and the situation he found himself in. For the next ten minutes, Jason sat in silence, fuming, as he watched the Colonel go through the thick folder before him. Picking up the file, Steel came around the desk and again sat opposite Jason. "Lieutenant, do you know what today is?"

Jason spoke through his teeth, "I am not a Lieutenant, remember? I don't know a thing. I'm just a misfit surfer."

Steel tapped Jason on the knee. "Let's start again. We need each other, Lieutenant. So do you know what today is?"

Jason didn't answer. With a sigh, the Colonel continued, "Today is Saturday, June 3, 1944. Tuesday, the invasion of Normandy begins. You are near Framlingham, England, on the base of the 390th Bomb Group, of which the 572nd Bombardment Squadron is part. That colorful tattoo you wear is impossible on two counts: first, technically, the color ink used in it did not exist at this time, and second, the squadron was not formed until the spring of last year, 1943, almost four years after you got the tattoo. You can now understand how Major Odin would have good reason to want to know about your tattoo."

Jason became alert. "I could tell him I was joking about everything. I got the tattoo just before I got here. I saw it on someone's jacket."

Colonel Steel pulled the thick file across the desk toward himself. He tapped the file with his fingertip. "Lieutenant, this should be your complete military file, but it isn't. Your induction medical records are missing, or, more plainly stated; your physical exam record when you joined the Army is missing. That is where it is noted any tattoos, scars, birthmarks you may have that might be needed for identification later. Based on what Major Odin said to you, your record did note your tattoo; he has it, so the Major wouldn't be impressed by your denial. However, maybe you can bluff your crew."

"I never enlisted in any Army."

"Wrong, not only did you join at eighteen, you have an outstanding record, skills, a battlefield commission, and a few medals to boot. You are hardly a misfit, Lieutenant."

Jason became engaged. "Really? Then what about everything I told Odin? The code name for an invasion that is three days away, an atomic bomb project, and a top-secret machine that broke the German code, that no one would admit existed till 1972? It got us into quite a mess!"

"Major Odin I can take care of. It is one of the privileges of a being a full bird Colonel."

"I guess it could have been worse. If the Major had mentioned Jimmy Doolittle, I would have gone off about *Pearl Harbor* and seeing Doolittle launch his planes off the *Hornet*."

Colonel Steel placed the file back down on the desk. "Well, I'm sure he is already impressed and will be more so as time goes on. I have a question for you. What does B.V.D. stand for?"

"Skivvies or underwear?"

"Anything else, Lieutenant?"

"No, just underwear."

The Colonel started to pace. "No, Lieutenant, I guess at this point that is what it should mean. You said you saw *Saving Private Ryan*."

Jason brightened up. "Yes, it was a great movie, one of the best. I mean the movie, not the invasion, I guess, at least not for those who were actually there."

Steel stopped in midstride. "What do you think would happen, Lieutenant, if the Germans know where and when the invasion will take place and most of the details?"

"Why, it would be a slaughter, a total defeat."

"Would it be fair to say, or at least reasonable to say, that the delay would give Hitler time to develop and improve his advanced weapons, like jets, rockets, and even atomic weapons, and that history as you know it would be much different?" Steel pressed Jason.

Jason could see where he was going. "My grandfather told me he was ordered to bomb Rommel's headquarters because his intelligence staff knew about the invasion."

"That is close to the truth." The Colonel sat back down. "The bottom line, Lieutenant, it is important for you to fly this mission and save the invasion."

"What!" Jason exclaimed. "Alex, Jerry, and you and everyone else on this base can call me a pilot, but I don't have the first idea about flying a plane, never mind some bomber."

Placing both hands on Jason's knees, "Please, look at me." Jason looked up into his eyes. "I'm asking you to become, in every sense of the word, First Lieutenant Jason Shawn Riley. That means knowledge, feelings, experience, emotions, the whole ball of wax."

"Is this some kind of reverse reincarnation?"

"There is no such thing as reincarnation. If you agree, this will be irreversible; you will be both yourself and Lieutenant Riley, one and the same, but never the same again." Jason started to stand. "Please, sit down, Lieutenant, while I try to explain what little I know."

Jason sat back down, and Colonel Steel maintained eye contact. "God has, for many generations, had his hand on your nation. I'll tell you, as a Brit, I have been an outside observer of this truth; He uses nations like He does individuals to do His will. I can assure you, the enemy of God and man does the same; this war is a testament to that fact. You know deep in your heart what I say is true. So you have been chosen; why I don't know."

"Don't I have a say in this?"

"You have, as always, the most powerful gift, free will, in this matter and, more important, in your salvation."

"What happens if I refuse?"

"In the case of rejecting God—"

"Sir, I know about that. My grandfather and my friend Nathan have shared with me the gospel. I mean, if I refuse to become Lieutenant Riley."

The Colonel picked up the file held it in front of Jason. "If you don't become Lieutenant Jason Riley, history as we know it will change, or maybe it won't. Maybe you will be only the first Jason Riley, and you will never be born. Lieutenant, I'm really just a soldier. I follow orders; I don't have all the answers. It is now up to you." With that Colonel Steel waited patiently for Jason to answer.

A few minutes passed; then, in a quiet voice, Jason said, "I don't know about this patriotism, but I need to save my grandfather and my father, so let's do it."

"You know what you are doing, and this is of your own free will?"

Jason let out a small laugh under his breath. "I guess as much as any twenty-year-old can know what they are doing. As for free will, that has been the subject of many theological debates, and to be honest, I haven't done much for anyone but myself. I guess it's time to do a little makeup. As you know, sacrifice and thankfulness are not very big with my generation."

Colonel Steel stood with a big smile, giving Jason's shoulder a gentle squeeze. "It's the right thing to do."

GROWING UP

"Is this going to hurt?"

"You should read the Bible, Jason. No one is ever worse off when dealing with God. I'm sure you'll not be tested beyond that which you can endure." With that, the Colonel started praying. Jason began to sweat and shake.

－－－－－－－－－－－－－－－－

Lieutenant Jason Riley, still where he passed out hours before, felt a chill go through his body as he opened his eyes. The birds in full chorus only added more pain, and his head throbbed with each pulse of his heart. Looking up into the overcast sky, he wondered how long he'd been asleep. He glanced at his watch. 0748 hours. Sitting up first, then he slowly rose to his feet. His body staggered to his left, growing weak as he watched his clothes fall from his body to the ground. As he stepped to his right, his watch went through his arm and fell on top of his clothes in the grass.

－－－－－－－－－－－－－－－－

The MPs stationed outside the door would later swear in written testimony that they heard a baby crying, and then what sounded like a child's voice. A few minutes later, there was a moaning sound. Worried, they knocked. When there was no response, they debated what to do and finally decided to see what was going on. Unlocking the door, they entered the commander's office and saw the Colonel looking exhausted, leaning back against the desk. Slumped in the chair in front of the desk was the young Lieutenant, who was soaking wet.

As the Colonel looked up, the MPs came to attention. "Sir, I'm Corporal Turner, and we were concerned—"

With a wave of his hand, the colonel stopped him. "Thank you for your concern, Corporal. It seems our young lieutenant had too much to drink last night. Please, let Major Odin know that I want to see him at 0900 hours. The Lieutenant really is fine; there's no need to lock the door on your way out." With that, the two MPs saluted, did an about-face, and raced out the door.

Just as the Colonel sat down behind the desk, Lieutenant Riley opened his eyes and immediately jumped to attention. "Sir, I'm sorry. I must have fallen asleep."

Opening the folder, the Colonel said, "At ease, Lieutenant." Jason assumed a sloppy parade rest.

Looking over the top of the folder, Steel snapped, "Lieutenant, please have a seat."

"Thank you, sir."

Once Jason sat down, the Colonel noticed a confused expression come over the young man's face. "Lieutenant, is there a problem?"

"Sir, something is wrong. I belong here. I don't, I'm …" he said, shaking his head.

As alarm spread across Lieutenant Riley's face, the Colonel dropped the folder and stepped around the desk and placed his hands on his shoulders. "Listen to me, Lieutenant; it is not your imagination. Now take a deep breath, and we will work through this."

With quiet words, hugging, and crying with the boy-man, Steel comforted Jason and Lieutenant Riley as they ran the gamut of emotions. From laughing to crying, from fear to calm, he assured them of their sanity. He took no offense, nor made any judgment on what was said and only showed love. When he felt that Jason and Lieutenant Riley had a handle on everything, he moved back to the other side of the desk. "You young men will struggle to keep your two lives in the right times, do you understand?"

With swollen eyes Jason/Lieutenant Riley replied, "What happens if we goof and get mixed up? I don't feel the same, my whole outlook is different, and I am so confused."

Steel set down the file. "There's only one Jason Riley, you happen to have two sets of life experiences in two different ages. Most of us change slowly, Jason; you just had a crash course in maturing. Lieutenant Riley, you now have a look into the future through yourself. With time, it will work out. You are normal; it's just that this process is not. As for what happens if you get mixed up, at best, Major Odin will you have put away as insane; at worst, you will change the course of history, which is unacceptable. If you fail to follow military orders, Jason—as you know, Lieutenant Riley—you will be court-martialed and maybe even shot, as this is wartime."

Jason said with indignation, "I'll fly that bomber to hell and back; that you can take to the bank."

Raising his eyebrows, Steel said, "Well, Lieutenant Riley, can you overcome this selfish dope-smoking student of Waterbury Community College?"

Jason stood up "Sir, I guess it's time to grow up. May I have your permission to stay standing?"

"You need to ask before, Jason, not after the fact. It's fine with me, but pay attention. We have about an hour to make sure you've got everything down in this file and a story about what happened this morning that is believable."

"Why don't you make a copy of it? I promise to study it." Jason leaned over the desk and asked,

"Jason, this is 1944. There are no copy machines; they use carbon paper."

"Of course, I know that; this is a nightmare." Jason hit his head.

The Colonel laughed. "Jason, just make believe your future life is one of my history lectures; with your ability to forget, we will be safe." Picking up the folder, he continued, "Lieutenant, I'll be jumping around to try to confuse you. Your full name?"

"Jason Shawn Riley, both times."

"We need only concern ourselves with our present time. When and where were you born?"

"August 29, 1980. Sorry. August 29, 1923, Olympia, Washington."

"What languages do you speak and to what degree?"

"German and French, fairly fluently."

"Wrong, Lieutenant. Only German from language school. No French; that was at Waterbury. What did you do, Lieutenant, before becoming a pilot?"

"Ranger unit assigned as a liaison with Canadian and British Commandos, mostly raids and reconnaissance in France. I was just promoted to sergeant when I was wounded, shot three times. He knew; you knew."

"Knew what, Lieutenant?"

"When I was … we were shot in the hospital parking lot."

"Yes, Jason, you can thank Lieutenant Riley for that, but you can also thank him for your physical fitness, despite your use of drugs and alcohol."

"Is that why I was in a daze, because of his drugs?"

Colonel Steel stood up and slammed the file on the desk. "No, Lieutenant Riley. It has only had to do with your physical body. You being in a daze is all on you, not Jason. Now pay attention: There is no Jason Riley of the twenty-first century. It's dangerous. You two have to get it together and become one, because you *are* one. No more speaking as if you're two different people."

"While I was recovering, I was sent to language school for German. I was reassigned to the Rangers, saw combat in Algeria, at Port of Arzew, and Oran. I received a field commission to second lieutenant. Someone got the bright idea to send me to pilot school and due to a shortage of bomber pilots; I was transferred and sent here."

The process went on without letup for the next forty minutes, until the Colonel looked at his watch. "Well, we have ten minutes to wrap this up before Major Odin and I have a serious discussion. So here is your last question; it's a repeat, what is a B.V.D.?"

"Skivvies," Lieutenant Riley said, holding back a smile.

Waiting a few seconds, until he saw the worried look on the Colonel's face, Lieutenant Riley broke into a big smile and said, "And the manufacturers of the B-17 bombers. B standing for Boeing, V for the Vega plant of Lockheed, and D for Douglas, B.V.D. I better not slip and say DVD."

Colonel Steel picked up his briefcase and, placing it on the desk, removed a sealed envelope and a folder that looked like the one already on the desk. "I think we're in fine shape, and you're as fine a pilot, Lieutenant, as you were a commando. You'll do fine; the Boss has a way of making good choices."

"Sir, do you have time for a few questions? What do you know about the crew, my friends?" Colonel Steel placed Lieutenant Riley's file in the briefcase and locked it. "The next time I see you, you can ask your questions, but right now we still have a lot to do." Reaching inside his coat, the Colonel pulled out a white envelope and handed it to Lieutenant Riley. "Inside, you'll find a thousand dollars. A good sum in these times."

"Sir, what do I need to do with this?" he asked, looking at the envelope.

Coming back around to the desk, Steel said, "I think you will find a use for it. Also, in the woods behind the 458th, where you passed out, is a footlocker. In it you will find what you need for this mission and your instructions. You need to get to it and store it away ASAP before someone finds it, and the same for your uniform and personal effects on the ground. Now as to meeting; if push comes to shove, here is the story you will tell…"

Lieutenant Riley snapped a smart salute, turned about face, and was just about out the door when he heard, "Again, Lieutenant, my official reason for our visit is to relieve the concern of an unnamed high-ranking officer at Eighth about your drinking and ability to fly."

"I understand, sir."

— — — — — — — — — — — — — — — —

Colonel Steel straightened his uniform as he glanced at his watch. *Well time to buy forty-eight hours of relief for Lieutenant Riley from Major Odin.* As he stepped out of the group commander's office, he walked over to the Sergeant and asked, "Sergeant, are the air exec and Major Odin in?"

The Sergeant jumped to attention. "Yes, sir. Major Odin is expecting you, and I'll tell the air exec that you would like to see him."

Colonel Steel had only a few seconds to wait before the Sergeant reappeared. "Sir, he'll be happy to see you. Please follow me."

Colonel Steel, who some would consider a large man, found his hand engulfed by the air exec's. "Colonel Steel, please have a seat. I don't believe we've ever met."

"Thank you for your time, sir. No, we haven't met; I've just been transferred to the Eighth. I don't wish to take up too much of your time, and I have a meeting with Major Odin to discuss some G2 issues. With the invasion coming, there are a lot of missions to attend to, so we are working around the clock."

The exec officer reached over for a pack of cigarettes. "You don't have to tell us here. What can I do for you?"

Handing over the brown envelope, Steel said, "First, extend my appreciation to Colonel Schilling for the use of his office. I'm sure you've been notified that these orders would be coming down; I just want to underscore that this is top secret. Only the 572nd is to fly this mission, and no one except you and Colonel Schilling are to know about it beforehand."

The exec tore open the envelope and said, "I'll handle this myself."

Colonel Steel watched as the air exec read and waited for the troubled look to come to his face. "They are to have no fighter escort once five miles inland?" The exec dropped the orders on the desk. "No fighters at all?"

"They won't be over land that long, and you can provide fighters going and coming. The target is the secret that will become obvious to you in time."

"I dislike leaving our bombers exposed like this."

"We don't have the luxury of liking our orders, just of following them, Colonel."

"Well, I will, but I don't have to like it."

"That is just how I feel about being here. Again, thank you, and thank Colonel Schilling for me."

- - - - - - - - - - - - - - - -

By the time Colonel Steel reached Major Odin's section, all goodwill was gone. When he walked in the G2 bay, the few staff working stopped.

"Gentleman, I need a private word with Major Odin."

Major Odin jumped up ready to protest as the red-faced Colonel leaned over his desk and snarled, "If I were you, Major, I would sit down."

The two men waited until the staff left. Colonel Steel threw the fake brown file on the desk. "I'm going to run this by you once and only once. If I don't like your response, I'll tear this office apart till I find Lieutenant Riley's missing medical records, then I will have you court-martialed."

"For what? Who do you think you are?"

Giving the Major a wicked smile, Steel said, "First, I am a full Colonel and outrank you, and second, you have ten seconds to produce those records so that we can forget this happened, starting now."

Reaching in the center drawer, the Major pulled out a thin folder. "It's right here. You see, there is something very unusual about the Lieutenant Riley. It's his tattoo."

The Colonel snapped the folder from Major Odin. "I haven't got the time to care about some wet-nose lieutenant's tattoo, Major. I have already wasted enough time as a personal favor to an unnamed General to hold this crew together so they can rotate out. Word came down that Lieutenant Riley's drinking was making him, shall we say, unstable."

"I would say that he tied one on last night. He was not making much sense when I saw him this morning. Did you see his tan and how disoriented he is?"

"Well, I had a long talk with the Lieutenant, and I think we've come to a firm understanding about him focusing more on his duty and less on the booze. He looked normal to me except for being a little drunk. I'll see that this gets back in the file where it belongs." As he started out the door, he turned and walked back. "A word of advice, Major: spend more time focusing on your planning and less on Lieutenant Riley. I would hate to come back and repeat myself. I trust I made myself clear?"

Major Odin, a little shaken by the exchange, replied, "Yes, sir, Colonel, I read you loud and clear, but I protest that something is very wrong."

"Major, when you have some real proof, look me up. Until then Lieutenant Riley is off limits, understand?"

"Yes, sir."

"Very good, Major. Let's focus on fighting the Germans and not each other."

"As you wish, Colonel Steel."

- - - - - - - - - - - - - - - - -

Walking up to the Sergeant at his desk, Colonel Steel threw Jason's fake file down. "Sergeant, I need your help, I've made a few confidential notes regarding my interview with Lieutenant Riley. He is being considered for a special mission; I want this file secured for the next week while we consider him. It is only to be released with my permission." Handing him a slip of paper, he continued, "Here is how you can reach me. I'd like to see how you are going to secure his file, please."

"Sir, yes, sir," the Sergeant said and placed the file in a locked cabinet.

"Thank you, Sergeant. Again, hold it secure for a week, no less."

As Colonel Steel walked out the front door, the Sergeant turned to his clerk. "I pity Lieutenant Riley being in the same office with him for hours."

SOMETHING NEW, SOMETHING OLD

In the small wooded area between the 572nd living area and 458th Sub-Depot, Lieutenant Riley found his uniform in a neat pile in the tall grass where he had passed out the night before. Reaching down, he picked up his watch and strapped it on. Next, he quickly transferred the contents of his pockets from the discarded trousers to those he currently wore. Finding the footlocker near by, he carefully loaded his duffel bag and then stuffed the thick envelope under his shirt as best he could. On the way back to the 572nd, he thought of where it would be safe and handy to hide the duffel bag then laughed as the idea came to him.

The hut was empty, so he spent the next forty minutes looking over the photos, maps, and instructions from Colonel Steel. When he was done, he knew why it would be the last flight of the *Golden Eagle*; he wondered what was going to happen to him. Stuffing the envelope under his mattress, he headed out the door and ran into Preacher, heading toward the hut.

Sergeant Nathaniel "Preacher" Campbell saluted. "Sir, I was looking for the Captain."

"No one here, Preacher, but us and the birds."

"Well, Lieutenant, we better get going to chow; we got twenty minutes."

"I'll be there in a few." Lieutenant Riley gave Preacher a dismissive salute.

-- -- -- -- -- -- -- -- -- -- -- -- --

Jason spent the next half hour exploring the base; it was new, yet common. For Jason it was exciting, and to Lieutenant Riley it was a place of death: planes coming in shot up and crippled, exploding on forced landings, of burning flesh and screams.

At an intersection, hearing the roaring engines, Jason looked left and spotted the *Golden Eagle* on the hardstand. Slowly he walked towards her, something new and something old. He rubbed his hand along her green metal skin. "I not only see you for the first time, but I have flown you. Well, girl, one more time. I'll see you later." To the ground crew working on her, Lieutenant Riley talking to the plane was typical for those that flew them. They remained intent on their tasks and bustled about the roaring engines of the plane.

He looked down at his watch, 1125 hours; he started jogging toward the mess. As he jogged to make it in time, he marveled at his new knowledge, hoping he could hold it together; he stopped suddenly. Looking at his hands, he noticed they were pale white. Taking off his right shoe and sock, he saw that his foot was also pale.

"Sir, is there something wrong?"

Looking up at the teenage Tech Sergeant, Lieutenant Riley replied, "No, I just got a pebble in my shoe, I mean sock."

Saluting, the Sergeant replied, "Have a good day, Lieutenant."

Lieutenant Riley, hopping around on one foot, returned the salute to the now amused Sergeant.

— — — — — — — — — — — — —

Lieutenant Riley was halfway down the mess line when he stopped the arguing within himself on why he should expect to still be tanned and noticed how basic the menu was. *No Pop-Tarts today.* As he looked down at the cold food, he thought, *I better not ask to have it put in the microwave either.* In a trance he walked past his enlisted crew.

Reb elbowed Preacher. "Gee, is he wasted or what?"

As Lieutenant Riley passed, all eyes followed him except for Tom, who took the opportunity to transfer food from three of the plates to his.

"You think he's wasted now; you should have seen him this morning. I had to help Jerry and Alex give him a cold dunking. It was wild; he was called on the carpet by the old man," Ox added.

"I better help him." Preacher got up.

Coming up behind Lieutenant Riley, Preacher gently grabbed his friend's arm. "Excuse me, sir, but you're in the wrong mess."

"You're right. Thank you." Jason looked around, confused.

The first to notice his food missing was Ox. "Who took my food?"

They all focused on their trays. Rodent screamed, "You rotten thief!" grabbing food off Ray's tray.

"What are you doing?" Ray protested, grabbing his food back.

Within seconds there was a mini riot. Lieutenant Riley glanced back and returned to the table. "What seems to be the problem here?"

All started to speak at once.

"Quiet!" he shouted. "On your feet, you misfits!"

Everyone was surprised at Lieutenant Riley pulling rank. "Sergeant Walker, in a few words, what is going on?"

"Everyone is stealing each other's food, sir," Walker replied.

"I take it, then, that no one knows who took what or whose food is on what plate?" he said with an evil smile.

When they nodded their heads in agreement, Jason took five metal trays with his free hand and dumped the food on the sixth, and then, using his hand, slopped the pile of food evenly back. As he walked toward the kitchen to wash off his hands, he looked over his shoulder. He saw the crew staring down at their trays. *Maybe*, Jason thought, *this lieutenant thing is not going to be so bad.*

Tom sat back down and broke the silence. "Are you guys going to eat?" One by one, they dumped their food on Tom's tray and walked out of the mess hall, leaving Tom alone with a pile of food to his delight.

— — — — — — — — — — — — — — —

Lieutenant Riley finally made it to the officers' mess hall and sat alone, lost in his thoughts. Alex looked over at Jason and nudged Captain John Riley. "Well Captain, it looks like Jason is a little anti-social today."

"I understand he was in the commander's office for two hours, and rumor has it that it was pretty wild. What did you two say about a tan?"

"Captain, ask Jerry. Jason had this deep tan; ask the Ox if you don't believe us."

"It's true, Captain, you never saw anything like it." Jerry nodded his head in agreement.

"I don't see any tan, just you two with a bad hangover."

"He was in worst shape, Captain. I have never seen him that bad off. If it wasn't for us he'd never have made it," Alex said.

"Alex is right, Captain. Glad we had Ox. They don't call him Ox for nothing, and have you ever seen him lift those fifty calibers? It's like me with this fork. By the way, I heard, Captain, it wasn't the old man he was with; it was a full bird from Eighth G2."

"Really? Alex, let's not leave Jason alone. Go over, finish lunch with him, and try to find out what is going on. I wasn't told a word about this. We have only three missions left to the magic thirty, and then we can leave this war to others."

"I take it, Captain, you want to see him?" Alex picked up his tray.

"No, let's have a full crew meeting. It's clearing up; let's do it over at the plane, say 1400 hours. I have to see the squadron commander right now. I don't want to talk to Jason until I find out what is going on. Jerry, come with me."

Jason didn't notice Alex staring down at him. "Jason, need some company?"

"Sorry, Alex, I was lost in thought; we sure tied one on last night." Jason looked up, startled.

"Speak for yourself; I'm not the one that had to have half a dozen buckets of water poured on me."

"I think Ox broke my arm. It would have been a bad scene if I didn't report in."

"What was that all about, and where is your tan?"

"Our friend Major Odin had a number of concerns about me. One was about my drinking, so I had to get the blessings of this Colonel. It sure was a bad call to get stoned, I mean drunk, last night, and I had a lot of talking to do."

"Why was Major Odin talking about your tattoo?"

"He doesn't know what he is talking about." Jason waved Alex off.

"You had it when you came to the crew, though." Alex pushed on.

"Just forget about it, Alex."

"I remember when you replaced Benny. Rough to lose a person you go through phase training with, ten different people, making us into a crew. He was great. Of all the dumb things, to get killed in an auto accident."

"I guess that's why my phase training ended early; they knew you guys needed me." He pushed his food around with his fork.

"Yeah, look how long after Ramsey got here with his crew, and you both went through Douglas together. So you got the tattoo the minute you got here?" Alex stuffed his mouth full of mashed potatoes and mumbled.

"Alex, you eat like a pig. I have more missions than you. I was a sub, like a relief pitcher, called in to strike the Germans out. What do you think?"

"Just when I think you're full of it, Jason, someone comes along and says it's true... our hero." Alex washed the remaining food down in a flood of powdered milk.

"Well, you're my hero, Alex. I need a big favor. I know you're the person for this mission with your expert skill." Jason threw two hundred dollars on the table.

"What do you need?" Alex stared at the wad of bills.

"And this." Jason opened the envelope threw down a bigger wad of bills.

"Wow, how much is here?"

"Twelve hundred."

"What did you do, rob a bank, Jason?"

"Yeah, I do it on the side when I'm not dropping bombs. Here is what..." For the next five minutes Jason explained what he wanted.

At the end of the conversation, Alex was excited. "Jason, you picked the right person. This is going to be tricky. I may need your help to convince the Captain to allow me to go over to the 389th Group. I can't get everything here, and I'll have to go over Hethel. There's a guy over there that is really into it."

"Don't say a word to anybody, and you better check first to see if he's still alive. One last thing, Alex: get a cigar box. The Ox must have one to spare. Make sure everything is wrapped watertight; this package will have a long trip home."

"Trust me, Jason, you will have the best. Oh, the Captain called a meeting at 1400 at the hardstand."

As Jason left the mess hall, he looked up at the blue flag flying. *Great,* he thought, *only day without a mission. Still it should be no problem for Alex to get over to the 389th with us down for the week for major repair and maintenance. But,* he continued to himself, *that can't be. We have our last flight in less than two days.*

— — — — — — — — — — — — — — —

On entering the hut, he came face to face with the Captain. Lieutenant Riley stood transfixed as his two relationships with the man collided. *How can I treat him as a stranger, my superior officer, when he is flesh of my flesh, blood of my blood, my grandfather, who opened his home and loves me?*

"Captain, I'm surprise to see you. Alex told me you were going to see the commander, so I didn't expect you here. I'm rushing to change; I wanted to spend a few hours going over to Framlingham after your meeting. That is, unless you have some plans for me."

"Well, I ended up at group. I heard you had a long and quite dramatic meeting with a full bird from Eighth. The story is it is about your drinking and some bull about Major Odin. I'm not buying it. You drink a lot less than most, and it doesn't take hours to tell you to knock it off. I don't like it when I don't know what is going on with a member of my crew. You should have told me."

"I was the most surprised person on earth to be in that office. I can guarantee you that, and I was hardly in the position to tell the Colonel what to talk about or for how long." He walked past the Captain.

As Lieutenant Riley turned to change, the Captain walked up behind him. "I'm still not buying it. You know a lot more than you're telling. Did you know that Major Odin had an explosive meeting with your Colonel and that your personal records are off limits?"

Lieutenant Riley spun around, jaw set, and faced the Captain. "That is a negative on both counts, sir."

"Try this on, Lieutenant Riley; your Colonel told Sergeant Wilson you were being interviewed for a special mission."

"He is not my Colonel, and if, and I mean *if,* I was interviewed for a special mission, it would no doubt be secret. So, say you are correct, what would you want me to do, tell the whole base?"

"I'll see you over at the hardstand and don't be late, Lieutenant."
He slammed the door on the way out.

Jason sat down on his footlocker, saying out loud, "No wonder
he became a prosecutor and judge." It hit him. *My grandfather knew
I was going to be his copilot when he saw me and pulled up my sleeve. Not
only that, he knew that all my friends would be his crew, and he never
said a word for nearly two years. He never talked about the* Golden
Eagle, *except two weeks ago, because he knew, and he said that he knew
Colonel Steel. I'll bet he does; they're in this together. So I lie now and he
already knows, or maybe he didn't, but he finds out later I'm lying, so he
lies later to get me back. But what does he know? Maybe he doesn't know
a thing; maybe he was made to forget the past as I was by Colonel Steel.
This is so complex. Which life am I living first?*

Moving over to the end of his bed, Lieutenant Riley reached
to open his footlocker and took out letters from his parents, sisters,
brothers, and Elizabeth, his girlfriend. He started to read one, then
picked them all up and threw them back in the locker. *I've read some
of these a dozen times since I got here. I must be out of my mind. I'm not
some punk kid, and yet maybe this is real and the future stuff is not. How
can I know? If I start shooting off my mouth, then the mission and I will
be in trouble. They'll ground me; the whole crew will be mad.*

Jason stared back at the locker. *What do I know about today? It's
Saturday, June third. Period. About tomorrow: not a thing. First thing I
know about is the invasion on Tuesday. No, wrong, I know about the last
mission. Grandpa said Monday, June 5, if it is not a lie.*

Lieutenant Riley started to stand and then sat back down again.
*I have two lives, if I'm not dreaming or making this up in my head about
being this surfer kid from the next century.*

*How can I find out? Colonel Steel is out of the question, so that leaves
the Captain to work on. Maybe my friends, the crew, but they don't seem
to have a clue what happened to them.*

*The cigar box is the only connection between then and now, or now and
then. I have nothing from this so-called future. Maybe it's not real; maybe*

this is some kind of military experiment. Upon hitting the mattress in frustration, the new quarter bounced into sight. Picking it up, he said out loud, "This quarter is real; that is a fact. So, then, is Waterbury."

As Jerry walked in, he asked, "Who you talking to, Jason?" He pointed at the quarter. "What is that?"

Lieutenant Riley jumped up, shoving the quarter into his pocket quickly. "It was a coin I got at a carnival, and there's nothing wrong with talking to yourself, even arguing with yourself. You're only in trouble when you argue with yourself and lose the argument."

"Well, this morning I think you were at that point."

"I've had a lot on my mind, Jerry."

Jerry poked his finger in Lieutenant Riley's chest and said, "We'd better get going or we'll be late, and there's no argument about that."

THE PRESIDENT

The Director of the CIA and President Strong had been friends since their days together at Yale. Deputy Director Odin, on the other hand, had worked for a number of presidents, mostly with mixed experiences, so he did not share the director's calmness as they waited. He had been going over every deal in his head. Now, the endless revolution of figures, people, and dates lost connection as the blood surged and swam through his gut before the first meeting with the president.

As the Chief of Staff came toward them, they both stood. "This is my Deputy Director, Aaron Odin. He heads, among other things, special operations," the Director said.

"I'm Carlos Martinez, glad to meet you. We have cleared a half hour, but you can have more time, if necessary. Let's see what this is about first," he said as they walked into the Oval Office.

President Strong, coming around from behind his desk, slapped the Director on the back said, "I haven't seen you around much, so I guess I made a good call sending you over to the spook house."

"You're just happy that I don't have time to make your golfing look bad."

"Well, that is not saying much. I take it you're Aaron Odin, one of many who make him look good."

"I do my best, sir." Aaron, smiling on the outside, making a mental note never to trust a smiling politician. With a warm smile and handshake, the President waved to the couches. "Please, let's sit down. If you don't object, I'd like Carlos to be in on this. There is coffee and tea, so help yourselves."

As the Director lifted the cup to his lips, he nodded to Deputy Odin to distribute the thick binders from what appeared to be a small aluminum suitcase. Placing the cup down, the director said, "What I'm about to say is in the introduction on the first page, the next few pages are the outline of major events, which I will also go over. The rest of the binder is an index to the source documents and summary of those files. The truth of the matter is, all the *Golden Eagle* files could fill up a couple file cabinets. First, the good news isthis all started in June of 1944, so anyone who can be blamed is dead for the most part. The bad news is, time has no meaning, and that is why we are here."

"You did say 1944?" The President stirred his tea.

"Yes, sir. I will go over the summary and the highlights, major events from the beginning until today, then Deputy Odin and I will *attempt* to answer your questions. I use the word 'attempt' without accident. Lastly, if we are in agreement, Deputy Odin will lay out a possible strategy."

President Strong waved his hand for the Director to move on.

"I would suggest we all open to the first page. I don't think it is an accident that this started this date in 1944. Let me give a background of events at the time. The war for us had been going for two and half years…" Twenty minutes later, uninterrupted, the Director stopped and asked, "What do you think?"

The President turned to his Chief and said quietly, "You'd better clear another hour."

After another half hour of questions, speculations, and frustrations, it was over. The President stood, saying, "So, someone then and now is pulling our chain. If this is real, life as we know it could be altered. In fact, it could be already, and we are what it has been altered to. Can you imagine what some crazy could do with this? Maybe we'll wake up tomorrow and find out Hitler won the war. If this is a very clever deception, we'll look like fools for buying into this."

"So I take it, Mr. President, that we need to go forward with this?" the Director asked.

"What choice do we have? Carlos, using the time to refill his cup, reflected on the issues before him and said, "None, boss."

"I guess, Aaron, it's your turn." The Director moved his binder from his lap to the coffee table.

"This better be good," President Strong said curtly.

Aaron moved a few items aside to make room for his briefcase. "I believe, Mr. President, that Judge Riley will lead us to his grandson, Jason. I don't think it is an accident, sir, that the Judge has hotel reservations on June fifth, the day of the last mission of the *Golden Eagle*, in France." Handing out an outline, Aaron continued, "The 572nd Squadron really saved the invasion. From both our debriefing of the few remaining crews of the 572nd and, after the war, with some of Rommel's staff, it is clear that the mission was one of courage and bravery. Through no fault of the surviving crews, they received zero awards but were banished from the 390th and history as part of damage control." Placing his briefcase on the coffee table, Aaron pulled out two sheets of paper. Handing one each to the President and his Chief, he continued, "Listed are the five members alive today of the 572nd Squadron who flew on June fifth, one of which is the Judge. Along with their names are close relatives, who, I would suggest fly with you on Air Force One, on your visit to France and then to

Normandy. If nothing else comes from this, the men of the 572nd will be given the proper recognition."

President Strong looked at his Chief of Staff. "Okay, I see no problem. Carlos?"

"No problem so far." Carlos shrugged his shoulders.

The Director took over. "Your guests would be able, if needed, to identify our young Jason Riley as Lieutenant Riley. I will, naturally, have your Secret Service detail beef up, both for your protection, Mr. President, and to make sure we can take the Riley's in tow. If we are wrong, or this is some type of a hoax, at worst, Mr. President, we have corrected a grave oversight in history by giving the proper recognition to the 572nd."

The President stood, signaling that the meeting was over. "Carlos, call over to the Pentagon, get them moving on this, and get our staff working on a press release, and I want a good speech. Maybe, Mr. Odin, depending on how things turn out, there could be six awards, one private."

As the Director slowly stood, he said, "Mr. President, we would like to take care of getting your guests to Air Force One."

"Carlos, you see any problems with them taking care of that?"

Carlos was already on the phone but countered, "I think the Army or Air Force would want to handle that."

The Director bent over, placing the fine china cup and saucer on the coffee table, and stared up at the President. "It seems like a long time ago when we drank cold coffee from dirty mugs."

"You're right, Jared, it has been a long time." President Strong nodded, indicating that he got the message. "I guess that would be normal, Carlos, but I want the Director's people to do it."

"I guess I can handle any ruffled feathers over at the Pentagon."

Deputy Odin bent down and lifted from his briefcase a clear plastic bag, holding it up for all to see. "One last thing, Mr. President. This was removed from the footlocker of Lieutenant Jason Shawn Riley, which, with everything else he owned, has been vacuum packed since

1944 until today. Before you land in Paris, Mr. President, we will have an answer to an important question, which is ..."

- - - - - - - - - - - - - -

Later, as they were leaving the White House, Deputy Odin pulled out his cell phone and made a call. "Mr. Higgins, we have a go. I'll be back in an hour; I need to eat before I faint."

The Director slapped his Deputy on the back. "Aaron, I'll buy. You deserve that, at least." Within minutes of their limousine leaving the White House grounds, five private charter jets were airborne; Operation *Golden Eagle* was in full swing.

- - - - - - - - - - - - - -

Watching the limousine go, the President turned from the window and said, "Carlos, are you buying this story?"

"It is unbelievable, but why not?"

"I've been in Washington for over twenty-five years, and nothing is what it seems."

"I understand that, but what can we do?"

With both hands firmly planted on his desk, Strong said, "First, trust no one; second, cancel me out of the Kennedy Center tonight. You and I are going over these binders with a fine-toothed comb. I smell a rat."

"A big one or a small one?"

"A military one. Knowledge is power, one of the hard and fast rules in this city. The military just hands over massive files and one of their best intelligence officers to another agency? No way."

"You're saying this story is hoax, but then we need to know how Deputy Odin got mixed up in it?"

"Correct, Carlos. My father told me that a good lie is ninety-nine percent truth. We just heard a good one." Pointing at Carlos, President Strong continued, "So what is the lie and what is the truth? That, my friend, is what you and I must find out, and we have about forty-eight hours, at best, to do it."

There was a soft knock on the door, then the president's secretary, Barbara, entered. "Excuse me, Mr. President, a call on your private line."

"Who?"

"I don't know his name, sir, just said to tell you *Golden Eagle* is on the line."

Moving quickly to his desk, he said, "You're right; it is important. Thank you, Barbara. I'll take it. Carlos, I want you to listen in."

When Carlos was in place, the President lifted the receiver. "Hello, whom am I speaking to?"

"A person on an unsecured cell phone by the West Entrance."

"How can I help you?"

"I need five minutes of your time to deliver a letter, sir. I'm sure Mr. Martinez can arrange my passage. Am I correct, Mr. Martinez?"

President Strong waved him off from answering. "Who is the letter from?"

"I don't think it best to say. If you send Mr. Martinez to the West Gate, this can be resolved in a few minutes."

"Why Mr. Martinez?"

"We're old friends."

"Okay, but I hope this is no trick."

"I'll be waiting, Mr. President."

Slamming the phone down, the president snapped, "Carlos, you have a friend at the West Gate. No records, no notes, just an old friend of yours who wants to meet the President, got it?"

"I'll be back in ten."

"I'll just sit here behind my big desk and work on my ulcer."

– – – – – – – – – – – – –

In fifteen minutes exactly and without knocking, Carlos re-entered the Oval Office with an arm wrapped around an elderly man in his eighties. Age did not demise the man's straight posture and purposeful steps. As the President walked out from behind the desk, Carlos introduced them.

"Mr. President, this is Major General Zachary Bloom. He was my commanding officer in Vietnam."

Shaking hands with the gentleman, President Strong said warmly, "It is a pleasure to meet anyone who can keep Carlos under control. I seem to be failing miserably."

"Yes, I understand. I didn't have much luck myself," Bloom replied.

The President escorted the General to the sitting area. "Please sit down and tell me about this letter you have for me."

Once seated, the General pulled out the letter. "From Deputy Director Odin."

Carlos was a little mystified and said, "He was just here with the Director."

"I saw them, also the ice-cream vendor outside the gate taking their photo. I would guess our Chinese friends."

The President regained control of the conversation. "This place is a fishbowl."

General Bloom handed the letter to the President "It's from James Odin, the current Deputy's father. It seems good agents can work from the grave."

"How did you get this, and why are you giving this to me now?"

"Jim Odin and I go back to the war when we were both with the Eighth in England. I went over to the Air Force, and Jim stayed in intelligence, working for what would later become the CIA. In 1975, he paid me a surprise visit while I was in Korea and gave me a large envelope. Jim told me that I was to keep it safe at all costs, that it was of the highest national security. I needed to develop a backup person, one I could trust without question. He told me that when I received a call that the *Golden Eagle* had left the nest, I was to open it and follow the instructions."

"Who called you, General?'

"I have no idea, sir, except he sounded like he had a British accent."

"What instructions?" Sipping the cold coffee, the President asked. Carlos reached into his pocket and pulled out the single sheet of paper the General had given him. "They were very simple, sir," he said. "The General was to use the enclosed key for a safety deposit box at Independence Federal Savings on Connecticut Avenue. Then, after delivering the letter to you, he was to immediately go on vacation for a month in Hawaii."

President Strong tapped the letter on the coffee table. "General, what was in the safety deposit box, and when did you last see Jim Odin?"

"The letter, ten thousand dollars cash, a note with the instructions and to have a good vacation, nothing else. I saw Jim about a year before he died. He exchanged the envelopes, four or five times over the years. He said that he was updating the information, and, I suspect, checking on me and my son."

"Your son?" the President asked.

"He is my backup, Mr. President."

"Do you know what this is about, General?"

"I have no idea, but if it is as big as I think it is, I don't think I need to know. I'm just a delivery boy." With that, he stood, and the President and Carlos followed suit.

"This was very important. Thank you again, General Bloom," he said, laying his hand gently on the General's shoulder; then he walked him slowly to the door. "Carlos, why don't you walk the General back. Oh, and tell Barbara no calls. No one. I don't want to be disturbed. When you get back, come on in."

When Carlos came back, President Strong was staring out the window with his back to the door. The torn envelope and letter lay on the desk. "Carlos, read the letter," he said, not turning.

After he read the letter, Carlos dropped it on the on the desk as if it had leprosy. "I need a drink. You want one?"

"You know better, Carlos. Help yourself. You know where it is."

Spinning around, he said, "I told you it was a military rat. Get General Thomas over here now!" he yelled, fire blazing in his eyes.

"Bad news. He's over in Hawaii at a planning conference, discussing a what-if scenario with the Chinese attacking Taiwan."

"Then get on a secure line and get him back here. When I take off, I want those missing files and cases of evidence on board, along with General Thomas and Secretary Wells. I also want Deputy Odin and his chief hangman for this. You know who that is?"

"I have his name and number here." Carlos fished in his pockets and pulled out a slip of paper. "I've never heard of him; it's a man named Higgins."

President Strong dropped down into his chair. "Did you say Robert Higgins?"

"Yes, Robert Higgins. Do you know him?"

"Yeah, he almost ended my career over an operation in Indonesia."

"When was that?"

"When I was over at the Justice Department."

"You want me to get him replaced?" Carlos asked concernedly.

"No, he's one of the best, if not a little headstrong and dangerous."

"You said dangerous."

"I don't want to talk about it, and don't tell Thomas or Wells a thing about *Golden Eagle*; just make sure those boxes and they get on the plane. When we're airborne, I'll call a meeting, and if anyone lies, I'll throw them out at thirty thousand feet."

– – – – – – – – – – – – – – –

General Wong saw the light coming out from under the door. He eased open the door, asking, "Major Lin, you are still working? A single young man like you should be enjoying the Washington nightlife."

Lin jumped to attention, half out of military courtesy and the other out of being startled. "I want to have this report ready for the General's eyes in the morning."

Walking over to the young officer, Wong said, "So what is so important for me to see, Major Lin?"

Lin handed the General the photo. "The CIA Director and his

Special Operations Deputy both worked long hours Saturday and then had an early Sunday morning visit with the President." Lin then handed Wong a second photo. "Then, right after that meeting ended, the President's Chief of Staff went to the West Gate and met a retired General Zachary Bloom."

General Wong laid the photos back on the desk. "Major Lin, do you have pictures taken of everyone coming and going from the White House? That would be thousands."

"Only when a person uses a cell phone to call the President, who was very disturbed." Lin replied with a slight bow.

"That is very interesting, Major. On a Sunday yet, we know how religious the President is. I can't picture the President of the United States in the habit of taking phone calls directly."

"It seems that General Bloom's code name is *Golden Eagle*."

"What did *Golden Eagle* want, Major?"

"He was delivering a letter to the President."

"Very good, Major Lin. This does seem to have merit. What is your plan?"

"To keep General Bloom and Deputy Director Odin under close surveillance."

"Goodnight, Major. I'll look forward to your more detailed report in the morning."

"Goodnight, Comrade General." Major Lin smiled at the acknowledgment that it was of interest.

— — — — — — — — — — — — — —

Three hours later, a simple typed message was handed to the CIA Director.

> Major Lin took note of your visit with Deputy Odin to White House. He took great interest in visit by General Zachary Bloom (code named Golden Eagle) with President and Mr. Martinez just after your visit. Be advised that Major Lin has assigned surveillance on Deputy Director Odin and General Bloom.

FIRST DAY OF THE LAST

A cloud of dust rose as the truck sped along the dirt road. The driver kept a watchful eye out for the MP motorcycle. Just passing the 458th Sub-Depot area, the driver took a sharp left turn, causing the crew in the rear to grab the sideboards and each other. It was a miracle that the crew riding in back didn't get tossed out. Preacher hit the top of the cab while he yelled at the driver, "What are you, German? You're going to kill us!"

The driver stuck his head out the window. "If it's not me, it will be the Captain if we're late."

Preacher continued hitting the roof repeatedly while shouting, "Slow down, slow down!" which produced no result until the driver came within sight of the *Golden Eagle*.

Seeing Reb jump off the back tailgate as if parachuting, as always, Rodent demanded, "Why do you do that all the time?"

Hitting him on the right shoulder, Reb replied, "Practice makes perfect, Rodent. Wish you would do that with your shooting. You can't shoot worth a crap."

"You should be stuffed in that ball turret for six, eight hours, see if you like it. Who else on this crew has whacked three of Hitler's best?"

Tom spoke up. "I think we have the record for the most bullet holes in our bottom. That last 190 almost flew into our bomb bay."

Rodent continued to protest, "If there are any holes in our bottom"—pointing to Ray and the Ox—"it's because those clowns were making them with their own fifties, half drunk."

As Rodent chased Reb around the hardstand, he jumped out of the way just in time to avoid being hit by the jeep with Alex behind the wheel.

"Darn, I had you in my sights." Alex laughed.

Lieutenant Riley jumped out of the passenger's seat. "Rodent, where is the Captain?"

Rodent replied smartly, "Over there with the crew chief," pointing to the tent.

Just then, the Captain came out of the tent accompanied by the crew chief. The line chief came up and saluted, saying, "Captain, just got the word; I guess my crews will have some extra hours."

"You guys are the unsung heroes of this war." He returned the salute.

"I need to move down the line Captain and spread the word." Saluting again, the line chief mounted his bike and headed for hardstand number seven.

As Lieutenant Riley watched the line chief, he commented to Alex, "He must be the only guy that salutes; he must think they'll transfer him to the flight crew if he doesn't."

The Captain, as he walked across the concrete hardstand, waved the crew over to the grass. Captain Riley bent down and felt the grass. "Looks dry; have seats." As the crew sat, the Captain remained standing and continued, "Well, this meeting is different than I had planned. I ended up going over to group; I wanted you to hear the news direct from me." Now squatting down, he continued, "I'll give you the good news first. The 572nd is no longer on stand-down; we'll be ready to go Monday. Now for the bad news—"

"If that is the good news, I can't wait for the bad," Rodent said, interrupting.

The Captain's cold, hard eyes stared at Rodent's interruption. "As I started to say, the bad news is that thirty missions is now thirty-five." With that, there were murmuring, heavy sighs, and a few dropped heads. "I understand they are going to pro-rate our twenty-seven missions, so we should have less than thirty-five. Like you, I was looking forward to a transfer, maybe going home, but as you may have heard, there is a war going on, an invasion is coming up, so that's it. Riley, Zandi, and Montgomery, I would like to see you."

The Captain, followed by his officers, walked toward the *Golden Eagle* and out of the hearing of the enlisted crew. "I know this is bad news. I'm concerned about morale, someone doing something stupid, so I want you each to pick a couple of the crew and talk this over with them."

Alex was the first to speak. "Just great, Captain. I'll talk with them, but who talks to me?"

Captain slapped Alex on the shoulder. "I'll tell you what; the next white flag with no missions, the drinks are on me."

"The last thing I need is booze; I'll take the Preacher and Walker," Jason said.

Jerry kicked a rock and said in a low voice, "We're not going to make it through this. What do I say? 'Cheer up and die like a man'?"

Alex turned and snapped, "No, Jerry, you shut up, listen to them, and then when you're done, go kick something more than a rock across a hardstand."

Jerry, red-faced, muttered, "I'll take Ray and Reb."

Alex shook his head and replied, "Great, I've got Rodent. I'll have to meet him in an icehouse to cool him down, and Captain, I need a minute with you, privately."

Captain looked at them. "You got it, Alex. Tomorrow I want the crew all over this plane helping the ground crew. Those guys are beat and could use the extra help, and it will give our guys less time to think. Make sure to tell them they're to report here at 0700 hours."

As the four officers walked back over to the crew, Lieutenant Riley called them to attention, and in a sloppy, slow fashion they came to attention. Lieutenant Riley, seeing that, made sure to give the Captain an extra crisp salute, and as the Captain walked away, Lieutenant Riley did a smart about-face and snapped, "Listen up, Stone and Jackson, fall out with Lieutenant Zandi, McBeth and Sorenson, the same with Lieutenant Montgomery. Campbell and Walker, stand fast; you're with me."

— — — — — — — — — — — —

As they got back in the jeep, Alex hit the steering wheel. "Jason, if you were a real friend, you'd trade with me and take McBeth; he's swearing up a storm. I had all I could do not to punch his lights out."

Slipping into the passenger seat, Jason looked at Alex. "I'm sure if anyone can calm the savage beast, it's you. How'd it go with the Captain?"

"We're in, Jason, I have until 100 hours. Tomorrow at first light I'll take off. At least I won't have to be with the Rodent all day."

Jerry pulled up his collar and buttoned it against the strange chill. "I don't even have a clerical collar. Will this do?"

"Well, I guess we'll all have an interesting night." Lieutenant Riley gassed the jeep forward.

— — — — — — — — — — — —

Lieutenant Riley had arranged to meet Campbell at a remote section of the base, near the chemical dump. He walked his bike down the trail to a small clearing where he found the Preacher's bike leaning against a fallen tree. Hearing a noise, Lieutenant Riley spun around and said, "Good to see you, Preacher."

Preacher pulled a blade of grass out of his mouth, "The same to you, Lieutenant Riley."

As they sat on the fallen tree, Lieutenant Riley said, "The Captain thought it would be good if we talked about the number of missions changing."

"Well, I can't say I'm happy about it, but if being happy is what life is about, then I wouldn't be here." Preacher picked away at the bark of the tree.

Lieutenant Riley let out his breath, waiting for the knots in his neck and shoulders to unwind. "So you're doing all right?"

"No, I care and love this crew, including you. So when I know we're going to die and some are going to hell, then I'm not doing okay."

That type of talk always made him uneasy. "Putting aside your concern for the others, how are you doing?"

"I'm fine. How about you?" Preacher stopped his picking.

"I'm having a lot of trouble. Look, I need a favor, and it's not a normal officer-and-enlisted type of favor." Jason stood and started to pace nervously.

"Please, sit down and relax. You're getting me nervous. There's not much of that in most crews; we're all just trying to survive, but I've heard of crews where it is, shall we say, more formal. Whatever is on your mind, Lieutenant, stays between us and this tree."

"Preacher, you're the only one that can help me." He sat back down.

"What makes you think so?"

"I know you're an expert on the Bible, a real Christian."

Looking into his eyes, the Preacher smiled. "Last night, I was praying and I had this vision. It seems we are about to go on our last flight on Monday, but you already know that, or we wouldn't be having this conversation."

"Yeah, I have the same feeling; that's why I'm having a lot of trouble." Turning away, he broke eye contact.

"Just a feeling? I don't think so. You're holding out, but that's your business."

"Okay, you're right. I won't lie, but events are beyond our control. I think you call it predestination."

"Predestination is a hot subject, the center of a lot of debates. Are we just puppets of God, so that no matter what we do the results are already in? Or do we really have free will to create our own history? To walk or not in his will?" Preacher laughed.

"Don't laugh, please, don't. I'm so scared" Jason lifted his gaze and leaned forward.

"I'm sorry, I didn't mean…" In shock, he fumbled with his words. *Is this the fearless Lieutenant Riley? Doesn't seem to be the same person*, he thought.

"Listen up, this is important. Would God get involved directly in helping us make choices?"

"Sure, he does it a lot; most of the time we are too stupid to notice, either in denial or we just plain don't care. We are not very God-centered as a rule."

"How so?"

"It all depends on if you have a personal relationship with Jesus Christ." The Preacher stood.

"Somehow I knew it would get down to this. Okay, what's the difference?"

Now Preacher was pacing. "It is an outside and inside approach. When a person has not made a commitment, then the Holy Spirit works on the outside. Then, when using free will, a person becomes a Christian and the Holy Spirit lives and works from the inside."

"So you have vision and I wouldn't; I would have a visit by an angel, and you would not, different methods, same result."

The Preacher picked up his Bible. "No and yes. In both cases it could happen the same to both of us…"

The next couple of hours flew by as the Preacher, with great patience, answered all his questions and helped him understand biblical answers to his questions. He thought of how he had known Preacher for nearly three years in his combined life, yet never heard Preacher out once. So much for his being open-minded.

"Well, Preacher, it's almost 10:30, I mean 2230, and it's just starting to get dark. Got to love this country. I wish I was home."

"You're not the only one. I miss my Anne and John."

"How is your little one doing?"

Preacher took a small photo of his wife, Anne, and son, John, from between the pages of his small pocket Bible. "See for yourself."

Jason felt salt drown his eyes as he looked at the photo and shoved it back. "He getting near one, isn't he?"

Sticking the picture back safely between the pages, Preacher said, "Yeah, in a couple of months. He'll be an old man soon."

"Thank you for your help, Preacher."

As Lieutenant Riley started to get on his bike, Preacher said, "Jason, I know."

"What do you know, Nathaniel?"

"That's the first time that you've ever called me Nathaniel, and it will be the last."

"First time you called me Jason, so stop playing games and spit it out."

"I will die, and you will live."

"I don't know that; I've been told a different story."

"You have been lied to Jason. I know the truth, but I'm ready. It really is okay."

Lieutenant Riley screamed, "Are Anne and John ready? Are they?" With that, Jason pedaled away as fast as he could, falling off the bike a couple of times, as if he could outrace death.

＿＿＿＿＿＿＿＿＿＿＿＿＿＿＿

When everyone came staggering back into the hut, Lieutenant Riley faked to be asleep; he wanted to be left alone with his thoughts. Staring up into the darkness, there was soon the sound of his sleeping friends, and in the distance the noise from the ground crews' 'round-the-clock dedication. He found himself once again in the struggle with his enemy, loneliness. It was not a new enemy, both as a teen going off to fight a war and as a young boy who lost the love of a father. He wished he could escape in his sleep, and when he woke up, he would be back in Waterbury, safe in his grandparents' home, or, better yet, with his parents and girlfriend, Elizabeth, in Olympia. The Preacher hit the nail on the head about a hole in his life, the deep loneliness that only God could fill. He could cover it over by the situation at moments like this, but if he was honest with himself, it was true even when in Waterbury or Olympia, even in a crowd, he could still be lonely and restless.

Nathaniel offered him an answer, and he knew it was not just cheap talk. He had seen Nathaniel live it out, not just his witness tonight in his faith of victory over death, but many times in the more dangerous subversive cultural war of the twenty-first century by his lifestyle. Nathaniel had placed a challenge before him, and Jason knew its truth. But just as he grabbed at it for himself, sleep robbed him of it.

THE DAY BEFORE

The first light of day was still over an hour away as Emily stood on the front porch waving as the taxi pulled away, taking John to the airport. She was confused by the various emotions that washed over her. On one hand, she was pleased John was going to surprise Jason, that they would go together to the D-Day anniversary, yet it was all so secretive, sudden, and strange. John normally had good judgment and a sense of the times, yet he asked for the last letter he wrote before he was shot down to show Jason. Why did he think Jason would care about some old letter?

- - - - - - - - - - - - - -

Glancing at his watch and seeing the time of 0727, Lieutenant Riley yelled, "Alex, wake up!" When there was no response, Jason looked over and saw Alex's bed empty. He jumped up and looked around. He saw the Captain's bed was also empty. Jerry's snores rose and fell in soft oscillations. Lieutenant Riley grabbed a pillow and threw it. "Wake up, Jerry!"

Shaking his head, Jerry mumbled, "What happened? Germans bombing the base again?"

"Where is he?" Jason pointed to Alex's bed.

"Gee, Jason, he went over to the 389th to see some B-24 puke." Jerry dropped his head back on his pillow.

"I forgot. Yeah, he told me he was going." He opened his foot-locker. "Where was the mission today?"

"I know you're not going to let me sleep, Jason." Jerry gave up any chance of more sleep, got up, and stretched. "Boulogne. Coastal defense again. I guess command is getting ready for the invasion."

"It's not even near there; it's at Normandy," he said before he could bite his tongue.

"Hey, guys, no more bombing Boulogne. Jason says it's the wrong place; it's Normandy!" Jerry yelled out over to the other section.

Lieutenant Joe Ramsey walked over and placed his hand on Jason's shoulder. "You know, friend, you get stranger each day."

Lieutenant Riley pushed his hand away. "Stuff it, Joe." snatching up some clean clothes, he pushed his way past the laughing officers of *Rita Bee* and *Hitler's Nightmare* out the front door.

Hopping on his bike, Lieutenant Riley headed out for a half-mile ride to the communal bathing site; there was rumor that there was hot water. *Well*, he thought, *with all the missions, I won't have to fight the other three thousand personnel on the base to use the showers, and with any luck there'll be hot water.*

Just as he got to the first intersection, he dropped his clothes and toilet articles. He got off the bike and gathered his possessions and laughed as he picked up the white and red can of Colgate tooth powder. *No toothpaste for this Army.*

Dark anger flashed and burned inside him as he remembered last winter. With one small stove to heat the barracks, one froze under a few thin blankets, needing to sleep with all one's clothes on.

Then there was the rotten food, lack of sleep, and being away from home and loved ones. As he picked up his bike, his hand started to tremble. Yes, there were an ever-increasing number of planes and crews not coming back, and tomorrow it would be their turn. Mumbling as he went, "All for what, Jason? So you, Jason, and that morally corrupt generation can squander this bloodily won freedom." Then a dark thought was voiced from Lieutenant Riley that scared Jason. "Maybe I don't have to go back. Maybe the Colonel can erase the future, and I can die here in peace with some purpose. Yes, purpose, that is the key."

Instead of turning right, he went left, and like a moth goes to the flame, he went to the *Golden Eagle*. Laying his bike down and waving to the ground crew, he reached up and grabbed the top of the hatch then swung feet first into the belly of death. He made his way up from the navigator/bombardier level up to the flight deck. Walker was just getting ready to leave and said, "Hello, Lieutenant. Here to check her out?"

As he flopped down into the black leather seat, he gazed at row upon row of instruments, the dozens of switches and levers, and he knew every one. "Well, how's she coming, Tom?"

"No new engine; they were able to repair it, a miracle. Try not to get it shot out again." Tom gathered up his tools.

"If this plane goes down, it will be because of your tools laying all over, not because of my expert skill." Reaching down, he picked up the hammer and threw it at Tom.

"Thank you, Lieutenant Riley," he said as it sailed past his head.

"You're welcome, anytime you leave tools laying around."

Lieutenant Riley slid open the side window and thought to himself, *That figures, no new engine, no break in time. We'll be ready to go.* His mind shifted to five missions before. He watched the pilot of the flaming *Jenny's Pride* struggle to get out the window with his chute on. Lieutenant Riley could almost hear him screaming as the flames spread up to the flight deck. Hitting his fist against the side of the cockpit, Jason thought, *No skateboarding or surfing for him.*

Sitting there, his mood grew darker as he picked up his thoughts from the night before. *What did I learn from the Preacher? That he, like me, knows this is the last flight of the* Golden Eagle, *information given to us both from the same source. I wonder which way is more direct: from God, Colonel Steel, or his vision? I wish I could lay it all out for the Preacher. He'd know if Steel's an angel; I'll bet he's not. I can't picture an angel actually smoking a pipe.*

Reaching over, Jason pulled a recent photo of his grandmother out of the Captain's window frame. The young smiling face looked up at him. He spoke to the photo. "Grandma, what does your husband know? Grandpa told both Alex and me that a dozen fighters jumped us. Well, I'm here. I've been here for a half year, so that is bull. We just about own the sky. Maybe some flak but not a dozen fighters." Lieutenant Riley, reaching under his seat, pulled out the holstered 45 cal. "I know that's a lie, because I can't afford to take the chance of being taken alive with what I know. So the Captain lied, but why would he? Who would ask him to lie and why would he do it? Professor Richford, a.k.a. Colonel Steel? I can't picture him doing that for anyone."

Two more hours found Jason mentally exhausted by his lack of understanding and combined years of chasing after things to give him purpose and worth, finally, as true wise men do, he dropped to his knees in surrender between the two seats and made the most important decision in his life.

Lieutenant Riley dropped to the hardstand with new joy; he almost landed on the Preacher. "I guess you're here to check everything out."

"Yeah, Lieutenant. This radio equipment has taken a beating; I guess the whole plane has more patches than most."

Lieutenant Riley pulled Preacher back by his arm and whispered, "About our talk last night, we, I mean I want to thank you."

"Thank God. That is why I'm here."

"Well, I'm off to get clean physically; I just took care of the inside." Jason picked up his bike and clothes.

"Are you saying what I'm thinking, Lieutenant?"

Lieutenant Riley bent over as best he could, being on a bike, and gave the Preacher a big hug, and then he started to pedal away, turning around with a big smile. "You got it, brother."

Both of Preacher's hands shot up, and he cheered so loud that it caused the ground crew to momentarily pause in their work.

— — — — — — — — — — — — — —

When the doorbell rang, Emily looked at the clock in disbelief. It was eight and she'd overslept. She jumped out of bed and, wrapping herself in a bathrobe, went downstairs. Peeking through the lace curtains, she saw an attractive young couple standing there. "Yes, can I help you?"

Agent Rolling moved her mouth close to the door and whispered, "Mrs. Riley, we're with the FBI, and we need to talk with your husband, Judge Riley."

Leaning against the door, Emily replied, "He's not here. He left about four hours ago on a trip. I would invite you in, but I'm not dressed."

"Mrs. Riley, we to need talk with you. It is very important."

As Emily reluctantly opened the door, the two CIA agents brushed past her while showing their FBI identifications. "I'm Jane Rolling, and this is Agent Robert Dowling."

Emily clutched her nightgown about her neck as she invited them into the living room. "I hope there's no trouble."

Agent Dowling continued, "Just the opposite, Mrs. Riley. We are here on behalf of the President of the United States. Your husband is to receive a high award for his service during World War II. The ceremony is at Normandy in two days, so we really need to reach him as soon as possible."

"Why, how strange. He's already on his way to Normandy as we speak. He's going there to meet our grandson and attend the anniversary ceremonies."

Dowling pulled out a small notebook. "Your grandson is there? Do you know where they are staying?"

"No, I don't. It was kind of a last-minute trip. Very strange, yes, strange." Emily bit her lip.

Reaching into his inside jacket pocket, Dowling pulled out a letter. "This is the official invitation from the President, inviting you and the Judge to fly with him tomorrow on Air Force One to Paris. Since the Judge is already there, we will arrange for you to meet him."

The invitation shook in Emily's hand. "This is such short notice."

Jane Rolling placed her hand on Emily's elbow and led her to the couch. "It will be fine, Mrs. Riley. We have a private jet waiting. If you can be ready in a couple of hours, we'll pick you up, and you can be in Washington this evening. Early tomorrow morning, you and the surviving veterans of the 572nd that served with your husband and their family members will travel to France."

"I want to go, of course, but a couple of hours?"

Agent Rolling continued in a soft voice, "The President is very sorry for the short notice, Mrs. Riley, a real goof-up. If you like, I will stay here to help you get ready, take you shopping for whatever you need."

"I don't know if I can actually go on such short notice. How many days will I be gone?"

"I'm afraid just four. The President will spend one day in Normandy and the next in Paris, meeting with the French president, so with two days of travel, plan on four days."

Emily stood, more focused as life returned to her body. "Well, if I don't get going, I won't make it. I'll be ready, but I do wish John was here."

"Again, Mrs. Riley, we are so sorry for the rush. One more thing, we've been traveling all night, and I'm afraid I drank far too much coffee. May I please use your restroom?"

"Why of course," Emily said and showed Rolling to the bathroom. On returning to the living room, Agent Dowling cleared his throat uncomfortably. "Mrs. Riley, as my partner said, we been traveling, and I guess the same goes for me, too much coffee. Is there another restroom?"

Emily pointed up the stairs. "There are two upstairs, one off our bedroom, had it put in during a major remodeling when our grandson came, but the more convenient one is off the hallway on your left. Our grandson uses it and I have not yet cleaned it, so use it at your own risk."

Dowling laughed. "I have a couple of teenagers, so this should be a low risk."

On entering the bathroom, Dowling locked the door and slipped on plastic gloves. He removed three plastic bags, which he placed on the toilet tank cover; next he laid out an assortment of swabs, Q-Tips, and tweezers. Five minutes later, he sealed the bags and carefully placed them back in his pocket. After a close visual check, he flushed the toilet and headed back down to the living room.

Dowling entered the living room just in time to hear Rollings say, "Mrs. Riley, thank you. We will be back at eleven to pick you up." Handing Emily a business card, "This is the hotel where we're staying. If you need to reach us or if there is anything you need, please call us."

As they started to leave, Dowling faked remembrance and asked, "I almost forgot, I was to ask you on behalf of the President's speechwriters if your husband happened to have any dairies or journals."

"No, he was never one to keep a dairy; he really spoke very little of the war and never about his last mission."

"Well, maybe he sent a last letter, where there could be a reference that they could use."

Emily walked over to the downstairs closet and said, "Yes, he wrote a very long letter, which was very unlike him. I found it strange, like he knew what was going to happen." She stopped and turned. "Oh, I'm sorry. I just remembered that John took the letter with him. He wanted to share it with our grandson, Jason."

The two agents darted a glance at each other, which was not lost on Emily.

While Rolling and Dowling were both using the bathrooms, Emily had used the time to slip into a housedress. Having walked them down the driveway, she waved goodbye. Turning to go back to the house, she noticed a trash barrel overturned at the side of the house. "Some people and their dogs," she muttered.

As she righted the barrel and put back half a barrel of trash, she stopped, there lay the old, beaten-up cigar box on top of the remaining trash. Why did John bury it? Didn't he tell me they would open it when Jason came back? As she walked up the front steps, she became determined that she and John would have a serious discussion, and on her terms.

THE CIGAR BOX IS BORN

Jason took a long shower, enjoying the rare day of little competition, but there was still no hot water; it had been another rumor. He dried off and put on his trousers, but when he pulled out a mirror, he noticed a hole in his right earlobe. He checked the other earlobe and saw another small hole.

"Your idiot, Jason," Lieutenant Riley said in Jason's mind. "Piercing your ears like some girl, I almost got tossed out of flight school between this, and getting the tattoo was nothing but trouble for me."

"You should talk, Lieutenant," Jason shot back. "I ended up shot to hell in a hospital lot because *you* wanted to be some type of hero."

Lieutenant Riley quickly replied, "Wait a minute, you shot me first; are you forgetting Indonesia? I thought it was a hunting accident; at least I was in a war, unlike you, putting my nose in other people's business, my hero. Don't get mad at me; how was I to know? That bright idea was the colonel's. So much for free will, huh."

"I'll bet the Captain knows." Jason stopped and stared. "It's unbelievable that the Captain will be … uh, is … uh, he's my grandfather."

Major Odin appeared out of nowhere. "Who are you talking to, Lieutenant?"

Jason dropped the mirror, startled, and watched it shatter. "You scared the crap out of me, Major."

Major Odin kicked a large piece of the mirror across the concrete floor. It came to rest against Lieutenant Riley's foot. "Looks like you've earned seven years of bad luck. Do you always talk to yourself, Lieutenant Riley?"

Lieutenant Riley stepped around the shard of glass and sat on the wooden bench. "Only way around here to have an intelligent conversation, sir."

"Very funny, Lieutenant. I understand you've become the group comic."

Lieutenant Riley put on his socks and boots without answering.

"Those look like bullet scars to me, Lieutenant."

Aware of the Major's intense scrutiny, he grabbed his shirt and put it on. "If humor helps get one through this war, so far, so good, sir."

"What about those scars, Lieutenant? Where and when did you get them?"

"A couple of Germans outside Dieppe didn't like me, sir."

"I thought that was a Canadian and British disaster."

"I was on a joint pre-invasion recon mission, Rangers and British Commandos. We were operating together. I missed the invasion. Guess they're calling it a raid now. I had a few buddies killed and a few more captured." Pushing the broken glass into a pile with his boot.

"Yes, I remember, you have quite the combat record. You don't seem the hero type." He pulled out a pack of cigarettes.

"I must have a split personality, sir." Lieutenant Riley bent down and picked up the pieces of the broken mirror, hoping that when he looked up the Major would be gone.

No such luck was granted as Major Odin leaned against the wall. "I understand all the 572nd has suddenly been taken off standdown. I haven't been informed about any missions for you guys. Don't you think that's a little strange?"

"That kind of stuff is way above my pay grade, Major. I guess the invasion must be near. As you know, we have thirty-three planes from group hammering away at Boulogne today, and we were just there on Tuesday."

"Yesterday you said it was going to be at Normandy," Odin said, hitting the pack of Philip Morris against his hand so one cigarette slipped out.

Lieutenant Riley walked over and dumped the glass in the trashcan, then, gathering up his dirty clothes, turned to face Odin. "I'm sorry about yesterday, sir. I had a very bad hangover and wasn't making much sense."

Lighting up, Major Odin took a deep drag. "You seem to have a protector, Lieutenant Riley. You are off limits; all your records are sealed. The group CO is mad as a wet hen about it, and I understand that he going to go all the way up to the Eighth. He's determined to get to the bottom of this."

"Major, as I said, this is all beyond me." Lieutenant Riley started to walk out the door when the Major blocked his path. "You know, Lieutenant, I'm going to get you."

Lieutenant Riley pushed past Major Odin's outstretched arm and glared at the Major. "You're barking up the wrong tree, Major. If I were you, I'd give it a rest."

— — — — — — — — — — — — — —

Hearing distant noises, Lieutenant Riley continued to go straight then turned left, heading for the edge of the runways. He counted the bombers as they landed; it was a good mission, only one missing, and only three emergency flares for priority landing: one red for injury and two green for damage. He tried to figure out which type of plane was missing, the newer silver model G or the older green F like the *Golden Eagle*.

The *Golden Eagle* was a good ship; she had been on over seventy missions and sent most of her previous two crews home. Every day there were fewer greens left, and tomorrow he knew there would be one less—his.

As he started to walk away, he heard the noise of the missing bomber come closer. Shading his eyes, he could see that the landing gear wasn't down. This was going to be a belly landing. He stood transfixed as the bomber skidded down the runway and then across the grass, smoke billowing. Jason braced for the explosion, but there was none. He raised his hand in a cheer as the crew leaped out, running for their lives; they would live to fly another day.

- - - - - - - - - - - - - - - -

Lieutenant Riley arrived at the squadron living site just as Alex did. "Alex, how did it go?"

"You would not believe it, Jason. It's like they wanted to give this stuff to me!" he said, holding up the wrapped packet.

"Hand it over, Alex."

"There's a guy over at the 389th who's a genius. He guaranteed me that it would seal so good it would last longer than an Egyptian mummy." He flipped the package to Jason.

"I was hoping to see what's inside."

"You wouldn't know what you're looking at. I got a cigar box from Ox, so let's go check to make sure it fits. I heard these great jokes while I was over there too." Alex grabbed the package back.

Lieutenant Riley pushed his bike alongside Alex as he told the latest joke. Jason's mind wasn't on the joke but on whether he and Alex would open the package together. "Gosh, Jason, that was a great joke and not a peep out of you. You're like the gloom of death."

As they entered the hut, Jason replied, "You're right, Alex."

"Well, the moment of truth." Alex went to his footlocker and brought out the cigar box. He took the sealed package and forced it down snuggly in the cigar box and handed it to Jason. "Mission accomplished, sir."

"Alex, we need to talk." He put the cigar box in his footlocker.

Noting the serious tone, Alex said, "Sure, what's the matter,

Jason?" Jason sat on his footlocker while Alex pulled the lone chair over. "Jason, whatever it is, you can count on me."

Lieutenant Riley jumped up, changing Jason's mind, and said, "I'm going to work on the plane for a few hours."

"But Jason, you said you wanted to talk."

"Yeah, but I need to think this out, Alex." Once out the rear door, he broke into a jog, not knowing where he was running, only knowing he wanted to run.

— — — — — — — — — — — — —

When Jason did not show up for four hours, Alex became worried and headed for the *Golden Eagle*. He found Jason sitting in his seat. Alex slipped down into the pilot's seat and saw Jason's swollen eyes. "Hello, Jason."

Jason, without looking over, replied shortly, "Alex."

"You still want to talk? We are getting worried about you."

"I watched a plane belly land earlier. I was waiting for the explosion, but there was none. I'm thinking, *Great*, as I watch the crew escape, *so few good things happen around here*."

"There are a few, but they do seem to be in short supply, Jason."

"When I got over here, I heard the ground crew talking about the ball gunner in the plane. It seems the electric system got all shot up. They couldn't even manually rotate the turret. He was trapped inside, and the landing gear could not go down. The pilot had a choice: run out of fuel and crash, or belly land and crush his gunner to death."

Alex reached over and laid his hand on his friend's shoulder. "Hang in there, Jason. We're all scared."

Putting his face in his hands for a second, Jason looked over and said, "Alex, what I'm going to tell you can't be repeated, got it?"

"Sure, Jason, you have my word."

"That meeting with the Colonel was not about my drinking but about the mission tomorrow."

"What makes you so special?" Alex sat up, tensing.

"That I can't tell you, but this is going to be the mission from hell."

Alex jumped up, "Why are you telling me? I don't need this."

"So you can make sure the crew write home, carry some extra food, and make sure they have their 45s. If I tried to talk to them, I would stand there and cry."

Alex grabbed Jason by the shirt and pulled him out of the seat and rammed him into the top turret. "Jason! Tell me what's going on!"

They heard the sound of someone and saw Captain Riley's hand appear below. Alex pushed Jason away and snarled, "We're not done with this, Jason." Alex pushed past the Captain.

Captain Riley struggled to keep his balance so he wouldn't fall to the lower deck. "What's with Alex, Jason?"

"Just mission jitters, sir. You're a Christian, aren't you, sir?"

Sitting in the seat just vacated by Alex, the Captain replied, "Yeah, not a very good one, I guess. Why do you ask?"

"Because today I became one."

The Captain slapped Jason on the shoulder. "That's great, Jason."

"Why didn't you ever tell me what would happen if I got killed?"

As if slapped, the Captain replied, "I had a good friend once; I shared with him about the need for Jesus and salvation. He became angry and said a few things that, while correct, hurt, so we were no longer friends. I guess I didn't want to take the risk anymore."

"I can relate. Never want to offend, live, and let live. I can't remember; do people use the term 'politically correct?'" Jason said softly, speaking to no one but himself.

"Never heard the term."

"In college I read a poem by Edmund Burke. There's a line that reads, 'The only thing needed for evil to triumph is for good men to do nothing.'"

"I didn't know you went to college, Jason. I read your record, and there was never any mention of college."

"Did I say college? I meant a college textbook... Anyways, at the time, I couldn't care less, but at least I'm doing something now." His right hand hung down and felt the 45 under his seat.

The Captain became uncomfortable. "I haven't known you to be very philosophical before, Jason."

"I guess I wasn't much of anything before now, nor the whole crew, you're the exception." With that he climbed out of the seat and went down the rectangle hole.

The Captain sat there, flooded with thoughts. No matter how bad the mission, he always felt they would make it back, but this time he had a bad feeling that was about to change. He reached over and pulled Emily's photo free from the window frame. "I think it's time to write you a long letter, my love."

— — — — — — — — — — — — — — —

As Alex walked in the enlisted crew hut, silence fell. He was relieved to see all the enlisted crew there and asked those from the other crew, "If you guys don't mind, I'd like a few private minutes with my crew."

Putting down a pencil, one replied, "No problem, Lieutenant. Roy and I will take a walk. Take your time."

"Thanks. I really appreciate it." Alex didn't have to ask for their attention; he had it. "I heard via the grapevine that the mission tomorrow is going to be rough. Make sure those 45s are ready to go; I want them with you, no leaving them behind this time. Also, take some extra food, and it wouldn't be a bad idea to write a letter or two."

Rodent threw down a deck of cards. "Great, you're just what I need, a visit from the Grim Reaper."

Alex rushed forward, grabbing Rodent by his shirt, and pulled him out of the chair. "I'll tell you what I need, to take your face and drive it into the wall."

Everyone jumped up to pull them apart with the Preacher getting between them. "Why don't we save all this good will for Hitler," he said quietly.

Alex stopped struggling. "Sorry, McBeth. The last thing I want is to be called the Grim Reaper," he said, brushing his sleeves. Alex started to walk to the door and stopped at Rodent's voice. "Alex, thanks for coming over, I really mean that. Sorry I was a jerk."

Alex turned around. "We all fill that role at times. Only by the grace of God are some of us learning to be less. If I've never told you, you're the greatest crew a person could ever be a part of." Giving them thumbs-up, he continued, "Here's to tomorrow."

They all returned the thumbs-up. The Preacher said, speaking to all and none, "It's time for those letters to be sent home, boys."

The old man took back his passport from the customs agent and shoved it deep down into his jacket pocket. As he exited the terminal, he waved over a skycap and a taxi parked nearby. As he was directing the skycap and the taxi driver in loading his luggage, he spotted in the side mirror a familiar face peeking from behind a newspaper. Tipping the skycap, the Judge slipped a piece of paper to the driver and said, "I trust that it's still standing. It has been fifty-seven years since I've been there."

Tucking the note in his shirt pocket, the driver replied, "Well, guv'ner, it's still a fancy place. I take it you were here during the war then?"

"Yes, it was heaven compared to the base."

Holding the door open for the Judge, the driver said, "My father, bless his soul, was RAF. Welcome back to England, and thank you for all that you did."

Looking past the driver at his tail, the Judge replied, "Do you know the hotel well?"

"I take a lot of fares there, and once I stayed there with the wife—you know, a little romance. We spent the night there."

"I need a favor. I seem to have picked up a person I would like to depart company from.

The driver remained facing forward. "You mean that chap in the blue suit with the newspaper under his left arm?"

"Why yes, how did you know?"

"I've been waiting here for a fare, and he reminded me of some wannabe spy. No offense, you seem a bit old to be in the spy business."

The Judge tapped the driver on the shoulder with his bony finger. "He works for a lawyer."

"They are the maggots of the earth, they are." The driver shook his head in disgust.

The cabbie ran into the hotel and soon appeared with a bellhop. With his help, they unloaded the suitcases onto a dolly. The driver made a big scene, thanking the Judge profusely for the tip until the Judge whispered in his ear, "Don't overdo it."

The old man waved to the desk clerk as he and the bellhop went by and continued out the rear exit to the waiting taxi. By the time the young agent realized that Judge Riley had not checked in and had given him the slip, the judge was on his way to the past.

A few hours later, when Lieutenant Riley came in, everyone was busy writing letters. The Captain stopped writing and looked up, saying, "It's getting late, Jason. No letters for you?"

"Just what I'm about to do, sir."

Lieutenant Riley got out the last letters he'd received and sat at the table thinking about what to write. Doubt crossed his mind. *Is this real?* Yet he had all the normal feelings, experiences, and memories. Starting to write, he poured out his heart for the next two hours in his last letters to his parents, sister, brothers, and his girlfriend, who, if not for war, would be his wife.

That night he silently cried himself to sleep.

At the Cherry Tree House a few miles away, the Judge lay awake despite his best effort to go to sleep. He became more frustrated as he glanced at the travel clock, knowing that in a few hours Colonel Steel would be coming for him. As the hours slipped by, he swore he could hear Lieutenant Riley crying as he had so many years before. *Or maybe it is Jason*, he thought. He wished now as he did then that he could comfort him, to be able to chase his fears away, but now, as then, he had his own demons to fight.

BRIEFING

The flashlight moved from one section to another, from bed to bed with the script greeting, "Sir, time to get up; breakfast at 0500, briefing at 0530."

As the door slammed, the lights came on, and the young officers of the *Golden Eagle*, *Hitler's Nightmare*, and *Rita Bee* struggled into their flight suits.

"My mother told me there were going to be days like this," Jerry mumbled.

"You never had a mother." Lieutenant Riley threw a shoe at Jerry.

From crew to crew, from squadron to squadron, the base came to the life with the death ritual in full swing. Trucks rushed the ground crews from the consolidated mess hall out to the waiting planes on their hardstands, combat crews to combat mess.

As the *Golden Eagle*'s crew jumped out of the back of the truck, Ox yelled, "This is where we separate the boys from the men."

Jerry pushed Ox out of the way. "Boys are not allowed in the officers' mess, sorry."

Lieutenant Riley reached into the leg pocket of his jumpsuit and pulled out nine toy crickets and threw one to each of the crew. "Here's a little gift, girls."

"What are we are going to do with these, Lieutenant?" Walker clicked his cricket.

"To start, drive the staff crazy in briefing. I'll tell you later."

Both the officers and the enlisted mess halls were built for far less use. Crowding, mixed with the high tension, made for more than a few cross words and shoving. As Lieutenant Riley pushed next to Alex, he nudged his forearm. "We need to talk, buddy."

Alex piled on fresh eggs. "At least we didn't get powdered eggs; good meals for the condemned," he joked blackly.

As they sat, "Alex, if we go down, and it looks like I'll be captured, if I can't prevent it, you have to."

"Have to what?" His fork stopped in midair. "I hope you're not asking me what I think you're asking."

"And what would that be, Alex?" he asked, picking at his food.

"To kill you, Jason."

"That is exactly what has to be done, Alex."

"Is this your idea of a joke?"

"No, Alex, this is no joke. I have topsecret information that, if it fell into enemy hands, could alter the war. I told you yesterday; it has to do with Colonel Steel," he whispered.

"Jason, I think the flak is getting to you; maybe you need to be grounded and get a rest."

Lieutenant Riley forced a smile for those that might be looking and put his arm around Alex. He pulled his friend tight to his side, pulling him off balance. His voice could cut steel. "I don't blame you; just keep in mind what I said. When we go to briefing, they'll brief everyone for Abbeville, but for the 572nd, the target will be Rommel's headquarters. We'll see then if I'm flak happy." Lieutenant Riley shoved Alex away. "I'm not happy at all, not at all." Lieutenant Riley pushed himself away from the table and made his way quickly out of the mess hall.

Outside he commandeered a jeep, turning heads as he roared back to the squadron area. Once there, Jason recovered the hidden duffel bag then continued driving like mad to the hardstand. He paused to throw the bag up into the *Golden Eagle*. He was back outside combat mess waiting for the crew in under fifteen minutes, no one the wiser that he or the jeep had left.

As the crew neared the briefing building, Alex and Captain Riley lagged far behind. "Captain, there's something very wrong; I think Jason's losing it." He told his commander about the conversations he'd had in the last few days with Jason.

With a little anger in his voice, the Captain said, "Alex, it has to do with that Colonel. Everything was fine with Jason until Steel showed up Saturday. Until then Jason was the best. We don't...*I* don't need this, and we have only a few missions left."

"What are we going to do?"

Captain Riley stopped in midstride. "We'll see how the briefing goes. If Jason has it right about the target, we'll have a very serious talk with our friend."

"And if Jason is wrong?"

The Captain continued walking with firmer strides. "We'll just have to see how the mission goes. What do you want me to do, Alex?"

"I, I guess nothing. I'm just scared; this is—"

"This is what, Lieutenant Montgomery? What is it?"

"It's all wrong, Captain."

"You got that right, Lieutenant."

As group commander, Colonel Schilling came in; a hundred-plus weary souls in various degrees came to attention. The group commander pulled back the black curtain. As the map was exposed, murmuring started. They saw a short red line across the map to Abbeville and then a little north up to Boulogne. The group commander yelled, "Your primary target today will be the airfield at Abbeville, kick the hornets' nest so to speak, and the secondary target will be Boulogne." He and the Air Exec sat down and nodded to Major Odin to get the briefing going.

Major Odin extended the long pointer and began. The lights

went out, and the cricket clicks were broken by some light chuckles and nudging shoulders. The Major shot a glance at his audience. The overhead projector went on showing aerial reconnaissance photos starting with the Abbeville airbase, then Boulogne. When the lights came on, the Major continued. "You can expect the following fighter…" As the Major lectured the group on the details of the mission, the black, ominous pointer jabbed and flicked against the yellow light and white projection of the plans that would dictate the men's fate.

When Major Odin was done, the Operations Officer spent the next ten minutes with information on flight and formation, escort, and altitude; then came the Weather Officer. The briefing ended with the Air Exec saying, "Since there are no more questions, we need navigators, bombardiers, and first officers for a separate meeting… It's a little different today, boys; we'll meet outside, and you will be directed from there. One more item: everyone from the 572nd, stand by in place. So let's process out and meet outside. One more thing, Captain Riley, would you be so kind as to bring in the rest of your crew?"

While everyone else went in separate directions, the 572nd stood in place as a group. Various squadron commanders pushed everyone else out to be processed. When all was quiet, Colonel Schilling had Major Odin join him up front and waited for Captain Riley. He spotted Captain Riley coming in with the enlisted crewmembers, and the second part of the briefing started. "Okay, I would like everyone to move forward. Captain Riley, could you join us up here, please?"

After a couple of minutes, the men settled down and quiet reigned. "If anyone should ask why you were delayed, you are to say it was to offer our congratulations to Major Riley, who will be your new squadron commander."

Shaking the new Major's hand, the Air Exec handed him a pair of gold Major leaves. With that, there was some hooting and backslapping.

The Exec yelled for quiet so the group commander could continue. "The real reason you're here is that you have been selected for a secret mission direct from Eighth, which our new Major Riley and the *Golden Eagle* will lead. You will fly one hundred miles south of

Abbeville. Your target is headquarters of B Army, and we hope that Field Marshal Rommel is home."

"I don't believe this is happening," Alex whispered to Jerry.

"Shut up, Alex. Let's listen up," Jerry whispered back.

"You have one target, and only one target, which is the chateau at La Roche-Guyon." Handing the stunned Major Odin a stack of photos to pass out, Colonel Schilling continued, "Major, give a set to each first officer and navigator." When every crew had the photos, he continued again, "As you will see, the target is small. What you can't see is the reinforced underground bunkers. That's why your planes have been armed with some very special five-hundred-pound bombs. You have one chance, and that is why you will be at fifteen thousand feet; there is no second chance. Let's just skip to the questions. Lieutenant Ramsey?"

Ramsey stood. "Their fighters, our fighters, and flak."

The Exec stepped forward and took over. "We do not expect you will have any trouble with fighters. The attack on Abbeville will serve as a diversion; they'll be too busy with the main group. You will have plenty of Mustangs, but when you break off, they will not follow. No one is to know your target until you're told you can tell. We have no idea about flak; we are hoping that you catch them off guard, flying so low that by the time they make the adjustment, you'll be gone."

Alex stood. "Sir, will we have any escort back?"

"Yes, after you hit your target, you continue south while you increase altitude. You will pick up escorts as you near your exit route, which will be fifty miles north of the Normandy coastline. Remember, not a word to ground crews, no one. Time is short. Navigators, bombardiers, and first officers, let's get to the usual places and get this show on the road."

The crew was hopeful that the Captain's promotion to Major would mean an early transfer home or to non-combat assignments as they drew their personal gear. The officers did the same, also checking in their wallets and personal papers. The first officers drew signal flares, which they hoped would return unused.

As the crew drove out to the hardstand, the base was roaring as over two hundred 1200-hp engines were preflight tested by ground crews. Just as they reached the hardstand, as if on cue, one engine after the other was shut down. As the crew jumped off the truck, Lieutenant Riley yelled out, "Watch out for those propellers!"

The crew replied in unison, "Yes, Mother."

As seven of the crew were getting into their electric suits, the conversation turned to the subject as Ox yelled over to Ray, "One of these days I'm not going to put this blue bunny suit right on my birthday suit. Maybe I'll stay warm."

Ray zipped up his flight jacket. "Yeah, Ox, you do that, you'll look like a lobster."

Tom couldn't stand it anymore and jumped into the conversation. "You guys are always complaining; you have all that nice, cool fresh air back there. I have to be up on the flight deck, always sweating."

Ox wrapped his thick arm around Tom. "I feel sorry for you, Tom. Yeah, why suffer? Give yourself a break. Come back and man one of the waist guns, get some of that nice thirty-below breeze blowing in about a hundred fifty miles per hour. Yeah, with a wind, the chill factor is about sixty below; that should keep you from sweating. You can get that frostbite look around your oxygen mask, look like the real man of this crew."

Tom tried to break Ox's grip. "Hear that, Lieutenant Riley? Ox doesn't think we're real men up front."

"Come on, girls; get those suits on. We have a war to fight," Lieutenant Riley urged.

As Lieutenant Riley started to swing up into the belly of the plane, Major Riley pulled him back down and, grabbing him, said, "Jason, Alex and I want to have a little talk with you." Lieutenant Riley pushed his hand away and continued to swing up, but this time he was pulled down with such force that he lost his grip on the hatch and fell backward to the ground. The Major pulled him up and, as Alex grabbed his other arm, said, "Time to talk, friend; we are your friends, right, Jason?" They slammed Lieutenant Riley's head against the plane; the ground crew moved and turned away. They had seen more than their share of combat crews fighting; they didn't want to be witnesses.

The Major got into Lieutenant Riley's face. "It's time to level, Lieutenant."

Lieutenant Riley knew the moment of truth had come, but not the real truth, just a version of it. "Okay, we're on our way, so there's no harm in telling at this point. Colonel Steel is the one who came down with our orders for this mission and a separate set for me. If we don't succeed in bombing our target, then I'm to bail and complete the mission and kill the B Army intelligence staff with the help of French Resistance."

Captain Riley loosened his grip a fraction. "You're full of crap. Do you expect us to believe that?"

Lieutenant Riley stalled for time, waiting for their next move. "I speak German and French. I wasn't too bad a Ranger; I'm maybe a little out of shape hanging out with you girls, though."

Just then Tom stuck his head out the hatch. "Lieutenant Riley, what do you want me to do with the bag? It weighs a ton."

Before Jason could answer, Alex reached up. "Just hand it out for now."

Alex lost his grip due to the weight, and the bag thumped to the hardstand. As Alex looked inside, he said, "Wow, Major, look at what our boy Jason has. Not one but two mean-looking knives." Holding up an M-3 submachine gun, Alex continued, "Look at this."

The Major let go of Lieutenant Riley, and, pushing Alex aside, he dug into the bag, removing four grenades, a compass, the cigar box, ammo, boots, and a large brown envelope that he threw to Alex. "Well, Lieutenant Riley, what is this about?"

Jason stood silent, hanging his head and on the verge of tears as confusion swept over him, watching those he loved grow more angry by the second.

As Alex ripped open the envelope, he yelled to Major Riley,

who now moved next to Lieutenant Riley. "Major, there are a lot of French francs, maps, some photos of a couple of German officers, aerial photos, and a drawing of a chateau."

Major Riley pushed Lieutenant Riley hard against the *Golden Eagle*. "Who are the photos of, Jason?"

"Both intelligence officers, the Oberst is from B Army and the Obersleutnant is from Fifteenth Army." Jason replied without resistance.

"How about in English with some names." The Major tightened both hands on Lieutenant Riley's collar.

"Colonel Walter Rietzen of B Army, his photo is in Alex's right hand. The other one is Lieutenant Colonel Helmut Meyer of Fifteenth Army. He's cleverer; he's the one who figured when and where the invasion is going to happen."

"Why aren't we bombing the Fifteenth Army headquarters?" He furiously pushed Lieutenant Riley harder against the plane.

"Meyer will be at B Army this morning." Lieutenant Riley, in one fluid move, broke the Major's grip and threw him to the ground. "Sorry, sir, we have a mission; it's time to get going. Lieutenant Montgomery, make sure you load up that gear." Lieutenant Riley swung himself up into the belly of the plane.

The first ray of morning light found Lieutenant Colonel Meyer fuming. It had taken over half an hour to form the small convoy. Turning to his adjutant, he yelled, "Major, I asked for an escort, not a division. What is that numbskull Keasling doing?"

"Colonel, he just got a KM ii half track."

"What! Major, you tell Keasling to get rid of it. We should have been on our way to B headquarters forty minutes ago. Tell him we leave now, or I'll take him out and shoot him myself!"

A few minutes later, Captain Keasling arrived, giving his best salute. "Sorry, Colonel, for the delay. We are now ready."

Meyer stood up in the back of the staff car and screamed, "Captain Keasling, we are late! Do you think the British and Americans are going to hold up the invasion waiting for you?"

"Yes, I mean no, Colonel; you are correct."

Still screaming, Meyer continued, "Let's get going! We are running out of darkness." With that Meyer fell down into the seat and, turning to the Major, shouted, "We will be sitting ducks in a couple of hours!" With that the four vehicles headed south, toward B headquarters.

TAKEOFF

When the alarm sounded, Judge Riley slammed it off, fearing it would wake up Cherry Tree House owner, Joan Hall. He looked at the time but already knew it would read 0500 hours. After a brief shower, the Judge struggled into his clothes. Looking down, he saw Colonel Steel standing next to a black sedan.

- - - - - - - - - - - - - - -

Around the *Golden Eagle*, final checks were being made as the last of the special bombs were loaded. Oxygen tanks were filled, ammo loaded to feed the twelve fifty-calibers, and everything checked and rechecked by both the combat and the ground crew.

Lieutenant Riley put on his shoulder holster and waited for the Major. "*I swear this plane won't get off the ground if he doesn't speak,*" he said to himself. Checking the 45 for the fourth time, he finally holstered it.

Major Riley reached up and felt the position of the toggle switch and broke the silence. "Lieutenant Riley. Fuel transfer."

"Off."

"Major, how is it going up here?" Alex came up to the cockpit.

"Intercoolers? Alex, why don't you ask Lieutenant Riley; he seems to be in charge," he said as he slid open his window.

"Cold. Look, you two, I didn't go to the Eighth and say, 'Why don't you give us this crappy mission?'"

Major Riley turned. "Fuel shut off? And why you?"

"Up and open. Fair enough, I was pulled from a Ranger unit out of Algeria. Someone got the bright idea to send me to flight school to work with the resistance movement. I had already operated in France."

"Landing gear, Lieutenant?"

"Set. I had already gone to language school. Instead, there was a bigger need for bomber pilots. So here I am, thanks to Colonel Steel."

"Jason, who is Colonel Steel?" Alex asked.

"I don't know, but it's a God thing."

The Major turned toward Jason. "God thing? Cowl flaps? Okay, Lieutenant, let's just get this over with."

Jason turned to them with pleading eyes. "Open. Really, you two, how many ways can I say it? This was not my idea."

A green warm-up flare shot up from the control tower, interrupting the conversation.

As the Major heard the banging of the belly hatch close, he said, "Alex, time to get this show on the road."

Alex leaned over and bent around to give Jason a kiss on the cheek.

Major Riley rolled his eyes. "Okay, lovers. Jason, fire them up."

Lieutenant Riley pushed Alex back and laughed. He turned to the Major. "We need to find that boy a woman soon." Then he flipped on the magneto switch for engine one; reached, turned, and held the start switch for ten seconds. He then held the mesh switch for about four seconds until the number-one engine roared to life. After a minute he repeated the process, firing up the number-two engine, then three, and finally engine four. The *Golden Eagle* was vibrating, like a fighter, dancing around in the corner, waiting for the bell to ring and the fight to start.

As Colonel Steel loaded the suitcases in the trunk, the judge walked over to what he thought was the passenger door. "Judge, are you going to drive?"

Looking in he saw the steering wheel. "How soon we forget," he said and walked to the opposite side.

As they drove from Hacheston, the Judge said nothing. It was only as they passed through Parham that Judge Riley spoke for the first time. "Strange how much it is the same."

Making a right turn, Steel replied, "Well, Judge, the base sure has changed. Time has not been kind."

"Nor to me. When I was young I thought I was infallible."

They pulled up to what used to be the control tower, now a museum. Dawn was just breaking as Colonel Steel asked, "How do you want to do this, Judge?"

"What do you mean?"

"Do you want to go by memory or be there?"

"You're not serious; we can really be there?"

"Not here, at the tower. You would look strange standing here with that clothing on, and I don't think Major Odin would be happy to see me." Pointing across the field where the main runway once was, Steel continued, "Let's go over to the other side, a little out of sight, but, more importantly, out of the reach of Major Odin."

They drove from the tower to the highway that ran diagonally across where the runways were. Turning left, they went a few hundred yards until they hit the small remaining section left of the main runway. Turning right, they went only a hundred feet until bales of hay stacked three high blocked them. Colonel Steel turned off the engine and said, "Well, Judge, this is the end of the line."

Getting out of the car, Judge Riley was concerned that the car was still on what had been the main runway. He turned to Steel and asked, "Don't you think we should move that car? It may cause a crash."

The Colonel walked off across the field and waved the Judge to follow. "Don't worry about the car; it's not coming with us. You'd better worry about getting off the runway. That would be something, getting killed by a plane you're piloting. Wouldn't Major Odin have the time of his life investigating that?"

Just off the side and toward the end of the runway they took up their positions. The Colonel removed his long overcoat and was in full uniform. "You're okay, Judge, but they might get nervous across the way if they spot two civilians."

The Judge jumped and was startled as the place roared with dozens of bombers. Looking across at the control tower, a red flare shot in the air, and the Judge said, "I don't believe … " The rest of his words were drowned by the screaming engines as the first bomber came racing down the runway toward them.

The *Golden Eagle* hardstand was near the end of the longest of three runways. This made it third in line and a very short taxi to get in position. As the plane stopped, Major Riley pushed the intercom button on the steering yoke and said, "Listen up, boys, we will be second out today. The 570th will lead out, so we are just waiting."

Ten minutes later, Lieutenant Riley cued the intercom, "Okay, gang, get ready. We are off." The *Golden Eagle* did a sweeping right turn onto the runway, and all four engines roared to a fever pitch.

Colonel Steel lowered his binoculars and nudged the Judge while yelling in his ear, "Here comes the *Golden Eagle*!"

At first the plane moved slowly under its full bomb load. The only thing going fast was the shaking, then her tail lifted, and Major Riley and Lieutenant Riley could see the runway ahead. As the bomber rushed into view and floated overhead, Judge Riley waved up to them.

The Major turned to Jason. "Did you see those two?" Then Major Riley noticed Jason's white face. "What is the matter with you? You look like you just saw a ghost."

Jason's deep voice shook. "I did, kind of. Two of them."

Up on the control tower, Colonel Schilling directed Major

Odin's attention to the two waving up at the *Golden Eagle*. Major Odin adjusted his binoculars. "Well, I'll be, my favorite Colonel." Rushing down the stairs two at a time, he jumped in the jeep, mashing the gears to speed toward the two men.

Colonel Steel picked up his overcoat and handed his binoculars to the Judge. "I know you're enjoying yourself, but look over at that jeep heading our way. Our friend Major Odin is on his way, and he is not too happy."

The Judge shook his head. "He seems to have a way of ruining things."

— — — — — — — — — — — —

They both jumped. The sudden rush of pheasant wings sprang up from the tall grass. The Colonel Steel put on his coat to cover his uniform. "Never can be too careful; I would like to see the major's face when he gets over here."

"Serves him right." The Judge laughed.

"If we plan it just right, we can do a head-on with him."

"Tell me, is Richard your real name?"

"No, it's really Andrew."

"Why do you use Richard?"

"It was the name of my boss. On earth, that is."

They drove past the control tower heading toward where the hardstand of the *Golden Eagle* used to be, up the dirt road to the 572nd that was now hard to spot. When they arrived at the squad area, only a few of the huts had anything left to them. Their broken windows and loose tin sheeting lay in ruin. One was being used for chickens and another for pigs, and, coupled with the weeds, the area looked little like its former self. Looking around first, the Colonel took off his coat. "At least your hut is still here. I have some work to do before we go."

"I need the keys to the truck. I need to leave Jason a package here, and I was followed in London."

Handing the Judge the keys to the truck, Steel said, "I already know, but we'll discuss that on the way to Duxford. Jason thinks he put one over on me with the cigar box, yet I gave him the money. I wonder what he thought I was giving him all that money for. Let me go first, and then you can do what you have to do."

"What's in it?" He looked at the sealed package.

Andrew beamed. "That is for Jason to show you. I don't want to ruin the surprise."

The Colonel opened the front door, walked through the first section of the *Hitler's Nightmare*, then that of the *Rita Bee*, and finally to the rear section of the *Golden Eagle*. He first went to Jason's footlocker, carefully wiped Jason's fingerprints off each item, and replaced them where he found them. Opening his shaver, he noted the blood on the razor and murmured, "They will think themselves so clever." With that he put it back. Next he bundled up all of Jason's mail, putting it in his pocket along with a stack of war bonds. Going through the uniforms, he found Jason's wallet where he was instructed to leave it. He put it in his pocket and finished by checking under the bed.

As he walked toward the door he was confronted by two MPs. "Sir, with everyone gone, we are just checking out the barracks."

"Good. You're very observant. I was just looking for Lieutenant Riley. I thought maybe he didn't go up today." He closed the door behind him.

Walking into the squadron orderly room, he announced, "Sergeant, I am Colonel Steel."

The Sergeant jumped to attention. "Yes, sir. How can I help you?

"I need to see the outgoing mail."

"But sir, I think you should talk—"

Steel put out his hand. "I'm not asking; I think there may be a security issue here. I want all the outgoing mail... now!"

After the Sergeant turned over the mail, Steel rifled through it, slipping out all the letters from the crew of the *Golden Eagle*. Handing back the rest, he said, "I don't want any of these to go out until Major Odin authorizes their release. Do you understand?"

"Yes, sir."

— — — — — — — — — — — — — — — —

Colonel Steel walked up behind the Judge from the opposite direction from where he left. "Well, Judge, it's all yours."

The Judge let out a weak yelp and said, "You're going to give me a heart attack, man!"

Reaching into the car, Steel pulled out the overcoat and slipped it on. "I'll wait here."

The Judge forced open the same hut door the colonel had used, now warped by decades of weather. The hut's interior had been stripped down to the concrete floor long ago. He looked up at the hole in the roof that once held the stovepipe from where the one miserable little stove had been. Walking out the rear of the hut, whose door had long ago disappeared, the smell of the pigpen hit him with great force. After ten minutes, the Judge gave up; frustrated that he could not find a safe place to hide the package for Jason.

As the Judge walked out the front door, he saw Colonel Steel leaning against the car and taking a long draw on his pipe. He pulled it from his mouth and yelled over to Judge Riley, "All set?"

Judge Riley waved his hand back and forth, indicating no. As he walked, the place he needed became clear; as he remembered, the group of brick buildings behind the control still stood. He turned to Steel. "Andrew, I need to go to the theater."

Andrew held the door open for the Judge. "Show me the way."

They drove in silence broken only by the Judge giving occasional directions. When they arrived, Judge Riley sighed at finding the large brick building in good condition. Picking up the sealed package, he turned to Andrew, saying, "I'll be right back."

He walked from the sunlight into a large dark room and waited until his eyes adjusted. The first thing he noticed was that most of the wooden floor was now gone, revealing the concrete floor below. Despite trying to focus on where to hide the package for Jason, his thoughts drifted to when this very room was transformed from a theater to the base chapel. He looked up at the small windows that ran the length of the room, and he moved to where he remembered the coffins had been set in place, that part of his crew that he loved like life itself. His hand moved involuntarily through the air. He could feel the smooth wood beneath his fingertips, the coffin that would travel back with him to Waterbury. He slowly turned and dropped to his knees, as he did that day so long ago, in rededication to Jesus. The tears fell on top of the package that lay on the dirt-covered floor.

"Judge Riley, we must get going."

The Judge lifted his head off his chest and rose slowly. The creaking and snapping of bones was followed with heavy breathing, a reminder of all the years of wear. A ghostlike figure moved toward him and he stepped backward. "Who are you?"

Stepping out of the sunlight into the darkness, the figure replied, "It's Andrew, Judge. Are you okay?"

Judge Riley had not known this fear for decades, but now, as then, the mission came first, to find the hiding place for Jason's package. "A little shaken up from these memories."

A growing beam of light cut through the darkened room, lighting up Andrew's face. "As you should be, Judge. It was a terrible time. You were and still are a brave man, John Riley."

The Judge started, seeing Andrew literally in a new light. "Thank you, Andrew." With that the Judge looked down at the package that seemed to glow in a second beam of light. Lifting his eyes, he saw it was not a miracle, but simply the sunlight coming through the square holes high above in the far wall, where once the film projector room had been. As he picked up the package, he instinctively followed the third beam that hit the wall behind him, lighting up at the long-forgotten wooden cross. "Andrew, maybe this is a miracle."

"Do you want me to put it up there for you, Judge?"

"No, thank you, Andrew, I'll do it. The truth is that I was always curious about what that sealed-off room looked like. Never could go in there. There was a fire danger if that nitrate film went off."

The Judge walked to the rear of the building and passed the long-deserted latrine. As he placed his hand on the first rusted rung made from rebar, he took a deep breath and began the slow climb. Entering the room, he ducked at what he thought were the fluttering of bat wings that blackened his view. Waiting for his eyes to adjust to the darkness, he spotted the square holes and laid the package on the eight-inch-thick concrete ledge.

Turning around to head back down the ladder, he saw the package in full view, yet he knew that it was safe.

On the drive to Duxford, Andrew gave further instructions and answered many of the Judge's questions, but he would not reveal anything about the future or about heaven, for that matter.

When they arrived at the airstrip, they drove over to the waiting jet, and Colonel Steel handed the Judge Jason's passport and Lieutenant Riley's wallet. "Needless to say, this must be protected. What Jason wants to do with it is up to him, and by this time tomorrow, my job will be done for now. I left a note inside for Jason."

"What is your job, Andrew?"

"That's easy, to do the will of God." His eyes filled as he said, "You know, John, I'd forgotten how it was to be back in the flesh, so to speak. Back to the pain, emotion, and temptations."

"Thanks for everything, Andrew, and tell that to the Boss too." They embraced like old friends.

"He knows already, John. Well, I have to get going. I need to save that grandson of yours, and I have letters to mail."

Riley looked surprised. "What letters?"

Holding up the letters from almost sixty years in the past,

Andrew explained, "The crew's. I didn't think Major Odin would mail them, and that would be hardship on all your families."

"So that's how. I never could figure out why they would mail our letters uncensored."

"One more of the many reasons Major Odin and company were more than upset when they figured I had gotten them first. I have to go; got to turn in the rental, or you'll be charged for another day."

"What do you mean *me*?"

Andrew held up the Judge's credit card and smiled. With a salute to Judge Riley, he disappeared in front of him.

━ ━ ━ ━ ━ ━ ━ ━ ━ ━ ━ ━ ━ ━ ━

Less than an hour later, the Judge was in Cherbourg, France, hailing a taxi. Heading north he passed through St. Mere Eglise. Thoughts rushed at the Judge as he looked up at the church steeple. A dummy was hanging from a parachute, depicting a member of the 82nd Airborne who was shot numerous times as he hung helpless on that fear-filled night.

In fair English, the taxi driver turned to the Judge and asked, "You are English, yes?"

"No, American. I was a bomber pilot."

"My father was in the Resistance. You are very lucky not to be like that poor devil on the steeple. My father said it was awful."

The judge's eyes flickered. "Is the church still used today?"

"Yes, not many attend. Mostly the white heads, old people. My father told me that there were hundreds of young lives wasted as the night drop scattered them off target. Many of them were pulled down by the weight of over, let me think…in pounds, over a hundred, drowning in the flooded fields and gliders impaled on the wooden stakes called Rommel's asparagus. He said they were still finding bodies hanging in the trees years later."

"Well, those soldiers saved my life."

"How was that, monsieur?"

"My B-17 was shot down near here."

"This is strange, no, impossible. Were you at a farm?"

"Yes, we held up there for the afternoon."

"That is my friend's farm that you stayed at. Often his father told me the story of your battle. You are very brave, and your country must have given you many decorations."

The Judge suddenly felt tired, barely able to say, "No, no medal."

When he arrived at the Chateau de L'Isle-Marie, the taxi driver had to shake him awake. "Monsieur, you're here."

As the Judge lift his suitcase, the driver waved him away from them and rushed inside yelling. Within a minute two young men had the judge's suitcases in tow, while the owner greeted him like a long-lost relative. The reason for all this excitement was lost to him due to his lack of understanding of French, but he knew that it somehow had to do more with Jason than himself.

The Judge went to pay the taxi driver.

"Your name, monsieur?

"John Riley"

"Not Jason?"

"Lieutenant Jason Riley was my co-pilot." A cold chill went over him.

"I cannot take your money, Monsieur Riley; it is I who should be paying you. You who were from that bomber are all heroes to us in this area. I can't wait to tell my wife!"

The Judge was mystified. "Thank you very much."

The owner upgraded his suite to the best available and insisted there was no extra charge. The Judge directed them to put Jason's bag in the one of the spacious bedrooms. When they left, he unpacked Jason's suitcase, taking care to throw a few items around to give the room a lived-in appearance. As he left Jason's room, he threw a few Euros and Jason's passport on the nightstand. He went into his room and unpacked his suitcase. He hid Lieutenant Riley's wallet, then lay down, falling fast asleep from exhaustion.

BOMBS AWAY

At the assembly point, signal flares shot out of the command planes to bring bombers from the various groups into formation. The 572nd's nine bombers had the distinction of being the last and in the low formation among those of the 390th. Somewhere midpoint of the English Channel puffs of white smoke came from the various B-17s as the crews tested their machine guns. It was at this point that the squadrons tightened up to present enemy fighters a wall of steel with little space to penetrate the formation.

Ten miles from the coast, Jerry got on the intercom. "Captain— correction, Major, we are ten miles off the coast. We'll be making the turn at fifteen."

Major Riley put on his sunglasses and responded, "Okay, I'm not used to this Major yet. Keep your eyes open; we may have company coming. Alex, go pull your pins."

Ten minutes later, Alex had the bombs armed, and Jerry was back on the intercom. "Major, new heading 179." No communications were needed to the other planes in the squadron as they copied the *Golden Eagle*'s banking south and drop in altitude.

Preacher's voice came over the intercom. "Major, I have radio traffic from *Rita Bee* and *On Target*. We've lost our fighter escort."

Hitting his hand against the yolk, "Nathan, you tell them no radio traffic." Reaching up as Lieutenant Riley bent over the center console, Major Riley knocked Lieutenant Riley's cap and headset off. "Sorry, Jason."

Lieutenant Riley put his cap and headset back on and responded calmly, "No problem; they didn't build these for luxury. We're at twenty thousand and descending."

Ray rubbed his crotch. "Ox, do you have an extra rubber?"

"If you didn't drool in your mask, Ray, you wouldn't need one."

"Funny, Ice Face, but it's not for the mic. Hurry up."

Two minutes later, the first bomb dropped over enemy-occupied territory. Ray yelled, "Here's to you, Hitler!" as the urine-filled condom fell to earth.

— — — — — — — — — — — — — —

The *Golden Eagle* entered its initial point sirens around the chateau were wailing, gun crews ran for duty stations, and the chateau occupants emptied into bomb shelters. Meyers, while hitting his driver's back, screamed, "Stop! Stop!" The Steyr truck following behind hit the rear of the Horch and sent the Major, standing behind the Captain, stumbling into the front seat.

Colonel Meyers was on his feet yelling orders in full fury, trying to get the escort vehicles in front to head back up the road away from the bridge as the valley erupted with the sound of dozens of eighty-eights aimed at the incoming squadron.

As Meyers jumped out of the vehicle, Captain Keasling protested, "Colonel, this is dangerous; we need to find some cover."

Pointing up, Meyers screamed, "You act like an old woman, Keasling! We are a mile away." He handed his binoculars to Captain Keasling. "Look up. Those are bomber contrails, not fighters;

they are not interested in a staff car. Make sure that the anti-aircraft crews don't fire. I have a feeling we have a long drive ahead."

Major Riley flipped over the row switches to Alex and his Norton bombsight. "Alex, it's all yours. Make them count."

Three miles from their target, the low clouds parted and the sky in front of the *Golden Eagle* began to fill with black bursts of flak. The crew scrambled into their flak vests and helmets. Alex kept his eye to the Norton sight. "Major, we're on target and clear."

Lieutenant Riley's voice came over the intercom. "Lots of flak ahead, boys. Make sure you have those helmets and vests on."

Alex felt the *Golden Eagle* make minor course corrections to keep the target in his crosshairs. Reaching down, he opened the bomb bay doors. The sky filled with deadly steel. As Lieutenant Riley glanced over his wing, *Hitler's Nightmare* took a direct hit; folding, the left wing went straight up.

"Ox, Reb, see chutes?"

Reb screamed from the tail, "Sorry, *Lady* is going down," as the *Golden Eagle* lifted up with a jolt.

"Hold on, everyone! We're near release." Alex yelled.

"Major, Major, we're hit! We need help back here. It's bad!" Ox screamed.

Major Riley was calm and measured. "Nathan, get back there."

Lieutenant Riley tore off his headset. "I'll go take a look. Be right back."

Major grabbed Jason and then changed his mind. "Hurry up and get back here."

Grabbing a portable oxygen bottle, Lieutenant Riley rushed to the rear, pushing past Tom, who was manning the top turret.

The Major said over the intercom, "Hold on, Nathan, Jason's on the way."

Lieutenant Riley pulled open the forward cabin door and was

hit by the cold wind. Halfway across the narrow rail, in the bomb bay, Alex pressed the release button, dropping a dozen bombs and lightening the *Golden Eagle*'s load. Another jolt caused Jason to fall to his knee, and he grabbed the guide chain with his free hand. Getting back on his feet, he watched his cap fall to earth. Sweat poured and heartbeats throbbed as he ripped open the radio room door. Preacher was gone, so he continued through the radio room, pulling open the final door. He was ready to jump over the threshold into midsection when he stopped, looking down at a huge hole at his feet. Most of the ball turret was gone, along with a chunk of the right fuselage. Screaming over the shrieking wind and pointing to his ear, Lieutenant Riley commanded, "Preacher! Preacher! Intercom! Intercom!"

Ox hit the Preacher and pointed to Lieutenant Riley. Preacher nodded his head, and Lieutenant Riley retreated back to the radio section. Fumbling around, Preacher plugged into the intercom as Lieutenant Riley picked up the headset. He heard the Major. "I got her, Alex."

Jason hyperventilated. "Preacher, Preacher!" There was no response as he was knocked off his feet when the *Golden Eagle* banked right and headed west. Flak hit the opposite side of the radio room. Lieutenant Riley spoke inward, *Come on, Jason, hold it together*. Jason took a deep breath and retraced his route back to the cockpit. He flopped back into his seat, sighing after noticing the bomb doors were closed. "Major, the ball turret is gone and a piece of the right side above it."

The Major shot up a hand to silence Lieutenant Riley. "We lost number three. The drag back there is pulling; we'll have to drop back." Pressing the intercom, he continued, "Alex, get back there and give me a report, and get Nathan on the radio."

Lieutenant Riley looked over at the Major. "We'll be heading toward Normandy; that is where the invasion will start tomorrow. If we have to ditch, I know a spot."

Major Riley was about to argue but instead said, "Jerry, Jason is coming down. Everyone listen up, we are dropping down and falling out of formation. Let's hope we don't have any company."

- - - - - - - - - - - - - - -

Everyone was awestruck as the chateau below them disappeared into a pile of flames and rubble. Before the last bomb exploded, Meyers was yelling orders to turn the vehicles south. His adjutant sensed the danger. "Colonel, where are we heading?"

"St. Mere Eglise, Normandy," Colonel Meyers snapped. Throwing the radio mic down on the seat, he continued, "Major, we are going to lose this war if we don't stop that invasion. We need to get to the Seventh Army as soon as we can. With the proof I have, even Hitler will order our Panzers forward. Pity those that make it off the beach. We will grind them up in their tracks."

The Major replied under heavy eyes, "It looks like we have a long day before us."

Slapping the Major in good spirits, Meyers said, "But a glorious one, Major, a glorious one."

- - - - - - - - - - - - - - -

Major Riley got on the radio and said, "*Rita Bee*, take them home. We're going down, and if things don't improve, we will bail at Normandy." At the same time, Jerry called up the first heading.

Alex and Lieutenant Riley arrived in the cockpit at the same time. Lieutenant Riley dropped into his seat and reported, "Rodent is gone, blew him right out. Ray just died. I have Nathan on right waist. I can't tell all the damage; there is one big hole back there. How is it going up here?"

Major Riley glanced over the instruments. "Three is out; losing some oil pressure in number two. The moment of truth is in about ten. Alex, you better get down there with Jerry. The way things are going, we'll be jumped."

As Alex left, Jason looked over at the Major. "You lied to me!

You said everyone made it back safe. Now Ray and Rodent are dead; there are no fighters."

Major Riley locked eyes with Jason. "I don't know what you're talking about. You're crazy. Alex is right. You're crazy. When we get back—"

"Two coming at twelve, one heading right!" Tom yelled into the intercom.

"Take her down now, now!" Lieutenant Riley screamed.

Major Riley violently pushed the yoke forward. He felt the number-two engine sputter. Tom's, Alex's, and Jerry's guns came to life; the *Golden Eagle* and the FW 190 were now in a game of chicken. Ox's fifty-caliber spit shells at the other fighter as it dropped out of the sun, shooting past the *Golden Eagle*. Just before impact, the 190 exploded. Instinctively Major and Lieutenant Riley threw their arms across their faces ducking from the flames and shrapnel that thrust outward and whirled toward the sky. Voices screamed from headsets as the Plexiglas bubble exploded, and a piece of the 190 imbedded itself into Jerry's head. Major Riley pushed the *Golden Eagle* into an even steeper dive.

The second FW 190 rolled belly up, keeping its armor-plated bottom toward the *Golden Eagle* and blazed a line of holes starting just in front of the rear wheel bay to the tail gun. When the enemy fighter pulled alongside, the Preacher repaid him with a few holes in his tail. Reb loosened his grip on the machine gun and fell sideways against the thin metal wall. *Strange*, he thought, *that I should fall*. He felt wet. Removing his gloves, he patted his chest. He examined his red, wet hands. They were lying before him, twitching and gleaming in the light, but he felt nothing. He yanked off his mask and tried to speak, but nothing came. He sat gasping for air, watching his life flow out with each passing breath. Reb slowly closed his eyes, slipping down into the puddle of blood.

Major Riley shouted for a count and got only four responses.

Leveling the *Golden Eagle* out at five hundred feet, he shouted in the intercom, "Get ready for a rough landing, boys."

As they dropped down to a hundred feet, the number-two engine sputtered and died. The Major shouted, "What the . . ." His voice drowned out as dozens of wooden poles tore at the plane and wire wrapped around the propeller. The tail section broke off on impact, just in front of the rear wheel well, and came to rest fifty yards away from the rest of the plane. Stunned and battered, the crew remained in shocked paralysis for a few seconds in disbelief. They couldn't believe they were still alive. As the *Golden Eagle* started filling with smoke, there was a sudden mad scramble for the exit.

Major Riley climbed out his window and tried to swing onto the wing, only to fall to the ground, spraining his ankle. Lieutenant Riley rushed down from the flight deck and grabbed his duffel bag. He almost landed on top of Walker, who, having pulled the emergency release handle, was now trying to kick open the belly hatch. Lieutenant Riley pulled Walker forward and found the place a mess. Jason turned his head away as he glimpsed Jerry's body. Alex didn't have the luxury of avoidance, with fragments of fresh brain matter staining his jacket.

Lieutenant Riley pushed Alex aside and took out an M-3 machine gun. He unloaded a full magazine at the Plexiglas bubble until it shattered into shards. Lieutenant Riley threw Walker out of the plane while yelling, "Let's go before she blows!" Alex pulled out his 45 and placed three carefully aimed rounds into the Norton bombsight. With a surge of strength and a scream, he lifted Jerry's body and went out the window.

Preacher was already on the ground as Ox turned to him. "We can't leave Ray; give me a hand."

Preacher had just helped pull Ray's body clear from the wreckage as he heard the 109 fighter closing in. Like the rest of the crew, Preacher was sprinting, yelling over his shoulder for Ox to get out.

Ox yelled repeatedly, "I'm not going to let this one kill us." He jumped back into the bomber and manned his fifty-caliber. He clenched the trigger. His body jerked with each spurt of bullets that sprayed toward the fighter as it screamed closer. The fusing sounds deafened his yell as the *Golden Eagle* and fighter exploded simultaneously.

The shock wave knocked the fleeing crew to the ground, sending chucks of metal flying in all directions. Ox shot up in the air like a rag doll. Everyone ran for a nearby hedgerow except for Major Riley, who made it for about forty yards then fell.

Lieutenant Riley saw the Major fall and threw Walker his duffel bag. "You and Preacher take cover. Alex, come on!" They hardly paused as Alex slung the Major's unconscious form over Jason's shoulder. Across the field, German troops poured over the side of the halftrack.

Lieutenant Riley grabbed his duffel bag from Walker. "Alex, get everyone to the other side." Then, pulling Preacher toward him, he asked, "Where is your 45?"

"Next to the radio, melted down by now." Preacher froze with heavy breaths.

"Take this, Preacher. I'll see if I can delay them." Lieutenant Riley took his shoulder-holstered 45, along with three clips of ammunition from the leg pocket of his flight suit. With Alex leading, Preacher and Walker carried the Major, fighting the thick vegetation to the other side. Lieutenant Riley stripped off his flight clothes and boots. He hid behind a large rock and dumped the contents of his duffel bag. He changed into combat boots, strapped on two knives, and loaded a full magazine into the M-3. The wait for the German troops to advance began. *Just like the old days*, he thought. He counted to ten and calculated his odds when, on the far road, a truck pulled up behind the halftrack, unloading a dozen more German troops. They went over to the broken tail section and soon discovered Reb's body nearby. Seconds passed as minutes as the second group joined the first group near the burning wreckage. Lieutenant Riley cocked his head to hear what the soldier was yelling as he knelt over Ox. Lieutenant Riley could not hear but soon saw the answer; they formed an assault line and slowly moved toward him.

Lieutenant Riley placed the four magazines and grenades in a neat row on the ground. *"Okay, Jason, do I die?"*

Jason said to his invisible tenant, Lieutenant Riley, "How do I know, Lieutenant? Everything I knew about this is a lie."

Lieutenant Riley mumbled, *"I must, Jason, because I don't remember you."*

"Colonel Steel said we're in this together. If I live, you do too."

"You know they lock up people who argue with themselves."

"That's not us; we are one and the same."

"Right, Jason. Here they come. Any ideas?"

"Pray. Best thing I know to do."

AIR FORCE ONE

In the early morning darkness, President Strong's motorcade entered Andrews AFB. The President, after a few brief words to the press, walked with his wife up the stairs, waved at the top, then ducked into Air Force One.

One could have noticed with simple adding and subtracting that one of the ground crew never got off the plane. No one did, however. What was noticed by the video camera of Chinese TV news crew was the large olive drab metal case getting special loading.

Once airborne, the President leaned over and kissed his wife. "I'll be right back. I'm going to greet our guests." As he walked down the aisle, he spent a few seconds with each person.

His military aide, Major Benson, introduced him to those few people he did not know. "Mr. President, Major Joe Ramsey and his wife, Margaret."

President Strong placed his hand on Major Ramsey's shoulder to keep him from standing. "Please, Major, stay seated. Major Ramsey and Mrs. Ramsey; it's an honor to have you on board. If there is anything you need, please feel free to ask."

The old man shook his hand. As the President started to move on, Ramsey asked, "I understand Colonel Riley is here, but I don't see him. Is he onboard?"

President Strong stopped and replied, "He's already in France. His wife, however, is on board."

Ramsey coughed and murmured, "Sorry, last time I saw Colonel Riley was in May 1945. He was visiting the graves of his crewmembers that died at Normandy. We were pretty close; our crews shared the same quarters."

The President was surprised at his good fortune and asked, "Really, Major Ramsey? So you were the pilot of the *Rita Bee*?"

Major Ramsey's eyes beamed. He hadn't thought the President would know the name of the plane. "Yes, sir."

President Strong patted the Major on the shoulder. "I have a little speech to give and maybe you could help me. Would you and your wife please join me for coffee?"

Ramsey broke into a big smile. "It would be an honor, Mr. President."

"I'll send my aide, Major Benson, for you in about ten minutes. Let me first greet the rest of my guests."

The President continued shaking hands until he got to Robert Higgins. Major Benson did the introduction. "Mr. Albert Shaw—"

The President interrupted, "I know Mr. Shaw. I take it that you'll be joining us for breakfast up front?"

"You know me, Mr. President; I wouldn't miss it for the world."

"Yes, I do know you," Strong replied coldly.

A young man interrupted, "Mr. President, I'm David Blake. I work on your staff."

Strong turned to Major Benson questioningly. Benson checked his list but didn't see Blake's name. Seeing the Major's discomfort, President Strong said, "Really? Refresh my memory, Mr. Blake."

Blake pushed on in youthful excitement. "I actually work in the executive building. I'm a graphic artist. It's an honor to be invited."

President Strong was mystified as to who the young man could be and why he was there. "Well, I'm glad you're enjoying yourself. Have a good time, Mr. Blake."

As he went back to his quarters, he stopped by his Chief of Staff's seat and whispered in Carlos' ear, "I'm having Major Ramsey and his wife for coffee in few minutes. Wait twenty minutes and then go to my office. One other thing: there's a young man named David Blake back there. He's not on the list; who is he?"

Carlos explained, "I just found out. He is a guest of Higgins and company," and waited for the expositive of temper. It didn't happen.

President Strong resigned himself to his fate. "Before you ask, Major Ramsey was in the same quarters as Lieutenant Riley. Knowing Higgins, I guess you don't know why this Blake is on board?"

Carlos wanted to get away from his boss, whose irritation was palpable now. "He just told me that everything would be explained at the meeting. I'll meet you with pad in hand."

After fifteen minutes of small talk with the Ramsey's, the president stood. "If you don't mind, Mrs. Ramsey, I would like to borrow the Major for a few minutes. I'm a bit of a history buff and would like a firsthand account from him on how the war really was."

"I hope you get more out him than I ever could."

Strong, as the perfect host, showed the Ramsey's the presidential section, with the planned final stop being the President's office. Strong nodded to Major Benson, who was waiting at the entrance, then gently grabbed Mrs. Ramsey's elbow. "Mrs. Ramsey, your husband should not be long."

As Strong and Ramsey entered, the President's eyes lifted. "Carlos, sorry, I didn't know you were here. Major Ramsey, this is my Chief of Staff, Carlos Martinez. Major Ramsey was the pilot of the

Rita Bee; in fact, his crew shared the same quarters with Colonel Riley. I asked him to share stories of his time with the 390th with me. Maybe you'd like to join us, if that's okay with the Major?"

"That would be fine, Mr. President."

For the next ten minutes, the President unsuccessfully attempted to turn the conversation to Lieutenant Riley, but then he hit pay dirt. "You and Colonel Riley were close?"

Ramsey was comfortable and plowed ahead. "Not really; he was closer to his bombardier, Lieutenant Montgomery. I was more close to his co-pilot, Lieutenant Jason Riley, the same last name, but not related."

"In our research of the 572nd and June 5, 1944, I seem to remember some talk about him being missing in action." Carlos paused from his note taking.

Major Ramsey looked down as his right hand began to quiver. He placed his left over it to try and stop the shaking. "After our last mission, everyone looked for him—I mean, everyone. He knew approximately where and when the invasion was going to be. But the way Jason disappearing was typical of him."

"I do seem to recall a Lieutenant Jason Riley. When did you first meet Lieutenant Riley, Major Ramsey?" The President leaned forward.

"We both had our training in Southwest Division, primary training at Ryan Field about twenty miles from Tucson. Then we split up for basic. Then we were together again on a train heading to Douglas Army Air Force Base for advanced. He stood out from everyone else, looked like he was seventeen. He was already a Second Lieutenant with a chest full of medals." Ramsey gripped his hands tighter.

"He'd been shot down before?" Carlos asked.

"No, he was a Ranger in Europe and North Africa. When he worked with some British Commandos in France, he got shot up pretty bad." His shaking increased as he thought, *Another interrogation*, and cursed Jason under his breath.

"How bad and where, do you remember?" Carlos took careful notes.

Major Ramsey thought, *How much harm can there be after so many years?*

"In the shower once, I counted at least three scars. You know, you just don't stare at another guy nude. I seem to remember a scar on his leg, his right arm, and somewhere on his back; I forgot the exact spot. Oh, there was one scar that ran along the side of his neck, so I guess four. So I asked Jason about them. He said the Germans were celebrating the Fourth of July by shooting him, but then he said it was really the night of the fifth, so he guessed it didn't count. I never did understand."

President Strong chimed in, "You said he was strange?"

Major Ramsey was ever cautious from past experiences when questions about Jason arose. "No, I didn't say that. If I were to say anything, it was that Jason was different. When we got to Douglas, we had to wait in the depot. It was over a hundred and five degrees, and everyone was in a bad mood from the long ride, nervous about advanced training, you know. Jason took it all in stride. He was more interested in the stained-glass dome in the depot ceiling than if transportation was sent to pick us up. I thought at first that was because of his being in combat, but that was just how he was."

"What was Lieutenant Jason Riley like?" Carlos pressed and focused his questions solely on Lieutenant Riley, not giving any pretense that Lieutenant Riley was not the subject of the meeting.

"He was a very complex person. He had a great sense of humor but also a kind of rebellious streak, which got him in trouble more than once. I figured the base commander, Colonel Wadman, would bounce him, but he was such a great pilot, and everyone really respected Jason. He was modest, didn't go on about what he did and what his medals were for. If we hadn't been friends, no one would know what I told you. He made jokes and dismissed what he did. He could be very sentimental. I saw him cry more than a few times over those killed or badly wounded, yet I know that he did his share of killing."

"This is important, Major Ramsey. Was he a religious man, a Christian?" The President made firm eye contact.

Ramsey was taken aback with the line questioning and stumbled over his words. "No!…Wait, let me take that back. I heard from his ground crew, and later, John Riley, that he became a Christian just before our last flight. I think he always believed in God but had a bad experience in church, like many of us. Jason, I think, got mixed up between church and God. He could be wild at times but always had good character, loved his country. I did see him pray once; he was going to get bounced out of advanced flight school."

"For causing trouble?" Carlos asked.

Ramsey felt pressured. "No, it was another strange Jason thing. It was his twentieth birthday in fact, August 29, in 1943. We went up together; we were in the same squadron since they assigned us by last name. When we landed, there was blood dripping from both of Jason's earlobes. Our instructor was excited and yelling that Jason's eardrums were ruptured. He rushed him over to the base hospital. As I said, it was a little strange, maybe typical with him. They found out that both his ear lobes had pinholes right through them that had caused the bleeding. No one on the medical staff could figure it out; they thought it was perhaps some kind of insect. It was like his tattoo; another thing he had done on his birthday, his sixteenth, or so he said. Even our last night at Douglas, or, I should say, early morning, there was crazy stuff going on. MPs came to arrest him for knocking out another MP, and they said Jason was nude at the time of battery."

"Sounds like a character." Carlos shook his head.

Ramsey realized that meeting had everything to do with Jason, so he decided to try to wrap it up in a polite manner. "Yeah, he missed the silver bullet on that one. We were all with Jason, packing and getting ready to go. In fact, we were just getting on the bus when the MPs came to arrest him. There was almost a riot between the

MPs and us; we knew they were full of it. Jason could not be in two places at once. But that MP seemed convinced and believable."

"How so, Major?" the President said.

"His face was swollen, he might even have had a broken jaw, and he described Jason really well, right down to his tattoo, the tattoo of the 572nd."

Carlos stopped writing. "Major, you're not making sense; maybe you need to start at the beginning."

Ramsey stood. "Never did, and never will. I need to get back to my wife. Thank you for the visit," he said, lying.

Carlos stood and said, "One more question, Major."

Ramsey came face to face with Carlos. "You seem to have missed the point, Mr. Martinez. I have been through this many times for many years. I have said too much already; go find someone else to interrogate."

Half an hour after the interview with Major Ramsey, Strong and Carlos walked into the conference room. Odin was there and introduced Higgins to the Chief of Staff. Everyone sat down, ready for business. President Strong spoke first, "Let's eat and talk. Time is passing very fast. Director Odin and Mr. Higgins, we seem to have gotten a break. Major Ramsey shared the same quarters as Lieutenant Riley; in fact, he went to a couple of the same training schools. He is very mentally alert and could be very helpful."

With that, Odin pushed a brown envelope across the table. "He's not necessary, except to confirm this. Inside this envelope, Mr. President, are two DNA reports. The reports are for two blood samples. The first blood sample was taken from a razor blade found in Lieutenant Riley's footlocker. The second blood sample was taken from a disposable razor found in Jason Riley's bathroom in Waterbury. The DNA on both matches perfectly."

"There can be no mistake?" The President speared half a sausage.

Higgins said, in his usual rough voice, "No, sir. We cut Lieutenant Riley's double blade in half and sent each lab a disposable razor from Jason Riley. Two different lab teams, same result."

Spearing the second half of the sausage with his right hand and handing the letter from Christopher Clark to Carlos, Strong said, "Give it to Aaron, and let's use first names, right, Robert?"

With a big grin, Higgins said, "Is this a sign of friendship, Mr. President?"

Stuffing the sausage in his mouth, Strong replied, "With you, Robert, let's say a temporary truce."

"Aaron, your father did not share everything with you, as you'll see in the letter. To get the *Golden Eagle* case transferred to the CIA so he could continue to track down Lieutenant Riley, he allowed a cover-up, a very complex one." Carlos threw the letter in front of the Deputy Director.

A few minutes passed. "Do we have the boxes?" Aaron dropped the letter on the table.

The President wiped his mouth with the corner of his napkin. "No, not yet. I didn't want this to spread, so I had General Thomas fly back from Hawaii to take care of this himself. It seems it was a more difficult task than it would first appear, but the general prevailed. I understand that some retirements were threatened. He is running late, hauling three large and heavy cases on board the last minute I'm afraid would draw the attention of our friends in the East, so Thomas and Wells will meet us in France with them."

"What's in the files and boxes, boss?" Carlos poured his third cup of coffee.

"Didn't ask. Less said the better with our Chinese friends now in the game. Robert, when did you become part of the ground crew?"

"When that Chinese news crew showed up with three cameras where one would do. I'm sure they will be waiting for us in Paris." He slid two passports over to Carlos. "You did well, Carlos. While David Blake is not an exact duplicate for Jason, he is close enough."

Carlos picked up the two passports. With raised eyebrows, he said, "So that's why you asked for a lookalike; Jason Riley becomes David Blake."

The President threw his napkin down onto the plate. "Okay, everyone. Let's lay it out."

"David Blake becomes Jason Riley." Aaron nodded to Higgins to answer the demand.

"We think that when we find Jason Riley, he will be wounded based on an offhand comment Major John Riley made to Major Ramsey in June of 1944. If that is the case, the last thing we need is for the French and the Chinese to be concerned or curious about a wounded Jason Riley. However, a David Blake, as part of your staff, we can handle."

"Why do you think we'll have a wounded Jason Riley, Robert?"

Higgins pulled out the pack of cigarettes and then cursed to himself, putting them back in his pocket. "I believe, Mr. President, it all started with that tattoo Jason Riley has and then it is on Lieutenant Jason Riley."

President Strong interjected, "Per Major Ramsey, Lieutenant Riley got it on his sixteenth birthday."

"I'm impressed. We couldn't get anything out of the old goat. ."

Strong picked up his fork, deciding that he was still puckish. "Kindness is a great thing, Robert. Does it say that Jason Riley was shot on July fifth, three times, two years ago?"

"Close, it was the fourth in the late afternoon."

A frown appeared on the President's brow. "That's strange." Now, deep in thought, he questioned, *Could it be the time difference between California and France?* "Carlos, have you got your notes of our conversation with Major Ramsey?"

"Major Ramsey said Lieutenant Riley, while a Ranger, was wounded in France on July 4, 1942, maybe in the early morning on the fifth, not really sure when."

Higgins pointed at the police report. "Just got it. Seems it went missing for a couple of years. It says that Jason was shot about five p.m. on the fourth. However, there was no sound; no bullets were found. I called Detective Tucker of Waterbury PD. He said it was a strange case. He couldn't put it in the report, but he swears Judge Riley knew about Jason being shot before anyone told him."

"Maybe someone told him."

"He was already in the hospital. Jason was shot outside after visiting him. When Judge Riley saw Jason for the first time, he passed out. That is how he ended up in the hospital. His son, Major David Riley, was killed in action in the Gulf War. There was no contact between them; Riley hadn't seen his grandson since he was nine or ten."

"Real shock: your grandson is your co-pilot. Did Jason have his ears pierced?"

"Yes, both." Aaron slid a photo of Jason across the table.

"Robert, let's get copies of that police report for everyone. I bet if we asked Mrs. Riley, we'd find out he pierced them on his twentieth birthday. Here's another little Ramsey tidbit. Lieutenant Riley, while at advanced flight training, on landing, for no reason both ears started to bleed. The bleeding seemed to be due to what appeared to be pinholes in his ear lobes; it was his twentieth birthday, August 29, 1943. We need to pull everything on Douglas Army Air Base from May through December 1943. You're right, Robert; what happens to one happens to the other. If Lieutenant Riley gets shot, then Jason has bullet wounds. I was doing the math in my head, time in France, nine hours ahead of California, bingo 5pm the 4th is 2am on the 5th in France. Jason gets a tattoo and Lieutenant Riley has one. That must have been something for a sixteen-year-old to find himself with a tattoo all of a sudden."

Higgins gathered up his notes. "Not as much as an old bomber pilot who sees his grandson for the first time in years and it's his co-pilot from WWII."

The President stood, pointing down at the police report. "Let's get the medical report that goes with that." Then, reaching down, he picked it up and handed it to Higgins. "For nearly two years, Jason has lived with Judge Riley, and he knows Jason was going back, but to what? What are they hiding? One more tidbit from Major Ramsey, Jason was almost arrested for assault on an MP his last day at Douglas, get this, while running around completely nude. Let's get those copies made and get to work."

ESCAPE

The troops made their way across the breezy grass toward Lieutenant Riley. He had just bowed his head for a quick prayer when two P-51 Mustangs roared over the dirt road, tearing up the field and German troops in a hail of bullets. Any thought they had of continuing came to a halt as the first two Mustangs pulled up and a second pair rushed over Lieutenant Riley's head and repeated the devastation of the first wave, plus wiping out the truck and half-track on the road.

Lieutenant Riley watched as the few remaining troops tried to aid their fallen comrades. Leaderless and devastated, they limped back toward the road looking up at the sky. Jason knew it was their time to pray; there was both relief and sadness in his heart; he saw no victories in killing.

When Lieutenant Riley found Alex, he was patching up the Major's leg. "How's it going, Major?"

With a little groan, Major Riley replied, "I guess you were right; that was our last flight. I hope you're right about this being the place.

It seems I have more than a sprained ankle. I have a few pieces of the *Golden Eagle* embedded in me."

Lieutenant Riley pulled Alex aside and asked, "What's the story?"

"He has a piece of steel in his right leg. I can't get to it; it would cause more infection and damage if I do. The one in his back is minor, but he needs help."

Major Riley sat up on his elbows. "Those P-51s screaming overhead almost made me lose it."

"I guess they were our escort. Better late than never. They must have seen the smoke; it was a slaughter. Those German troops didn't stand a chance out in the open."

Alex was about to give Major Riley morphine when Lieutenant Riley said, "Alex, I need him alert; he has to remember everything."

"He's in pain, and this will help."

"I said no, and I mean it. We can't afford to have him out of it, you understand?" He grabbed the morphine from Alex.

"Okay, Jason, no morphine."

"Cap it, we may need it later. I'll be right back; I'm going to go see if I can find help." He handed the syringe back.

Twenty minutes later, Tom and Preacher dove for cover as they heard voices approaching. Tom jabbed Preacher. "Is that German?"

"No, I think it is French." Preacher listened intently.

They both raised their 45s. Preacher reached into his jumpsuit pocket and pulled out the toy cricket and clicked it. Lieutenant Riley returned the signal as he led the farmer through the hedgerow. Tom and Preacher slapped Lieutenant Riley on the back in greeting and out of relief that he had found help.

"You're just full of surprises," Tom said upon seeing Lieutenant Riley for the first time in full combat gear and with an automatic weapon.

"This whole mission is full of them. Stay alert; we may not be forgotten." Lieutenant Riley nodded in agreement.

Pushing his way down the hedgerow, Lieutenant Riley went back to the Mmajor and Alex. Alex, hearing the rustle of Jason's passage, turned around, pointing the 45 at the hedgerow. "Alex, you'd be dead. First sound, use your cricket, and if no reply, shoot."

Alex stood, and Lieutenant Riley's companion rushed forward and embraced Alex, speaking a flood of French. Lieutenant Riley laughed at Alex's blank expression and said, "This is Monsieur Henri Colbert. Unfortunately, he doesn't speak any English; however, we're on his farm. His house is a couple of fields over, and he says there's a lot of Resistance activity and, as always, German patrols."

Major Riley tried to stand up, forestalling Colbert's attempt at an embrace by waving his hand. "Sounds good to me; I think I can make it."

Alex placed his shoulder under the Major's arm and steadied his weight. "I don't think you're going to be able to walk far."

Lieutenant Riley checked his map. "Good news is we're just south of St. Mere Eglise. I would suggest, sir, that we hole up at Monsieur Colbert's farm. Tomorrow, if I remember correctly, we can head into town and hook up with our troops."

"Okay, Jason, so far you've done good by us, but I want to know how you know." He pressed Lieutenant Riley on his uncanny knowledge.

"I watch movies," Jason replied flippantly. He turned his attention to the farmer and, after a brief conversation, watched him walk away. Lieutenant Riley turned to Alex and Riley. "He'll be right back with a wagon."

"Can we trust him, Jason?" Alex asked.

"We have to. Didn't you see how excited he was to see Alexander, Liberator of France?"

"I'll leave the liberation to others; I'll just be glad to get back to base."

Jason swatted at a fly. "Major, why don't you take it easy? It may be a half hour before he gets back. I'll go down with Tom and

Preacher and reconnoiter. Last thing we need is for the Germans to kill our host."

In less than the time promised, Tom and Campbell helped Major Riley into the large hay wagon. When everyone was covered and hidden by the hay, the farmer headed back to the farmhouse. The trip was uneventful except for a flyover by four P-51s.

Jason was concerned that the German troops would discover their hideout, so for the safety of their host and his family, he convinced Colbert to leave and send back some local Resistance members to help them with their escape. He had the Major placed outside the rear door if a quick escape was needed.

Tom and Preacher were outside protecting the Major as Lieutenant Riley stepped out the back door. "There's some food inside; I'll stay with the Major while you two get some chow."

Preacher looked up. "I'm not hungry; I keep thinking about the crew. Half of us are gone, and we're not out of this yet."

Lieutenant Riley nodded at Tom, who grabbed Preacher. "Then you can watch me eat. Alex needs some company." They started to go in when the sounds of battle erupted close by. Alex rushed out with his 45 in hand as two P-51s flew over the farmhouse.

The members of the *Golden Eagle* waved in rapid swats at the plane, jumping up and down. The pilot waggled his wings in acknowledgment as he headed east, back toward England.

Lieutenant Riley pushed Alex toward the door. "Okay, guys, go get some food. Stay alert; whatever those birds were shooting is close by."

Finally alone with Major Riley, Jason reached into the knapsack for the cigar box. "I need you to keep this safe for me. No matter how long it takes, I promise I'll come and get it."

The Major looked inside the box at the sealed package. "What is it?"

"Let's just say it belongs in the future."

He reached into his pocket and pulled out a small notebook and pencil. A couple of minutes later he put the note he wrote and the new, shiny New York quarter in the box. "This is my proof that I'll be back. Don't tell anyone; it's just between you and me. Just remember that I will come back."

"Okay, Jason. I give you my word. I'll keep the box and keep it as our secret. It will be safe and waiting for you when you come to get it." Reaching into his pocket he pulled out a few photos. "Throw these in too. It feels like it's going good for us."

"To tell you the truth, I'm scared. This is a lot more than I was thinking it was going to be." Jason said, wrapping the two heavy elastic bands around the cigar box.

Major Riley winced in pain. "From what I heard about you from Joe Ramsey, you've been in worse."

"He talks too much. One part of me has, the other part has not," he said, handing his grandfather the cigar box.

"You're right, Jason. Those who think war is glamorous should try one on for size."

"We just have to lay low Major, for the next twenty-four hours. Our airborne troops will be landing tonight; we will hook up with them." Jason mumbled to himself, "Lay low, and we're out of here, is that what you told me?"

"You know a lot, Jason, even French."

"One of the few things I listened to my grandfather about. He was big on me learning French; now I know why. One more thing, this is important, for our nation and for our family. Do whatever you have to make sure I'm here, even lie if you have to. It's really important."

"Lie? I don't understand, who should I lie to?"

"To me, lie to me!" Their conversation was interrupted as Jason heard vehicles coming toward the house. "You'll make it, and me? We'll just have to see. I love you." Jason rushed back into the house.

Major Riley looked down at his hand covered with blood from

his reopened wound. He pulled the cigar box close and said aloud to no one in particular, "I hope you're right, Lieutenant Riley, I hope you're right."

— — — — — — — — — — — — — —

For the second time that morning, Colonel Meyers came out of the roadside ditch screaming, "Hurry, we are running out of time!"

Captain Keasling looked around in shock; more of his men lay dead and wounded. Under his breath he mumbled, "I should shoot this madman before he gets us all killed." Keasling rushed over to Meyers. "Herr Colonel, I have men who are badly wounded; they are in no shape to travel. We can radio a patrol and get them help."

Meyers brushed the dust off his sleeve and pointed at the one remaining radio, which was riddled with bullets. "What do you suggest we use for a radio, Captain?" Not waiting for a reply, Meyers turned to his adjutant. "Major, how far are we from St. Mere Eglise?"

Looking at a map, the adjutant replied, "I would guess seven or eight kilometers." Seeing chimney smoke, he pointed and said, "Looks like a farmhouse. We can leave our wounded there."

Meyers looked up, searching for more enemy planes, irritated at the burning anti-aircraft troop vehicle. "That fool Goring is going to cost us the war. Don't we have any planes left? Let's take care of the men." When his riddled staff vehicle started, he thought it was a miracle. With the only remaining escort vehicle, the Steyr, and no radio, they made the dash to the farmhouse. As they drove up the dirt road, they were unaware that the eyes of the *Golden Eagle*'s remaining crew were upon them.

Keasling dropped down from the truck passenger seat and ran over to the staff car; he gave a smart salute. "Colonel, none of my detail speaks French. We were wondering if you or the Major would assist us."

"I'll do it myself; everyone take a five-minute break." He paused as he took out a pack of cigarettes and watched, as the wounded were unloaded. "Major, did you ever get that feeling of coming doom?"

"Yes, Colonel, every married man understands that feeling." The Major laughed at his own joke.

Laughing, Meyers replied, "You're right. Wives do that at times; yes, they seem more dangerous even than American Mustangs."

Lieutenant Riley grabbed Alex. "We missed him. That is Lieutenant Colonel Helmut Meyers." Jason reached into his shirt and pulled out a photo to show Alex. "He knows about the invasion; that's what he is doing here."

Tom grabbed the photo and peeked out the window. "It looks like him."

Alex rushed to the window. "It's him!" Pulling out his 45, Alex aimed it at Meyers. "We can't let him get away."

"You crazy?" Lieutenant Riley grabbed Alex away from that window and, at the same time, flipped off the M-3's safety. "He was supposed to be at the Chateau. Now, he's here, walking right up to us. How strange, or is it?" Lieutenant Riley gave orders before anyone could ask questions. "Tom, Preacher, go out back. One right, one left. Come along the side to the front. When you hear me open fire, come around the corner firing; don't let them see you until then." Throwing Alex a hand grenade. "Alex, you and I are the frontal attack. Just follow my lead."

Alex looked down at the grenade. "What is a frontal attack?"

Waving Alex toward the front door, Lieutenant Riley snapped, "We're going out the front door."

Alex dropped out the partially full magazine and replaced it with a full one. He pulled back the slide of his 45 and chambered a new round. He watched as the one already in the chamber ejected past him and hoped Jason did not see it, or Alex would never hear the end of it. "Why didn't you just say that?" he asked.

As Preacher went to the back door, he stopped and turned to Lieutenant Riley. "This is what I saw, Jason. You know, the vision. You'll be okay." Then he rushed out after Tom.

Jason paled as the Major leaned against the rear doorframe. "Major, you can't be here," he said, but Alex grabbed Lieutenant Riley's arm. Meyers flipped his cigarette aside as Lieutenant Riley opened the door and started firing. Meyers, his adjutant and security chief, went down in one burst. As Lieutenant Riley was changing magazines, Alex pushed him aside and threw his grenade then continued laying down fire. Tom and Preacher opened fire from the sides of the house, causing Alex and Jason to duck. Usually 45s against assault rifles was no match; however, Lieutenant Riley's use of surprise had leveled the playing field.

Hearing the gun battle, the Resistance fighters ran across the field, not stopping until they came upon the carnage. They brought down the last fleeing German soldier, as he was halfway down the road.

"Well, I guess our mission is accomplished." Lieutenant Riley crawled next to Alex.

Alex used every bit of strength he had left to sit up against the staff car. He could see Walker and Preacher spread out where they'd fallen. Pointing over his shoulder, he said, "I would guess there's a briefcase or two in there that should be liberated."

Lieutenant Riley, holding his hand tight against his side, stood on his good leg and pulled out the only briefcase from the back of the car; he watched as it fell to the ground. He slipped back down to the ground and dragged the briefcase toward him. A quick look inside and he knew they had hit the mother lode of intelligence. Jason pulled himself over to sit closer to Alex. "Now I remember. This is how my dad told me it was."

Alex tried to adjust himself into a more comfortable position. "What, Jason?"

"Children should listen more closely to their parents."

"Jason, did you get hit on the head? How bad are you hit?" Alex forced his words over the pain.

"Never been worse, not even in the hospital lot."

"What lot, Jason?'

"Never mind, it was a long time ago, more like a lifetime. How are you doing, Alex?"

"I'm hurting, but we're better than Tom and Preacher."

Lieutenant Riley grabbed hold of one of the Resistance fighters who appeared to be the leader and gave instructions, fighting to keep conscious. Crawling on both knees, pushing back the pain until he was over Preacher, he picked up his 45 and fished around in the Preacher's pockets till he found a new clip. He had done all he could not to break down. He wanted so much to reach down and hold Preacher in his arms. Preacher had just given his life to save his, but there was still danger and much to do. Sitting next to him, Jason patted Preacher's hair. "You knew, Nathan, you knew."

A large hand engulfed Jason's as he looked up at a giant of man who nodded in understanding. With a slow pivot, the stranger lifted Jason's hand away and put Nathaniel "Preacher" Campbell over his shoulder. In excellent English, he said, "I lost my brother last year. I know your pain, but he is safe now." As he turned to walk away, Preacher's small Bible flew out of a pocket and into the bushes next to the house. Jason didn't see it happen through his tears.

The dead were loaded into the staff car and escort vehicle then driven into the barn. The tracks left by the vehicles were swept away, bullet casings picked up, pools of blood shoveled into the field to fertilize the living. Two wagons pulled up, and Alex and Lieutenant Riley were loaded on one while the second one for Major Riley, who was found slumped over the front window frame.

Major Riley's last image of Lieutenant Riley and Alex alive was only for a minute, as they lay in the back of the wagon covered in blood, looking more dead than alive. As the wagons separated and went in different directions, Lieutenant Riley gave him a thumbs-up.

SEARCHING FOR ANSWERS

Judge Riley woke at the knocking on the door. He fumbled with the latches and doorknob. Once open, he faced two serious police inspectors. They held up their identifications. "Good afternoon, or, should I say, evening? Judge Riley, may we come in?"

The Judge stepped aside, and as they entered the sitting room, the younger one spoke. "This is a very nice place. Did you know Chateau de L'Isle-Marie was once the site of a Viking fortress?"

"No, I did not, but I'm sure you didn't drop by to give me a history lesson. How may I help you?"

"As I understand it, you could sure give us one. We are, as you would say, messenger boys. Your wife, Emily, is on her way here with your President. It seems that you are to be given a high award tomorrow, with others from ... " He checked his notepad. "Sorry, the 572nd."

"She'll be here? An award? When?"

The other inspector spoke for the first time. "She is already in France. Your President landed a couple of hours ago, and the motorcade should be here at anytime. I'm sorry we don't have more information, but this was very fast. Did you know your President is staying nearby at Chateau de la Brisette?"

"No, I didn't know that. If I recall, the President normally visits every decade on the anniversary of the invasion. The next would be 2004."

"That is correct. This is all very different." With that, they shook the Judge's hand. "Congratulations on your honor. Oh, is your grandson here? I believe your wife said you were going together to the ceremony."

The Judge opened the bedroom door; he noticed they pushed forward to look in. "I was taking a nap; I guess my grandson is out right now. You know, you can never keep young people still for very long. Thank you for coming by."

The inspectors bade farewell to the Judge and left.

As the convoy of military police vehicles arrived, MPs spilled out taking over the guard posts and surrounding every major building in fenced formations. The base telephone switchboard, radio room, and control tower became primary targets that would assure the 390th was sealed off from the outside world. The PA system, or, as the English called it, the Taney, was screaming orders restricting all personnel to their living areas. Five trucks and a jeep proceeded to the 572nd area. Hut by hut, with yelling and shoving, all the personnel were rounded up and pushed into the backs of waiting trucks. The same was going on at the hardstands with the ground crew, all being taken down to the briefing building. Even those hospitalized did not escape and found a MP standing guard by their beds.

Squadron Commander Major Claus pushed the MP Major back. "You lay a hand on me, you ground pounder, it will be the last thing you'll remember. I'll go when I'm ready to go."

"Major, you need to cooperate." Since the MP was facing the door, he saw General Hughes, Thirteenth Wing Commander's silent entrance. His legs locked and chin rose to attention.

Failing to notice the General, the Squadron Commander replied, "Cooperate with you and your goon squad? Fat chance." Sensing the change in the major, he turned and snapped to attention.

The young Brigadier General Hughes nodded at the MP. "Major, if you will leave us, we'll be down shortly." The Major saluted then retreated.

"Sorry about this, Major Claus," the General said. "It seems that your Lieutenant Jason Riley has caused a stir all the way up to the Eighth Headquarters, and I suspect beyond. Colonel Schilling and Major Odin are still at Supreme Headquarters. I'm sure both are wishing they were here. It seems that Lieutenant Riley revealed to Major Odin the location of the invasion tomorrow and some other important information and, judging by the reaction, very serious. I understand there will be some heavy-hitting G2 types landing any time, along with the Division Commander."

The Squadron Commander's lips parted. He searched for words. "I'm sure there's a reasonable explanation. Lieutenant Jason Riley is a fine pilot, and the whole crew is one of the best, or was the best. They didn't come back. We lost two planes up near the target area and one just off the coast here; that accounts for all the missing, lost four out of seven. Two planes got shot up so bad they'll never fly again except as spare parts."

"Math may not be my best subject, but two at the target area and one in the ocean is three, not four, Major Claus."

"I just received word from their P-51 fighter escort of an F-type bomber burning, the tail section was broken off near the wreckage, with the Group Square 'J'; the *Golden Eagle* is the only plane not accounted for."

"Where did it go down, Major?" He placed his briefcase on the desk.

"Near St. Mere Eglise in the Normandy area, General."

"You see this is one of the problems, Major Claus." He held up the thick file.

"General, my problem is, I have some good men up at the hospital, a couple holding on by a string and a prayer. I hope the brain child up at Eighth that came up with this mission is satisfied."

The General dropped Lieutenant Riley's file on the desk. "Well, you see, that is another of the many problems here. If it's any consolation to you, there was no order from Eighth." General Hughes waved toward the file. "Look at it, Major."

Major Claus picked up the file and rifled through it. "I don't understand, sir. How can this be? Just blank paper."

"We all seem to have our own problems. I'm not looking forward to handing this file to General Dartenhill and telling him it's Lieutenant Jason Shawn Riley's complete personnel file."

The Major grinned nervously. "Maybe they'll send us home."

The General laughed. "We should be so lucky. I don't know what happened, but I can tell you, this is so big that they're not going to care about us. They're going to be busy covering their backsides and tearing up France trying to find Lieutenant Riley before the Germans." General Hughes paused. "If I'm not mistaken, I think I hear company landing."

– – – – – – – – – – – – – – – –

It was less than a half hour after the inspector's visit when there was a rap on the door. Judge Riley opened it to see Emily. She gave him a big smile and hug. "John, this so wonderful!"

"I'm so glad to see you, honey. I was surprised to hear you were coming, and with the President, no less. You travel in high company." He gave her a light kiss.

"One of the advantages of marrying a famous person," she said, stepping into the room.

Deputy Director Odin and Higgins followed her in, carrying her suitcases. "This is Mr. Higgins and Mr. Odin. They are with the President and were so kind to help me. Gentlemen, my husband, Judge John Riley."

The Judge focused on the two and said in a soft tone, "Thank you for your help. I'm so surprised. I'd like to ask you a few questions."

"We had the same in mind, sir." Higgins handed over the suitcases.

"It will be a minute." The Judge carried Emily's suitcases as she followed him into the bedroom. "Emily, you must be beat. Maybe you'd like to take a nap or refresh yourself."

Looking around, Emily nodded. "We left in the middle of the night, so that would be nice." Her gaze returned to the Judge. "Where's Jason?"

The Judge put the small bag on the bed, the other on the stand. "I would guess he's in town. Emily, we'll talk in a while. There's a fine restaurant close by." Giving her a kiss, he closed the door gently.

The Judge walked back into the sitting area where they were seated and waiting. "Well, Mr. Odin, you look like your father. I take it that Mr. Higgins also works for the Company?"

"I know you may find this hard to believe, but my dad respected you very highly." He gave the Judge a nod of respect.

The Judge sat across from them. "Really? He had a funny way of showing it. Let's get down to business; I don't want my wife involved."

"Where is your grandson? He's not in there," Higgins demanded, pointing to the other bedroom.

Aaron sensed that was not the right approach and cut in. "Judge Riley, let's start at square one. Call me Aaron, and this is Robert. Let me level with you. We have DNA proof positive that your grandson, Jason, and your co-pilot, Lieutenant Riley, are the same person. Major Joe Ramsey flew over with us, and I am sure he can identify your grandson. We were very impressed with his keen memory. He told the President how Lieutenant Riley was shot three times in France. Strangely, it happened on the same time, and at the same age of your grandson Jason being shot in the hospital parking lot. Did you know that when Jason had his ears pierced on his twentieth birthday, Lieutenant Riley, on his twentieth birthday, bled from his ears?"

The Judge hung his head down, speaking more to the rug than Odin, "I didn't know that, but it doesn't surprise me."

Higgins took out a cigarette, but Odin shook his head no, knowing with Higgins it was of no use, and continued, "Mr. Higgins and

I are also impressed, Judge, with your ability to predict presidential elections so far in advance. You seem to have a magic gift, so I think you can connect the dots and see how this is and was major a security issue for my father and now for me."

Higgins tapped the butt of his cigarette against the arm of the chair. "Not to be rude, Judge Riley, but as you said earlier, let's get down to business. When did you realize your grandson was Lieutenant Riley?"

Judge Riley shifted slightly and relaxed. "When Jason showed up to attend college. The tattoo was what convinced me; Aaron's father had a thing for it. It was a major shock to me, as you can believe. When did you know?"

"It started with your passport applications. We've been keeping you company. Every picture of your crew obtained over the years has been blurred; the photos of Jason's friends were missing or blurred. Until a few days ago, the focus was on you, not Jason." The smoke quickly clouded the room.

The Judge stood and picked up his suit coat, draped it over the back of the chair. Reaching in his inside pocket, he threw down a quarter and two photos of the crew and said, "That was a brand new quarter when Lieutenant Riley gave it to me on June 5, 1944. I had the answer right in front of me all the time and missed it."

Aaron picked the New York quarter up and, after looking it over, handed it to Higgins, who placed it in a small plastic bag. "If it's all right with you, Judge Riley, I'd like to have our lab look at this." The cloud bulged to the edges of the room, fighting to slip under the door.

The Judge shrugged his shoulders. "It's just another quarter, no problem. The black-and-white is a photo of the crew. I pulled it out of the *Golden Eagle* just before she blew up, and the color Polaroid was taken by Emily the night before Jason left."

Odin and Higgins looked at the photos, pointing and holding them carefully at different angles. They both nodded. "First clear photo of your crew and Lieutenant Riley as your co-pilot, and the other is a good photo of you and your grandson."

"What do you mean, me and my grandson?"

"What do you want us to say, Judge? Okay, it is an excellent photo of you and your grandson." Higgins threw the photos down on the table between them.

The Judge picked up the two photos of the crew just as Emily entered. He stood. "I'll let you know if I hear more about my co-pilot. As I said, the last time I saw him and my bombardier, they were in a wagon, both badly wounded. Maybe that will be helpful in completing this historical chapter."

Odin and Higgins also stood. Odin turned slightly to Mrs. Riley. "Thank you for being so patient with us history buffs, sir. Good-night, Mrs. Riley, enjoy your visit."

Higgins bowed slightly. "Thank you, Mrs. Riley, for allowing us the time with your husband. It was an honor."

As Judge Riley ushered them out the door, he slipped Jason's passport into the Deputy Director's hand. Then he turned to Emily. "Well, is my favorite girl ready for dinner?"

A cold stare met the Judge. "I found the old cigar box hidden in the trash can. Where is Jason?"

"He should be here anytime now."

"Then I guess we'll just have a very quiet night here waiting for him." She turned and shuffled back to the bedroom. The door slammed.

As he sat alone, the Judge felt for the first time that he'd held the package for his co-pilot for nothing.

- - - - - - - - - - - - - - - -

After four hours of interrogation, the remaining members of the 572nd stood at attention as the Wing Commander entered. "I'm sorry about all the security; I came over here to congratulate you on the mission today. I know it came at a high price, but the success of the invasion hangs on it. As you can imagine, tomorrow we'll be putting up every plane that we have. I trust that the 572nd will make us proud. Colonel Schilling, carry on." With that the General hurried to a waiting plane, cursing Lieutenant Riley under his breath.

Colonel Schilling had just arrived and looked worn. "I'll make this short. The 572nd is being deactivated, and you will all be reassigned into other squadrons for the next few missions. I know I speak for all of us in the group that your service has been outstanding, and, as such, you represented the 390th with pride. Go get some rest; we all have a busy day ahead."

Lieutenant Ramsey and his crew were the last to get back to the 572nd site. Gone were the MPs, replaced by trucks already loading the 572nd's equipment and supplies. As the officers walked back into their hut, a wave of despair washed over Ramsey. Eight of the twelve officers that had called the hut home that morning were killed or missing. Lieutenant Ramsey's mood darkened as he looked down at the names on the top of the footlockers walking through *Hitler's Nightmare* section. In his own section, his co-pilot's name reminded Ramsey that even then his friend and comrade was struggling for his life. Without realizing it, Lieutenant Ramsey held his breath as he walked to the rear section. He let out a gasp that brought the rest of his crew over. All evidence of the existence of the *Golden Eagle* officers' was stripped away, clean to the concrete floor. Everything was gone.

Dusk found Major Riley standing in great pain as he limped out the rear door of the farmhouse. He wished he understood French because the farmer's wife was screaming at him as she ran out the front door. Luck was with him, as he found an old weather-beaten rubber poncho thrown over a nearby bush. He'd always wondered why he carried the pocketknife from his youth. Maybe it was just for this time. With careful strokes, he cut a section from the poncho and walked for what seemed like hours. It was less than fifteen minutes before his eyes fell on a large loose rock in a field wall. He opened Jason's note for the first time; after reading it he looked to the sky and sighed. *Alex is right; Jason is losing it. But a promise is a promise, and not a fickle one that John Riley would break.* He placed the note back in the box and wrapped the rubberized cloth around the cigar box and 45. The wetness returned to his leg. He reached down as its warmth spread to his hand, which was soon covered with blood. He pulled more loose rock out of the small hole to make ample room. Placing the bundle in the hiding spot, a brief inspection was followed by a prayer for the niche to be safe from humans and the weather. He fixed in his mind the location and moved off in a different direction from the wall.

Major Riley fell asleep as he leaned against a tree and woke at noise coming from his right He went for his 45 and cursed under his breath as he remembered he'd placed it with the cigar box. Just as he attempted to stand, he heard the sound of the toy cricket. Reaching into his jumpsuit, he withdrew his cricket and made the proper response. Colonel Richard Steel, in full combat dress, came out of the darkness into the pale light cast by the sole miserable light that hung over the rear door of the farmhouse.

The farmer found Major Riley lying against a tree. He was looking up at the stars, silent twinkles against a black abyss, and humming to himself. The soft ground and gentle breeze that rustled through the grass provided physical and mental relief. In the distance, the sound of anti-aircraft guns and small arms echoed through the night. Major Riley forever kept secret the visit and conversation between himself and Steel, even till his own fiery death.

"If I were a drinking man, this would be the time," the President said, slowly pacing.

"Well, I'm going to have a stiff one; this situation is getting out of control. We get paid to have things under control, and I feel we are on the sidelines," Carlos said, having gotten up.

"Where is General Thomas? How much longer?"

"Got delayed. His plane had mechanical problems; was forced to land in England. I think half our military equipment is down at any given time. He landed in Caen a half hour ago. Should be here any second." He dropped the ice cubes into his glass.

The President picked up the binder next to his chair. "I was reading the autopsy reports of the crew."

"That means what?"

"Carlos, read the autopsy report on Sergeant Nathaniel Campbell, fourth page, second paragraph, aloud." Strong handed him the binder.

Carlos said in a bored tone, "Due to his position for three days in the staff car, it would appear normal that both..." As what he was reading hit him his head jerked up.

"That's right, Carlos, a staff car. It was not one of ours driving around here in Normandy a day before the invasion. Not one word any place about any staff car or whose, except in the autopsy report of Sergeant Campbell. You can bet if I spotted it, James Odin did. I think it was his way of making sure that if General Clark failed, we would still have a trail to the truth."

"Why did they do an autopsy?"

"Remember, Ramsey said, or did I read it, he'd never heard of such a thing, but what happened that day and the following weeks was not normal. The military went crazy."

"I would, if I were them, have gone crazy. Imagine you have a Lieutenant, one of two hundred thousand Army Air Corp officers fighting the air war, telling you about your invasion location. More importantly, he gives you code names for an atomic bomb project and the machine that breaks the German code. I would if them, have gone crazy, as Major Ramsey said. What is next?"

The phone rang, breaking the contemplative silence.

President Strong walked over and answered, then hung up. "The answer to your question may be in three very heavy metal boxes on their way to Paris."

AT PEACE

Lieutenant Riley and Alex lay next to each other in the pitch-black basement as the new day started with the sound of British bombs exploding. In a couple hours, the bombing sound had been replaced with that of small arms fire. Alex turned to Jason. "You there?"

"Where do you think I am?"

"They're close and yet so far. I don't think I'm going to make it. I'm really hurting, Jason." Alex winced in pain.

"You should talk. If I can, you can. That's either the 82nd Airborne or 101st, I can't remember. Anyway, those are our troops coming to town. We just need to hang on."

"Let's get out of here; I want to see the stars, Jason."

With Alex dragging the briefcase and Jason the M-3, they emerged from the basement short of breath. They slid down the rear wall of the building to the ground. Their clothes became more soaked by the blood of their wounds. "Alex, maybe this wasn't such a good idea."

Alex forced words through gritted teeth, "If I'm going to die, I want to be under the stars rather than in some stinking basement. When I look up at the stars, I can almost think I'm home. You think you're so smart. Did I ever tell you that the Major came home with me on leave to Waterbury? My family really liked him."

"No. So that's how he knew about Waterbury." Jason re-checked his 45. "Talking about good ideas, Alex, did you ever talk with Preacher?"

"Only a fool would be in this war and not take care of business with Jesus." He coughed up blood.

"Until yesterday, I guess I was a fool," he said, pulling the briefcase toward him and sliding it gently under Alex's head.

Alex flinched at an explosion close by. "If we don't bleed to death, we'll get killed by our own troops." Alex glanced in the distance. "Jason, did I ever tell you I love you?"

"Next, you'll be kissing me."

Alex grabbed Jason's hand and, holding it, said, "Be serious. Not like that. Like a brother."

"Alex, I know, the same is true for me. Just the thought of you not making it …"

"I love the stars. I miss my family and the ocean. I guess we could be worse off." He coughed up more blood.

"How is that, Alex?" He moved closer to Alex and rested his head on his shoulder. Alex managed to say, "We could be living for nothing rather than dying for something." Several shallow rasps followed, and his grip loosened. Jason felt for a pulse and then fell across Alex's body. Quiet sobs moaned into the night.

Jason jerked, scared that he had passed out. The battle seemed to be winding down, but a bigger battle was waging in his mind: whether to avoid being a POW or returning as part of a wasted generation. He knew what the latter entailed and felt its possibility, shivering. He was so tired and growing cold. To the night, he said, "You're right, Alex. It's better to die for something than live for nothing." Using the last bit of his strength, Lieutenant Riley raised the 45 to his head. A shot thundered into the night.

Colonel Steel picked up the M-3 submachine and reached into the pocket of his field jacket and pulled out his cell phone. In perfect French he said, "I'd like to report a shooting. The victim has been shot twice and is in bad shape. He is in front of …"

At the sound of the 45, eleven soldiers hit the ground. Two picked themselves up and rushed forward. They were about to open fire when they heard the clicking cricket sound and saw a figure with his hands up. "Who is in charge?"

The Lieutenant was about to answer when a Major from behind answered, "I am. Who's asking?"

"Colonel Richard Armstrong." Steel dropped his hands slowly.

"Sorry, Colonel, who is that?" The Major was looking down.

Bending down, Steel closed Alex's eyes and lifted the briefcase from under his head. "This is Second Lieutenant Alexander Montgomery, bombardier of the B-17 that crashed nearby this morning. In this briefcase are some very important intelligence papers. Everything here needs to be secured, Major, until G2 arrives. I would suggest you give a couple of your men a break and guard this. I never did get your name or outfit, Major."

The Major reached down and covered Alex's body with his poncho. "Major Charles Bond, 505th of the 82nd, and your outfit?"

Steel slung the M-3 assault weapon over his shoulder. "I don't think you would recognize it. Let's just say I'm an old warrior passing through." Steel walked into the darkness and out of World War II with his mission accomplished.

— — — — — — — — — — — — — —

The first responding officer to Steel's cell phone call arrived, fearing that the badly wounded and nude young man was the missing staff member of the U.S. President. He placed a phone call to the chief inspector's home as instructed. He'd been told there was to be no radio traffic to alert the media traveling with the President.

The chief hung up and sat down. His gaze fell through the window but became blurred. How strange the phrase "swept under the rug" was at this time. He recalled Secret Service Agent Higgins explaining the idiom as the ice clinked in their glasses. *"We don't want this to become the latest gossip at this conference. Let's just file it away for our next private meeting, and let it be swept under the rug for now."* How sensitive the Americans were and wanted this to be, as they called it, "swept under the rug."

－ － － － － － － － － － － － － － － － －

At the three hospitals in the area, teams were already in place; each hoped that the missing staff member would not show up at their hospital.

The chief inspector, his assistant, Deputy Director Odin, and Higgins all arrived within a few minutes of each other.

The stakeout leader casually walked over to the Deputy and Higgins. "Sirs, it is David Blake, tattoo and all. I got a minute or so with him alone. He's in bad shape, one shot in the right side of his back, one front entry, in the right thigh, both large caliber. Glancing wound across his forehead with powder burns looks like an execution that went bad. Strange, he had a lot of powder markings on his right hand and under his right eye. He was covered with a lot of blood and completely nude, no watch, nothing."

Deputy Odin slapped his shoulder. "Good job, Carl. Let's keep it all quiet with the media and all. The President is going to be upset, having a staff member grabbed by some terrorist. Call the other teams and thank them. We'll take it from here."

Walking over to the chief inspector, "I'm Aaron Odin, and I believe you met my assistant, Robert Higgins. I'm afraid that is David Blake, the young man we reported missing earlier."

Odin handed the chief inspector David Blake's passport with Jason's picture. The inspector looked through it and then over at Jason. "It is a shame; he just arrived yesterday."

"Yes, he flew over with the President. With so much of the world's media here, if they found out about this, it would overshadow the President's main purpose in being here." He lowered his voice and leaned forward. "An incident like this could hurt the economy so dependent on tourism and with so many being very old veterans. Americans and British don't like the idea of being victims of terrorists."

"Who said anything about terrorists?" The inspector's head shot up so fast it almost smacked Odin's chin.

"Not us, but ..." Aaron put his arm across the shoulders of the inspector. "You know how the media is, especially when the medical staff start talking about a wound to his head. Many would think an attempted execution, then terrorists."

"This is not something either of us wants then." The chief inspector took out his handkerchief and wiped his brow. The Deputy led the chief inspector to a remote corner of the emergency reception room. "I have an idea of how we can work this out. Mr. Higgins here was a detective once in New York. If he and your assistant could work together, then this could be kept between us. I understand the President's medical staff will be here soon. We can fly Mr. Blake to a military hospital in Germany. It would be out of your hands, so to speak."

The chief inspector shook Aaron's hand in vigorous warmth. "I will make sure that everything is kept private, that no one talks."

"One more thing,"—he held out his hand—"Mr. Blake's passport"

- - - - - - - - - - - - - - - -

The Judge let in Deputy Director Odin. "Sorry it's so early, Judge, Mrs. Riley. Ma'am, I would like to have a private minute with the Judge if you don't mind." Emily was more than a little miffed and stormed out of the room. Sitting down, Odin apologized, "Sorry, I seemed to have upset her."

"You're just one more straw, Aaron. This whole affair, with Jason not being here, has been a strain on us all." The Judge sat down.

"I'm afraid I have bad news but not unexpected. Jason was found; he was shot up petty badly early this morning, about 2:30. He's in critical condition and in protective custody. We'll be moving him to Ramstein Air Base in Germany."

Judge Riley was very worried about Jason and the CIA. "What are your plans, Odin?"

"To find the truth." He stared into the Judge's eyes.

"Or to bury the truth?" The judge's voice hardened.

The Deputy attempted a small smile. "We just need to talk with him…and you."

Judge Riley leaned over and stuck his finger in the Deputy's chest. "I'll talk if you guarantee me his safety. He is no danger to you."

The Deputy stood. "A person who can time travel is no danger? I think you are wrong. You and Emily will be with him at all times, right after the ceremony." His eyes softened. "I want to say, on a personal note, that I can't imagine what a nightmare this has been to you. My job is to get to the bottom of this, not to make your life miserable or to harm Jason in any way."

"Thank you. I guess it's time to share the truth with Emily." The Judge stood.

Odin walked to the door and, turning, said, "You'll be picked up in an hour; the ceremony is in three hours. We will be moving Jason while the media is there; you and Mrs. Riley will go from the cemetery to the airport."

"We will be ready and on time, Mr. Odin"

The Deputy placed his hand on the doorknob and again turned back to the Judge. "We are using the name David Blake for Jason. He is a staff member to the President. We suspect that Mr. Blake was the victim of terrorists; the local authorities are very grateful that we are taking this off their hands and keeping it quiet."

"I understand." The Judge nodded.

——————————————————

The Judge walked over to the bedroom door and tapped. Emily opened the door and, seeing the expression on the Judge's face, she threw her hands to her own and wiped her tears. Judge Riley, putting an arm around her waist, led her to the sitting room. "Emily, please sit down. It's time for that talk."

A half hour later, emotions exhausted, they had no time for dwelling on their thoughts with the necessity of packing and the ceremony looming. When the Judge retrieved Jason's wallet, Emily was closing her suitcase. "I take it that is Lieutenant Riley's wallet; should we tell them about it?"

Finding a small plastic bag in his suitcase, Riley wrapped the wallet and placed it in his pocket. "If this was a security issue, I would agree, but this is between God and them. Just like the package in the cigar box. So many times I would have liked to see what was inside, but I always trusted Lieutenant Riley to show up."

"John, I want to go see Jason now."

"No, Emily, you are going to have to be the good soldier this time. Follow orders and bear it."

--- --- --- --- --- --- --- --- --- --- --- ---

The Riley's arrived at the American cemetery of Coreville Sur Mer almost an hour before the ceremony was to begin. It was their first visit. There were over nine thousand white crosses as far as the eye could see, interrupted only by their two motionless silhouettes blackening against the sunrise. Even without engravings, the crosses spoke of bravery and the evils of war. The Judge found Deputy Odin looking up at the large battle maps on the walls. "Emily is on board. It took everything for her not to go see Jason. I'd like to take her to visit some of the crew; it has been too long a time since I have visited them."

"If I remember, it was May 25, 1945. The one and only time, correct?"

"Only one time, but they weren't here. Close by, but not here. They were moved a few years later."

"I took the liberty of looking up their locations." He pulled the map from his pocket and handed it to Judge Riley. "This is where you will find them."

The Judge took the map, and his eyes filled with tears. "You know that is exactly what Joe Ramsey said to me as he handed me a map."

Twenty-five minutes later, the Judge substituted the wallet for a dirty spoon in his overcoat pocket. After a careful examination of his work, he bent over and kissed the white cross. Wrapping his arm around Emily, they walked as two young lovers. As they passed a trash-can, the Judge reached in his pocket and handed the spoon to Emily. She dropped it in as they passed, and their soft steps continued.

- - - - - - - - - - - - - - - -

The ceremony was small but impressive as the President stood before the five elderly men reciting the grim statistics of those lost from the 572nd on that last mission. He apologized about the delay caused by the classified status of the mission, which prevented that day from happening earlier when more veterans of the 572nd could have attended. For the next few minutes, he praised the mission against the Chateau at La Rcohe-Guyon for the thousand of lives and the invasion it saved.

Stepping aside, the President was replaced by a young army offi-cer who read the official military order first for unit citation, then the posthumous awards for the crews, in plane assignment order. He turned and faced the five who now stood, one with great effort in front of his wheelchair, tears flowing from old opened scars, invis-ible and silent. The President paused before each man and placed a medal around each neck. He then spoke a private word. After a sol-emn cock of the wrist and slanted hand, he moved to the next man. The President closed with a few remarks. A cloud of microphones and tape recorders swarmed the five recipients in a fluttering storm.

- - - - - - - - - - - - - - - -

As the presidential motorcade headed to Paris, one nondescript vehi-cle turned unnoticed at the exit for the Caen airport. The dark sedan pulled up next to a military medivac jet. As Emily and the Judge got out, an Air Force Captain held the door open and smartly saluted them. Within ten minutes, the jet was lifting off the runway.

Once airborne, a tall, distinguished officer came down the aisle and bent down. "Judge and Mrs. Riley, I'm Colonel Weatherly. I will be overseeing your grandsons care. We are very sorry about the attack against Mr. Blake. He will get the best care possible. If you would like to go forward, you can visit him now."

"The truth, Colonel, how is he doing?" Emily demanded as she stood.

"If he was not young and in good physical shape, I don't know if he would have made it. As it is, he will fully recover. It will be fast. It was mostly the loss of blood that was the main danger. I have to admit, Mrs. Riley, I was surprised."

"You mean, at how he is doing?"

The doctor looked down at his clipboard. "No, that the President's medical staff had that much blood with them. His blood type is O negative, which is not common. A person with O negative can only receive O negative, so, as luck has it, he and the President must have the same type. We can expect him to regain consciousness anytime."

FOLDERS AND METAL BOXES

Three dark green metal cases were neatly spaced against the far wall. The tense silence was occasionally broken with Carlos stirring the ice cubes in his drink. When the soft knock came, it clapped like the release of thunderclouds. Barbara stuck her head in the door. "Mr. President, General Thomas and Secretary Wells are here."

The President waved them in. "Please, send them in, Barbara."

After introductions, the President began. "General Thomas and Secretary Wells, I take it you both read the report of events up to now." As each nodded, the President continued. "Carlos, you will brief us about what we have here. That should bring us all up to date. Carlos, let's get to it."

"First, General, Mr. Secretary, we are sorry for the change of plans. By the time you both arrived in Caen with your cargo" He pointed over to the metal cases. "Our Chinese friends had the place staked out. The last thing we needed was for them to see you hauling in these."

"What are the Chinese up to?" Secretary Wells asked.

Carlos picked up two large folders off the center metal case.

"Like you, Mr. Secretary and General Thomas, before you read that report, the Chinese knew something important was going on, but unlike you, we hope they will not know what this is all about." Picking up a large stack of photos off another case, Carlos explained, "Director Odin, here is what your father led us to, a cover-up that is like an onion—you peel away one layer to find another. First, there was that failed intelligence that Field Marshall Rommel was back home in Germany, which we now know is open history. Next, the bombing of the chateau that saved the invasion that resulted in heavy losses of the 572nd was another lie."

"Mr. President, less than six hours ago, you gave out awards and said the 572nd saved the invasion." Aaron's jaw hung open.

Carlos started to answer, but the President interrupted. "In a sense, it is technically true. Part of the 572nd did, the crew of the *Golden Eagle*, or more correct, four members of that crew. We will get to that. Carlos, continue."

Carlos frowned but continued. "More importantly, the 572nd was never ordered on that mission, at least not by the US Army."

"Who did then?" Higgins pulled out a cigarette.

"Colonel Richard Steel, Colonel Richard Armstrong, Professor Richard Richford, or, if you like, the mystery agent on the cemetery road. Take your pick."

"Richard Armstrong? That is a new name," Odin said.

Carlos handed the folder over to the Deputy. "In the folder is an interview with a Major Bond about Colonel Richard Armstrong. We're getting ahead of ourselves." Lifting the liquid courage to his lips, he continued, "With the crash landing of the *Golden Eagle* in Normandy, we now have Lieutenant Riley full of military secrets that only a few know about, running around in enemy occupied territory." Carlos opened up each of the three metal footlockers. "In two of these cases is the physical evidence from the autopsies, weapons from both the *Golden Eagle* crew and Germans from the farmhouse and where Lieutenant Montgomery was found dead. In the other are folders of the interviews of all the surviving members of the 572nd, including Major Riley. In fact, there is a folder for each of the interviews with the Judge, one for every day until June 20, when he flew back with Lieutenant Montgomery's body."

"Farmhouse? Shootout?"

"After the plane crash, Lieutenant Riley and three other members of the crew, along with Major Riley made their way to a nearby farmhouse. It was there they ambushed Lieutenant Colonel Helmet Meyers, his adjutant, and a security detail. That farmhouse is just about two miles from where you found Jason this morning. Colonel Meyers was an intelligence officer for the Fifteenth Army, and he knew about the invasion by infiltrating the French Resistance leadership."

"We know the Judge survived. Did anyone else?" Higgins stood and walked over to look down into the case of weapons.

"No one else. Lieutenant Montgomery was found at the same location as Jason; however, that was June 6, 1944. The Judge is the only living witness to what happened in the front of the farmhouse." Carlos pointed to the case of reports. "The French Resistance found him in the farmhouse. Again, all the action was in front. It was something out of the Wild West, a shootout at the OK Corral."

"I take it that is Colonel Meyers' vehicle?" Aaron held up one the photos from the stack piled on the coffee table.

Carlos leaned over to check the photo of the bodies in the staff car taken three days later. "Yes, G2 treated both sites, where the battle took place and where they found Lieutenant Montgomery, as crime scenes: lot of photos, detailed reports, and interviews. So here we are."

The President poured himself another cup of coffee. "General, Secretary, anyone, questions?"

"This does not make any sense. I can see their concern about the Germans getting hold of Lieutenant Riley, but we're talking about a cover-up that has lasted now near six decades over some wet nose Lieutenant missing in action," Higgins said while shaking his head.

The President stirred his coffee with a slow swirl and laid his spoon aside. "You know, Robert is right. They had no idea about the connection between Jason Riley and Lieutenant Riley. General Thomas, on whose order was this carried out?"

General Thomas reached in his inside pocket and handed the President a yellowed sheet of paper. "None other than the Supreme Allied Commander himself, one of your predecessors, Mr. President, General Dwight David Eisenhower, dated June 15, 1944."

"It seems, Robert, the plan was not for decades, but to be secret for at least a century, I would guess they hoped it would be secret forever." The President looked over the document then handed it to Higgins.

"To keep classified till June 15, 2044. I still don't understand." Higgins passed the order to Deputy Odin.

"Sorry, I don't have the answer. Aaron, let's hear the details about this morning." The President rubbed his eyes.

Odin pulled from his briefcase a brown envelope and a plastic bag that he laid on the coffee table. "These were removed from Lieutenant Riley. They are both 9mm, I would guess from one of those MP.40 Schmeisser submachine guns." Gesturing toward one of the metal boxes, he continued. "The one that is not mushroomed was a front entry in his right thigh. Hit some object before entering, so it went sideways or it would have gone through. The other was a rear entry in the right side of his back. It almost exited out front, so the bullet was just under his skin." He reached in and pulled a dozen photos from the envelope, throwing them on the table and handing the bottom two to Higgins.

"It's a miracle he is still alive." Carlos picked through the photos.

Higgins held up the last two for all to see, a front view of Jason's face and a close-up of his forehead. "The real miracle is that Lieutenant Riley was not successful in his suicide attempt."

"Suicide?" the President asked in disbelief.

"You give us those boxes. After about twelve hours, we'll have answers." Higgins stubbed out his cigarette.

"I'm sure our Chinese friends would like that also. I understand they are across the street watching."

"Mr. President, it is time." Carlos looked at his watch.

The President stood. "Sorry, gentlemen, I know this was rushed, but I have a meeting with our so-called ally, the French president, and then a state dinner. You can go through all this and stay at it. One more thing, Robert; you have more than twelve hours, more like eighteen. We will be taking off at eight a.m. tomorrow for Ramstein Air Base."

They now all stood in shock. Carlos managed to ask a single-word question. "Ramstein?"

"I'll take care of Lieutenant Riley personally, and we won't have to play cat and mouse with the Chinese. General Thomas and Secretary Wells, good to have you both with me for the next couple of days as we do some surprise inspections of a couple of military bases in Europe, starting with Ramstein."

Emily and the Judge took turns staying beside Jason's bed, out of range of the cameras set up to monitor Jason and the military police there to "protect him." They discussed their fears of what his mental health would be. The Judge broke down more than once. Emily thought it was just over Jason; she knew nothing about the crew.

Emily was awakened in the early morning hours by Jason's screaming. Before she could sit up, he was held down and injected with a mild sedative. After a minute he turned his head toward her and was trying to speak when he slipped back into unconsciousness.

Four hours later, as the Judge dozed, he was awakened by the sound of soft crying. Looking over at Jason, Judge Riley saw that Jason was staring at the ceiling, mumbling and crying. The old man reached over and held his grandson's hand as Jason fell back to sleep.

An hour later, Jason woke up complaining about being hungry. Both of his grandparents were in the room, but Jason did not seem to notice. Looking confused, he tried to rise, but pain kept him in place. The MP started out the door but was pushed aside as a half dozen medical staff rushed in. Jason kept trying to get up, and a young nurse nudged him down with the tips of her fingers. "Mr. Blake, please lie down. You have been seriously wounded."

"I'm Lieutenant Riley." He fell back.

Doctor Weatherly bent over Jason, taking his pulse. "Mr. Blake, you have had a rough time of it, but in a week or so, with proper rest, you will be fine."

"There is no more crew; they all got killed except for the Major." He started to cry. "Sorry, it was a little rough." He cleared his throat. "How did the invasion go?"

"What invasion?" Weatherly's brow lowered.

"Why, Normandy. What happened to Major Riley?"

Doctor Weatherly nodded to the nurse. "Mr. John Riley? Your grandfather is right here."

"How did you find out he was my grandfath—" The sedative continued to swim through Jason's veins as he fell back to sleep.

Doctor Weatherly rushed from the room to the nearest phone and pulled out a crumpled slip of paper with a phone number. "Mr. Odin or Higgins, please. They are presidential staff."

It only took milliseconds for satellites to bounce his call from Germany to Virginia then back to France. "Mr. Odin, Colonel Weatherly here with some good news. Mr. Blake is awake but a little delirious. He was talking about World War II, about a crew being killed. Something like that is to be expected. We will stay with him."

Weatherly nodded. "Thank you very much, Mr. Odin. Yes, he will be completely fine."

The Judge quietly came up behind Weatherly. "Mr. Odin wanted to talk with me?"

Weatherly spun around. "Sir, Mr. Riley would like a word with you." With that, he gave the Judge the phone and stood back.

The Judge's voice warned the other. "Aaron, old buddy, John here. He's awake and talking about World War II and such. He's still out of it, and the staff is concerned, if you get my meaning."

As a cheerful act, Riley replied, "He could be fully awake in an hour. The staff is great; they are with him every second. When he sees me or continues with his war dreaming, they will be right there to help, cameras and all…Yes, Doctor Weatherly is right here. I'll see you later." He then handed the phone back to the Colonel.

Within minutes all the cameras had been removed, along with security. Jason could feel the Doctor Weatherly's cold stethoscope against his chest. "Mr. and Mrs. Riley, it looks like Mr. Blake will be fine. Dr. Baker just arrived from Washington, part of the Presidential medical staff, and will be taking over. I have been told there is no more threat to him. It seems they captured the robbers."

"Robbers, not terrorists. That is good." The Judge mocked surprise.

They shook hands, and the Colonel assured them. "If there is anything you need, please ask," and left.

Unknown to all, Jason followed the exchanges. As Doctor Weatherly walked out the door, Jason spoke. "Grandpa, Grandma, I guess I'm back."

They rushed to his side. Emily grabbed his hand. "Oh, Jason, Jason, I'm so sorry for you." Soft sobs drowned her gasps.

Lieutenant Riley lifted his gaze to Major Riley. "Sir, are you sorry?"

The Judge bent down and kissed him on his forehead. Lieutenant Riley could feel the dampness trickle down on his brow. "Jason, more than you know."

Their hands locked and squeezed.

"What does it take to get a good meal here?"

Deputy Odin placed the phone down slowly. "That was the Director. We pulled all the security, Our boy Jason is coming to." Higgins held up the Schmeisser and the test-fired rounds. "This is the one that almost did Lieutenant Riley in. How is he doing?"

"Yelling about the invasion, crew getting killed. Why we pulled out the video cameras and security; last thing we need is a video to spread this. Baker should be there any minute with his staff to take over and put the wraps on this."

General Thomas was a man who found keeping his thoughts to himself a good course in life and spoke little. As he continued through the hundreds of files, he found a sealed envelope. Cutting it open, he pulled out a single folder sheet and a key fell to the rug. While he was fluent in Spanish and not Swiss, he still realized what he had found. Three of the four signatures of the Swiss bank stationery he recognized right off. "Mr. Higgins, you have that photo of Lieutenant Montgomery?"

Higgins searched through the stack and found a dozen. "Which one?"

General Thomas reached over. "One with a briefcase will do." Taking the photo, he put down the letter dated June 14, 1944, and sat. He motioned, "Gentleman, please sit down. I have a little story to tell before my stop in Zurich."

As Jason ate, Emily went on about the President, the ceremony, who was there, and what happened when he was found. The Judge added corrections or a little detail. Jason hardly spoke a word during the meal, except to ask if Alex had dropped by.

Emily's eyes darted between them before she wiped her mouth. "Only one person. He said that he borrowed, you know, one of those things you wrap around your leg when you surf. Maybe his name was Alex."

Jason looked at his grandfather, who reached in his pocket for the color Polaroid of the crew and put it down on the bedside table. Jason turned away. "Your grandmother thinks that's a good picture of you and me. In fact, everyone who sees it does."

Jason pushed the bedside table away. "It's called a leash, Grandma. I'm a little tired."

"Sorry, Jason, we got carried away. I love you." She saw the tears again in his eyes.

"Has anyone told my mother anything?"

"We haven't. We didn't think you wanted to cause her any anguish." Emily replied, blushing.

"You're right. I'll tell her myself, so don't say a thing." He paused. "I'd like to ask Grandpa a few questions alone, if you don't mind, Grandma." Jason attempted a weak smile.

Hand on the doorknob, she turned and said, "Always man business."

As the door closed, Jason turned to his grandfather. "Why did you lie?"

"Because Lieutenant Riley asked me to. Remember behind the farmhouse?" The Judge reached over and picked up the photos off his bedside table.

Jason nodded. "Yeah, I did, didn't I."

"The truth is, Jason, I would have anyways. If I told you the truth, would you have made the sacrifice? I don't mean to be harsh, Jason, but I feel your generation is corrupt and spoiled and, I would dare say, at times without a clue about morality, patriotism, or sacrifice. As Lieutenant Riley, I trusted you with my life. But as Jason, I couldn't take the risk."

Jason could feel the weight of the reality as he spoke. "They are all dead."

Handing him the black-and-white photo, the Judge remarked, "Remember when that guy from *Rita Bee* took this?"

Lieutenant Riley held the photo. "He was a tail gunner from Detroit. Bill Murphy. I'm glad you pulled this out before she blew. All my friends are gone. How about my family and girlfriend in Olympia?"

"I don't know, Lieutenant Riley. Your military records were blank. Colonel Steel took all your letters right after we took off." The Judge laughed. "Remember when we took off, how you went pale? Unbelievable. My waving up at us as we took off. Jason, with him, it's like time has no meaning." He shook his head. "There I was, waving to myself taking off."

"Everything is gone." He forced himself up more.

He pulled out the map of the cemetery. "Only the cigar box and your wallet."

"You have my wallet?"

"No one knows about them except your grandmother. They are safe but not here. The cigar box package is up in the projection booth at the base, and your wallet is buried behind the cross of Jerry Zandi's grave. Remember it is Gerald not Jerry. As for the crew living in Waterbury, your grandmother does not know that."

"How can that be? Alex nearly lived at our house."

"I don't know how; I'll investigate."

"Why go through all the trouble of hiding, all the secretive stuff?"

"You're a national security threat, Jason. Think about it; time traveling? You're a guest of the CIA, not the military."

"What! It's not me, it's Professor Richford and Colonel Steel."

Their conversation ended when a young doctor entered. "I'm Dr. Curtis Baker. I'm going to be taking good care of you. So how are you doing, Captain? It looks like you are eating fine."

"I'm a little beat but ready to go. You said Captain, not Mr. Blake?"

Just then two more staff showed up. One cleared away his tray, and the other placed a big bouquet of flowers on the nightstand next to the bed. Jason was handed a small card, which he read. "Wow."

His grandfather tried to find his reading glasses, then glanced at Jason. "What does it say, son?"

"Your promotion is only the beginning of the appreciation of a grateful country. Signed, President James Strong."

--- -- -- -- -- -- -- -- -- -- -- -- --

The reporter nodded to the camera crew, holding the earpiece with one hand while clinging to the microphone with the other. "That roaring noise behind me is Air Force One as it lifts off. With Secretary of Defense Wells and the Joint Chief of Staff General Thomas at his side, a few minutes ago the President made the stunning announcement that he would be extending his visit to Europe by two days. Planned are a number of surprise inspections of military bases in Europe. The first is Ramstein Air Force Base in Germany. When asked, White House Press Secretary Ed Butler only said, 'No comment.' This is ... "

In a quiet corner of a deserted projector room, a sealed package loomed in the shadows, awaiting Jason.

UP AND AWAY

Once airborne, the President convened the conference. "This is a short flight; since we all read the various reports, I trust Aaron and Robert will present us a complete picture. So, who will be first?"

Odin nodded to Higgins. "I guess I'll start and summarize the last twelve hours or so of Lieutenant Riley's part of World War II. As you know, after escaping the crash of the *Golden Eagle* and under the protection of their P-51 escorts, the five surviving crewmembers of the *Golden Eagle* made it to a local farm. Lieutenant Colonel Meyers, the intelligence officer of the Fifteenth Army, and his heavily armed security detail were on the way to the Seventh Army to warn them about the invasion. If you can believe it, which I do not, they happened per chance upon the same farmhouse where Lieutenant Riley was."

Odin slid a photo of Lieutenant Colonel Meyers across the table. "This photo was found next to Lieutenant Montgomery's body, along with this photo." Odin slid a second photo across the table. "This is Colonel Reitzen, Meyers' counterpart, with Rommel's B-Army, who was killed in the bombing raid on the chateau."

"Where did these come from?" Secretary Wells picked up the photo of Meyers. In interviews with Major Riley, Lieutenant Riley had them with him, along with a duffel bag of weapons."

"So Meyers was set up from the start." Wells placed the photo back down.

"So it would seem." Higgins resumed. "Lieutenant Colonel Meyers, his adjutant, Major Schmidt, and the head of the security detail, Captain Keasling, were cut to ribbons at the farmhouse door. Each had at least a half dozen 45cal wounds, which is consistent with what the Major Riley heard and the little he saw by the time he made it to the front. He said that Lieutenant Riley had an M-3 submachine gun. It was a slaughter, despite being armed with only 45s, an assault rifle, and a couple of grenades. They were credited with twelve of the eighteen killed."

"By my count that leaves six." Carlos held up six fingers.

Higgins put up one finger. "All that was admitted to by the French is that they killed one fleeing soldier. The other five killed were all bandaged. None, by the way, were killed by 45 cal. The theory is that they killed the wounded. Under the circumstances, that seemed reasonable."

"I can believe killing wounded seems reasonable to you, Higgins," the President said sarcastically.

Higgins looked up from his notes and, in solemn iciness, said, "Shall I continue, Mr. President?"

"Sorry, folks, old history. Mr. Higgins, please continue."

"This came at a cost because killed were Sergeant Thomas Walker and Sergeant Nathaniel Campbell. Ballistic results showed a Schmeisser submachine gun, in the box tagged number two, killed Sergeant Campbell and it was the same gun that almost did in Lieutenant Riley. In all likelihood, Sergeant Campbell, the crew called him Preacher, saved Lieutenant Riley. At first there was confusion, since Corporal Walter Winterstien, the shooter, was killed by Lieutenant Riley's 45. When no weapon could be found belonging to Sergeant Campbell, a check of powder residue on Sergeant Campbell matched Lieutenant Riley's 45. It would make sense that Sergeant Campbell would have borrowed Lieutenant Riley's 45."

Deputy Director Odin took up the story. "Based on dried blood on Lieutenant Riley, his blood loss–"

"Hold on, Aaron. Higgins, you said Sergeant Campbell was called Preacher?" the President asked, shaken.

"Yes, it was what Major Riley called him in one of the interviews."

The President looked at his notes. "Carlos, you remember Major Ramsey saying Lieutenant Riley became a Christian just before the flight, the day before?"

Carlos searched through his notes. "Yes. He said the Judge told him about it."

"According to his grandmother, Jason is a heathen surfer. Then he goes back in time and becomes a not very religious Lieutenant Riley. Yet on the last flight is a Christian."

"Sir, where is this leading us?" General Thomas leaned forward.

"I think that is the real question. Jason is a sideshow to something bigger. Aaron, please continue."

Aaron spread his hands on the conference table. "After the battle, Lieutenants Riley and Montgomery were taken to where we found Jason yesterday. Major Riley, newly promoted to Major, ended up not far away. As to the major, he said that the last time he saw alive Lieutenants Riley and Montgomery they were in the back of another wagon. They looked badly wounded. Our next witness was from a unit of the 82nd Airborne, who came across our mysterious Colonel Richard Armstrong bent over the body of Lieutenant Montgomery." Odin nodded to Higgins to take up the tale.

"Yesterday or June 6, 1944, if you like, per the interview here." Higgins held up a folder. "Major Charles Bond, later killed in action, with his patrol, came across a Colonel Richard Armstrong. He was bent over the body of Lieutenant Montgomery. I'm sure if he was a few seconds earlier he would have come across Lieutenant Riley. So we find Jason Riley covered with a lot of dried blood, as well as fresh bleeding, in an area that he would be found easily within a few minutes. If it was June 6 of 1944, that would not be the case. As I said, two Major wounds from a German weapon, but the grazing wound to his forehead was not from the battle at the farmhouse. We did a quick lab test, and the powder residue on Jason's forehead and right hand was consistent with the ammunition in his 45, which was wiped clean of fingerprints. As for Lieutenant Riley, only his clothing, dog tags, watch, photos of Meyers and Reitzen, and his 45 were left behind. The Army at the time checked the serial number, and it matched the one issued to him; the M-3 submachine gun was never found. I would guess Colonel Armstrong took it. Anyway, yesterday morning we find Jason nude. I would guess when we interview the Judge, we will find the trash bags he had at Waterbury Cemetery with Jason's clothing and personal effects."

The President let out a low whistle. "So it is true, our Lieutenant Riley feared living more than dying. Not only did he know military secrets, but our future, and he elected to die with that knowledge rather than be taken alive."

As Higgins sat back, the Deputy stood and gathered the photos and reports. "Yes, sir, that seems the case. Fearing he would be captured, he attempted suicide; he just waited too long, did not have enough strength and failed. That would fit. Everyone said Lieutenant Riley was one tough Ranger and, with combat experience and the elements of surprise, succeeded in taking out Meyers and saving the invasion and more."

"And the more is?"

The drumming of fingers came to a stop, and General Thomas added, "The reason why Eisenhower did not want the truth to be found."

It was the moment that Wells, Odin, and Higgins had been waiting for since Thomas' return from Zurich. Thomas slid across the table the signed agreement and a key. "Mr. President, this may be the answer."

The President studied the document for a minute and then slid the Swiss bank stationery to Carlos. "I recognize Eisenhower and Rommel. Who are the other two signatures?"

"Their adjutants. All are dead, some sooner than later."

"General Thomas, I trust you are going to tell me what this is about." He sat twisting the key between his fingers.

General Thomas picked up a glass of water and took a slow drink. "The agreement and key were found in one of the files in those metal cases. I just got back from Zurich and can tell you both are very real."

"So you are saying"—President Strong pulled back the document to check the date—"that they met in Zurich on June fourteenth without anyone knowing?"

Thomas pushed across the photo of Lieutenant Montgomery looking at peace with his head resting on the briefcase. "A few knew, maybe too many for Rommel. A short time later, he was forced to commit suicide. There has always been a rumor of a signed protocol that the Allies would not interfere with the attempted killing of Hitler, code name Valkyrie, and keep certain names confidential in exchange for certain considerations. Paris was taken without a fight, and the German army fought hard against our Soviet allies right to the end, giving us needed time to access resources and save lives, ours. In fact, our landing on the moon, you could say, is one of many results."

"General, are you saying that briefcase under Lieutenant Montgomery was the cause?" He looked down at the photo.

"Part of the rumor is that there was a list from the German high command of the conspirators against Hitler."

The President placed the safety deposit box key on top of the agreement. "That would be some leverage. I'm sure they saw the handwriting on the wall. They were smart and knew the end game. I just wonder what Eisenhower was thinking about our Lieutenant Jason Riley as he signed this agreement. He must have known Lieutenant Riley told Major Odin on the second that the invasion was the sixth. Eisenhower didn't even know that himself; he changed it the last minute from the fifth because of weather. Eisenhower for sure knows the Valkyrie list was the result of Lieutenant Riley and that he had disappeared."

"It is true it was all falling in on them, but for some it was a moral issue. For a variety of reasons they felt they had to get rid of Hitler. They did try but failed. I have no idea what was going on in General Eisenhower's mind at the time."

"Strange, we have the only key." President Strong slid the agreement and key back to Thomas.

"There were two, but I suspect Rommel may have taken the second with him to the grave. We don't know for sure, though whoever possesses the other key will find it of no use till June 15, 2044. The Swiss are very serious about these things, and there is nothing we can do until then." Thomas placed the document and key back in the original envelope.

Carlos leaned forward. "It makes sense. There was no love lost between the Soviets and us. A case can be made that using the atomic bomb on Japan had more to do with the Soviets than Japan itself. Can you imagine the reaction from the Russians, even ten years ago, if this went public? That the US cut a deal with the Nazis?"

"Carlos, never mind ten years ago, they would have a fit today. I'm going to have a private dinner with . . . is it Jason, Lieutenant, or Captain Riley, General?"

Thomas rubbed the back of his neck, giving himself time. "Mr. President, he never was discharged, and he's been listed as missing in action. There's a lot of back pay; I don't know if we could pull that off. Also, there are a lot of military awards. There is no question with all interviews of the time and physical evidence he was instrumental in saving the D-Day invasion and, with what was in that briefcase, a lot more. Under normal circumstances and with proper recommendation of Major Riley, we would be talking about awarding him a Congressional Medal of Honor."

"The media would like that, awarding a twenty-one-year-old the Congressional Medal of Honor for heroism during World War II. Now that would be some story." Carlos laughed.

The President handed Carlos back his notes. "I want your questions for Jason and the Judge in my hands in two hours after we land, and don't put down what was in the briefcase. I have that as one of my questions. Also, see if you can come up with any ideas of how we can help a surfer, skateboarder, typical underachiever who finds himself an officer and a hero on how to deal with this."

Carlos pushed his coffee cup away. "I suggest we all get together, say about a half hour after we land to work up a list."

President Strong stood to signal the meeting's end. "I want to thank you all for a good job. I think we are getting close to knowing what and how. Now we just need the why and whom, and I have my theory there. General Thomas, I need to see you for a couple of minutes in my office."

As Higgins headed for the door, there was a tap on his shoulder. Turning, he looked into the President's eyes. "I want to apologize for my remarks, Robert. That Colombian operation nearly cost me my job. It, as they say, rattled my cage. I would like to have you over for lunch when we get back. Just you and me."

Higgins shook his hand. "I would appreciate that."

Doctor Baker bent over Jason, checking his bandages. "Remarkable what thirty-six hours can do. At this rate, I give you a week and you'll be ready to go. We are going to do a little housecleaning here, starting with changing your bandages. Then you have a visitor."

As soon as Baker left, a tall, dark man entered. "Hello, Captain, I'm Sergeant Walters. I have a Class-A uniform, shoes, underwear, the works for you."

Jason looked up at the Sergeant. "Who is my visitor?"

Walters laughed. "Who am I to spoil the surprise?" He hung up the uniform and cranked Jason's bed to the sitting position. A figure stood in the doorway observing then entered with medals hung collaged in gleaming rows.

Jason was so absorbed in staring at the uniform; he didn't hear his grandfather whisper until Judge Riley tapped him on the shoulder. "You're an important man, Jason."

Jason did not have a chance to reply, for as the Sergeant left the room, a bull of a man entered with four stars on each shoulder. Lieutenant now Captain Riley sat up straight. "I take it you're Colonel John Riley. I'm General Thomas, Joint Chief of Staff."

The General walked to the front of the bed, and Captain Riley saluted, which the General returned. "Captain Riley, relax. You have, needless to say, caused a stir for near sixty years. I find you nothing short of a miracle. Let me correct myself. You *are* a miracle. What you and the crew of the *Golden Eagle* did saved thousands of lives and maybe even the war. I need to clarify your official status as strange as it is, Captain Riley. You were never discharged. You have been officially listed as missing in action since June 6, 1944. You will be in uniform in two hours, at seventeen thirty hours." Turning to the Judge, General Thomas continued. "Judge Riley, you and your wife, along with the Captain, are invited to a very private dinner with the President of the United States." The General turned to see frozen dumbness grip Jason's face. "Captain, after dinner, you and your grandfather will have an open, honest, and private discussion with the President. I want to remind you, Captain Riley, that the Ppresident is the Commander in Chief. Are there any questions, Captain?"

Jason was stunned. "Yes, sir. I mean no. I understand." With that, General Thomas tapped the brim of his cap toward the Judge and left.

- - - - - - - - - - - - - - -

A half hour before his dinner with the President, two nurses came in and woke Jason, helping him to clean up and shave. Doctor Baker followed and was pleased with his progress in such a short time. "Captain, you're doing great. Just move slow and easy for a few days; I'll check in with you later."

Jason looked in the mirror and straightened his tie as his grandfather came in. "What are these medals for?"

The Judge explained most, but there were a few he did not recognize. "It looks like they took your service record, but that is wrong; Steel has it. They must have figured out what you had and converted them to current awards." Jason felt warm arms embrace him. "You are very impressive, Jason, in more ways than one."

A Major entered. "Captain, the President will be here soon; please follow me."

A nurse with a wheelchair appeared. Jason sat up. "How far do I have to walk?"

The Major pointed. "Just to the next room, Captain Riley."

Jason waved the nurse away. "Let me give it a try." He walked slowly with his grandfather as support.

The hospital room next to his had been transformed into a combination dining and sitting area. Jason found his grandmother there already. He gave her a kiss and lowered himself with a slow descent into a chair. Five minutes later, General Thomas walked in with a tall, thin man. Captain Riley managed to stand at feeble attention and saluted.

Thomas returned the salute. "Captain, you look very good in uniform. This is Secretary of Defense Wells. The President is just finishing up with the press and will be here shortly. Please, sit down."

The General and Secretary asked a few general questions until the Major reappeared and whispered in the General's ear. Thomas stood. "Well, the President is on his way up. Remember, Captain Riley, you have your orders."

Secretary Wells shook hands in farewell, saying, "I just wanted to see you in the flesh, Captain. If this were 1944, your picture would be on the front page of every newspaper and cover of every magazine. As it is, there are only seven of us outside your family that know the story. I suspect it will remain that way, but you have your country's deep thanks." Secretary Wells and General Thomas saluted the young man.

Captain Riley returned their salutes. "Thank you, sir, but I don't feel like a hero. I was just another college kid doing what had to be done." Only after they had left did he realize who saluted first.

The three of them were alone for a couple of minutes when the door opened and a Major reappeared. "The President of the United States is here." The President entered, followed by a Major who closed the door.

People seeing the President for the first time often mistook his ordinary appearance and manner for a lack of inner strength and power, often to their undoing. Jason stood at his best attention and held his salute, while the President shook his grandfather's hand and kissed his grandmother on the cheek. Less than a foot in front of Captain Riley, he returned the salute and then unexpectedly hugged him. Holding him tight, he whispered in his ear, "Welcome back, Jason. You're safe with me."

The action shocked Captain Riley, and he felt a tear form. "Thank you, sir."

President Strong released Jason with care and went around the table to pull out a chair for Emily. "Please, sit down, everyone. Before we start, I want to remind you of a few ground rules and how we will proceed tonight. First, there are six others that know about you, Captain, no one not authorized by me ... "

The meal was pleasant, with exchanges about their personal lives. What impressed Jason was the President's humor. After the meal, Emily excused herself as she had been instructed previously, and the three men went over to the sitting area. The steward placed the drinks they'd ordered and half dozen pads and pens on the coffee table.

"Thank you, Howard. Could you please ask Major Williams to come in now," the President said.

After Major Williams placed the three sets of notebooks and numerous files from two briefcases on the table, the President dismissed him. "Major Williams, we will be starting our meeting now. Captain Riley will have you secure all this when we are done."

Passing out the notebooks, the President continued. "Judge Riley, the gray notebooks are the summary of the work of Major James Odin, later CIA Deputy Director, and his son, Aaron Odin, current Deputy Director of CIA Special Operations. The white file folders are the FBI investigation of both of you and all your family members. The red notebooks are what the army kept back about your action against Colonel Meyers at the farmhouse. Needless to say, the result of your action and what was in his briefcase not only saved the invasion; it did much more. Captain, why don't you start a detailed review of your life?"

For the next two hours, save a five-minute break, the President continued to write as he told about his life as Jason Riley and Lieutenant Riley. The President and the Judge had to struggle to keep their composure as Jason told his tale of love, sacrifice, and faith of the last few days. Only the cigar box and the wallet were not mentioned.

The President put down his pen at last. "You mentioned the two photos. May I see them?"

The Judge laid them on the coffee table.

"I take it the tall one with the green t-shirt is Alex; he looks like a surfer," the President said.

"Odin and Higgins couldn't see the crew." The Judge picked up the photos.

"They couldn't?" He rubbed his chin.

"Neither could Emily." The Judge handed them to Jason.

"So, Judge, do you think there is something more? I'm sure they have a fine photo lab on base that can make copies. I'll see you get one set, and Captain, I'll see that you get the originals back."

"I would appreciate that; they mean a lot to me." Jason handed the photos to the President.

"The least I can do. Captain, you and your grandfather will spend tomorrow morning with our CIA friends. Tell them everything except about the crew in the color photo." The President reached into his pocket and pulled out an envelope, dropping it on the table in front of Jason. "Captain, you will have full access to wide-range military resources by calling the number inside. Your orders are to remain here until the twelfth to fully recover, and then you have a two-week leave. You will, on the twenty-seventh, report directly to General Thomas, who will inform you of your appointment time at the White House for us to meet and review any new insights we have and where to go from here. In the meantime, we will each have to search within for the true purpose of all this." As the President stood, he continued. "Captain Riley, Major Williams will secure this when you are both done. Try not to keep him up too late. Judge Riley, could I please have a minute with Jason alone?"

As the door clicked behind the Judge, the President continued. "Jason, please sit down." Once they were both seated across from each other, the President softened his voice and said, "I didn't want to bring this up in front of your Major, your grandfather. I have a few questions about what was in the briefcase, why you tried to commit suicide, and a story I was told that you did not make any reference to."

Captain Riley moved the folder labeled *Troy Riley* closer. "Sir, the first question is easy, the second more complex, and the third I need to know what you are talking about. The briefcase was jammed with the usual maps and orders, which I didn't have much time to look at. You have to remember the situation I was in and what had just happened, but I did find a list."

The President tapped Jason on the knee. "Was it a list of conspirators, Captain Riley?"

The tapping on his knee reminded him of how Professor Richford and Colonel Steel had done the same. He looked into the President's eyes and wondered if he could be … then chased the idea from his brain. "Yes, over two hundred. There were some high-ranking officers, and some, I suspect, were not all military or at least they had no rank. Even I knew a couple of the names."

"You are never to say a word to anyone about that list, do you understand? That is a direct order."

"Yes, sir."

The President, satisfied, prompted, "The attempted suicide?"

Jason did not speak until the President repeated his question. "We each had our reasons. The most logical one was not to be taken prisoner. The other more complex reason was not to return."

The President moved in close. "I take it the military reason was the idea of Lieutenant Riley. Seems logical, but why, Jason, for you not wanting to coming back?"

Tears filled Jason's eyes as he heard the President getting it right. "As my friend Alex was dying, he said it was better to die for something than to live for nothing. Sir, I just don't know if we both agreed or not." Jason turned his face away from the President.

Strong sensed that Jason did not need to be pushed on the subject. "Major Ramsey, your old friend, mentioned you almost got arrested, Captain, at Douglas. What happened, and why didn't you tell me about it?"

Captain Riley was irritated at Ramsey's big mouth. "I almost did, but I never did know why. I was accused of hitting an MP. There was no doubt someone whacked him. His face was swollen. He identified me from a class photo book."

"What photo book?" He made more notes on the yellow pad.

"Not really a photo book. It was a class book, like a yearbook. That's how he picked me out. He even described me down to my tattoo. He seemed convinced and sure as hell something had happened to him, but it had nothing to do with me."

"When you found yourself back in time in England, you were nude, and when we found you yesterday, again you were nude. Captain Riley, Ramsey said that the MP claimed you were nude when you hit him, correct?"

Captain Riley placed his hands on both sides of his head. "Yes, that's why my tattoo stood out in his mind. But I swear I never saw him, nor was I ever near the administration building or the runways. I was on the other side of the base, packing up. Everyone saw me. I had a couple dozen witnesses."

"When exactly was that?"

Captain Riley rubbed his chin and looked up at the ceiling for the answer. "We graduated the day before. As luck had it, we had to catch a train the next day, so we were up early, more like the middle of the night. It was about three or four a.m. on the tenth."

"September the tenth?" the President verified.

"No, I'm wrong. It was the tenth we graduated. It was nine-eleven, September eleventh."

"Let me make sure I have this correct. Douglas, Arizona, September eleventh, three or four a.m. Is that correct, Captain Riley?" the President said as he wrote.

Captain Riley nodded. "Yes, sir, September 11, 1943."

The President stood up and laid his hand on Jason's shoulder. "Captain, enjoy your leave, and be careful. I don't want anything to happen to you."

Outside the door, he found the Judge sitting and waiting. He placed a hand on the old man's shoulder to keep him from rising. "Sorry it took so long. He needs a few minutes to himself." President Strong pointed to Jason's room. "One other thing; there's a little surprise in his room. Judge Riley, give my best to your wife for me." And he left.

Jason and the Judge spent the next hour looking over the files and notebooks. At last the Judge closed them with a sigh. "So the last mission was not about bombing the chateau but about getting you to that farmhouse. Now you know why I wanted you to learn French."

Unnoticed, Jason slipped a sheet from the FBI report on his brother, Troy, into his rear pocket. He heard the voice of Captain Riley within agree they would kill Troy's drug suppliers if needed.

LESSONS LEARNED

When Jason and Judge Riley returned to his room, the surprise was that everything of Lieutenant Riley's that was taken from his hut was there, along with a large manila envelope. At first Captain Riley was tempted to keep the leather jacket with the painted bomb-carrying *Golden Eagle* on the back. Surrounding the eagle were bombs and swastika symbols for bombing missions and fighters shot down. By the end of the week, he decided that the jacket belonged to history. As a result, he watched as the olive green metal case was loaded on a C-130 and heading for Davis-Monthan Air Force Base in Tucson, Arizona, with the final destination next door to the base, the 390th Bomber Group Memorial Museum. He wondered if the 572nd Squadron would ever be acknowledged as part of the 390th. Captain Riley kept everything from the envelope: his orders, new military ID card, a summary of his "new" military records, and a very sizable untaxed check, in part retroactive flight pay and travel pay and an assortment of creative loopholes. It was a lot more than the $250 a month he made as a First Lieutenant during the war.

Jason, wearing baggy jeans, loose t-shirt, earrings, and his baseball cap on backwards, he suddenly felt foolish. He removed the earrings and turned the cap around. All his life in this time, he had been driven by image, being the surfer, the skateboarder, and the party animal. Now he was determined that whatever his image was going to be, it would be genuine, from the inside out.

A jeep drove up and a young Corporal saluted. "Captain Riley, your plane is ready."

On the way back to Caen, France, the Air Force pilot invited Jason up front to try his hand, giving him the controls. "Well, Captain, word is that you're an Army flyboy. What are you qualified to fly?"

Captain Riley, busy looking over the controls, found some missing and some new ones and said, "Primarily B-17s and little B-24 bombers."

"Very funny. Seriously, what?" The pilot laughed.

Feeling a little more comfortable, Captain Riley smiled. "Who's joking?" By the time they got to Caen, France, Captain Riley landed the plane with a little advice from time to time. His first order of business was to pick up the rental, have breakfast, and find a modest bed and breakfast nearby.

Early the next morning, Captain Riley headed for St. Mere Eglise to buy flowers for his visit to the crew. Along the way, he spotted a familiar-looking farm from a couple of weeks before. Captain Riley pulled along the side of the highway and walked up the paved road to the farmhouse; a modern barn had replaced the old wooden one. He looked around as the memories of the day not long ago to him, but distant to others, flooded his mind. He started to walk away when he heard someone address him in French, saying, "Good morning. Can I help you?"

As Captain Riley turned and faced a man in his mid-fifties,

he replied in French, "Good morning. I was wondering if this was where a battle took place the day before D-Day?"

The farmer became animated as his eyes beamed. "Yes. I'm Jason Riley Colbert. My family has owned the farm for over a hundred years. My father was here at the battle."

Captain Riley's eyebrows lifted with his eyes. "Jason Riley?"

The farmer replied with a big smile, "After the famous pilot. Please come in. You know about this?"

Captain Riley tried to find the right words but failed. "Yes, more than you can imagine."

An hour later, after a good breakfast, Captain Riley heard the tale that had grown over the years. He left with a gift, a small pocket Bible that Jason Colbert's father had found in the bushes two weeks after the battle, and the investigation that followed.

Sitting in the rental car, he opened Nathan's Bible and removed a slip of paper that listed the crew. Seven names had a line through them and a date after each. The date for Lieutenant Riley was June 5, 1944, the day he became a Christian. He rested his head on the steering wheel and reflected on Preacher and the gift of life he shared.

As Captain Riley started to turn the ignition key, he looked down on his lap where there was the small yellow photo faded by time: Nathan's wife and infant son. After fifteen minutes, his emotions were settled, and he was able to drive to St. Mere Eglise. Like his grandfather, the week before, Jason looked up at a church steeple. Seeing the dummy hanging from a parachute, a wave of depression began to rise within.

■ ─ ■ ─ ■ ─ ■ ─ ■ ─ ■ ─ ■ ─ ■

As he walked across the Colleville Sur Mer cemetery parking lot toward the visitor center, he felt his stomach turn and slight weakness in his legs. At the visitor center he got a brochure about the history and general layout of the cemetery. Now armed with that and the map his grandfather had given him, he braced himself to visit the crew. As he walked among the thousands of graves, Jason reflected with shame how, at the Waterbury cemetery, the crew, all drunk and drugged out, would urinate on the graves around the World War II monument. Jason mumbled, "Well, here you're safe from us ingrates."

Carved in the first white cross was,

RAYMOND W. STONE
SGT. 572 BM SQ 390 BG
NEW YORK JUNE 5, 1944

"Well, Ray, you never became a druggie. Glad you truly lived in a different time. Thank you for your friendship and for showing me courage." Jason bent over and placed the flowers in front of the cross, stepped back, and Captain Riley saluted. He paced his steps down to the next cross, landing the final step in the soft grass, next to the memory.

BILLY R. JACKSON
SGT. 572 BM SQ 390 BG
ALABAMA JUNE 5, 1944

"Reb, you always protected our rear ends. I'll miss that yell, and thank you for teaching me enthusiasm for life." Jason placed flowers in front of the cross, stepped back, and Captain Riley saluted.

PAUL O. SORENSON
SGT. 572 BM SQ 390 BG,
INDIANA JUNE 5, 1944

"You big dummy, Ox, you wouldn't even abandon a dead comrade. Thank you for showing me loyalty." Jason left flowers on the side so the name could be viewed by all and Captain Riley saluted before making his way to the next headstone.

GERALD E. ZANDI
2nd Lt.572 BM SQ 390 BG
MAINE JUNE 5, 1944

"My fellow officer, guiding us to and from many dangerous missions. Thank you for showing me how to be real." Captain Riley knelt, glanced around, then dug in the soft soil, shaking the dirt off the plastic bag. He removed the wallet and placed it in his rear pocket. Bending over, he placed the flowers in front of the cross and Jason stepped back with a salute.

As he looked at the brochure, his interest picked up on the Garden of the Missing. It took Captain Riley fifteen minutes before he found his name among over 1,500 on the wall of the missing.

JASON S. RILEY
1 LT 572 BM SQ 390 BG
WASHINGTON JUNE 6, 1944*.

What does the asterisk mean?

As Captain Riley re-entered the visitor center, he turned to the elderly gentleman behind the counter and asked, "Can you help me? I have a question."

The old man replied with a deep French accent, "I hope I have the answer."

Captain Riley pointed to the photo in the brochure. "I was looking at the Wall of the Missing, and I noticed Lieutenant Jason Riley has an asterisk after his name? What does the asterisk mean?"

The old man's eyebrows raised as his hands shook. "That is the talk of the whole region. It is in all the newspapers and on television, very strange."

Jason felt cold sweat run down his back as the old man pushed a local newspaper across the counter toward him. "You see, the asterisk means they found the person, or, I should say, his body. The last time an asterisk has been put into the Wall was well over fifty years ago."

"What idiot did that?"

"Excuse me, what did you say?" The old man leaned over the counter.

"May I please have the paper?" he answered in French.

"Yes, of course. What is your name? You look very familiar." He switched to his native language.

"Thank you for the paper. I'm nobody, not important. Thank you." Jason ran out of the visitors' center, leaving the old man scratching his head at the odd behavior of the American.

- - - - - - - - - - - - - - - - -

Driving up the coast a few hundred yards, he pulled over. After a short walk through a field, he found a quiet spot on the cliffs that overlooked Omaha Beach. Sitting down on a section of what had once been an artillery fortification, he reached back and pulled the recovered wallet out of his rear pocket. "My tricky friend, you left me a note." Pulling out the note, he began to read the fancy, flowing script.

> Dear Jason,
>
> Once I led those I loved into battle and suffered from the loss. I can assure you that one day the One that loves you and me beyond our understanding will wipe your tears away.
>
> You may ask why you had to go through this ordeal. That is not for me to say. I only know that like God, the devil is real, and many have elected not to break bonds with his evil. In fact, some are so foolish as to join forces with the Evil One, so we war within families, our nations, and ourselves. In this great conflict that you shared, nation against nation, over fifty-five million would die before this war ended.
>
> When I was with your grandfather on that grim night, I forgot to tell him that I was once an overnight guest at Framlingham Castle. You should visit it, since you flew over it so many times.
>
> The blessings of the Trinity upon you, your country, and your President.
>
> Andrew Grey, Earl of Westminster
> Adjutant to Richard Couer de Lion

Captain Riley refolded the note and tucked it back in his wallet. He then took out the photos of his family. They were bright and clear, not yellow and faded as he expected. He hoped time would not change his family and girlfriend, like him and the wallet, but deep down he knew that it would be impossible, but he would need to find out.

Jason spent the rest of the day visiting the various battle sites in the Normandy area. He felt both pride that as Captain Riley he had answered the call to duty and sadness for his generation. But what was his generation? Which one was wasted? He thought about his own life in recent times. Is slow death of never being worse than a violent end? Which is the greater sin, the killing of six million in concentration camps by mad men or a nation under the name of choice killing one and half million babies a year decade after decade? What was the seed in the greatest generation that gave so much and yet produced such a generation as his mother's? What went wrong?

The next morning, he dropped off his rental car and headed to the waiting Army OH-58D Kiowa Warrior helicopter. Walking toward it, he took off the light jacket that hid his uniform. Captain Riley knew trouble was coming when he saw the Major give him the onceover and then realized that the helicopter had no place for a passenger.

"Captain Riley, Major Stanley, I guess you're my co-pilot today."

Giving the major a crisp salute, which was sloppily returned, he said, "I hope not or we will be in the North Sea. I'm fixed-wing pilot."

"Really, Captain Riley, with all your decorations? You're twenty-one or twenty-two; I figured you had to be a helicopter pilot, some type of special operations."

"Nope, just an old bomber pilot."

"Just as I guessed, with this VIP treatment you're black ops."

What is black ops? He wondered.

"Maybe I should fake a heart attack to see if you're lying, Captain."

As they neared the English coast, Captain Riley asked the Major to swing over Framlingham Castle. How often the *Golden Eagle* crew would cheer when it came into sight. It was near noon as they landed close to the old 390th control tower, which had become a museum. The visitors were already stirred up by the arrival of the two RAF vehicles. When the rotors were still, Captain Riley jumped out of the helicopter and was greeted by four Royal Air Force officers. Captain Riley came to attention and saluted the Brigadier General, who, on returning the salute, said, "Welcome, Captain Riley. I'm Bill Frank."

"Thank you, sir, my pleasure." He did not expect, nor welcome, a greeting party, with a General no less.

During the next half hour, General Frank explained the various memorabilia in the tower and how the base operated. Captain Riley did all he could not to correct his errors. As they exited the control tower, he thanked him for his time.

"I was very pleased to see your President acknowledge the men who flew from this base. My father and your grandfather, I understand, served together here at the same time."

"There aren't many veterans left."

"Wait until you see my father. You'll think he has another eighty years left." General Frank glanced at his watch.

"Is he here?" He held his breath, waiting for the answer.

"Not yet. He had mechanical problems. His car is stuck on the side of a road; he was really mad, as he wanted to meet you so much. He made a point of making sure I would ask you about Lieutenant Jason Riley, your namesake." He took a mental note of Captain Riley's worried look.

"Yeah, I was named after him." Jason pulled out a pad, wrote his grandfather's address, and handed it to the General. "He was my grandfather's co-pilot. Here is Grandfather's address. If your father writes, I'm sure my grandfather will reply."

"Thank you, Captain." He gave it a quick glance before stuffing in his pocket.

"My grandfather is very good at writing back."

"You know, he's very famous, him disappearing and all." He

placed his hand on Jason's shoulder and walked him toward the parking area.

"How is that, General?" he asked, playing dumb.

General Frank stopped and turned to face Jason. "Part of the mystery, Captain Riley. Not just his disappearing, but how a mere Lieutenant who knew the most closely held secrets of the war simply vanishes. Don't you think it's fascinating, Captain Riley?"

Jason sidestepped to break eye contact and started walking. "Being named after him is a lot different than knowing him." He turned to face General Frank and continued. "I can tell you my grandfather never told me anything about Lieutenant Riley. You can take that to the bank, General."

"What are your plans, Captain?"

"I'm going to visit the castle and the American Cemetery at Cambridge." He wished to be done with the man and his intrusive questions.

"Captain, I will leave you my driver and vehicle for your use."

"Thank you, but I've already rented a vehicle."

"We cancelled your rental, Captain. You are now the guest of Her Majesty's Government."

"Thank you, but that is not needed." He could feel his nerves sear with each minute.

General Frank glanced at his watch again. "We would not have it any other way." Shaking Jason's hand, he continued. "Well, I'm off; it was very good to meet you. I had hoped my father could have met you … One other thing." The General handed a camera to his driver. "Corporal, please take a picture of Captain Riley and me." Jason protested as the camera clicked, and the General smiled as he slid his hand into his trouser pocket and felt the old photo his father had given him of the *Golden Eagle* crew.

After the General and his aides left, Jason told the driver that he wanted to see where his grandfather's barracks were. They drove on the dirt road until the overgrowth prevented further advance. As Jason got out, the driver insisted that he would go with him until

Captain Riley finally had to order him to stay with the vehicle. As he walked around the 572nd site, it was hard to believe it was less than two weeks since he'd woken up there. Pushing open the warped door, he walked to where his bunk used to be and stood silently, giving in to his emotions. Walking out the back door, he looked around, and the odor of the pigs made him retreat back inside the hut. Reaching the young driver, he returned the salute and, like his grandfather with Andrew, directed the driver to the base theater.

He had the driver park just out of sight of the theater and ordered him to stay with the vehicle. Captain Riley walked down the road and around the curve. Once he was out of sight, he doubled back through the woods, where he watched the driver pull out a cell phone. Captain Riley wished he were closer so he could hear. After another ten minutes, Captain Riley was satisfied that he was not going to be followed.

Jason did not go into the main building at first, but up the rusty rebar ladder into the projection booth. As his grandfather promised, Alex's wrapped package was out in the open, sitting on the ledge. As he picked up the package, it fell from Jason's hand to the floor, and he followed it.

When Jason came around the corner from the rear of the building, the Corporal was startled. Eyes swollen, Jason did not look like the same person he'd driven. "Sir, I was worried about you and…" Seeing the package in Jason's hand, the Corporal stopped midsentence. Jason walked past the Corporal as if he were invisible. A wave of unknown fear sent the driver running back to the vehicle.

Inside, Jason closed his eyes for a minute and then opened them with caution. As he hoped, they had adjusted for the darkness. Jason looked at the far wall, and the stream of light cutting across the darkness hit the old wooden cross. Walking toward it, he struggled with what he should do or say, but he knew he was in God's presence. He felt it in and around him. Jason bowed his head and, as best he could, came up with a one-sentence prayer. "God, in Jesus' name, help me not to be anyone except in you."

- - - - - - - - - - - - - - -

Captain Riley, wearing his uniform, stood out from the other tourists. In the gift shop, he paid for the self-guided tour and was given an orange wand. Walking along the top walls of Framlingham Castle, he stopped before each sign that gave a short paragraph of history and a number to punch into the wand. He was bored as he listened, until a couple of sentences struck him.

"This castle, as you see it, was built after King Richard granted the land back to the Bigods. While it has never been confirmed, it has long been rumored that King Richard was the overnight guest of Roger Bigod, Second Earl of Norfolk. The story has been passed down to those who own the castle and the villagers in the area." After the second rerun, Jason ran down the stairs to the gift shop.

He tried to wait until the clerk was free but could not stand it any longer and leaned over the counter to say, "I'm sorry to interrupt: King Richard, Couer de Lion?"

"What about King Richard the Lion Hearted?" the clerk replied in measured tones.

"And Andrew Grey, Earl of Westminster?"

The elderly clerk stocking shelves overhearing. "Captain, how may I help you?"

"I was asking about Andrew Grey, Earl of Westminster." He relaxed his tone.

The elderly clerk gave Jason a good looking over. "When I was a young lady, Captain, there were lots of you Yanks over here. Don't see many today." She led Jason over to a small office. "My late husband was a tour guide here for many years. It was before those ugly electronic wands. I fear one day we will all be replaced."

"I would hate to see that happen, ma'am."

The office was small and cluttered with piles of books and stacks of paper. The top of the small desk was hardly visible and seemed ready to collapse under the weight. She knew just where to look. "I seem to remember the name ... Yes, he was a minister of some type to King Richard." She pulled out a copy of an old document. "Here it is, Captain."

He leaned closer but still could not read what was written. It was in a language he did not recognize. "Ma'am, what does it say?"

"Why, I'm surprised, Captain. You don't recognize orders when you see them. It is Latin, the official language of the Church, appointing Andrew Grey, Earl of Westminster, as King Richard's adjutant in Jerusalem."

Jason thought of the words of the note, "... *Once I led those I loved in battle and suffered from the loss ...* "

"Are you talking about the Crusades?"

"Yes, Captain, one of the longest struggles between men: Christianity versus Islam. Between good and evil. Which is good and which is evil depends on your viewpoint."

Jason held the package close to him and felt a chill.

In London the night before, Captain Riley had forcibly dismissed his driver and rented a car for the long drive to Cambridge. Early afternoon found Jason back in civilian clothes as he entered the Cambridge American Cemetery, the final resting place for many members of the Eighth Army Air Force.

He searched among the hundreds of names etched in the wall of those whose bodies could not be recovered. Finally he found the name he was looking for, next to a statue of an air crewman holding a 50 cal machine gun. He moved his fingertip across the name.

STEVEN H. McBETH
SGT. 572 BM SQ 390 BG
CALIFORNIA JUNE 5, 1944

"Rodent, you have no grave. You belong to the sky in which we flew. Thank you for showing me how to overcome weakness. If Preacher has it correct, I'll see you in heaven." Jason bent over and placed flowers at the base of the wall and Captain Riley stepped back and saluted. When he turned, he faced a small group that had stopped, fascinated at a young man who was so moved. Wiping away a tear, he moved across the walkway, heading to the long, circular row upon row of white crosses and an occasional Star of David.

THOMAS P. WALKER
SGT 572 BM SQ 390 BG,
INDIANA JUNE 5, 1944

"You were always there. In the end, your bravery was typical of you. Thank you, Tom, for teaching me about humbleness." He repeated his ritual of placing flowers and saluting his fallen comrade.

NATHANIEL Q. CAMPBELL
SGT. 572 BM SQ 390 BG,
ARIZONA JUNE 5, 1944

Pulling out the small Bible, "I have your Bible and the list, but I guess you know that. You knew we were going to die. No concern for yourself, even during the battle. In so many ways, you showed your love and concern for us. I hope your list is wrong, that we all make it to heaven. Thank you, Preacher, for loving me into eternal life." Again he placed his flowers in front of the cross and stepped back. The photo fell out of the Bible and down to the grave, falling to his knees, moaning, "I'm so sorry, I didn't even have a chance to tell your wife and son. I'm so sorry…" Soon his words were lost in waves of sobbing.

Visitors nearby turned their backs, except for an occasional glance. The glances increased, until finally a couple ran for help. A large black hand reached down and picked up the photo. Squatting down before him, the man lifted him with gentle hands, holding him close to his chest. "Let it go. Don't hold back."

With glassy eyes and rubicund face, Jason paced with the gentle giant for about thirty yards before regaining a degree of control over his grief. As he pushed away from the man, he looked into the eyes of Robert Higgins.

"Please, Jason, have a seat."

"I just want to go back." He sunk to the bench.

"Is that why you tried to put a 45 in your brain?" he said, fishing in his pocket for the pack of cigarettes.

"I don't know; the thought was there, as was being captured, when I pulled the trigger." Heading hanging down, he spoke more to the ground than Higgins.

"I know the feeling." He nodded in reflexive agreement.

"What are you doing here, Higgins?" He reached for the pack of cigarettes and then pulled back.

"Watching out for you."

Jason refused the cigarette and said sarcastically, "I can't be trusted, is that it? Need to get rid of the witness, like Indonesia never happened, but you know I'd protect you. I promised."

Higgins stood up and, in a firm voice, replied, "I know I can trust you, Jason, even more now that you're Captain Riley. Get up, and let's take a walk." With a slow lock of the knees, Jason got up. As they walked in silence among the hundreds of graves, Higgins broke the silence. "I was not assigned; I asked to be with you. You think, Jason, you're the only one who has it rough, my father was killed too, only in Vietnam. When I was marching down Broadway, you know, the Gulf War victory parade, all I could think of was that half of those cheering and throwing confetti would have spit in my father's face on two counts: one for being black and the other for Vietnam." He paused to light his cigarette. "So, Captain, you lost your crew in a just war, a good war, if there is such a thing. I lost twice that many. Two full teams, sixteen out of twenty-one in a stinking Colombian jungle for a stupid drug war. I can't visit them. They don't have graves to put flowers on. No medals, no nothing."

Jason stopped in silence. Then he looked around and said quietly, "Sorry, I misread you."

Higgins draped his arm around Jason's shoulders. "Come on, let's get out of here and join the living. One other thing, Jason: if you haven't noticed, we are being watched."

Jason looked around but couldn't see anything unusual. "I don't see anyone, but then I'm not CIA. I believe you though and need a favor."

"What can this humble servant do that you cannot?" Higgins dropped his cigarette and crushed it.

"You have diplomatic shipping or whatever you call it. I have a package to send; it is personal. My grandfather gave it to me. It's not a security issue." Captain Riley bent down and picked up the crushed cigarette out of respect.

"Don't think I know where we are. I was going to pick it up." He took the cigarette butt from Jason. "Strange way your grandfather has of giving you a package, leaving it at the base. The British would like to get their hands on it." Jason started to speak, but Higgins held up his hand to silence him. "Let me make a call and find out; trust is not a commodity we deal well in."

-- -- -- -- -- -- -- -- -- -- --

For the next couple of days Jason and Higgins, except for a quick visit to the American Embassy, acted like typical tourists. They visited many historical sites and museums. While over fifteen years of age separated them, their common pain allowed an understanding bond to grow between them.

TROY

Jason and Higgins passed through customs at JFK. As they loaded their bags on the conveyor belt to transfer to their domestic flights, Higgins placed one of his bags on the floor and pulled out Jason's package. "I never asked what was in it. I was afraid of the answer."

"But the trip to the embassy?" He took the package and examined it closely.

"Just for show, for our British cousins." Higgins laughed and threw the bag on the conveyor belt. "Little bro, here's my card. On the back is my private cell. If you need anything, anytime, give me a call. I should be in Washington at least a month. You've caused a lot of paperwork and meetings."

"I'll let you know what I find in Olympia about my family. I'm going to Seattle to visit my other family first."

"I don't think the visit to Olympia is a good idea, Captain. Don't forget, you have till the twenty-seventh to report. Be careful. You're a valuable national resource."

"Everyone keeps telling me that. When I get to D.C., I'll give you a call. I'd better call my mother and tell her I'm on the way."

Higgins pointed at Jason. "Nothing foolish."

Before boarding, Jason called home, and Troy answered in a slur. When Jason told him he was flying in from New York, he was met with indifference. The phone slammed. Jason vowed to take care of business when he got home. By the time the plane touched down, Jason had a plan for dealing with Troy's drug problem.

Throwing his suitcases in the rental car, he headed to what he used to call home. It had only been a little over three weeks since he had last been there. In reality, it was a lifetime. Then the professor's words echoed in his mind. *"Summer can be a lifetime."*

As he entered the house, his mother ran to him and enveloped him in a hug. "Jason, why didn't you let me know you were coming?"

"I did call. I told Troy, but I guess he was so drugged out he forgot," he whispered in her ear.

"He may smoke a little pot, so does most of the population, but that does not make him a druggie." She quickly released her hug.

"You're wrong, Mom. He has a serious problem."

"I don't know what your problem is. Do you just hate him? Is that why you keep putting him down?"

"No, Mom, it's because I love him, and we're losing him. I need to take a shower. I'm beat." Picking up his suitcases, he went to his room.

Closing his bedroom door, he dialed the access number. "Captain Riley here."

"Sorry, I'll try to remember code first."

"Yes, my code is Zebra, Charlie, Roger, 1600."

"Maybe this is out of line, but I need your help …" After explaining Troy's drug problem, he was promised a call back.

Ten minutes later, Jason was getting out of the shower. The phone rang, but before he could answer it, he heard his mother's voice.

"Hello."

"There is no Captain Riley here; my late husband was Major

David Riley." "Yes, Jason is my son. He has never been in the military, thank God, much less a Captain."

Jason came up behind her and took the phone. "Sorry for the confusion, Zebra, Charlie, Roger, 1600." By the time he hung up, he had written down the information he requested.

"Well, Jason, what was that about?" she said, fuming.

"One of my friends, we play these war games. You know, like Troy with his 'Dungeon and Dragons.'" He slipped the paper into his pocket.

"You would be better off playing D&D than that murdering military stuff."

"Sorry, Mom, I am into Jesus, not Satan. Let's not get into anything, and let me finish getting dressed."

Jason had no desire to contact old friends. He went out in the kitchen and asked, "Mom, how about a cup of tea and a little conversation?"

"So a few days in jolly old England and you become an English gentleman, not coffee but tea." She put the kettle on the stove.

"We had coffee; with all the rationing I saw, many British learned to like a little coffee during the war." Captain Riley flopped down at the kitchen table.

"What did you say?"

Jason stumbled around his words. "The English started drinking coffee during the war, not just tea. We started drinking tea; just a little history lesson." Jason wiped his brow at the close call.

For the next two hours, Jason mostly listened as his mother went from subject to subject; much of it was moved by his subtle questions. Toward midnight Jason asked, "What time does Troy have to be home?"

"It's summer, no school. He doesn't have a curfew. He may not come home."

Jason felt his blood pressure rise. With good military discipline, he held his temper in check. "Aren't you concerned about where he is?"

"You haven't been here, for what, the last three years. You spent one year surfing around the globe and two at your grandparents.' It has been hell. Troy comes and goes as he pleases; I tried to ground him a couple of times, but he went out anyway. All we do is argue and ... " She started to cry.

Jason came around behind her and placed both his hands on her shoulders. "What's the matter, Mom?"

She held his hands, and her reply was broken. "I never told a soul, but just after your last visit, I found him stealing money from my purse; we had another argument, and he slapped me."

He felt awkward trying to comfort her. Troy was out of control. When he felt she was okay, he gently kissed her on the cheek. "Goodnight, Mom. I'm beat, but we'll talk more in the morning. I love you."

— — — — — — — — — — — — — —

Instead of going directly to bed, Jason pulled out his father's footlocker from the back of the closet. He felt around the inside of the doorframe and located the key. He unlocked the trunk. If his mother ever knew what was in it, she would have never allowed him to have it. Unlike Captain Riley's mother of an earlier time, who knew everything that was in his room, Jason of the enlightened generation gave rights both unearned and destructive. Captain Riley selected a knife that was close to one that he had used as a Ranger. He'd learned in the last couple of years to hope for the best and prepare for the worst.

Another night, a different place, he thought as he looked up at the dark ceiling before another mission. Jason thought of the all the times, both good and bad, he'd spent with his brother, Troy. He was more like Troy's dad than a big brother. He felt ashamed now that he had never once given any consideration as to how his brother would feel about him leaving to surf around the world or go off to college. He tried to count how many times he'd visited in the years he'd spent at Waterbury. How many times had he called? He came up with two brief visits and the same number of phone calls. How different and far away it all seemed. A gentle boy turned into one who slapped his mother, but drugs do that, along with a lot of other bad things. It was all about to change; he rolled over and fell asleep.

- - - - - - - - - - - - - - -

As the helicopter touched down on the carrier deck, the commanding admiral came out to greet its passenger. "Welcome aboard the *Abraham Lincoln*, Mr. Higgins."

Higgins checked his watch and cursed under his breath; it was past nine. "Thank you, Admiral. Has Major Johnson and his team arrived?"

"Yes, over an hour ago. They're down in the conference room."

As Higgins entered the conference room with the Admiral, all stood to attention. "Thank you, Admiral. We are also expecting Captain Murelli of Seattle PD."

"I'll see that the she gets down right away."

"She?"

Admiral Kensington smiled. "Captain Murelli is a piece of work. I'm surprised you've never run across her. As I understand it, she was once CIA before she joined the SPD. She is still a chopper pilot in Army Reserve. Rumor has it she still has a connection with CIA, a rough customer, but you know how rumors are." Kensington left, closing the hatch to the conference room.

Higgins sat down and scanned the Brave Shield Team. Marine Major Edward Johnson, even in civilian clothing, was one mean-looking person. His bullet head blended into his shoulders, and it appeared as though he had no neck. Team executive officer, was Army. Captain William Morris, who was the mirror opposite of Johnson, was thin. With wire-rimmed glasses, he appeared more like an engineer. One would expect to see a pocket protector filled with pens, but in reality, Morris was the more deadly of the two. Benson he recognized, but not the other three.

"Major Johnson, who are these three goons?"

After a short introduction by Johnson, Higgins threw down a stack of photos. "I trust you all got a copy and read the FBI investigation on Troy Riley." When everyone nodded, he continued. "This comes direct from the President. Our orders are to make sure that nothing happens to Army Captain Jason Shawn Riley, the one in the photo before you. This is a matter of the highest national security; I'm not authorized to go into why. I can tell you this young officer deserves your highest respect. Last night, he contacted his resource connection. It seems he is going to force his brother into a drug rehab program. The danger is that his brother's suppliers may have other ideas, and they are some rough players."

Morris raised his hand. "Do we have photos?"

Higgins was about to say no when out of his peripheral vision he saw Captain Murelli enter. "Morris, I don't—" he turned with an extended hand—"but perhaps Captain Murelli does."

"It has been a long time, Mr. Higgins, I'm Chrissy Murelli."

"I must have missed our first meeting."

"Brave Shield team; it figures." Looking at the faces around the table. "You wouldn't remember me, Mr. Higgins. You were pretty shot up at the time. In my spare time as Major Murelli, I flew in and pulled what remained of your sorry butt out of Colombia."

"Then a thank-you is in order," he said, giving her new respect and offering her the empty seat next to him.

Captain Murelli took the chair and swung a thin briefcase in front of her. "Good morning, gentlemen. I'm Captain Chrissy Murelli of the Seattle PD. Most of what you've read is what my detail prepared for the FBI." She took a stack of photos and threw them on the table. "There are enough for everyone, but I want them back. Johnson, right?" Johnson nodded. "If you look at the sheet that

GERALD "JERRY" DOW

accompanies the half dozen photos, you'll see the two on top are Alberto and Raymond Rodriguez; the other two are their so-called employees." Murelli held up a photo of the Compton warehouse. "The Rodriguez brothers run out of this warehouse, as a front, an appliance repair business. They are the only tenants in the dump." Next she held up a photo of Jason's house. "This was taken at first light. Jason's mother's house with the rental car in the driveway; had to take it myself."

Higgins stood. "Bottom line, we need to find Troy before Jason does and secure him." Glancing down at Captain Murelli, he continued, saying, "We are to do whatever is necessary to make sure that nothing happens to Captain Riley. Whatever use of force needed is to be used."

A half hour later, three teams, armed for a minor war, left the dock area in rental sedans in search of Troy Riley.

Jason was up early and found a twenty-four-hour drugstore. An hour later, looking in the mirror, Jason was pleased with his spiked, bleached-white hair, oversized baggy jeans, large hoop rings through each ear, backward baseball cap, and an ill-fitting Raiders jacket. Captain Riley thought it was silly but knew it was needed. When Jason walked into the kitchen, his mother gave him a big hug and told him how good he looked. When he sighed at her comment, she gave him a dirty look, so Jason inwardly told Captain Riley to be quiet.

Over breakfast, Jason sprung the plan on his mother of how he was going to force Troy into rehab and that an agency would arrive within hours to take him. After her violent protest, he persevered. Mentally exhausted, she gave her word that she would sign the needed papers. Jason reached over and laid his hand on hers. "Mom, I love you, and I will find Troy. This will work out, I promise you."

In turn, she laid her other hand on top of his. "Thank you, Jason. You better get going; Seattle is a big city." Jason bent over the table

264

and kissed her; the saltiness of the kiss was salt in his heart, and a tear of regret formed.

－－－－－－－－－－－－－－

As same time Higgins had landed, Jason was pacing about for the bank to open. When the doors unlocked, he approached the young woman behind the new accounts desk. "I would like to open a checking account, please."

Looking up at him as if he were an insect, she did not invite him to sit. Instead, gave a lecture of the bank's rules for checking accounts. "First, it takes at least a hundred-dollar deposit, and you'll have to wait for three to four days for any check you deposit to clear, so you can't get cash out right away."

Still standing, Jason reached into his pockets and threw down five thousand dollars on her desk. "I think if you count that, you'll find that is more than one hundred, and since it is cash, I assume that I won't have to wait three or four days to use my account, is that correct?"

Her lips curled inward as she stared at the bills. "You're correct, sir. You don't have to wait, but I'll need to get the manager. Please, sit down. I'm Carol Books, and you are … ?"

"Riley. Jason Riley."

Twenty minutes later, after a little hassle with the manager, Jason was able to transfer a thousand dollars to a California agency.

－－－－－－－－－－－－－－

The city was not that big to Jason, especially when he knew where to look. More than once Jason had scored drugs down on the waterfront. Moving from brick building to brick building, he wondered why they had not fallen down in the earthquake a few months back; they were such dumps. After an hour, he saw a group of teens hanging around with a couple of transients. As he neared them, they started to walk away. Recognizing one of the boys, he yelled, "Hey! Bobby!"

A youth with blond dreadlocks and bloodshot eyes squinted at Jason. He gave him a three-stage handshake. "Hey, dude, what's up?"

"I'm looking for Troy." Pulling out a pack of cigarettes.

"Well, I haven't seen him for a while." Bobby started to back up.
"Bobby, where is he?"

With both hands down by his side, palms up, Bobby's hands carved a "what's up?" motion. "My name is Tyrell now, dig it?"

"A smoke, Tyrell?" As Bobby stuck out his hand, Jason slipped a pen between two of his fingers and crushed all three together.

"You fu—" was all Bobby could say as he felt his breath halt, and he was jerked up on his tiptoes.

"You can call yourself Tyrell, but I'll call you sorry if you don't tell me where my brother is," he said with a voice that could freeze water.

"Okay, okay, he is down at the shooting gallery."

Squeezing Bobby's fingers harder together, he confirmed, "Shooting gallery?"

"You know where it is. It's the old Compton warehouse, where, where everyone up, gets up." In between gasps, Bobby babbled.

"I got it. One last question, friend, and I'll ask only once. Who is supplying my brother?" He released the pressure a bit so that Bobby's heels sank to the ground.

"The Rodriguezes. You know, the brothers, Alberto and Raymond!"

Removing the pen from between Bobby's fingers, he placed it back in his pocket, and slapping Bobby on the back. "See, Bobby, you could have been more cooperative right away and saved yourself a lot of pain." He stuck a cigarette in Bobby's mouth. "A word of advice." Reaching into his pocket, he pulled out a lighter. "Go home, Bobby. Now." He reached over and lit the cigarette. "We never saw each other, right?"

Bobby's eyes darted away between heavy breaths. "Never saw you, psycho dude."

A couple of blocks away from the abandoned warehouse, Jason hung up the phone. The money was received, and the agency would be at his mother's house in a few hours. Reaching behind his neck, he assured himself that the knife was firmly in place, and in his best hip-hop walk, he headed toward the warehouse.

The Rodriguez brothers walked across what had been the warehouse's main floor. It was empty, except for a few old appliances against the walls, their so-called business. Raymond looked into what used to be an office.

"What is he doing here?" Raymond slapped Troy Riley full force across the face. There was no response from the boy.

Alberto pushed Raymond aside. "You idiot! Feel for his pulse." He knelt down, placing his finger against the Troy's carotid artery. "You can hit him all day, idiot. He's dead."

"It's like that ad about the roach motel." Raymond laughed as he kicked Troy's body. "He is the idiot. That makes four in the last month."

"It's not like we have quality control. Ray, get Sammy and Ace in here. We'll dump him in the bay. Where are those two?"

"They left an hour ago to pick up a washer for repair. Would you believe, we have a real customer."

"Tell them to leave it on the truck. We'll take it over to Benny's for repair. We don't want anyone to complain about our service." Alberto brushed the dirt off his pants.

As they walked out of the office, they laughed at how they lost money for every customer of Rodriguez Brothers' Repairs.

— — — — — — — — — — — — — — —

Thanks to Captain Murelli, the Brave Shield team had staked out the correct warehouse. Captain Morris was the first to spot Jason walking toward the warehouse. "Three, we have subject heading this way."

Major Johnson replied, "Two. Just some hip-hop teen, no show of principal. One reports principal is not home, so heads-up."

Morris picked up his binoculars, focused them on the teen, and hit his partner. "Take a look, Wright." He handed over the binoculars to his partner.

"That's him. White hair and all."

Morris got back on the radio and said, "Three, the principal is heading this way. Instructions."

The Major hit the steering wheel. "Two. Hold in place."

The radio crackled. "Two, your exact location."

Morris gave Wright the radio. "One, we are on the southeast corner."

Higgins typed in the information on his laptop. "I got it, Three, Two. I'm on the way, a couple out. Three, meet at Two's location. Everyone pull up the target building. Suggestions?"

Major Johnson looked down at his laptop screen. "One, this place is a nightmare, has a half dozen known exits. Figure a like number of unknown exits. Suggest area coverage."

Higgins snapped his laptop shut. "I agree, Three."

Morris slipped down lower in his seat. "One, we have activity. Second vehicle pulled up by entrance. Blue Ford, pickup, mid-eighties, two white males, biker-looking types, heading in the southwest front entrance. Principal is sixty to ninety seconds out from same entry point. This is getting tight."

Alberto grabbed the six-pack out of Sammy's hand as they neared the rear office. "Save the beer. We have another body in the office. You two dump him in the bay and give me your keys."

Sammy and Ace headed for the office as Alberto and Raymond headed out of the warehouse. They were halfway across the warehouse floor as Jason stepped in through the main entrance. The two brothers stopped in their tracks. As Jason walked toward them, Raymond reached for his Glock 9. Jason didn't miss the movement.

Alberto was the first to recognize Jason. He yelled out a greeting in hopes of warning Sammy and Ace. "Jason Riley! Long time no see, man!"

"I'm looking for my brother, Troy. You know him." He shook hands with Alberto and Raymond.

"No, I never met him. What's he into, pot?" Alberto pulled out a few joints, handing one to Jason.

Jason took the joint. "More than that; I heard he was hanging here." Jason lit up, making sure not to inhale. "How about I look around?" He held up the joint. "Thanks, Alberto."

"I don't think that's a good idea. This building is falling apart and can be dangerous to your health," Raymond said, grabbing Jason by the shoulder and spinning him around as he started to walk toward the office.

"Thanks for the warning, but my mother is really worried. He didn't come home last night." He pushed Raymond's hand off his shoulder.

Sammy and Ace came out of the office carrying Troy's body. Jason rushed toward them, and before they saw him, he was on them, yelling, "Troy! Troy!"

They dropped the body, and Jason fell to his knees. "Troy, I'm sorry... so sorry!"

Higgins wasted no time in deploying. "This is fly-by-your-pants. Johnson and Wilkins, take the rear. Morris and Wright, get in there! Benson and I will take the front entrance. Let's go!"

Higgins slipped an optic cable around the corner then backed off. He saw the scene on the warehouse floor and reported, "Everyone, we have four with principal, confrontation seventy-five feet at two o'clock from entrance. We have a body on the deck; principal's reaction indicates brother. Three make entry into the rear office area. You'll be twenty feet away. Two, your location?"

Morris whispered into the sensitive mic, "One on low crawl along front wall, I make it we are eighty feet at eleven o'clock. Two body carriers are sighted."

Raymond placed the Glock against the back of Jason's head. "Stand up, or I'll shoot you where you are."

Jason stood and placed his hands on the top of his head. "You're going to pay for this."

Morris' whisper froze Higgins' blood. "One, we have a weapon to principal's head."

Higgins motioned to his partner, Benson, to hide behind the

pickup. "Two, adjust on threat. On exit, we will neutralize carriers. Hold fire if possible. Allow Three to position." Morris acknowledged the order and sighted on Raymond.

Alberto motioned to Sammy and Ace. "Take good care of my friend's brother. We have business to attend to."

Higgins reached into the open Ford pickup and pushed down on the horn.

Raymond pushed Jason down to the floor. "Ace, find out what's going on!"

After a couple of moments, Ace came back in yelling to Alberto and Raymond, "All clear. Must have been on the street." Picking up Troy's body, Ace and Sammy stepped out the front door and holes appeared, ever so silently, in each of their foreheads. Before Troy's body hit the ground, they were both dead.

Raymond pulled Jason back up while keeping the automatic to his head. "Time for business. Step into our office, and keep those hands on your head."

The horn delay gave Johnson the time needed to rush across the rear office, as luck would have it, the right one. He pressed himself against the inner wall while Wilkins waited outside, covering the window. Major Johnson tensed as he heard Morris in his earpiece. "Three, Two with principal heading your way."

Raymond grabbed Jason by his collar and spun him around. "Turn around, pothead! I want to look into your lilywhite face as I kill you." He pushed Jason backward into the office. Jason's knife remained tucked away, unnoticed.

As Jason backed in, he saw the Major pressed against the wall, automatic in hand. He hoped the man was a friend. His right hand inched slightly down the back of his neck as he drew Raymond deeper in the office and into the Major's kill zone. "You're both dead."

Alberto pushed Raymond forward into the office. "Bravo, Jason! Such brave words, amigo. You should have left. Nothing personal, but business is business."

Raymond stopped two-thirds of the way into the room, and as he raised his weapon, two rounds exploded his head. Alberto got off one round as Jason's knife flew through the red mist and imbedded itself in his throat.

Alberto slammed against the wall while clawing at the knife; the hilt hit the doorframe and drove it in deeper. Alberto dropped to his knees and, with begging eyes, looked up at Jason. Jason slowly reached down and pulled the knife out, releasing a fountain of blood, assuring a quick death. "Nothing personal, Alberto." He stepped over the quivering body into the Higgins' arms, who hugged him tightly as he once did in Indonesia. He led him over to Morris. "Take care of Captain Riley."

Morris stood with his hands at his side, lost at what to do. Yell at him. Hit him. All were possibilities. Instead he managed to hold out a hand. "Captain, come with me. Mr. Higgins, are you coming?"

"I need to call Captain Murelli first." He pulled out his cell phone.

"Mr. Higgins, you don't have to." Pointing toward the entrance.

As Morris walked by Captain Murelli with Jason, she gave him a look that could kill along with a volley of cursing. By the time Murelli reached Higgins, her hands were dug into her sides above her hips, and her heavy huffs pierced the silence. "Saw two outside. How many total?"

Higgins held up four fingers. "Had no choice."

Murelli pushed past Higgins as the Rodriguez brothers came into view.

"Just great! Higgins. This cover-up is going to cost you dearly."

OLYMPIA

The police officer noted the stairs and front porch were in need of repair and paint. He thought, *Another single parent*; little did he know it was death, not divorce, in this case. As he knocked on the front door, Jasmine Riley pushed open the door. "You're the agency; I was not expecting a uniform."

"Ma'am, I don't know anything about an agency. I'm Officer MacClenny. Am I speaking to Jasmine Riley?" He was confused by her remark.

"Yes. You've been here enough over the years. You should know."

"Ma'am, I've never been here."

"Sorry, I'm a little upset. I was expecting my sons here hours ago. You can come in and wait if you want."

"I think there's some confusion, ma'am. I'm sorry to have to tell you this, but your son is in the hospital." The young officer was thankful that he did not have to deliver the death notice; that would be for others this day.

"Jason was right about Troy." She placed her hand to her mouth.

"No, ma'am, it's your son Jason. There was an accident." He gently placed a hand on her right elbow in an act of compassion.

"What happened? How serious?" She trembled.

"I don't know any details. I just got the call and land-lined—I mean, phoned in—and was told to transport you to the hospital. Can I help you with anything?"

"Please come in. I need my purse. I'm so sorry; this has been a terrible day. We are sending my youngest son off to rehab, and I was expecting an agency for him. My older son, Jason, was out looking for him." Confused, she paced about the living room, then the kitchen, mumbling to herself while looking for her purse, until she remembered it was in her bedroom.

The young officer stood by and watched her helplessly, but he was powerful in another way as he prayed silently for her.

As they started out the door, she remembered. "I'll have to leave a note for the agency," she said, and then she turned back. "I better not. Troy might see it."

As they drove, the officer felt guilty about what he had not said. Lies take many forms. As they approached the gate of the naval base, Jasmine tapped him on the shoulder from the rear seat. "Officer, you said Jason was at the hospital."

He passed his identification card to the guard. "Mrs. Riley, here to see her son Jason Riley at the hospital." While the guard was on the phone, Officer MacClenny turned in his seat to look her in the eye. "I was told that he's here at the base hospital."

"What is he doing here?" she shouted. Her demand was met with silence.

As the patrol car pulled up, Higgins, having been called by the front gate, met Jason's mother. "Mrs. Riley, I'm Robert Higgins. Please, come with me. Jason is in fine shape."

"What is he doing here? No one answers me."

Higgins did not reply right away but led her through the front entrance, starting down the long corridor. "Jason will explain."

She stopped in midstride and looked up at Higgins. "I don't like the sound of this one bit."

As she was led into the treatment room, the doctor excused himself. "Captain, you should be good as new in a few days." The doctor nodded as he walked by Jason's mother. Higgins followed the doctor out, knowing that Jason needed a private moment.

His mother looked at his blood-soaked clothing. "What is going on, Jason?"

Jason wrapped his one good arm around her and said, "Mom, Troy is dead."

"Captain? Troy dead? Is this your sick idea of a game?" She pushed him away and slapped him across the face.

Jason stood frozen, tears filling his eyes. Waiting outside the door, upon hearing the screaming and the slap Higgins busted into the room. "Jason, do you want me to get her out?"

"No, it's all right. Could you have Troy brought in?"

Not a word was spoken between Jason and his mother, not even in response to the soft knock on the door. Two orderlies came in and pushed aside the examination table from the center of the room. A few minutes later, they returned and wheeled in a gurney; one gave an awkward salute to Jason then turned and left.

Jason grabbed the edge of the white sheet and pulled it down.

"My baby! What happened to my baby?" She collapsed across Troy's body.

"I'm sorry, Mom. I was too late for Troy. He was already dead. There was no pain; it was an overdose." He stood next to her as she sobbed over her youngest son's body. Hours seemed to pass as the sobs rose and fell, with Jason frozen and helpless.

Without warning, she stopped crying and lay motionless over Troy's body. She stood and turned placing her arms around Jason. "I'm so sorry. Please forgive me." It was as if, in that moment of agony, she remembered her other son.

"We both have a lot to be sorry about, Mom. Let's get out of here." He placed a soft kiss on her cheek.

"We can't just leave him. I can't leave him."

"He's fine now, Mom. They'll take good care of him." With a gentle nudge, he led her out of the room.

Higgins was waiting outside the door. "Jason, this is Chaplain Jordan. The base commander has made a private area available for you and your mother while we clear up matters here and in Washington."

"Mrs. Riley, I regret the loss of your son Troy, and sir, your brother. If you will allow me, I can offer you considerable help in this matter." Chaplain Jordan bowed slightly.

The cottage was cozy and next to the bay. With the help of the Chaplain, an outline of the memorial service and burial was completed within an hour. Every time his mother would bring up the cost, Jason assured her not to worry. Higgins had already given three thousand dollars cash to the chaplain as a down payment. Finally, Chaplain Jordan excused himself to start making arrangements.

As the Chaplain left, Jason told his mother how he had found Troy in the abandoned warehouse. He guessed a drug pusher had wounded him, and police were investigating.

"Tell me about this Captain thing, Jason."

"I joined the Army instead of going to school; I just became a Captain."

"You're telling me your grandparents were in on this?"

Jason hated getting his grandparents in more trouble with her but said, "Yeah, in a way. They had no choice, you could say."

Jason waited for the explosion, but instead Jasmine said in a matter-of-fact tone, "Well, at least you're still alive. More than I can say for your brother."

A young seaman carried in one of Jason's suitcases. He also put down two cell phones, an address book, and a set of car keys. "Captain, the gray phone is secure. The other is in your name. Is there anything else you need?"

Jason stood. "Thank you. I will be fine, Seaman." He returned the salute while dismissing him.

"I guess I'll have to get used to having a military man around again," she said as she watched his easy manner of the use of authority.

Knowing he had to bring his grandparents on board fast about not living in Waterbury, Jason gave her the unsecured cell phone. "Mom, why don't you call your parents while I change. If you don't mind, I'll call Dad's parents and let them know."

"That is a good idea. Tell them I'll call them later. Don't worry, Jason, I'll be nice."

Two hours later, Jason was driving his mother back home when the music stopped. "We interrupt with this fast-breaking report from Cameron Smith. Cameron?"

"Thank you, Linda. Police responded to an abandoned Compton warehouse, one of a number of warehouses along the waterfront…"

Jason reached over to shut it off when his mother's hand covered his. "Leave it, Jason."

"Responding to a call of numerous shots fired and a fire, police found only what could be described as something out of the thirties: four victims with hands and mouths taped, hanging upside down from the rafters. All had been shot dozens of times by automatic weapons. Two of the victims have been identified as Alberto and Raymond Rodriguez, brothers well known to law enforcement with an extensive criminal history, especially drugs. This comes on top of a report, just a half hour ago, that another local teen was found floating just below the West Seattle Bridge. Authorities would only say that the victim is a seventeen-year-old white male and appears to be victim of a drug overdose. If this proves correct, this will make the fifth teen overdose in the last month. So it looks like the drug situation here in Seattle is heating up. This is Cameron Smith. Back to you, Linda."

The female announcer's voice returned. "We continue now with music from the eighties…"

Jason flipped the switch.

"Which is it, Jason, the warehouse or the bay?"

"It was the warehouse, but the bay is what the police will tell you, and that is the official story."

"What about the four in the warehouse, Jason? Is there a story with them?"

"Not one you need to know about. All you have to know is that those who killed Troy won't be doing any more killing." He gave her a quick glance.

"You know, Jason, I'm not violent."

"Mom, I would never kill anybody in cold blood. Please forget about the warehouse. It can only cause trouble and complicate things more."

"You know, Jason, you have a lot of your dad in you. I have a feeling he would be proud of you." She stared at him.

"I know, Mom. I know."

She reached over and laid her hand on his thigh. "Maybe there is evil that we can't turn our backs to. Maybe you, your dad, and your grandfather have been right and I have been wrong. Everything is not so simple." She looked away. "What I can't deny is that I'm going to bury a son."

Jason pulled off the highway and a mile later found a suitable pull off. When all was quiet, he pulled his mother toward him. "Mom, sin makes us all wrong, and we all sin. Don't beat yourself up. It's not God's way." With his mother's head on his shoulder, he looked up into the trees and heard the birds. It could have been morning in England in simpler times.

‒ ‒ ‒ ‒ ‒ ‒ ‒ ‒ ‒ ‒ ‒ ‒ ‒ ‒

Three days later, the black limousine pulled up in front of the First Baptist Church. Jason helped his mother and grandparents out under the cameras of the media. They entered the packed church. Jason was wearing a dark suit he had planned to wear at the Normandy ceremony. He remembered that the last time he'd worn a suit was when they had buried his father.

After opening prayer and hymns, Jason's mother moved behind the pulpit. "It has been many years, actually, since my youth that I have been in a church, except for weddings and to be with others who say good-bye to those they love. I'm not here to share with you my failure to instill godly values in my son. I, like many of my generation, some say the rebellious sixties, who glorified Woodstock, tolerated sexual expression, what we called independence, and yes, even the use of drugs. Today, for what I failed to do, I now join four other grieving mothers in this area whose sons, like Troy, were recently dumped like trash in the bay after overdosing. I can't bring my son back; all I can do is beg you as friends of Troy's and Jason's, those of us who are parents and grandparents, to consider what we are letting drugs do to our families, the nation. Look at all the corruption and death that drug money causes in other nations. While I have lost one son, I found in these terrible days an awesome son" She gazed for a moment at the Judge and Emily. "and renewed relations within my late husband's family. It is said that good can come out of evil. That is my hope for all of us."

Jason mounted the platform. "Two years ago, as I elected to go off to college, my life took a turn from what I had planned. I found myself in the Army. I cannot begin to share with you all how I feel and the experiences I have had in the time I have been gone. I can share with you the most important change in my life. Four days ago, I went in search of my brother. My purpose was to have Troy placed in a drug rehabilitation program, by force, if necessary. I was too late for him; however, I'm determined not to be late for you. I want to share with you the story of my friend Nathan, whose patience, love, and forgiveness saved my life twice ... "

For the next fifteen minutes, Jason was careful to hide the historical details in his sharing but was bold and open about his commitment to Jesus Christ. When the minister closed with an invitation to make Jesus Christ both Lord and Savior, over a hundred came forward, most combined friends of Troy's and Jason's.

While the Seattle memorial service was large and open to the public, the graveside service the next day in Waterbury was small, private, and brief. It was so brief due to the airline schedule that Jason and his family had just enough time to place Troy next to his dad. As they walked across the sun-drenched lawn and back to the waiting limousines, Higgins stopped Jason, handing him a secured cell phone. A brief conversation followed. Jason ended with, "Yes, Mr. President. We are just leaving the cemetery ... Thank you for calling ... Yes, my mother is right here."

Jason's mother felt a tap on her shoulder.

"For you, Mom."

Unlike Jason, with only a brother, Troy, Captain Riley had a number of brothers and sister. In the silence of the drive back to Seattle, Captain Riley reviewed his visit to his home in Olympia. The house and neighborhood he had grown up in was long gone, replaced by a large shopping mall. The only member of his family left was his younger brother, Ralph, who had retired from the postal service several years back. Captain Riley found Ralph seated on the top of the front steps. Strangely, he showed no recognition of him, but Captain Riley had figured that would be the case. "Are you Ralph Riley?"

"Why, yes." Sipping his coffee.

"My name is Ryan Neil; I'm writing a history of the local area, especially interested in families that lived here during the forties, during the war years." He sat down next to him and shook hands.

Ralph looked into Jason's eyes. A feeling he couldn't put his finger on rose within him. "Let me see, during the war years, my father worked on the waterfront, my mother took care of us kids; I was the youngest. My brother Joe was in high school, my older sister Gail went to work at the Boeing factory. In fact, we joked that she was making Jason's plane, our older brother, the only one in the war."

"Mr. Riley, tell me about your brother Jason." "He was a great brother, very giving, smart, and patriotic. He enlisted and was in the Rangers for a period of time, then became a B-17 pilot. He was killed on a mission over France." Tears filled his eyes.

"Do you have any letters or photos from him?"

"Had a lot of them until about 1947. There was a house fire, and we lost everything. That's why we moved out of the old neighborhood." He drained the last of the coffee from his cup.

"Where is your brother Jason buried?"

Ralph's eyes narrowed. "The Army version is he was killed in Normandy. He was shot down during the invasion. I remember my parents were upset because they didn't get a telegram until late September, and we knew he was already dead or MIA in June."

"How did you know?"

"In his last letter, he just about told us, and he mailed us all his war bonds. He knew all right." Ralph placed the cup down.

"His war bonds?" He was surprised that the letters and the bonds made it through the censors.

"That's what I said. The last week in June '44, we got a call from the pilot of his plane, Major John Riley. He had the same last name, no relation. He was in California; he'd come back with the body of one of his crew. He told us about them being shot down and Jason being missing."

"But the Army told you he was dead?" Captain Riley pulled out his wallet.

"If our congressman hadn't raised a fuss, the Army may have never told us anything. I thought you were interested in the old neighborhood. You seem to be more interested in my brother." He thought about other questioners over the years like this young man.

"Sorry. I'm also a military history buff, so I got carried away." Jason pulled out eight photographs from his wallet and showed them to Ralph. "My staff came upon these photos; think you could help me identify them?"

"Where did you get these?"

Jason laid them out on the porch between them. "I didn't. One of the college interns who are helping me with research last summer put them together. I understand the photos were found during an interview with relatives of the late owners of O'Hare Drugstore. They had boxes of old photos, I guess duplicates, lost and missing when people sent in to have their film to be developed and never picked them up."

"It was something in those days to get film developed. Took over a week, and we're talking just black and white. Yeah, those days were something."

Ralph took time with each photo, identifying everyone correctly, including Jason. However, Ralph didn't connect the photo of his brother with him physically in front of him.

Despite the years, it was obvious that Ralph still loved his brother; a tear fell to the porch. "If you don't mind, I'd like to keep these. I only have one photo of Jason."

"I'll have copies made for you. May I see your photo?"

"Sure, it'll take a minute. I'm sorry, I forgot your name." He stood and picked up his cup.

"Ryan Neil." He screamed inward, *Jason Riley, your brother!*

Captain Riley stood to stretch his back and was just slipping the photos back into his wallet when Ralph handed him a small photo. "This is the last picture of me and Jason. He was home on leave between training schools."

Captain Riley looked at the picture of him and a much younger Ralph, faded to yellow by time. "Joe never could take a picture."

"How did you know who took this?"

"What?"

"My brother's friend Joe Ramsey. How did you know he took this?" Ralph snatched the photo back.

Captain Riley realized the slip. His breathing became shallow. "Sorry, I was thinking out loud. My brother's name is Joe. He never could take a good picture; they were always tilted like that one. It still hurts after so many years, doesn't it?"

"Jason was one hell of a person, as well as a great brother. I wish we could have found out what happened to him." He slipped the photo into his shirt pocket.

"But you said the Army told you what happened."

Anger rose in Ralph's voice. "It was all a lie. Major Ramsey, his friend who took the picture, called us after the war and told us they were full of crap. In fact, the government came here in 1947, asking us all a bunch of questions: reading all of his letters and trying to get fingerprints, like he was a criminal. If it wasn't for the house fire, I'm sure they would have come back and taken everything of his."

"Your parents must have been overwhelmed."

"No, they both died in an auto accident in 1946. The one that took it the hardest was his girlfriend. Even four years ago just before she died, she still hoped we would find out what happened. Elizabeth loved Jason until the end ... Such a pretty girl, never to get married."

"I think it's time I left. I'm sorry I brought you this pain. Maybe I'll come back another day." Tears ran down the sides his cheeks.

"Maybe that would be best." As Jason went down the walkway, Ralph came halfway down the steps. "Don't forget those copies of Jason's photos." Ralph thought, *How strange for the young man to cry like that.*

NO PLACE LIKE HOME

Jason was in a daze. He could not remember driving back to Seattle. It was a miracle the trip was not interrupted by an accident. Entering the house, he greeted his maternal grandparents. "Where is that beautiful daughter of yours?"

His grandmother hit him on the arm. "She's in the backyard. How was your trip up to Olympia?"

Jason gave her a peck on the cheek. "My trip was all right." He went out the back door and found his mother dozing on the chaise lounge. The book she had been reading rested on the ground, her fingers just brushing the cover. Bending over, he placed a gentle kiss on her forehead. "It'll take you a long time to finish at this rate, Mom."

"I guess I must have dozed off."

"Good guess," he said in a flat tone.

"How was the drive, and did you find your friend?"

"Yeah, I found him," Captain Riley remembered with sadness.

"You sound down, Jason. Are you okay?" Shielding her eyes from the sun.

"A lot has happened in a very short time, Mom. It's just overwhelming. I need to report back soon and wanted to visit Waterbury for a day or two before I head back. Is that okay with you?" His voice became distant.

"When are you planning to leave, Jason?" She stood slowly.

"Tomorrow morning, if it's okay with you."

"Sure, Jason. You've been great. Your grandparents will stay here and help me pack. It's going to be strange to live with them again, but I think it will be good for all of us." She pulled Jason toward her and hugged for life while giving him a kiss. Holding him, she thought, *Lately you have changed so much, Jason. What is happening to you, son?*

"I'll go and start packing everything that's mine, so I'll be ready to leave tomorrow," he said quietly and gently pushed her away, when he really wanted was to stay forever in her love and embrace; he was so weary.

"If there's anything of Troy's you want, take it." She stepped back.

"I guess I better go find some boxes and get started."

Looking down at the clouds, Jason wondered if there would ever be a time when he wouldn't think of the *Golden Eagle*. As he leaned back, staring out of the window, the reverie was broken by the announcement-requesting passengers to put their seats in the upright position.

As he came out of the lower-level baggage area, his grandfather was waiting. There was no greeting. The old man began ranting about how he hated LA and all the traffic at LAX. Jason smiled and gave him a hug. "Just pretend all those cars are flak, and you're going right on through."

The Judge grabbed for one of Jason's suitcases. "I do, Jason, and throw a few bombs their way. Why did I have to drive to this hole? You could have flown into Santa Maria."

Jason took the suitcase from his grandfather's hands. "It's okay;

I'll get them. We're going over to Torrance; I still haven't opened the package. You *do* want to see what's in it, don't you?"

The Judge pointed across the street. "I'm parked over there; and yes, since I protected it for fifty-seven years, I guess I do, but…"

"But what?"

"Only if you want to. There's no danger." He stopped in the middle of the street, causing cars to honk.

"I want you to, and the only danger I see is from you. If we don't move, we're going to get run over."

"The heck with them." Cars swerved to avoid them.

"You're getting a little cranky in your old age, Grandpa. Come on, and you'll see what you've been protecting all these years."

— — — — — — — — — — — — — — —

After getting lost once, they arrived. "Here's the place, Grandpa. I'll drop you off in front and go find a parking spot."

Getting out of the car, Judge Riley looked at the sign and then ducked his head back in through the car window. "Whose bright idea was this? You two or Alex's?"

"I guess you can say it was teamwork all the way."

The Judge looked at the store sign again. He shook his head. "You've got to be kidding me. I have half a mind to walk home, boy."

"Hurry, it's almost three. Besides, a hundred-sixty-mile walk would take you a week at least."

"Good! It would give me time to think of ways to kill you, boy. Darn you, Jason!" Shaking his finger at Jason.

Jason parked the car and, with the package in hand and his grandfather walking behind, went up to the counterman. "I have an appointment with Roger Pace."

"Your name?" The balding middle-aged man looked up from his work.

"Jason Riley." He laid the package on the display case.

"I am David Pace, his brother. Have you ever been in our store?"

Hearing his grandfather clear his throat. "No, excuse me, this is my grandfather, Judge John Riley."

"Pleased to meet you, Judge. Look around. Home Plate is one of the biggest stores of its kind. I'll go get my brother."

"Of all the stupid ideas" The Judge fumed.

Before an argument began, a taller version of the counterman appeared. "Hello, I'm Roger Pace." He shook both of their hands. "I see you've already met my brother, David. Are you a collector, Mr. Riley?"

"No, I'm not a collector. What I know is just what I read in here." Jason picked up the latest edition of the *Becket Price Guide* off the counter. "I had a good friend that was really into it, though." His grandfather kicked his ankle.

"Why does everyone kick me in the ankle?" Turning to his grandfather, Jason asked plaintively.

"It's your mouth. It's always been a problem." Judge Riley grabbed the package off the display case. "This was left to my grandson here by one of my crew members from World War II."

Roger looked at the package. "You mean it has been sealed since ... ?"

"June 4, 1944."

Roger ushered them to a rear section of the store. "David, do you have your video camera handy? Is it Mr. Riley or Jason?"

"Jason is fine." He glanced nervously at the camera.

"Please, sit down, gentlemen. When David is ready, we will open her up." Roger pulled out a chair at the oak table.

"That's fine. I just don't want to be in the video." Jason noted how his grandfather put the package on the table with caution.

Roger put on a pair of latex gloves and slid the package closer. "No problem, Jason." With David doing the videotaping, Roger opened the package with delicate skill. He laid before them an assortment of over two hundred baseball cards, candy wrappers, and matchbook covers in mint condition. Among the collection there was a small box and an envelope with Jason's name on the outside. Picking up the envelope, Roger looked at the name. "I guess this belongs to you. Strange that it has your name on it."

The Judge grabbed the envelope and quickly slid it into his inner coat pocket. "I told him that my grandson was going to be named after my co-pilot."

David couldn't hold out any longer. Putting down the camera, he pulled on white cotton gloves and opened the smaller box. Scratching his head, he picked up the *Becket Price Guide.* "Do you know what you have here, Jason?" David asked.

"No, but I'm sure you're going to tell me."

"A 1919 White Sox team set, twenty-five cards. There's only one known complete set, up until now."

"That's good, right?" The Judge could feel his heart dance.

"About fifty-thousand-dollars good, Judge," Roger replied, still shaking his head.

Jason poked at the items with the eraser end of a pencil. "I don't know why Alex got so many Babe Ruths. Matchbooks, candy wrappers; I spent good money, I told him ... " Jason felt a sharp pain again from under the table.

"That candy wrapper, as you call it Jason, is worth about a thousand dollars." David pointed out to both Jason and the Judge in the guide.

The brothers spent the next hour going over the cards, explaining to Jason and the Judge as they went along, grading the quality and giving them an estimated value.

"This is incredible. You have over two hundred thousand dollars' worth" David concluded.

They walked to the parking lot with a signed agreement, an accurate inventory list, and a sizeable advance; Jason placed a hand on his grandpa's shoulder. "Grandpa, half of this is going to be yours."

"Keep it, Jason, I made enough with your presidential predictions."

"You did what?"

"Two can play this game. Must be something in the blood." He slapped Jason on the back while chuckling.

On the long drive home, Captain Riley told the Judge about his visit in Olympia with his brother. "Did you know about the bonds?"

The Judge pointed to the sign. "The 101 North is the next exit. Bonds, no. When Andrew visited our barracks, he must have taken all your bonds. I know he went and got the crews' letters from the orderly room; said that he was going to mail them. He figured the Army wouldn't if they found them."

"Thank you for calling my family."

"It was the least I could do. I called all the families of the crew. They let me come back with Alex, since I was still recovering." He stretched his legs. "Now, let me sleep."

"What do you think of Joe Ramsey calling?"

"For crying out loud, Captain; that was stupid. Your family must have really gotten upset. You sure have a way of picking friends." Sitting back up, Judge Riley yawned.

"Come on, Major, he just talks a little too much." He checked the rearview mirror and changed lanes to exit.

"Like someone else I know; I'll bet he enjoyed spilling the beans to the President. Now, let me sleep," he said waspishly, looking over.

He kept up his own conversation as the car wound along the 101 northbound, somewhere around Santa Barbara. The Judge's strained face relaxed, his eyes closed, but the snores were drowned out by his monologue. About ninety minutes later, they pulled into the barn-like garage. He shook the Judge awake. "Hey, Sleeping Beauty, we're home."

The Judge awoke and pushed open the door. "What are you going to do with the money, Jason?"

"I guess by now Preacher has grandchildren. So I want to see what I can do to help. I just feel so bad about not being there for his family, especially his son." He opened the trunk.

"It worked out perfectly." The Judge slammed the passenger door closed.

"What did?"

"The money I won on the Kennedy election put him through college. I knew that would be what you wanted to do, and you happened to make it possible," he said, lifting out the lightest suitcase.

"This is from both of us, Grandpa." He gave the Judge a warm hug.

"Stop talking like that, Jason. There's only one of you."

"You do it all the time—Jason this, Captain Riley that,"

"I can get away with it. You are now Captain Riley, and your first name is Jason, right?"

"You know what I mean."

"You know what I mean, you're going to get in trouble one day, anyway. Maybe when you're in Washington, D.C., you'll have a chance to meet Congressman John Campbell from Arizona."

"A congressman; well, I'll be. What does he know about me?"

"All they ever knew was that you were well off and had set up a trust fund for the crew's families."

"You mean there is such a thing?" He pulled out the second suitcase and slammed the trunk close.

"Nathan's family had the biggest need, him being married and all. With most of the others, it was their parents, brothers, and sisters. I'll go over it all with you later. Your grandmother is waiting."

"How about Rodent? He had a girlfriend named Betty. She had a kid or was going to." He handed the car keys to the Judge as they neared the steps.

"If he did, I didn't know about it. I hired a good private detective to do a background on all the families. When did he tell you?"

"I think a week before I left here."

"You see, Jason we have a problem. There is no 'here'; your friends never existed in this timeframe except for me and you."

"You're telling me that it was like a big dream? I'm sure if I went down to McDonald's, the owner, Mr. W., would remember them for sure."

"After our conversation with the President, I went down to McDonald's and had a talk with Jim Winfield. He never heard of any of the crew, but he seems to know you real well."

"Well, I'll be. How about Jimmy Wright and Laura Smith?" Jason was growing more excited and louder.

"Be quiet, Jason," he whispered and nodded toward Emily standing on the porch. "Alive and well, just not the crew. We better get moving, Jason, or your grandmother will start yelling."

"Any money left, Grandpa?"

"No. The last of it is gone. The Foundation closed a couple of weeks ago."

"Foundation?"

"Um hum. The Foundation of Time, and don't get any ideas about money; Andrew used the last of it, your five-thousand-dollar check…"

The rest of the reply was lost for all time in the emotional welcome "home" from his grandmother. Like the very first she enfolded him in a tight hug.

After dinner Jason went up to his bedroom, then came running back down. "Grandpa, the letter from Alex."

Judge Riley reached in his coat pocket. "Wow, can you believe I forgot? Sorry, Jason."

— — — — — — — — — — — — — — —

As his bedroom door swung open, his sinful past overwhelmed him. It had been three weeks, yet it seemed a lifetime. Dropping his suitcases just inside the door, he sat on the edge of his bed and ripped open the letter from Alex. At the cry of Jason's anguish, Emily dropped her cup of coffee and jumped from the chair. The Judge reached over and grabbed her hand. "Please, sit down, Emily, don't. He needs to work this out."

"What do you mean? Work what out?"

"Let's give him a little time, okay?" The Judge stood and walked over to the sink for a dishrag.

As he wiped the table, they could hear the sounds of crying, loud banging, and then abrupt silence.

"John, this is ridiculous"

"Trust me, Emily" Another ten minutes of silence passed. "Okay,

Emily, let's go check on him." Halfway up the stairs, they could hear Jason sobbing. Outside the door, they hesitated. Each nodded, and the door creaked.

Emily cried, "Jason!"

Jason was seated in the middle of the floor. Posters were ripped off the walls, CDs thrown about, clothes ripped to shreds. Clutched in his hand was the letter. Looking up at them, he said brokenly, "Grandma, I need a trash barrel and a couple of bags." At a nod from the Judge, Emily headed out of the room, clutching her chest.

The Judge almost had to pry the letter from Jason's grip. As he read the letter, tears filled his eyes.

My brother Jason;

I like the sound of that. I never had a brother, and if I did, I would want one like you. I'll make this fast since this 389th puke is bugging me to hurry up so he can seal this package.

If you're reading this letter, it means I'm not there as promised to open this together and for me to pull it from your hand, so I'll assume the worst has happened. I told the Captain if anything happens to me to see that I'm sent back to Waterbury, even if it means digging me back up. I just want to go back home.

There's a hill in the cemetery that overlooks the ocean and the town. It's one of the most beautiful places on earth. I went into this war with my eyes wide open, and I have seen many braver than me die. I know for those who went and fought in the Great War the town set aside a section of the cemetery. If they do the same for us, I would consider it an honor to be with them versus in the family plot.

I want you to visit my family. Tell them it's okay, that I'm with Jesus, and it does not get any better than that.

When you raise your glass and toast me, say, "It is better to die for something than to live for nothing.

I have to go. I love you, Jason, and hope to see you on the other side of life.

Your brother,
Alex

Jason got up from the floor and sat next to his grandfather on the bed. "Is that what I have to look forward to? Crying even after sixty years?"

"At the rate you're going, I don't give you sixty days, never mind years," he grumbled.

Emily entered the room with the items requested. She sat on the other side of Jason. "What is that, John?" she asked, gesturing to the letter on his lap.

"A letter that Alex wrote."

"So Alex left you a letter?

"No, Alex left it to Jason."

"This is so unfair, to be here in this filth again. My brother dying because of it and the crew all dead." Jason stood, kicking the plastic bags.

"Jason, please don't be so hard on yourself." She reached over, grabbing Jason's hand.

"Jason, these things are junk, they have no meaning. It's your character. You have a lot of that; I'm proud of you." The Judge waved his hand around the bedroom. "Please sit down with us, Jason." Emily searched her memories through the years and realized how few times she had seen John cry and never Jason, until this month. She leaned over and whispered in Jason's ear, "Trust God and lean not on your own understanding."

The three sat together in the midst of chaos and confusion but with the inner peace of God leading them forward from that time and place.

— — — — — — — — — — — — — —

The old lady ended her prayers. Her withered, veined hand placed flowers on the young man's grave. She stood and looked down as a shadow crossed the gravestone. She spun around and looked into Captain Riley's eyes. "My God, My Lord, as you promised!"

"Easy, Ruth." The Judge put his arm behind her sagged back.

"You're Alex's sister, Ruth?" Captain Riley backed up.

"Lieutenant Jason Riley, you're the answer to my prayer." She stiffened under the Judge's grip and moved forward.

"I don't understand."

Reaching into her purse, she pulled out of her wallet an old photo. She held it up for him to see. "Your uniform is different. Tell me that this is not you."

Captain Riley looked at Alex and him by the *Golden Eagle*. As hard as he tried, no words came from his trembling lips. The Judge reached out and took the photo from Ruth's, glancing at it, he handed it back to Ruth. "You've upset my grandson, Ruth."

"John Riley, be silent before you lie, especially on this day and in this place. Do you remember what today is, John?"

"Yes, Ruth. It's the anniversary of the day we buried Alex."

"It's also his birthday, the twenty-fourth. He always gave me a hard time for being two months younger."

"Alex once wrote me that you were a person of integrity. I guess it is true. You don't look a day older than your photo, but I knew that. I knew you would come."

"How did you know?" He didn't hear the camera's click.

"A vision from God; your secret is safe with me. All I want to know is about your time with my brother. You were with him when he died." She also missed the camera's click.

The Judge pulled his car keys out of his pocket and handed them to Ruth. "In the trunk there's a blanket. Please get it and give us a few minutes with Alex, alone, then we'll talk." As they watched her move slowly across the lawn, the Judge pulled out the bottle of Wild Turkey from the plastic bag. Two shot glasses appeared, and he slowly filled them. "Not one for drinking myself. Seen too many lives ruined. The last time I had a drink was when I buried your dad, Jason. One of the worst things is for a parent to have to bury their child, no matter how old they are."

Captain Riley took the shot glass from his commanding officer, Jason from his grandfather. "Ready, Major?"

They both stood at attention, and in unison they held up their glasses. Together they said, "It is better to die for something than live for nothing." They downed their shots in one gulp.

They refilled the two glasses and poured it on the flat granite stone, watching as it flowed into the carved lettering. Jason started to laugh. The Judge stopped pouring. "What is so funny?"

"That last night we were up here, Alex pissed on his own grave."

The Judge frowned. "We don't need that kind of language. I hope you're not going to emulate him."

"Don't be silly, Grandpa. His sister is coming back."

A half hour later, with the Judge on one side and Jason on the other, Ruth walked back to the parking lot unaware of Jong and Zeng slipping down the other side of the hill. The last two weeks had seemed like a waste of their time watching an empty cemetery, but now their respect for Colonel Lin grew. As they sped north on 101, they shared hopes that newly promoted Colonel Lin's pleasure with the film and license plate numbers would lead to their own promotions.

THE OVAL OFFICE

President Strong had two offices for two different purposes. His working office was piled with paper and knickknacks, while the Oval Office desk was one of order and show. It was this important image that made the two framed eight-by-ten enlargements, the color Polaroid, and the black-and-white of the *Golden Eagle* crew on the credenza seem so out of place. Lost in his thoughts, the President placed the black and white back down. Staring out of the window at the clouds, he thought about the *Golden Eagle* when a loud thump spun him around. It felt as if he were in a dream as papers blew off his desk in slow motion. Centered on his desk was the thick military folder labeled "Riley, Jason Shawn, RA21280135." It was as it had been on the day it was removed by Colonel Richard Steel, although Strong didn't realize it.

Fear and curiosity warred within him. The file had seemed to fall from the sky, it had appeared so suddenly. Breathing deeply, he sat down and, with caution, touched the file. He almost expected it to be hot. Courage outweighing fear, he opened the file, then spent the next fifteen minutes in utter amazement learning about the colorful career of Lieutenant Jason Riley.

As he picked up the phone, the flat side of a large sword pinned his hand on the receiver. From over his right shoulder, he heard, "Mr. President, I would not use that phone except to make sure we have some private time together."

The sword lifted, and a figure moved toward the front of the desk. The President turned pale. There stood, in the full armor of the late twelfth century, Earl Andrew Grey.

"This cannot be; I must be dreaming."

"I assure you, President Strong, that you are not dreaming. No more than John or Jason Riley, to mention a few. I'm Andrew Grey, former adjutant and servant to His Majesty, King Richard the First of England; I now serve the true King." Andrew sheathed his sword.

"How much time do you need?"

"We have much to discuss, and your country is in great danger. Let's start with the rest of the hour."

"Can I have my Chief of Staff?"

Andrew picked up a bronze bust of Lincoln and examined it. "Let me ask you, what does he think of the crew photos?"

"He thinks they look better in uniform."

"Since he can clearly see both, it will be fine if he attends. I hope I served Richard as well as Mr. Martinez serves you. Please, make sure no one else is aware of this meeting."

"I can't wait to see the expression on Carlos' face."

"I'm glad I can provide some humor to your humble life." Andrew laughed.

- - - - - - - - - - - - - -

The Pentagon, or, as the residents call it, the Five-Sided Puzzle Palace, was a massive relic from World War II. It covers over twenty-nine acres and is surrounded by another sixty-seven acres of parking lots. Captain Riley found himself in a sea of Colonel's and General's, hopelessly lost in the building's seventeen and a half miles of corridors. Finally, a full Colonel stepped away from a group that had gathered at the uncertain gaze. "Captain, you seem to be lost. Can I help you?"

"Yes, sir, I am lost. I hadn't realized this place would be so massive."

"Big mission, big building. By the looks of those decorations on your uniform, seems you've been on a few missions too. What type of outfit?"

"Rangers, sir."

"Really. That's not what your shoulder patch says." He spotted his aviation wings. "You're a flyboy? Black Hawks? Apache?"

"Sorry, sir. I would like to carry on this conversation, but I need to report in or I'll be late."

The Colonel waved over his fellow officers. Green suits trapped Jason. "First thing, Captain ... " He looked at his nameplate. "Riley, break out your ID."

Captain Riley started to protest, but their presence was suffocating. He handed the Colonel his ID card. "Sir, please, I need to get going."

The Colonel searched the card and handed it back. "Looks like it's fresh off the press, Captain. A captain at twenty, you look even younger, I'm impressed." He handed back the ID with a big smile. "Why don't I escort you to where you need to go. That way, you won't get lost again."

"Sir, directions would do. You don't have to go out of your way."

"I'll bet. Who are you reporting to, Captain Riley?"

A prayer rose under his breath. "Please Lord." He looked up. "General Thomas."

"Our young Captain is to report to none other than the Chief of Staff. Is that what I'm hearing, Captain Riley?" He laughed, as did the group.

"Yes, sir. That is how I remember he introduced himself to me."

The Colonel slapped Jason's shoulder. "This, Captain, is going to be a pleasure." Everyone else joined in the laughter.

Five minutes later, as the colonel and Captain Riley walked into the reception area, General Thomas looked down at his watch. "Captain Riley, you are late."

Captain Riley stood at attention. "Sir, I had a problem finding my way. I was stopped by the Colonel, who found my uniform and identification card of interest, if you know what I mean."

"I do, Captain Riley." General Thomas turned to the colonel, who was also standing at attention. "Colonel, you have problem with Captain Riley?"

"No, sir, I thought..."

"You thought what?" The veins swelled on his forehead.

"He's so...so young, and...and to have all those decorations, maybe in wartime, but, but..." The Colonel wished for a hole to escape in.

General Thomas pointed his finger within inches of the Colonel's nose and barked, "But what? Remember his name, Colonel. He's one of the bravest soldiers you'll ever meet." He wrapped his arm around Jason. "Thank you, Colonel. You are dismissed." He escorted Jason into the office. Thomas closed the door and walked behind his desk. "Well, Captain?"

Jason's reply was casual. "Yeah?"

"Is that it, a yeah? It is, 'Yes, sir.' You better stand at attention and report in like a soldier." His voice bounced of the walls.

Captain Riley jumped at the sound. "Yes, sir!" Snapping to attention, his hand slashed to his forehead. "Captain Riley reporting as ordered, sir!"

"At ease, Captain. Don't let that act fool you. Got it?"

"Yes, sir."

"If I had my way, you would be up for a court-martialed for being stupid. What were you thinking, Captain? That you're some type of Rambo?"

Jason started to speak. "I—"

"Shut up, Captain. Do you know how many IOUs you caused? To start with, the Seattle Police Department and the Navy. Shall I go on?"

"No, sir, but my brother needed help." He stared forward. It wasn't the first time he'd been dressed down by a superior.

"Which brother, Captain, Troy or Ralph, whom you visited despite a warning by Mr. Higgins, correct?" As he sat, he reached down on the floor and slammed a tan folder on the desk.

"Yes, sir. The General is correct." He knew words would have no meaning.

"It seems this came special delivery to the President three days ago. Do you know what it is?" He opened up the thick folder.

"Yes, sir. It looks like my military records."

"That is correct, Captain Riley. I'll bet it's been some time since you've seen your record."

"No offense, sir. It's been about four weeks since I saw it." He waited for the General's wrath.

"Yes, you're right, Captain Riley. For the Army it's been fifty-seven years. Captain, be at ease, have a seat. Your record is very impressive. We have underestimated your accomplishments. I guess a few more awards are in order."

"Sir, may I speak freely?" Inwardly, Captain Riley told Jason to shut up.

"Granted."

Jason pointed to the patch on his left shoulder. "I feel foolish enough as it is. When that colonel stopped me, I didn't even know the patch I was wearing. Then he asked me what I flew, rattling off names, I guess about helicopters. I'm no soldier."

"Really, Captain? Then what are you, a surfer?" He mocked subtle intrigue.

"In these times, yes, sir." Jason nodded his head.

The General reached over and pressed the intercom. "Joanna, has the Colonel arrived? ... Good, please send him in." The door opened and Colonel Richard Steel entered.

"I believe, Captain, when a senior officer walks in, military courtesy is to stand at attention," General Thomas bellowed.

Slow to rise, Jason said, "But General, he is ... "

Thomas stood. "But nothing, Captain Riley." Walking around his desk, Thomas continued. "I'm going out for a cup of coffee. That gives you fifteen minutes to get your act together, Captain. Colonel, he's all yours."

"Thank you, General," Colonel Steel replied at attention.

"Not my idea. The President, I hope, has good reasons for all this." He brushed past without a glance.

The door slammed, and Colonel Steel's shoulders sank with a sigh. "Captain Riley, please sit down before you fall."

"Well, here we are again," he said as he sat across from Jason.

"I can't take it anymore." Jason trembled.

Gently, Steel touched Jason's knee. "I guess you could say that's a paraphrase from the cross for you and for us. He never gave up."

I'm not God. Are you, Andrew?" He flinched at Steel's touch.

"Not even close. But in Him I'm a lot closer than not." He laughed at some inward joke.

"Why me, Andrew? Why you?" It was now Jason who tapped him on the knee.

"I know why He selected me. You know anything about the Crusades, Jason?" he pulled out his pipe.

"Wars between Christians and Muslims, I think."

"That's all you need to know for now, my young knight. You'll find out more soon. Time will tell, but you have an important mission ahead."

"Last time you asked me about war, I found myself in the middle of one. Please, I have killed so many. I'm tired." Tears filled Jason's eyes as he thought *I couldn't handle the Crusades.*

"Evil does not give us the luxury of rest. Only fools and politicians that cater to them think you can comprise with evil." He put the pipe back in his pocket, knowing the General's intolerance for smoking in the office.

Jason looked into his eyes, sensing the sadness of the other man. "I have so many questions. Is there going to be another war for me?"

"I can't answer that. This is not the time."

"I can tell, it's the Crusades, right, I'm a young knight?"

"No, no, Jason, it's not that Crusade. I guess I better watch my terms." As he stood, he thought, *How Christian to call it that. No, Jason, it will be called the war on terrorism.*

"I was worried for a second."

"Please stand and let me pray for you." His voice softened.

"Last time I let you do this, it was life changing."

"As it should be, Jason, as it should be. And as it must be." He placed his hands on the crown of Jason's head.

— — — — — — — — — — — — —

Many who knew Barbara Bucklew accused her of being a control freak, which she always denied by saying she just didn't like surprises. As she glanced over at Colonel Steel, she struggled for a reason why he made her so uncomfortable. Never would she admit that since his arrival, all the unfolding changes had remained beyond the grasp of her control. In all her years with the President, she had never seen such changes and activity as in the last week. After the President's abrupt cancellation of a week of scheduled events, she thought she was going to have a quiet week. Instead, the Oval Office had become a revolving door. "Congressman Campbell is here, Mr.

President... Yes, sir. Also, Mr. Martinez called in and is running ten minutes late. Yes, sir. I'll send him in."

Placing down the phone she came around the desk, announcing, "The President is ready for you, Congressman."

Standing in the middle of the office, the President looked strained as he welcomed his guest. "Congressman Campbell, always good to have one of the loyal opposition party visit."

There was no greeting from the Army Colonel that followed him in, nor an introduction of him. The Congressman made a mental note of what he thought as rudeness. A little distracted, he replied, "Thank you for honoring my father and all the members of the 572nd. I didn't know how or why he died until then."

"It was long overdue. So what is the talk on the Hill?" He ushered him over to the seating area.

"It's not just on the Hill; it's all of Washington. You've cancelled everything. Rumor is that you're ill, yet I understand you've had a lot of visitors this past week and are burning the midnight oil. Then there's this strange story of a photo being passed around, first by Mr. Martinez, then to those who visit here."

"You're right. Many have come, but you're the only one invited to come alone; that means you're special. Please sit down" As they sat slowly, Colonel Steel did the same across from the Congressman.

"I would guess a thank-you is in order for the special honor."

"Maybe you are thinking I invited you because you're the chairman of the Armed Services Committee? The truth as to why you are here is, you are the son of Sergeant Nathaniel Campbell, radio operator of the *Golden Eagle*."

"I don't understand." He noticed the two picture frames facedown on the coffee table before him.

"Congressman, pick up the picture to your left. Tell me what you see." Colonel Steel said.

Campbell felt the anger of pride. *No introduction, and now ordering me around like some private*, he thought. But he knew he was at the mercy of the President. As he turned over the black-and-white photo of the crew, his eyes filled up with tears. "Where did you get this?"

The President knew the ways of powerful men. He said quietly, "Colonel John Riley, anew major back then, gave it to me after the Normandy ceremony." Strong slipped a smaller copy into Campbell's hand. "This is a copy for you to keep. Now, do you have every face fresh in your memory, Congressman?"

Campbell placed the smaller photo next to the larger one. "I always have; my dad sent this same photo in his last letter, along with every photo I think he had. I know each of them by heart." He wiped a tear. "It's all I had of him."

"You're wrong, Congressman. You have true faith, the faith of your father. Please pick up the other picture," Colonel Steel said.

Campbell never thought of himself as brave, even though he'd won more than his fair share of medals in Vietnam, yet he felt uneasy. As he turned it over, it slipped from his hand and fell to his lap. "I don't find this funny."

The President stood and handed a copy of the Polaroid to Congressman Campbell. "This is no joke, Congressman. Just be patient, and you'll have your answer." Strong walked over to the door and stuck his head out the door, saying, "Barbara, who's the agent on duty outside?"

"Why, it's Agent Forster, Mr. President."

"Excellent. Please tell him I need him in here for a minute." Closing the door, he walked back to the seating area and continued, "We're in luck, Colonel, the foul-mouthed Agent Forster is on duty."

"Mr. President, is there a problem?" Forster entered a few feet into the office.

"No, not at all. Please come over here. Just need your trained powers of observation for a moment, Agent." Picking up the photo from the coffee table, he asked, "Congressman, may I please have the picture on your lap?" He handed both framed pictures to the agent. "We got into this discussion of who looks like who in each photo."

"The old man in the color photo of course does not look like any-one in the old photo, but the kid is a dead ringer for that lieutenant. Look at the end of the back row on the right," Agent Forster said.

"Agent Forster, please point out to the Congressman who is the dead ringer."

The Congressman stood and looked over Forster's shoulder, mumbling, "Lieutenant Jason Riley."

"How about the others, Agent?" the President asked.

"Sir, what others?"

"In the color photo, Agent Forster." Congressmen's finger was stabbing at the color photo.

"You mean in the black and white, sir?"

"What don't you understand? In the *color* photo." His voice was animated as he held up his small color photo.

Agent Forster was unsettled at the congressman's insistence. "Just like the big picture. The old man and the kid." He looked to the President for permission to escape from the mad Congressman. "Mr. President, is there anything else you need?"

"Yes, there is. Please have Barbara come in and then watch the door, Agent. No one, I mean no one, except Mr. Martinez comes in, and no phone calls. Thank you, you've been a big help, Agent Forster." He took photos back.

As Barbara walked into the completely silent office, a chill went up her spine. They all stood.

"Mr. President."

"I want you to join us, Barbara, please sit down."

"Sorry I'm late, sir." Carlos came rushing in.

"Since we all know each other, I guess I don't have to do any introductions." The Congressman glanced at the Colonel and wanted to correct his host but kept silent. "Everyone, please, sit down. "Carlos, I just invited Barbara to join us. Agent Forster just pointed out Lieutenant Riley to Congressman Campbell. Barbara." Handing Barbara the two framed photos.

"You want them in their usual places, Mr. President?" she asked as she stood.

"Please, Barbara, sit down. What do you think of them, Barbara? You've had a couple of weeks to study them."

"At first, I thought they were weird, or, I should say, some trick photography. Then I figured it out."

"Really? Which is?" He smiled at the thought of what was about to take place.

"That group of kids in the color photo went to one of those places that dress you up to make it like an old-looking photo, like the Civil War or Wild West, but in case it was World War II."

Carlos and the President laughed, Congressman Campbell's remained expressionless, and Colonel Steel was smiling. The President continued. "Well, Barbara, that's a good idea, but the truth is they were taken over fifty-seven years apart."

Barbara laughed. "That is impossible." All other laughter had stopped. She looked around. Things were out of control. She didn't like it.

"Barbara, I know how you don't like surprises, so please try to relax. Congressman Campbell and Barbara, let me formally introduce you to Colonel Steel who—"

"My father wrote about a Colonel Steel. You can't be ..."

"Yes and no. His real name is Andrew Grey, and he will tell you the real story about your father and Lieutenant Riley."

The Colonel leaned forward. "What I'm about to tell you is going to be hard to believe, so I'm going to make it easy for you." His figure swirled and unfolded into the Earl of Westminster.

－ － － － － － － － － － －

General Thomas pondered what to do with the sweat-soaked Captain Riley passed out in the chair. With Captain Morris waiting outside, Thomas finally shook Jason's shoulder. "Wake up, Captain."

"Sorry, sir! Where's Colonel Steel?" Captain Riley bolted from the chair.

"You're a mess, Captain." Pointing to his private restroom, he continued, "Go into the head and try to get presentable." As soon as Captain Riley left, he buzzed in Captain Morris.

"Captain Morris reporting to General Thomas as ordered, sir!"

"Captain, please sit down." He opened Morris' service file. "I have a very special mission for you, Captain." For the next four minutes, he explained the glorified babysitting assignment in very general terms.

As Jason stepped from the bathroom, "Captain Riley, I should have known." Morris stood up and glared.

"I never did thank you, Captain Morris." He extended his hand in a gesture of reconciliation.

"You caused a lot of trouble in Seattle, Riley." He looked down at the extended hand with contempt.

"If you two warring dogs can please sit down. Captain Morris, you need to forget about that situation." He handed each a pair of photos, "Captain Morris, please give me your observations. Captain Riley, I already know yours."

"Sir, when was the bomber crew photo taken?" Morris said, looking at the black and white photo.

"Captain Riley, when?"

"About two months ago. Sorry. End of April 1944." Captain Riley scratched his head while searching his memory.

"Captain Morris, I'm waiting." He smiled as he saw Morris recognize Captain Riley in the crew photo.

"They are the same group except that the old man is not in the black and white, and the captain is missing in the color one."

General Thomas pushed Lieutenant Riley's military records toward Captain Morris. As the folder neared the edge of the desk, he said, "You're wrong, Captain Morris. The old man is the captain of the B-17 crew. Before you ask, the color photo was taken about on June 2."

"There must be an error, sir. It's impossible, sir." Morris was left searching for words. Erring in naming a commanding officer crazy was inexcusable, but a General or the Chief of Staff? It was military suicide.

"This, Captain Morris, are First Lieutenant Jason Riley's records until I and the President promoted him about three weeks ago to captain. Go ahead, Captain Morris. Read them; we'll wait."

"This can't be real." After four minutes, Captain Morris had read enough; he was in total confusion.

The General nodded to Captain Riley, whose voice filled with pleasure as he said, "Captain Morris, I really was considered a decent B-17 pilot until I went MIA on D-Day."

"You were at Normandy?"

"Yes. I didn't see the invasion itself. We were shot down the morning before, on the fifth. Then I, shall I say, disappeared in the early morning hours of the sixth." He was enjoying mentally tormenting the Captain.

"You two will have plenty time to swap war stories on your own time. Captain Riley, wipe that silly smirk off your face. I explained to Captain Morris his assignment. He is to observe, coach, protect, and advise you as you go to Ranger-refresher training. Then for four weeks, you'll join him in a special operations team. We'll see if you're still as good as your record says."

"But sir, I joined to fight a war. How can you force me now?" Jason protested viciously.

General Thomas turned red. It was all he could manage not to deal with Jason right then in front of Captain Morris. Taking a deep breath, he proceeded in formality. "Captain Morris, could you excuse us? Oh, and one last thing before you go: I need you to sign this." Slipping the form across the desk and holding out a pen, "Just a friendly reminder of the consequences of disclosing any knowledge of or anything related to Captain Riley."

"First time I ever met a national secret." He signed the paper, snapped to attention, saluted, and left the room. The fuming General and Jason sat alone.

THREE-DAY WEEKEND

Captain Riley lay on his back in the cutting sand, inching his way under the barbed wire. Machine gun tracers licked the sunset sky above him. He jumped up and ran to his right but was knocked off his feet by an explosion that sprayed rock and dirt down on him. Crawling again, he felt an elbow in his side as Morris thrust a radio at him. "Robert twelve."

Another explosion threw a rock, slicing his cheek. "Repeat!" he yelled, reaching for the pain, pulling back his fingertip covered with blood. "Yes, sir, I'll tell him."

As Captain Riley was relaying instructions to Morris, a fiery ball shot up. A dozen enemy soldiers flickered under its glow, ready to descend on their position. Overhead, two Apache helicopters rained down shell casings. He remembered casings from bombers flying in higher formation would do the same, once almost killing Alex when one came through the bubble window. Jason watched as the cardboard enemy was cut apart. A third chopper swooped in to extract Captain Morris and Riley. Morris's boot just landed on the skid as the chopper lifted and banked away from the mock battlefield.

"Well, Morris? Is he a soldier yet?" Major Johnson yelled, pulling Captain Riley farther into the craft's belly.

"He is a keeper, Major. Glad we saved his sorry butt!" Morris yelled, giving the thumbs-up.

"General Thomas will be pleased to hear that." Johnson slapped Morris on the back, sending his helmet bouncing to the deck.

Instead of landing, the helicopter flew over the field compound heading toward the airstrip. Captain Riley and Morris stopped working on their weapons and looked at each other, mystified as to the meaning. Once on the ground, Colonel Williams met them. "Riley, Morris, you two have five minutes to turn in those weapons and field gear to Sergeant Andrews here."

"Yes, sir," both said and saluted in unison.

Colonel Williams handed them orders and pointed to the waiting C-47 transport. "It seems that General Thomas wants you two fast. Your personal gear is already packed and on board." They both saluted and started to walk away. "One more thing, you two."

"Sir?" Morris asked first as they turned.

"Congratulations, I understand you're both off to West Point."

"Thank you, sir. That was the deal."

"What is it, Riley?"

"The deal was that I come here, do my best, and I go to the Point."

"Was I part of the deal, Riley? I graduated already," Morris said, looking over at Captain Riley.

"I understand you'll be teaching history. What do you think of that?" Colonel Williams said.

"I can't believe Colonel Butler would request me, sir. I was not his favorite history student."

Colonel Williams decided to walk them to the C-47. As they started to board, he yelled, "Morris! He didn't request you. The new department head did, Colonel Richard Steel."

Germane Jones tried not to draw attention as he moved to his usual table, but the limp and the ugly scar that ran down the length of his face made that impossible. What few had seen were the gunshot and knife scars, and no one saw the mental scars from the Colombian jungle. Throwing his taxi cap on the table, he slowly lowered himself into the corner booth, giving him a clear view of the café and out the front window to his cab. Leaning back, he felt a digging in the small of his back. He pulled his cap off the table to the set it next to him and placed the .38 automatic under its rim.

Five minutes into his meal, he looked across the room and watched a black male, about twenty-six, enter his cab and drive away. *Another stolen vehicle, a way of life in D.C., especially in this neighborhood,* he thought. *Well, that's the way the boss wanted it. Leave the door unlocked and don't do a thing if anything should happen.*

Twenty minutes later, Germane wiped his mouth and reached for the check. A large hand covered it, causing Germane to look up.

"We don't get a chance to visit much." Higgins sat down across from Germane and lit up a cigarette.

"Bad habit, bro, going to kill you."

"Well, how's it going, Germane?" he said, taking a deep drag.

"Better since getting away from you." He lifted and moved his bad leg over with his hand.

"Thousand dollars, tax free. Too bad your cab was stolen, won't be able to work tomorrow, but then, you deserve a Saturday off." He slipped the plain white envelope across the table.

"You know, Commander, I was just kidding." He placed the envelope on top of his cap.

"Germane, screw-ups cost lives." He pointed over his shoulder toward the window. "I suggest you change seats and face the wall. Don't want to give the police the wrong idea. Good to see you, until next time."

In the five weeks since Zhoa and Huan had taken over surveillance of Deputy Director Odin, nothing of significance had occurred until today. As they followed the large black limousine that carried the CIA Director and his Deputy, Zhoa attempted to contact the other surveillance teams, but the radio was full of static. There would be no switching off between them and the other team.

As the black limo approached the intersection, the light turned yellow. The limousine driver stepped on the brake, slowing down, then quickly accelerated as he sped through the intersection, forcing Huan to accelerate and enter the intersection on the red light. The impact of the stolen taxi hitting the passenger door threw Zhoa into Huan. Only Huan's professional training was all that saved their vehicle from losing control. Zhoa tried to kick open the passenger door while yelling and cursing in Chinese. The young black driver of the taxi fled on foot through the gathering crowd. As the large crowd gathered around, Huan and Zhoa shook themselves off, knowing that their minor pains would be nothing compared to reporting to Colonel Lin that they lost Deputy Odin.

D.C. Parks Department's wooden barriers blocked the dirt road that led to the parking lot above the foot trails. Only few vehicles were at the far end. A week ago, it had been different, but now public school was back in session and Washington was already emptying out for the weekend.

"Sergeant Taylor, in the trunk is a SWAT vest and an M1; put it on and make sure no one gets past." As Higgins pulled up to the wooden horses, he hit the automatic door locks and the trunk release.

"Yes, sir, consider it done"

"You did a good job at that intersection. Perfect timing."

As instructed, Taylor dragged away a couple of the barriers, and Higgins pulled into the lot next to Director Henning' limousine. Exiting, Higgins was met by hostile stares of the Director's bodyguards.

Odin climbed out of the back of the Director's limousine and handed Higgins a trunk key. "Good job back there, Robert, and thank Sergeant Taylor. Put the briefcase in the trunk." Odin pointed to the nondescript black Ford Crown Victoria on the other side of the limo.

Higgins opened the trunk of his sedan and pulled the briefcase from under a blanket. As he walked over to the Crown Vic, he took a moment to count half a dozen snipers. From experience, he knew there was at least that many more that he didn't see. He placed the briefcase in the Crown Vic's trunk. The license plate was covered with a cloth. He paced back to Odin. "Must be some important meeting." He dropped the key into the Deputy's hand.

"It is very."

"Don't forget to remind whoever to take the safety off. They have sixty seconds exactly." He passed over the small detonator.

"One more time, Robert, for the record. Ten fifty hours." He put the detonator and key in his pocket.

"For the record." Higgins almost laughed at Aaron's terminology. The *last* thing there would be was a record. "Yes, sir, 1050 is correct."

"Our guest will be the first to leave. Who is at the gate now?"

"Taylor."

"He's a good man, Robert. I want you back out front and make sure his back is to our guest's vehicle as it nears. You can do the plate unveiling." Heading down the trail, he turned. "Robert, it is best that you don't look at the driver or license plate. This whole thing could turn out very bad, so protect yourself."

Odin entered the small clearing and found Director Henning and General Wong seating on a fallen tree trunk. They were visiting as if they were old friends. As he approached, they both stood. The Director was the first to speak. "General Wong, my Deputy, Aaron Odin."

The General shook Odin's hand and bowed slightly "I've heard so much about you, Mr. Odin. Especially lately from Colonel Lin."

Odin dropped General Wong's hand. "It's not Major but Colonel Lin, sir."

General Wong moved to where two trees intersected. "The perfect place as designed by God. With Colonel Lin, what is your term? Cracking the *Golden Eagle* and Lieutenant Jason Riley, he will find great favor."

Odin felt weak and was glad for the tree to sit on. General Wong, seated, looked over at the director. "Jared, Vietnam sometimes seems just like yesterday. You and I against the Russians, our common enemy at that moment."

"Now the Russians are our so-called friends, and China?"

"Another common enemy, or at least for those that Lin works for. We are divided, which makes it a very dangerous time."

"Who does Colonel Lin work for, General?"

"Mad dogs of war, Mr. Odin. The last time the world had a capitalistic economic system with a dictatorship was when Hitler came to power. Your people should remember that as they swarm to buy from China. Not even the downing of your spy plane a few months back seems to stop their stupidity," he said in contempt.

The Director nodded to the General, who reached down and pulled up his briefcase. He laid it on the tree. A hard push was needed to open its bulging sides. Placing a photo down on the log. "Mr. Odin, this photo is compliments of Colonel Lin. I'm sure you recognize Jason Riley and his grandfather. Do you know who the woman is and where the photo was taken?"

"It's at the Waterbury cemetery at the grave of Lieutenant Montgomery."

"Very good. And the woman?" General Wong gently picked up the photo and slipped it into a large brown envelope.

"No, I don't recognize her."

Wong handed the thick envelope to Director Henning while

keeping eye contact with Odin. "That is unfortunate. Colonel Lin did." He turned slightly to his friend. "Inside, Jared, is the police report on the accidental death of Ruth Montgomery a couple of weeks back. There are also a few photos and pages from the records of two of Lin's people out of our consulate in San Francisco. The woman's death was no accident."

"They killed her?" Odin took a sharp breath.

"Come now, Mr. Odin. Are you not about to kill to keep the secret of Jason Riley, or should I say Lieutenant Riley? They will kill to obtain it." He closed the briefcase and pushed it toward the Director. "I'm sure, Jared, you can arrange a fitting end for them, as I will on Sunday for Colonel Lin. We do what we have to do."

"Aaron, Mr. Higgins is where?" The Director asked, handing the envelope to a trembling hand.

"In the lot, at the entrance."

"Aaron, I'm sure you can have Mr. Higgins take care of this." The Director's eyes moved back to General Wong. "What time will this happen?"

"What is the time, Mr. Odin?" General Wong asked.

"Mr. Higgins says 1050, sir." He reached into his inside jacket pocket and pulled out a single sheet of paper. He handed the sheet to General Wong. "Here's the plan. Mr. Higgins has no idea it is you, General Wong."

Director Henning gave his Deputy a warm smile. "We will be up shortly, Aaron. You better get going." Aaron jumped off the log and started to walk away when the Director stopped him. "Did you forget something?"

"I was told to remind you, sixty seconds. Don't forget the safety." Walking back and red faced, he handed the key and detonator to General Wong.

"Thank you. If all goes as planned, you'll have a second briefcase."

Having walked partly up the trail, Deputy Odin looked back as the Director handed the General two small photos and CD with the virus and heard him say, "This is what you need, my friend."

"How can a nation so clever with technology be so blind to an evil heart? So Colonel Lin is correct. The United States has defeated time? This the mad dogs will go to war over this." He placed the photos and the CD in his pocket.

The Director stood and picked up the General's briefcase and wrapped his arm around his friend's shoulders. "Not really, friend. God still controls time and history."

— — — — — — — — — — — — — —

The Judge and Emily had never been to the White House, even as tourists. Now they were to be guests of the president. Carlos Martinez, greeted them and escorted them to the Oval Office. "Since you saw him last, he has been working late. Mostly into the early morning hours."

"I heard he was the 'early to bed, early to rise' type," the Judge replied.

"He was until Colonel Steel showed up." He nodded at Barbara as he escorted the Riley's past.

"Colonel Steel has been here?" The Judge stopped in his tracks at the door.

"He just about lives here. Come on, he's very anxious to see you." He opened the Oval Office door.

As they entered the office, the President stood up behind his desk. Bags had begun circling under his eyes that blinked in heavy, slow dabs. "Welcome, good to see you both again. This will be a very busy weekend." Strong walked around the desk and kissed Emily on the cheek and then shook the Judge's hand. "Jason is, as we speak, on his way here."

As they went toward the seating area, Emily caught sight of the two photos on the desk. A deep-rooted groan proceeded as she collapsed backward, and Carlos caught her and carried her to the couch.

The President rushed to the door. "Barbara, we need water fast!" The President's secretary bolted out of the chair.

Emily's eyes blinked through the blur as Barbara patted her hand. "John, are they all gone?" The fresh memory of a house full of youth and laughter now flooded through her.

"Yes, dear, they're gone," the Judge, kneeling beside her, whispered.

"For two years you knew. How could you stand it, John?" She retraced her thoughts and met her husband's narrowed eyes.

The President reached down and wrapped his arm around Emily, shifting her to a sitting position. "Because your husband is a patriot."

— — — — — — — — — — — — — — —

The flight from the California desert was long and rough. Coupled with the end of three days of field training, Captains Riley and Morris were sound asleep when awakened by the Sergeant's barking calling them to attention. Jumping to their feet in their shorts, they came face-to-face with General Thomas and the Commanding General of Quantico Marine Base. "Welcome to Washington, gentlemen. It's a beautiful Saturday afternoon," General Thomas warmly greeted them.

"Yes, sir," they replied as one.

Thomas pulled out four cigars from his inside pocket. "Captains Riley and Morris, in four hours, you two will be driven to the White House as the President's dinner guests." He pointed to their bags. "I hope you have your class A's with you?"

"Yes, sir, but they may be in sad shape, a little wrinkled and all," Captain Riley answered for them.

"General Schlange, can you help these two troopers out for a good cigar?" Thomas handing him a cigar.

"You can always trust the Marines to bail out the Army." He grinned and snapped the cigar out of General Thomas' hand.

Jason looked at the Marine general's nametag and smiled, which did not go unnoticed by Thomas. "What is it, Riley?"

"The General's name in German means snake, General Thomas." Morris cringed, but instead both Generals broke out laughing.

"Well, Thomas, it looks like the Photo Club has a wise guy for a hero."

Captains Morris and Jason's eyes met before a unison. "Photo Club?"

Thomas shook his head. "Never mind the Photo Club for now; you'll find out later. Why President Strong likes you, Captain Riley, I have no idea why." Thomas threw them each a cigar. "Don't look so stunned, Captain Morris. By the way, Captain Riley, your paternal grandparents will also be there."

"General? Did you say my grandparents?"

General Thomas reached down for his briefcase, which had gone unnoticed by the captains. "Yes, Captain Riley." General Thomas opened his briefcase and waved a report under their noses. "I received a glowing fitness report on you, Riley.

"Thank you General Thomas."

"It seems you even fooled Captain Morris here that you're fit to be an officer in this Army. Is that right, Morris?"

"Yes, sir. An outstanding officer."

Thomas reached in and withdrew two packets, throwing the fitness report back in. "Since you've both been on vacation for the last eight weeks, events have taken a turn. What you have in your hands is the press package released to the media today. It seems, Captain Riley, you will be awarded the Medal of Honor on Sunday. It will be posthumously, of course. Later, in a private setting, you will receive it in the flesh. Can't be giving that out to some misfit."

Jason stared, remembering, and said, "Misfits, sir? With respect, sir, none of us turned out to be misfits."

THE LORD'S DAY

The cameraman made one last walk in front of his subject. He stopped and nodded to the announcer.

"It's a beautiful Sunday morning here in the Rose Garden, in sharp contrast to that day over fifty-seven years ago when young men made history and changed the world storming the shores of Normandy. In a few minutes, President Strong will posthumously award the Congressional Medal of Honor to four members of the Army. These young men were part of the crew of the B-17 bomber called the *Golden Eagle* and participated in one of the most guarded secret actions of World War II." He held up a binder. "This report, just released to the media is what books and movies are made from. It looks like the ceremony is ready to start, so we take you live for what could only be described as an incredible event."

The Army Major read the formal order of notice, ending it with, "Sunday, the Day of Our Lord, September 9, 2001." He stood at attention as the band played 'Hail to the Chief.' When President Strong and General Thomas took their positions behind the Major, the band stopped. With a smart about-face, the Major handed the read order to General Thomas, saluted, and did a right face before marching away.

General Thomas stood behind the lectern and waited for the three hundred guests to sit down, along with the President. "Distinguished guests, members of the media, family, and friends, I want to introduce those who will accept the Medals of Honor as a token of a grateful country for those who gave their lives so today we can have the freedom we currently enjoy. Standing behind me and from my right Congressman John Campbell of Arizona will be accepting on behalf of his father, Sergeant Nathaniel Campbell. Colonel John Riley, captain of the *Golden Eagle*, and a friend of Second Lieutenant Alexander Montgomery. Mr. Ralph Riley accepts on behalf of his brother, First Lieutenant Jason Riley, and finally, Major Joseph Ramsey, friend and former commanding officer of the *Rita Bee*, accepts on behalf of the family of Sergeant Thomas Walker."

He folded the white paper and slipped it in his inner pocket. He then opened the binder and continued. "It is my pleasure to introduce to you now the President of the United States, James W. Strong."

The band started up again and the President shook General Thomas' hand before taking the binder. On his first signal, the band stopped, and on his fourth attempt, he was able to get everyone seated.

"A little over three months ago, in Normandy, I recognized members of the 572nd Bomber Squadron for actions of valor that were way overdue. Because of the secret nature and delicate aftermath of that mission, the whole story was never fully understood or revealed. I would like to remedy that by telling you what took place on that fateful June 5, 1944 …" Strong held up what was claimed to be the original 1944 report by Major Riley. An expurgated tale followed.

Fifteen minutes after the ceremony ended, Congressman Campbell pushed his way to the President. "Mr. President, don't you think it's time to meet our guest?"

"You seem anxious, Congressman Campbell."

"Yes, sir, the last two months have been hard. To finally meet the man my father died to save." He glanced around to make sure he was not heard.

The President shook a few more hands and shared a few kind words with veterans present. "To tell you the truth, I am with you," he whispered to the Congressman.

Colonel Lin paced about and glanced at his watch; General Wong was fifteen minutes late. Their appointment at the Russian Embassy had been scheduled for eleven. Feeling pressured, he was ready to call General Wong when there was the soft knock on the door. Eng stepped in, closing the door behind him, and said, "General Wong is here, sir."

Eng opened the door and ushered the General in. "Good morning, Comrade General." Colonel Lin was slow to stand, which received a stare from the General. General Wong felt the detonator in his pocket. "Comrade Lin, good morning. We have important issues to settle, but first." He handed Lin a pair of photos. "I would suggest that you look at these."

Colonel Lin slowly sat down while studying the photos. "These are what are being passed around by the President's people?"

General Wong now sat down, ignoring the lack of military courtesy in Colonel Lin's seating himself uninvited. "Yes. I got them from a very reliable source."

"So I was right all along. I will put them in the safe."

"Let us take them with us; we may need them to trade with our Russian brothers."

Colonel Lin sat behind his desk while he kept eye contact with General Wong. "I don't understand." He answered the imperious ring. "Yes, I see … General Wong is with me now." Beads of sweat formed above Lin's lip. "Nothing, I'll call back."

"Something wrong, Colonel?" The General smiled.

Colonel Lin started to shift as his shoulders tensed. "There was what the police are calling a robbery. A couple of our people in San Francisco were murdered. It happened early this morning or very late last night."

"That is unfortunate, Comrade Lin. We can talk later, but we must hurry and gather everything we have on the *Golden Eagle*." The General looked at his watch and wondered why the clever Lin was not watching the ceremony at the White House.

Lin unloaded the safe into his briefcase and turned around to find General Wong going through the drawers of his desk. "You won't find anything there, Comrade General. I have it all."

General Wong nudged the mouse and the computer screen came to life; Colonel Lin was logged in. "I was looking for tissues, Comrade Colonel. I think I'm starting to get a cold." Lin almost laughed at his suspicions. "Sorry, Comrade General. They are in the top right drawer."

General Wong sat down and pulled it open. "Are you sure you have all intelligence regarding the *Golden Eagle*?"

"Yes, Comrade General." He nodded.

"Then get Eng and Fu in here. We need to get going." As Colonel Lin stepped out of the office, he inserted the CD he been given earlier and instantly the virus began devouring every file and program in the embassy. The timing was perfect; he slipped the disk back in his pocket as the door opened. As they started out the door, he turned. "Security Colonel Lin, you left your computer on; we'll use my personal car." Normally alert, Colonel Lin was now the victim of mental warfare; the news from San Francisco, the photos, and his own breach of security clouded his conscience.

- - - - - - - - - - - - -

"What is this private church service about? Why didn't I know about it sooner, Kelly?" Vice-President Ronald Davis pulled his Chief of Staff over by the elbow.

"Because I didn't know. We are being closed out. Martinez is working sixteen hours a day, and I don't have a clue on what." He yanked his arm back.

The Vice President shook another hand. "Yes, it was a nice ceremony." He turned back to Kelly, saying sarcastically, "Maybe it's time I praise the Lord."

"I'd like to see that, sir."

A shock wave erupted from the explosion spreading rapidly across the spacious White House lawn and toward the Rose Garden. Secret Service agents pushed their charges to the ground, covering them with armored briefcases. Other agents circled the group with automatic weapons drawn. A minute later, the Vice President's limousine pulled up, and he was thrown in the back. Kelly ran and was able to leap in as the armored car sped away from the President, who was rushed inside within a huddle of agents.

The gathering for the church service went virtually unnoticed by the media in a wave of confusion as pagers and cell phones went off, it seemed simultaneously, with reports of an explosion outside the Russian Embassy. Director Henning pulled the President aside. "Mr. President, we have a report of a car bomb outside the Russian Embassy."

"Our meeting with Andrew is in less than a half hour, Jared." The smoke from the blast drifted harmlessly past the window.

"It's the perfect distraction for the media, a cover for the tightened security for the next few hours and will keep your guests' coming and going secret. As we speak, the Vice President is heading away from us."

"It is almost too perfect, Jared. Did we have anything to do with it?" The President's jaw set as he faced the Director.

"Some questions, Jim, you should not ask." At Martinez's signal, "Mr. President, your guests are waiting in the Oval Office. Carlos will sort everyone out."

As the President came into the Oval Office, everyone stood, but coffee cups were still full. "Please, ladies and gentlemen, sit down. I want to assure you that that explosion was—"

"It was a car bomb," The Director said, interrupting. "I would suspect Chechnyan rebels. It looks like they brought their war with the Russians here."

"Please, don't let this upset you, and don't let your coffee get cold. Taxpayers don't like us wasting their money."

A few minutes passed without interruption. President Strong reached over to Jason's brother. "Mr. Riley, may I please have your brother's medal back?"

Ralph stared in stillness for a moment. "Why, yes, Mr. President." He handed over the medal. "Thank you, Mr. Riley." He slipped the medal into his pocket. Carlos led Major Ramsey over. "I hope our time, Major Ramsey, will be more pleasant for you than last. Please let me introduce my old friend from Yale, Jared Henning, Director of the Central Intelligence Agency. He has a couple of photos to show you."

The Director pulled out two small sets of photos from his suit pocket. "Mr. Riley, Major Ramsey, brace yourselves." He handed them each a set.

They stared at the photos then at each other, their eyes begging for an answer. "I don't understand the meaning of this. I don't … *we* don't understand, Mr. President," Major Ramsey said.

"You will in a minute" He smiled and looked across to the Judge. "Judge Riley, we are ready. Please bring your grandson in."

The Judge would never forget the look on Ramsey's and Jason's brother Ralph's faces as they came face to face. Minutes later, President Strong was still hard-pressed to put a stop to the celebration. But time was pressing, so he announced, "Everyone. Please, please. We have a couple hundred of our brethren waiting."

As they walked from the Oval Office to the map room, everyone stood. This time there was no band or secret service surrounding the President. "Please sit down." He remained still and stared. He then continued, breaking the expectant silence. "First, I want to tell you a story about a hero among us. Then Senator Geraldine De Ramos will lead us in worship, and finally, Sir Andrew Grey will address us."

The President pulled out a simple index card of the main points. "This is a true story; it is the story behind the photos that you all saw while many others failed to see." He gazed at Andrew standing in the rear corner and swallowed. "One that Sir Andrew Grey, I'm sure, will do his best to clear any doubt in your minds about." He paused. "Where do I start? From whose viewpoint do I tell the story?" At some point, President Strong made a decision to end his talk. The President reached into his pocket and pulled out the medal. "While I, as the President, have the great honor of presenting this medal to Captain Jason Riley, I feel that one of us would be more appropriate to bestow it." Walking to the front row, he handed the medal to Congressman Campbell.

Campbell bent over and kissed his twenty-year-old daughter, Janelon the cheek. She returned his affection with a hard squeeze to his hand while touching Jason gently on the knee.

As Jason stood at attention, tears of joy and pain rolled down his cheeks. Friends and relatives clapped. An inner voice spoke. "Well done, good and faithful servant."

EPILOGUE

Deputy Chief Chrissy Murelli managed to balance her coffee and the cardboard box as she unlocked the door to her new office. Sliding the box on the desk, she still marveled at the chain of events from her encounter with Captain Jason Riley and Robert Higgins.

She could almost hear the former occupant of this office screaming at her about how screwed up the Compton warehouse case was. What was she thinking putting that idiot Sergeant Fisher in charge of such a high-profile case? Even reminding him about the fire and that paramedics and media had all arrived before the police department had all but destroyed the crime scene; that it was his idea to assign the mayor's nephew, did little to calm him. It did not surprise her that he had a reported heart attack, for in little time, the former deputy chief had both retired and was hired as security director for a firm outside of Washington, D.C. What did surprise her was who would want the worthless piece of human debris.

She unpacked the framed photo of her and the governor at the announcement that Seattle PD had received the largest grant ever given by the Office of Criminal Justice Planning (OCJP). She, as the grant author, had accepted the check as attempted payback. Looking for a place to hang the photo, she spotted a large cabinet that, when opened, revealed the fifty-inch flat-screen TV. *So much for the taxpayers' money*, she thought.

She started to call her mother in Sierra Vista, but, glancing at her watch, a thought tightened her lips and caused her to frown. Arizona did not change to Daylight Savings Time. Fearing she would wake her mother, she decided to watch the news. She would call from the airport. She found the remote on top of the TV and was walking away to continue unpacking when she spun around at the name of Lieutenant Jason Riley.

As she sat, she mulled over the connection, if any, between the order from President Strong to save Captain Jason Riley and seeing the Medal of Honor being awarded to a Lieutenant Jason Riley. As she pondered, the sound of the explosion made her jump to her feet.

- - - - - - - - - - - - -

Following trends, the car bombing outside the Russian Embassy had been captured on video. The Russian Embassy had released copies of the security videotape almost immediately to the media, in a show of the new openness and freedom far from that of the former Soviet Union.

The twenty-four-hour news channels reran the security videos, mixed with various government press releases. The Russians voiced their outrage at the terrorist attack on its embassy. The United States sent condolences at the loss of life from such "a cowardly act with the promise to fully investigate." The Chinese mourned the untimely death of those who had served their country so well.

By Sunday night, viewers had the video burned in their minds: The red Ford Escort being parked out in front of the embassy with the "terrorist" running from it…Two minutes and eleven seconds later, the black Ford Crown Victoria sedan parking behind the Escort…The sedan driver getting out and pulling a briefcase from the trunk and handing it to one of the three passengers…The four walking next to the parked Escort, and then a white light that "blinded" the camera for a moment…The Escort almost vertical, falling back down to earth, partly on the sidewalk, as fire and smoke drifted over what looked like bodies on the sidewalk.

While the police and media scoured the area for witnesses, there was a fascinating story of two tourists: Paul and Ramona Miller from Massachusetts. They told how, as they were walking toward the embassy, a young black male stepped out from an alley with a gun and demanded their money. The explosion down the block knocked them all to the ground. The robber recovered first and fled the area, leaving the Millers unharmed. They claimed the attempted robbery had saved their lives.

Ten minutes farther in the tape, never to be shown to the media, the police and fire departments raced about in chaos. "Police Sergeant Higgins" unlocked the white Ford sedan trunk, removing the briefcase belonging to Colonel Lin while "Police Lieutenant Odin" pulled open the ashtray and shoved the detonator and computer disc into his pants pocket.

Following his modus operandi at the Sunday service, Pastor Corpus of the Fort Lauderdale First Valley Baptist Church asked for praise reports. Guest speaker Chandler Brownlee, National Director of CS-US, stood to share a mysterious thirty-thousand-dollar donation made to Christian Surfers–United States in the name of Nathaniel Campbell, a member of the Waterbury, California, chapter. Brownlee went on to explain that while there was a very active chapter in Waterbury, no one knew or had ever heard of Nathaniel Campbell, but the cashier's check was very real and was much appreciated.